His wildest imaginings couldn't have prepared him.

He didn't think anything could have prepared him for the way he caught fire when he touched her, kissed her. And anything beyond that didn't bear thinking about. But he thought about it anyway, and shuddered under the impact of imagining them intimately entwined, her silken skin bare against his, her long, curved legs wrapped around him....

He slammed the mug down on the table before the window, swearing at himself for letting his fantasy get out of hand; all he'd done was torture himself with that rising, yearning ache that he'd been battling since he'd first seen her again. A burning ache that was compounded by the fact that she still didn't trust him.

Of course she doesn't, he told himself. She's spent the past fifteen years blaming you, hating you, for killing her father. You're not going to change that in fifteen days. But at least, he consoled himself, they were talking. They were communicating. And kissing ...

Dear Reader,

When two people fall in love, the world is suddenly new and exciting, and it's that same excitement we bring to you in Silhouette Intimate Moments. These are stories with scope and grandeur. The characters lead lives we all dream of, and everything they do reflects the wonder of being in love.

Longer and more sensuous than most romances, Silhouette Intimate Moments novels take you away from everyday life and let you share the magic of love. Adventure, glamour, drama, even suspense— these are the passwords that let you into a world where love has a power beyond the ordinary, where the best authors in the field today create stories of love and commitment that will stay with you always.

In coming months, look for novels by your favorite authors: Kathleen Eagle, Marilyn Pappano, Emilie Richards, Kathleen Korbel and Justine Davis, to name only a few. And whenever—and wherever— you buy books, look for all the Silhouette Intimate Moments, love stories with that extra something, books written especially for you by today's top authors.

Leslie J. Wainger
Senior Editor and Editorial Coordinator

JUSTINE DAVIS

Suspicion's Gate

SILHOUETTE·INTIMATE·MOMENTS®

Published by Silhouette Books New York

America's Publisher of Contemporary Romance

SILHOUETTE BOOKS
300 East 42nd St., New York, N.Y. 10017

SUSPICION'S GATE

ISBN: 0-373-07423-9

First Silhouette Books printing March 1992

All the characters in this book have no existence
outside the imagination of the author and have
no relation whatsoever to anyone bearing the same
name or names. They are not even distantly
inspired by any individual known or unknown
to the author, and all incidents are pure invention.

Printed in the U.S.A.

JUSTINE DAVIS

lives in San Clemente, California. Her interests outside of writing are sailing, doing needlework, riding and driving her restored 1967 Corvette roadster—top down, of course.

A policewoman, Justine says that years ago, a young man she worked with encouraged her to try for a promotion to a position that was, at that time, occupied only by men. "I succeeded, became wrapped up in my new job, and that man moved away, never, I thought, to be heard from again. Ten years later he appeared out of the woods of Washington state, saying he'd never forgotten me and would I please marry him. With that history, how could I write anything but romance?"

Chapter 1

"At the gate which suspicion enters,
love goes out."
—Dr. Thomas Fuller

Nicki had been hearing the whispers for several moments before the sounds began to coalesce into words in her weary brain.

"Did you see him?"

"I can't believe it! After all these years."

"He always did have more gall than sense."

"But to turn up here, now! Of all the nerve!"

"He looks...different. Not just older—"

"He looks like what he always was. A troublemaker."

Her heart caught in her throat at the familiar appellation that brought back so many memories. *Troublemaker.* She lifted eyes still gritty and sore from a night of tears, searching the gathering.

Only one person had ever inspired such universal disfavor in the small town of San Remo, and she knew all too well who it was. It took her only seconds to spot him; he stood at least two inches taller than nearly everyone gathered in the mist that was clinging rather grimly to the green expanse of the cemetery lawn.

"Travis," she breathed, the name a mere whisper of sound that went unnoticed by the people clustered around her. As if he'd heard her, his head came up. His eyes, those incredible gray eyes that had always seemed to have the power to look clear through to her soul, fastened on her as if he'd known all along exactly where she was.

For a split second the old joy leapt in her, an instinctive response she couldn't stop. She'd never been able to stop it, not when Travis Halloran turned that consuming gaze on her. And for an instant she saw the answering leap of emotion in his eyes, a softening in the cool gray.

And then she remembered. She didn't think her expression changed, but she saw his eyes go icy, and the mouth that had gentled for a moment thinned as his jaw tightened. She looked hastily away, wondering why she had thought he wouldn't know exactly what she was thinking. He had always known. She only wished she knew why he was here.

She tried to concentrate on the minister's words, but she didn't need to hear them; she had said her own private farewell in the dim, harsh light of dawn. But Reverend Porter's voice was having the same effect now that it had had on her as a child in church; it sent her mind flying anywhere to escape the droning buzz. Even to Travis Halloran.

He'd changed. Not that he was any less compelling than he had been when she'd last seen him; more so, she thought rather breathlessly. He was still tall and lean, but he'd filled out to the adult male muscularity that had been promised in the breadth of his shoulders and the strength of his arms in youth. The dark hair was just as thick and still worn a bit long, but fell with the careless ease of a good haircut rather than the tousled shagginess that spoke of a wallet that didn't stretch to regular trips to the barber.

His eyes were just as softly, thickly lashed, but they were harder now, as cold as the granite stones whose color they matched. His features were just as striking, high cheek-bones, strong jaw, and that unexpectedly soft, mobile mouth. But where he had looked reckless and a little angry then, he looked only forbidding now.

She wondered if he ever smiled anymore. Wondered if he ever let loose that devastating, lopsided grin to wreak havoc on the pulse rate of any female in the vicinity, that grin that had made even the "nice" girls in town watch with avid expressions as he walked by, and the younger ones giggle, blush and whisper from afar. Judging from the set, grim lines of his face, she thought it unlikely.

"That son of a— Can you believe that?"

Her brother's exclamation brought her out of her reverie. Richard, who was as usual a beat behind the rest of the world, had only now noticed the tall, lean figure standing apart from the throng. He took a step in that direction, but Nicki's slender hand on his arm stopped him short.

"Hush," she whispered sharply. "Not now."

Richard looked a little surprised, as if the shock of seeing the man who had once been his friend had driven all else from his mind, even the somber reality of the occasion. He turned his head away and she felt him go slack, sagging back into his usual slumping posture.

Her palm stung, and Nicki realized that the recurrent, sharp pain was from the thorns of the single rose she held. She eased her tense grip, straightening the crushed florist's paper as she became aware of the silence.

They were waiting, she thought, for her. Always for her, although Richard was the oldest, and the only surviving man of the family now. She smothered a sigh.

When she looked up, she met an assortment of stares that both comforted and puzzled her. The ones of honest, pure sympathy she understood; it was the touch of anticipation in others that puzzled her. That is, until she saw one of those glances slip sideways to Travis, then back to her.

What were they expecting? she wondered with a spurt of sudden bitter anger. An explosion? Something to liven up a bleak occasion? Well, she wasn't about to oblige them. The child she had been would have; the woman she'd become had left that kind of thing far behind.

She stepped forward, to the edge of the gaping hole in the lush carpet of grass. Without meeting any of the staring eyes, yet feeling the gaze of one particular pair as if it were a physical thing, she tossed the rose down onto her mother's casket.

He hadn't wanted to come. He'd never wanted to set foot in this town again, and if it hadn't been for that attorney's dogged insistence, he wouldn't have. He'd shed the dust of this place fifteen years ago when they had cast him out, and he had never looked back.

Well, almost never. But Travis Halloran tried not to think about the times when one image battered its way into his resistant consciousness, when the one bright, shining picture from those dreary days pounded on the door of his mind and refused to go away until he'd let it in to be looked at, to be remembered in all its vivid clarity, to be savored in all its sweetness. The only sweetness he'd ever known in that long ago, bitter time.

It had stunned him to find that the image he'd carried around for so long was so wrong. Gone was the coltish, gawky girl; in her place was a lovely, poised woman, long-legged and femininely curved. A woman who caused a lightning-fast response of tension and heat in him. Nicki Lockwood had grown up, and he couldn't help feeling that somehow she'd passed him in the process, never mind that he was nearly three years her senior.

But for the briefest second, a frozen moment in time, that young, innocent girl had looked out of those wide blue eyes, the girl he'd known before the world had crashed in on him, wiping that look of near-worship out of her eyes forever.

It was no more than he'd expected. Why should she be any different than everyone else in this town? Just because, for a while, she seemed to see past the defenses of an angry, rebellious spirit to the frightened boy inside?

No, she was no different. The look of distaste that had narrowed those huge eyes mirrored the look of everyone else in this place, and any tiny hope he had ever harbored that she, of them all, might not believe, might not hate him, went down to a quick, lonely death. And with it, some lingering, soft part of his heart quivered and gave up the fight against the encroaching stone.

Still, it tore at him when she stepped forward, a slender lonely figure, nearly as isolated as he was as she tossed the solitary rose into the grave. Where the hell was Rich, why wasn't he with her, supporting her—?

Because when it came to the crunch, Richard Lockwood had as much backbone as a jellyfish, he thought sourly. And who knows it better than you, Halloran? Why the hell are you here, anyway? That damned lawyer...

"It's imperative that you be present, Mr. Halloran," the lawyer had told him.

"Imperative?"

Travis had said it idly, unimpressed by the urgency implied by the word. He'd been too busy speculating that this man, this lawyer, who had come to San Remo long after his own inauspicious departure, was probably the only man in the small town who would ever call him "Mr. Halloran." To everyone else he'd always been just "that Halloran boy," "that drunkard's son" or, more simply, "that trouble-maker."

"Yes," the man had said, oblivious to his gaffe by San Remo standards. "Not for the funeral, necessarily, but for the reading of the will."

Curiosity, he thought now as he drove the familiar yet changed roads to the big, sprawling house on the hill, was going to be the death of him yet. The attorney had refused to divulge any further details, and he'd been forced to satisfy his inquisitiveness in the only way possible; he'd come back to the town he'd been born in and had sworn never to come back to in his life.

And, he muttered grimly to himself as he pulled in beside a long, white Cadillac convertible, if you think your reception at the cemetery was cool, wait until you walk into that damned house.

He got out, noting with a vague interest that the plate on the long, spotless car read LOCKWD1. Richard, he thought immediately. The senior Lockwoods had never gone for that kind of personal advertisement, and Nicki would find it . . . ostentatious in the extreme.

He felt a tug of nostalgia as the word *ostentatious* floated up to him from the depths of memory. How many times had she said it, with all the self-assured wisdom of a fourteen-year-old who looked upon her own comfortable world with the disdain of one who'd never known any other?

He'd said that to her the first time she'd used the word to describe a different car, also shiny, new and expensive, that had sat unused in one bay of the huge garage behind the house.

"It *is* ostentatious. Richard can't even drive yet, he's such a klutz, but there it sits, rusting away." She'd wrinkled her nose in that way that always made him uncomfortable, although he couldn't have said exactly why. "Ostentatious and blatant."

"Blatant? I can understand ostentatious," he'd said, reaching out to tweak her sassy, upturned nose; somehow it made him feel better. "I think you just like the word. But why blatant?"

Instead of answering right away, she had looked at the big house that was her home. "I'm not sorry we have money," she said honestly, "but that doesn't mean I like to flash it around like that. It would have been better, would have made Richard better, made him appreciate it more, if he'd had to work for that car."

She hadn't said "like you did," but the implication had been there, along with the subtle compliment. She did that often, and it made him feel awkward even as it warmed him. He was sixteen years old, with the practiced, cool remoteness affected by so many boys his age. Only in his case it was all too real, brought on by too many confrontations with the limitations and grim reality of his life. He'd learned to live with that; the problem came when he tried to reconcile the cavalier, impudent image he felt compelled to uphold with the boy who was flattered, even moved by the honest admiration of a fourteen-year-old girl.

He'd tried to brush it off, act like it meant nothing to him. He'd teased her mercilessly, yet she had always seemed to see beyond his defenses. And he had never realized how much it had come to mean to him until he'd lost it forever. He shook his head sharply, clearing out the mist of memory as he walked past the conspicuous car.

He'd underestimated, he thought as the heads swiveled toward him as he came through the front door. You could freeze Hawaii with the looks he was getting. And this was just the company staff and friends of the family. He was obviously going to be severely testing the thickness of the shell he'd built over the years. That is, if he didn't cut and run right now.

Not, he thought, a half-bad idea. But then the thin, almost emaciated frame of John Langley, the attorney who had come to him with this ludicrous request, appeared in the doorway of the library.

"Damn," he muttered when it became obvious that the man had spotted him.

"Ah, yes, Mr. Halloran, thank you for coming. We can begin now that you're here."

It was almost worth the chill when he saw the stunned expressions around him. He wondered if it was because he was being invited into the inner sanctum, or because of the almost deferential air granted by the lawyer to someone they remembered only as barely—if at all—deserving civility. The thought braced him, and he slipped back into the mental armor that had been his weapon ever since he'd walked out of this house fifteen years ago, with the acid of betrayal eating at his gut.

"We're waiting in the library. Right this way—"

"I know where it is."

The man looked startled. Travis couldn't help a wry smile. "You're new in town, aren't you, Mr. Langley?"

He didn't wait for an answer, just walked past the man toward the heavy, carved doors of the library. He couldn't help the shiver that rippled through him as he remembered the last time he'd been here, the night that had ravaged his life. The night when a woman he'd trusted had turned on him, and an adoring young girl had looked at him with stunned, tragic eyes. He'd put on the old armor, he thought ruefully, but he hadn't checked it for chinks. He shrugged, shoring up the weak spot.

He heard a gasp as he stepped into the paneled room he remembered so well. He didn't know who it had come from; his gaze had shot immediately to the slim figure still clad in the simple black dress she'd worn at the cemetery.

She was sitting in the chair she'd always favored, a big, overstuffed twin of her father's recliner, the chair he'd sat in so often himself. Her long, silken legs were curled up under her, and she looked small and fragile. And bruised somehow, not with physical marks but in the darkness shadowing her eyes. His stomach knotted at the sight of her.

"What the hell?" Richard had come to his feet behind the big, mahogany desk that dominated the room. Despite the man's obvious anger, all Travis could think was that he looked like a boy playing at his father's desk.

"Hi, Rich," he said casually, as if he'd seen him only yesterday.

"Isn't it enough that you . . . you desecrated my mother's funeral?"

"Desecrate?" One dark brow rose sardonically. "I didn't think I was that important, Richie."

Richard fumed, reddening, but he made no move to come out from behind the big desk as he sputtered, "What the hell do you think you're doing here?"

"I've been asking myself the same question," Travis answered dryly.

"He is here at my request," Langley put in quickly, looking more than a little wary at the intensity of the undercurrents he clearly didn't understand.

"You asked him here?"

Travis watched as Richard whirled on the man. Perhaps it was just the contrast with the spare attorney, but Richard looked almost fat. Soft, at least, pudgy, as if he'd regained the baby fat lost in adolescence. Or maybe he'd never lost it at all. Travis couldn't remember. He couldn't remember much of Richard at all; he'd spent too many long, solitary hours blocking out those memories. His images of Nicki were so much clearer, had always been so much more vivid—

"Where do you get off inviting him here? Do you know who he is, what he did—"

"Do you?" Travis said it quietly, almost gently, and watched as Richard's eyes widened in shock. My God, he thought. He's even got himself believing the Lockwood version of the truth. "Never mind, Richie. You're safe now."

"Don't call me that," Richard snapped. "Get out. Just get out."

"I asked him here," Langley cut in with a sudden firmness that surprised Travis. "On Mrs. Lockwood's behalf."

"My mother?" Richard looked stunned. His eyes flicked from the lawyer to Travis.

"Relax, Rich," Travis drawled acidly. "She probably just left me a ticket straight to hell, with her blessing and her loving family to deliver it."

It still stung, he realized in carefully masked amazement. After all this time it still stung that this woman he'd respected, admired, and yes, even loved, had turned on him at the worst time of his life, and delivered the final blow that destroyed what little there had been left of youth and trust in him. It had taken him years to convince himself he didn't care. And more years to stop thinking himself a fool for believing in Mrs. Lockwood in the first place.

"If you will sit down, please, Mr. Halloran?"

"I'd rather stand, thanks." Travis sliced a sideways look at Richard. "Wouldn't want anyone to think I planned on staying."

Richard, still red-faced, glared at the attorney, then shifted his gaze to his sister as if searching for support. She'd said nothing at all from where she sat with her eyes fixed unwaveringly on her lap.

No, Travis thought, on her hands. Slender hands, with long, graceful fingers that were now laced together so tightly the knuckles were starkly white.

"Let's get this over with," Travis said suddenly, in a tone of command. Whatever last blow Emily Lockwood wanted to rain down on him from beyond the grave, he didn't want to drag it out. And he told himself firmly it was for his own sake, not Nicki's.

It seemed interminable. There were bequests to various relatives and to several long-time employees of Lockwood, Incorporated. Then came the house, and Travis barely restrained himself from pacing as the endless list of items went on and on.

No one, he thought, should have so damn much stuff that it took three days to bestow it when you finally had to admit you couldn't take it with you. Or you shouldn't be so picky about where it all went. One line would do it. House and contents. Three little words, and it could have been over. It was all going to go to Nicki and Richard anyway. Of course, that wouldn't explain why he was here. But then, he wasn't sure he wanted to know why he was here.

He felt suddenly uneasy, afraid that somehow Emily Lockwood was going to reach out and smash him to bits all over again. Langley read on.

The will, he thought, was exactly like Emily Lockwood had been: carefully worded, precise and detailed. He'd admired that then, the contrast with his own rather slovenly household, he supposed. And he'd been properly struck with grateful reverence when she had taken an unexpected interest in him.

He hadn't seen then how unlikely it was, that the queen of the Lockwood clan would genuinely care about the son of the town tavernkeeper, no matter that he had saved her precious son from a brutal beating. But she'd made it clear to him that night, in this room, in front of that son, and a stricken, wounded-looking Nicki, just how fleeting that caring had been.

As he thought it he felt a tingling at the back of his neck. He turned suddenly and found those wide eyes fastened on him. They were different now, masked, and except for that split second this morning, totally unreadable. So unlike the young, innocent girl he'd known, the girl who, without his realizing it, had wormed her way into some secret, untouched part of him. And when she'd turned away from him, she'd forgotten to give that part back. He had ached from the loss for a long time without knowing what had happened to him or how. But he'd learned it this morning, in the harsh gray mist, when he'd looked up to see those eyes once more and realized that part of him had been missing all this time.

It was absurd, really. She'd been little more than a girl that first day that Richard—Travis hadn't yet shortened it to Rich, he'd been too intimidated by the Lockwood name— had brought him home. He'd also been awed by the grandeur of the elegant, twenty-room house, but his pride had kicked in and he'd been coolly nonchalant about it while wondering how anybody could stand to live with all this; he'd be scared to breathe. It seemed cold somehow. And empty.

And then there had been a shriek of laughter as a bundle of fiery-haired energy had come sliding recklessly down the exquisite, polished banister to land in a heap of grubby denim at his feet.

"Oh, geez, Nicki, grow up, will you?" Richard's face had been red with embarrassment. "You're fourteen now, why don't you act your age?"

"And be an old fuddy-duddy like you?" she retorted, undaunted as she tried to untangle legs that seemed too long for her slim, straight body. "No way. I—"

She stopped, abruptly realizing that her brother was not alone. Her gaze traveled upward, from a pair of worn, black leather running shoes, over an equally worn pair of faded blue jeans with a rip in each knee, and a faded dark blue T-shirt.

He saw recognition dawn in a pair of big blue eyes when she reached his face; even people who had never met him seemed to know "the troublemaker." He waited. The trepidation he usually saw didn't appear; the blue gaze held steady on his face.

"My sister," Richard said with all the strained patience of an aggravated big brother.

Travis never looked away from her. "I gathered." He saw her chin come up. "Nice flight," he said mildly, "but your landing could use a little work."

She grinned, undaunted and apparently uncowed by his presence, and he felt something odd and warm break free in his chest.

"I know. I'm practicing," she said. "You're the one, aren't you?"

The one? So that was it, he thought. She was one of those. One of the ones who found him intriguing, perhaps just a bit frightening. He almost laughed. If she'd been a little older, if she'd been of the age he knew found his edge of disreputability fascinating, if she'd been the kind who sent off all kinds of sexual messages, he'd have given her the expected answer. *Yeah, I'm the one, all right. The one your mother warned you about, isn't that how it goes?*

But she wasn't, she was barely old enough to be aware of those things, and he was some kind of weird for even thinking that way. "Sure," he drawled, a sour undertone marking his voice. "How did you ever guess?"

He'd meant it to be sarcastic; she took it literally. "Because you're the only one of Richard's friends I've ever seen who looks like he has the guts to stand up to those jerks."

It took a lot to startle Travis Halloran, even at sixteen years old. He'd seen and dealt with too much in his young life already. But Nicki Lockwood had done it.

"Oh," he said, rather blankly, only now remembering the reason he'd been invited here at all; rescuing the heir to the Lockwood family fortune had had benefits he'd never expected.

Of course, he hadn't known that the battered, bloody shape he'd pulled out from under that pile of out-of-town punks had been Richard Lockwood at the time, he'd only done it because he hated stacked decks. And five to one had seemed very stacked to him at the time, enough for him to use his considerable strength and his tough appearance to send the punks running. Little did he know that there would come a day when even those lopsided odds would look favorable to him.

Of course, if he had realized it was a high and mighty Lockwood, he might have done it anyway, just for the perverse pleasure of having them in the awkward position of owing him.

The spell of memory was broken when Nicki looked away from him abruptly. Another way she'd changed, he thought. She'd always faced things head-on, never let herself be intimidated by anything or anyone. Unlike Richard, who'd taken his sense of self-worth from his family's position and wealth, Nicki had had an assurance that sprang from within, from her own indomitable strength. Had she lost that, over the years?

Then he realized that she had looked away because John Langley had mentioned his name. He looked up to see the man holding something out, waiting, obviously, for him to come and get it. Aware of the burning stares of everyone in the room, he started forward.

A book, he realized as he got closer. She'd left him a book? Somehow that was worse than anything he'd imagined; it brought back too many memories of when he'd sat in this very room while she prodded, pushed and forced him into using his mind to grapple with questions he'd never thought about. Memories of when he'd believed she meant it, believed she really cared. For nearly a year and a half she had—

"You'll notice an envelope inside, Mr. Halloran. I must ask you to refrain from opening it for a few moments. Mrs. Lockwood was very specific as to the order in which this would be done."

"I'm sure she was."

Travis felt the crackle of tension at his flat tone, and he stepped to one side, out of the direct line of fire of those heated stares. He looked down at the book in his hand, at the leather cover in a deep, rich green, embossed with gold that was, no doubt, real. Nothing less than 24-karat in the Lockwood library.

He didn't have to look at the title; he knew what it was. His mouth twisted into a wry, reminiscent smile. *Huckleberry Finn.* He'd held this book before, often, and listened to Emily Lockwood's quiet yet imperious words. He'd been angry at first, his pride rising up fiercely in the face of her arbitrary judgment of him, but he'd found it impossible to walk out on her. And that had made him angrier; he didn't like feeling intimidated.

"I read it," he'd said shortly when she'd first handed it to him. "I do go to school, you know."

She had brushed off his anger. "I mean *really* read it. It is a classic. Hemingway said that all American literature comes from this book."

"He also said you should stop reading it at chapter thirty-one," he'd said, glad for once for the memory that seemed to soak up the oddest details, "because Twain cheated on the ending."

That light had come into Emily Lockwood's eyes, a glow of eagerness he had seen before but didn't quite understand. She had leaned forward, speaking earnestly, and it had been the first time Travis had ever seen a real resemblance between the formal, perfectly coiffed and attired woman and her live-wire daughter.

"You have such potential, Travis. You could go anywhere, do anything, be anything. Don't let your...cir-

cumstances keep you down. You are as independent and
contrary as Huck Finn—but I believe your heart is just as
good. With your brain, the possibilities are endless.''

It had been, he had often thought in retrospect, incredibly arrogant and condescending. It had also been, for the
autocratic Mrs. Lockwood, amazing behavior. The queen
of the manor, lowering herself to encourage the proverbial
kid from the wrong side of the tracks. And it had been only
the beginning, then. For over a year she had pushed, prodded and berated, forcing him up to the level she told him she
knew he could reach. She had made him try, made him
fight, but worse of all she had made him believe...and then
she had taken it all back. She had—

A sheaf of papers thrust into his hand disrupted the reminiscence, and he nearly jumped. He shook his head; it
wasn't like him to go off into never-never land like that.

"These papers are the dispensation of Lockwood, Incorporated, including the gravel and concrete operations. I assure you this is all in accordance with Mrs. Lockwood's
wishes." Was it his imagination or did Langley sound a little nervous? Travis lifted the sizable stack of stapled papers, but the lawyer's next words stopped him. "You may
open that envelope now, Mr. Halloran."

With Emily Lockwood's royal permission, even after
death, he thought wryly. He was tempted to ignore the directions and read the papers first, but with a sigh he reached
for the rich, ivory-colored piece of vellum that had been
tucked inside the flyleaf.

His name was written across the front in an unsteady
version of Emily Lockwood's elegant hand. He stared at it
for a moment, aware that, could she have helped it, that
shakiness would never have been evident. She must have already been quite ill. Perhaps she had already known she was
dying.

It gave him an odd feeling, one that it took him a moment to recognize as sorrow. It brought him up short, angry at himself. The woman he would have grieved for had

never really existed, and he hated it when his heart couldn't seem to remember that.

Jaw tight, he moved to rip open the expensive envelope. He stopped mid-motion when he saw, in the same hand, a notation on the flyleaf. His eyes flicked over it quickly.

Travis—
Everything I told you was true; it was I who didn't live up to it. See that you do.

Emily Lockwood

For a moment his throat tightened. Handing out orders even now, he thought. And when it was too late for him to throw them back in her face. When it was too late for him to tell her to go to hell. When it was too late for him to ask her why.

He opened the envelope and slid out a thick sheet of stationery, her name embossed in script at the top, and covered with the same unsteady writing.

Travis,
   If you are reading this, then I will be trying to balance my sorry books with a far more powerful accountant than you. Yet that does not frighten me nearly as much as you do, for it is you for whom I must answer.
   Nothing can make up for what has been taken from you. Only now, when time has become so precious to me, do I realize the grievousness of stealing it from someone. I won't ask for your forgiveness, for I don't deserve it. I will only ask for your understanding; I hope you have it in you to give.
   Richard is my son. He is not the son I would have wished for, I think you know that, but he *is* my son, and I did what I thought I had to do to protect him. That it would be at such cost to someone who was everything I wanted in that son was something I didn't realize at the time.

I know you will not want what I have given you. I beg you to give it time; don't make your decision in the heat of anger, or out of the hatred I'm sure you bear for me. Wait, think, and do what is best for you. I know that if you give yourself that chance, you will make the right choice.

I realize that I am giving you a great deal of power. While Richard, I'm sorry to admit, deserves, as do I, whatever comes to him, I beg you not to use that power against Nicole. She is innocent in this, and I regret that I haven't the courage, even now, to tell her the truth. I love her too much. I'm sure you will tell her, as you should. I know I shall lose her love, as well; she adored you, and would never forgive or condone my betrayal. I'm thankful at least that I won't have to know about it.

While it is true that this offering is given partially out of my own guilt, please believe that it is also given out of love. For I did, and do, love you, Travis, like the son I never had, for everything I saw in you, everything you are and can become. My final sorrow is that I never told you when it would have mattered to you.

Emily

He nearly crumpled the heavy sheet of stationery with the force of his grip. What the hell was she talking about? And how dare she do this now, when it made so little difference, when there had been a time when he would have paid any price to hear those words from her?

"Damn her," he muttered, furious at the stinging of his eyes. "Damn her."

"I...don't understand," came Richard's confused voice. "What does all this stuff mean?"

"I understand."

It was Nicki's voice, cool and controlled as she stood up, the sheaf of papers in her hand. She crossed the room in a smooth, graceful stride that made him wonder where the loping, always-in-a-hurry girl had gone.

"Congratulations," she said as she came to a halt before Travis; her tone was as chilly as the atmosphere in the room. "It seems you've wound up with all the marbles."

His brow furrowed. "What?"

"Read it," she said shortly, gesturing with the papers. "It seems you've inherited half of Lockwood, Incorporated. Welcome to the company, *Mr.* Halloran."

Her voice was bitter, harsh, a tone he would have thought impossible for the girl he'd known. Her face matched her tone, and she turned her back on him. Then, from the door, she looked back over her shoulder and fired a final, piercing shot.

"Not bad, for the man who killed my father."

Chapter 2

"I don't know how you did it, Halloran, but you're not going to get away with it! We're going to fight this! You haven't got a prayer! You're nothing but a con artist! Mother must have been out of her mind to—"

The front door mercifully cut off the rest of Richard's furious tirade. Barely aware of his own movements, Travis made it to the edge of the steps. He stopped and leaned for a moment against the upright post of the porch. His mind was spinning, racing in so many directions at once he felt almost dizzy with it.

He was vaguely aware of the book and papers still clenched in his hand, but made no move to look at them. John Langley had made things quite clear in the stunned moments after Nicki had gone. Emily Lockwood's final blow had been the very last thing he'd expected, yet it was no less demolishing.

A movement in the distance, a slim, darker shape in the shadows of a huge willow tree, caught his eye. He knew who it was; that cool, shady spot beside the man-made pond had always been her favorite place. They'd spent many long hours there, hours that had been both the brightest and the most painful for him to remember. Hours that had both sustained him and tortured him during all the years since.

What would she do if he went to her? If he joined her there in that place where she had confided girlish dreams in a very unlikely confidant, and he had basked in the first freely given admiration and respect he'd ever gotten in his young life?

Get real, Halloran. She'd do exactly what her brother had done; tell him to go straight to hell. Well, he'd been to hell, and he had no intention of going back. And if there was going to be a confrontation with Nicki Lockwood, he would just as soon it be now, and out of earshot of the shocked occupants of the big house. More importantly, out of earshot of her brother.

He saw her sit down on the cool grass, curling long legs under her. For a moment he stood there just looking at her. And feeling things he didn't want to feel, wasn't ready to feel. Not for Nicki Lockwood, who had been the real friend her brother had only pretended to be. Things he shouldn't be feeling for the woman she'd become, Miss Lockwood, of Lockwood, Incorporated. Nicole.

Who, he added silently with an inward sigh, quite probably hated him. He started down the steps. She didn't look up when he parted the trailing strands of the willow and stepped into the quiet, secluded, and heart-wrenchingly familiar spot. The spot he'd thought of so often, that had remained so bright and clear among his memories of the darkest time of his life.

He hesitated for a moment, but when she didn't look up or protest, he sat down a careful three feet away from her. He tried to think of something to say, but no words seemed adequate. He turned over sentence after sentence in his head, but before he could settle on one, she spoke, still not looking at him.

"I remember all the time we spent here."

He wasn't sure if it was a reminiscence or merely an observation of fact, but her voice was low, calm, and he felt a trace of encouragement.

"So do I."

"I never realized what you were doing then. Until today."

"What I was...doing?"

"You obviously did it well. Well enough for my mother to do this."

She still wouldn't look at him, but her words told him what he would see in her face if she did. He realized the calmness he had interpreted as cause for hope was only the outward sign of a hatred too great to be vented in words.

"I don't—"

"No wonder you came."

"I didn't know about this."

Her gaze flicked to him then, disdainfully, and just as quickly away.

He let out a short, harsh breath. "I didn't. How could I have?"

Her gaze stayed on him longer this time, steady and unwavering. At last she smiled, a bitter, cool smile. "You have a point. I suppose not even you would think that all the groundwork you laid back then would survive what you did to my father."

He went rigid, his expression going flat, emotionless, his eyes chilly.

"Oh, yes," Nicki said brittlely, "I forgot, I'm supposed to believe that that wasn't your fault. Just like I'm supposed to believe you didn't know that you were going to inherit half of Lockwood."

His grip tightened on the book in his hand, the book that held the letter from her mother. The image of that letter, of the shakily written words, danced before his eyes. Show her, some little voice inside him screamed. Make her stop looking at you like that. It's so much worse from her...

In the act of reaching for Emily Lockwood's letter he stopped. No, damn it. She should have known. She never should have believed it in the first place. He'd bared his soul to her, trusted her with his deepest thoughts and emotions. She'd known him better than anyone ever had; she should have believed him.

How could she? that little voice spoke up. How could she, knowing what believing you would mean? How could she have made that kind of a choice? She'd been just a girl . . .

A girl. Well, she wasn't a girl now. She was a woman, a full-grown woman who had turned out more beautifully than even he could have guessed, although he'd always known the seeds were there. He wondered idly if Richard ever felt foolish for all the times he had teased her about being a gangly, rough tomboy.

His eyes went over her, from the burnished auburn hair, worn in a sleek, smooth sweep, to the clear, sky blue eyes rimmed with thick, heavy lashes, to the sassy nose and pert chin. And the rest of her was all woman, too, ripely curved in all the female places yet still long, taut, and supple. He felt a twinge he suppressed before he even had a chance to admit what it was.

No, she wasn't a girl now. And if the woman still didn't believe him, he wasn't about to beg. He had gone too long without any pride at all to easily surrender what he had gained now.

"What was in the letter . . . she left you?"

He nearly jumped. Trust her to read his mind; she'd always been uncannily able to do so. The temptation to tell her rose in him again, but this time it was that tiny pause in her words, that catch on the word "she" that stopped him. If he showed her, told her, it would destroy her vision of her mother forever. *I know I shall lose her love,* Emily had written. His gaze went to her pale, strained face, to the dark shadows beneath her eyes.

He couldn't do it. He couldn't be the one to add the straw that might break her fragile strength. Not now. Besides, the letter didn't prove anything except that Emily Lockwood had felt guilty for some unspecified reason. Just like her to leave the dirty details to someone else. And just like her to drop this bombshell in his lap without warning.

"It's . . . personal," he said at last.

"And none of my business?" She laughed. It sounded harsh. "I'd say it's—or at least it *was*—quite literally 'my business.'"

"I don't want it." His voice was flat, inflectionless.

"I'm supposed to believe that, too? Believe that you don't want half of an operation that grosses over thirty million a year?" Her voice went from bitter to sarcastic, and it bit deep. "Oh, I suppose you're so successful now you don't need it, right?"

For just a moment he wanted to throw the book, the letter, and the business papers in her face. He wanted to shout his achievement at her, make her see that he wasn't the failure everybody had expected him to be. He didn't do it; he wasn't at all sure she'd even care. Not only was she no longer a girl, there was no trace of the girl he'd known in the icy, distant woman before him.

"I never would have figured you for such a superior bitch," he ground out.

For a split second something showed in her eyes, something alive and pained, glittering as she scrambled to her feet. "And I never would have figured you for a liar, a killer, and now a . . . a thief."

His breath left him in a rush, as if her words had been a lethal blow. Pain knifed through him, slicing through old, buried scars. Oh, yes, it was so much worse from her.

She turned and ran toward the house. The only resemblance to the girl who had raced that path so often came when she bent to tug off her high heels so she could run barefoot through the lush grass. But in those days she had run it joyously, not in anger and hatred.

Wearily, Travis got up and followed, trying to piece together the mental armor she had shattered so easily. She, of all of them, had the power to get to him, to pierce that thick shield he'd worked so hard to build.

And he was going to need that shield, he thought as he saw Richard come out the front door, followed by John Langley. He heard the lawyer say something in calming tones, but Richard wasn't listening. He was tugging at his rather lank, dull brown hair, as he always had when upset, and his words carried easily across the wide front lawn.

"I don't care what you say, Langley! This is the most outrageous thing I've ever seen. We're not going to stand for this." He looked up and saw his sister. "Are you coming?"

"Where?" She sounded as tired as he felt, Travis thought. This had to have been rough on her. She and her mother had been close. Not, he reminded himself rather fiercely, that he cared.

"To see Frank Hartford! A *real* attorney, one with the brains to stop this farce! He'll put this con man in his place."

He saw Nicki look at Langley, who shook his head. "As I've told your brother, the provisions are unbreakable. Your mother was of sound mind, and quite explicit in her desires." He went on in the tone of one who had explained this far too many times. "Her interest in all the Lockwood holdings are now Mr. Halloran's, and by the terms of the will, non-transferable for a period of six months. After that he may dispose of it as he wishes."

Richard snarled something unintelligible, then turned back to Nicki. "Are you coming, or not?"

She sighed. "All right."

"Good." Richard clambered down the steps, moving awkwardly, as if they were much steeper than they were. He came to a halt when he realized the Cadillac's door was blocked by an immaculate black Mercedes. "Who the hell left this here? Langley, is this yours? Move it, right now."

"Not mine," the man said hastily.

For the first time since he'd admitted to himself that he'd intentionally driven the Mercedes instead of the Jeep, Travis was more glad than rueful.

"So sorry, Richie," he said blandly as he pulled the keys out of his pocket and unlocked the door. He didn't even try to smother the little spurt of satisfaction he felt at Richard's gaping stare. He tried to ignore Nicki's look of doubt as she stared at the expensive car.

"That's yours?" Disbelief rang in Richard's voice, and it scraped over nerves already raw.

"No," Travis snapped. "I stole it." His eyes flicked to Nicki, the memory of her words still burning deep in his gut. "But I'm sure that wouldn't surprise you, would it?"

He yanked the door open and slid into the driver's seat, anxious to put this place that seemed to be the scene of every crisis in his life behind him. Fool, he berated himself silently. That's what you get for thinking you could impress anybody in this town.

He turned the key and shoved down the accelerator; the powerful engine roared to life. He heard the tires squeal as he raced the car out of the long, curving driveway, but he was beyond caring. And he denied inwardly that it took any effort at all not to look in the rearview mirror as he left.

"And so, Mr. Halloran, that is essentially it. Both Lockwood children hold the half interest left them by their father, twenty-five percent each. You hold the other fifty percent."

Travis leaned back in the leather chair, his elbows resting on the arms as he steepled his fingers in front of him for a moment before he spoke. "So what you're saying is, there is no majority."

"Exactly."

Langley sounded pleased. Since there was nothing he could see to be pleased about in the arrangement, Travis assumed it was because he had understood the implications of what Emily Lockwood had done.

"Mr. and Miss Lockwood together can match, but not outvote you. If one of them was to join with you, of course, you would have a decisive majority."

"And it might snow here on the Fourth of July."

"Er...yes, I gathered there is...some tension there."

Travis chuckled dryly. "You have a flair for understatements." He looked at the attorney behind the big oak desk curiously, then scanned the office. After a moment, phrasing it carefully, he said, "No offense, Mr. Langley, but why did she come to you? The Lockwood's legal affairs have been handled by old man Hartford for years."

Langley coughed. "Yes, I'm aware of that. Mrs. Lockwood explained the situation. She said in this instance she most particularly did *not* want to deal with Mr. Hartford's firm."

"Because?" Travis prompted when he hesitated.

"I got an idea—strictly an impression, you understand—that she was afraid he would try quite adamantly to talk her out of what she intended to do."

I'll bet he would have, Travis thought sourly. Old man Hartford had hated him from the day he'd let the air out of the tires of his new Lincoln when Travis was ten years old. He would have thought she was crazy, Lockwood or not. He met Langley's bland, professional gaze, and thought he saw a spark of, if not curiosity, at least interest.

"And you were new in town. You didn't know enough to try and stop her. Am I right?"

"I've been here only a few months, yes. But in any case, it's not my job to judge. I'd like to think I would have fulfilled her wishes in any case."

Travis studied the man for a moment. Yes, he thought, maybe you would have. "Did she tell you . . . why?"

Langley didn't pretend not to understand, and Travis liked him even more for that. "Not really. No details. Just that it was to pay a huge debt. One that was long overdue."

Travis closed his eyes. "And far too late," he murmured.

"Pardon?"

"Nothing. It doesn't matter."

"The answer? Or the payment?"

Travis smiled slowly, in acknowledgment of the man's perception. "Both." He let out a long, weary breath. "I don't want it."

Langley never blinked. "I see," he said, as if people turned down millions of dollars in his office every day. "Hmm. I'm afraid the conditions are unalterable. The percentage, and the income, are yours whether or not you decide to take an active part in the business."

"I don't want it," he repeated.

"I'll have to consider this," Langley said, brow furrowed. "I suppose there could be a way, a trust, perhaps. Of course, as I explained, in six months it becomes yours free and clear, and you may sell it, turn it back, or do whatever you wish."

"I don't want it, now or six months from now."

Langley studied him for a moment. "You do realize the amounts we're talking about here? The concrete operation alone—" he paused and shuffled through some papers until he found the one he wanted "—pours an average of a thousand yards a day, five days a week. At a current rate of about sixty dollars a yard that's—"

"Three hundred thousand a week. Fifteen and a half million a year. I know."

"Yes. And with the gravel pit operations on top of that, you're looking at—"

"I know how much it's worth. Believe me. I spent a great part of my life envying it."

"Oh?" For the first time, Langley looked startled. "I shouldn't have thought that you would envy anyone."

His mouth twisting wryly, Travis answered the unspoken question. "Did you think I've always been where you found me?"

"No, but—"

"It was a long haul to that office. Speaking of which—" Travis sat forward suddenly, fixing his gaze intently on the other man "—that is between you and me. No one else is to know."

After a moment's hesitation, Langley nodded. Travis didn't miss the pause, and his gaze narrowed. "You've already told someone?"

"Not exactly."

" 'Not exactly'?" Damn, Travis thought, he would have sworn he could trust this man. And these days he wasn't usually wrong; he'd learned the hard way to judge people. But if he'd already been flapping his mouth...

"I mean, I haven't told anyone who... could tell anyone else."

"What does that mean?"

"It... took me quite some time to locate you. My client was concerned that I wouldn't be able to do so in time. So when I did, naturally, I had to reassure her."

"You told...Mrs. Lockwood? About Willow Tree? That I...?" He was stunned, the emotional turmoil that had finally abated after he'd left the house—and Nicki—rising anew.

"Yes."

He tried to bite back the words, he didn't want to ask, didn't want to admit that it mattered. And then he was asking anyway. "What... did she say?"

As if he understood the dilemma of the man across his desk, Langley answered quietly, gently. "She knew the company name immediately. When I told her you owned it, she said, 'Of course. I knew he would do it. It would take more than a foolish, wicked old woman to break Travis Halloran.' And," he added as Travis closed his eyes as if against great pain, "she said it with more pride than I've ever heard from anyone. As if she were speaking of...a beloved son."

Something broke deep inside him, and Travis felt the hot, flowing relief of a festered wound lanced and cleaned at last. It was the release of a pressure carried so long it had almost been forgotten, yet the relief was almost dizzying.

For the first time he thought, not of what he had gone through since that fateful day in the Lockwood house, but of the hell Emily Lockwood had lived with. She had been a polished, discriminating woman, with most definite views on right and wrong, and the wrong she had done must have gnawed at her no less than her betrayal had eaten at him.

More so, probably, he realized now. She had had a lot farther to fall; he had only begun to climb when she had knocked him down to the bottom rung once more.

I love you... My final sorrow is that I never told you when it would have mattered to you.

It matters. Damn it, I don't want it to, but it does, Travis thought, trying to control the urge to blink against the stinging behind his eyelids, unwilling to betray so much even in the unexpectedly neutral company of John Langley.

Neutral, he thought suddenly. Neutral only because he didn't know. But he would, soon. As soon as the amazingly efficient grapevine of San Remo passed on the news of Emily's will, the eruption would be heard for miles.

"... research this. When I have some options, where can I contact you?"

Yanked back to the present by the words, Travis noted with appreciation that Langley had assumed he would not be at the Lockwood house. When he opened his mouth to answer, the words that came out were not at all what he had planned to say moments ago.

"No. Let it stand, for now. I need to...think about this."

Don't decide in the heat of anger, or out of hatred, she had written. Well, he wasn't angry now. And he wasn't sure he hated anymore. What he did know was that he was tired. He'd driven since before dawn to get here; that and the confrontation with Nicki had drained him thoroughly.

Richard, he could deal with; his hate meant less than nothing. But the realization that Nicki so utterly and completely loathed him had shaken him. He had hoped—foolishly, he admitted now—that over the years she might have softened a little. He supposed she would always blame him for her father's death, but he'd thought when the initial grief had passed, she might remember how close they'd been, might think about it, and begin to wonder.

Right, he told himself scathingly. You never believed in Santa Claus, and he's a lot more likely to exist than a believing or forgiving Nicki Lockwood.

"I'll be staying down in San Clemente," he said abruptly. He pulled a piece of paper out of his jacket pocket and read off an address and phone number.

"No room number? A residence?"

He nodded. "I'm borrowing it."

Langley nodded and wrote it down.

"I won't be there until tomorrow. I have some arrangements to make at home."

"I imagine so."

There was no expression in Langley's voice, merely an acknowledgment of fact. Despite himself, Travis smiled.

"You don't give much away, do you, Mr. Langley?"

The thin man raised an eyebrow. "Hardly appropriate, in my line of work."

The smile widened. "I think I'm glad she came to you."

"Thank you." He studied Travis for a moment. "You've changed your mind, then?"

"I don't know. I'm going to think about it."

"Good. It's not a decision to be made in haste." He began to gather up the papers on his desk.

Travis lifted an eyebrow. "No advice?"

"I don't recall you asking for any."

With a wry laugh, Travis said, "I didn't think lawyers waited to be asked."

"Some don't." He shrugged. "It's clear to me that there are things involved here that I don't know about. Any advice I might give would quite possibly be useless, or even harmful. Besides," he said, eyeing Travis assessingly, "some people need advice. I don't think you do."

Travis stood up. "I don't think you do, either. So I won't bore you with the gruesome details. You'll hear about it all soon enough, I can promise you that. When it hits the fan, I'll leave you to make your own judgment."

And hope like hell I'm not making a mistake, he thought as he drove down the coast. But I have to trust him, for now. I don't have the time or the energy to deal with the details now. It's going to take all I've got to handle facing one Nicole Lockwood for the next few days.

* * *

Nicki rubbed at her forehead, then propped it in one hand as she dropped her pencil on top of the stack of papers on her desk. She couldn't seem to concentrate today. It was as if there were some gnawing, annoying thing flitting around the edges of her consciousness, distracting her without revealing itself so she could do something about it.

It wasn't the usual distractions; she'd long ago grown accustomed to the constant noise, the rumble of material trucks arriving every few minutes and off-loading tons of sand, rock and gravel, and the rolling sound of the mixers that had been loaded. She'd learned to ignore it all, to tune it out, to relegate it to the background as she worked, as she had once done her homework over the background of the rock and roll blaring from her headphones.

But today that ability to concentrate had deserted her completely. Every time she yanked her mind away from the knowledge that, just down the hall, her mother's office sat empty, it seemed to go to the shocking fact of Travis's presence. And the even more shocking realization that he now owned half of the company she'd devoted the past five years of her life to.

Work, she ordered herself silently, turning back to the pile of papers on her desk.

Richard had done it again. He'd sent out forty yards of concrete to a buyer who already owed them several thousand dollars, tying up four mixers they'd needed elsewhere, for paying customers.

She couldn't count the number of times in the past six months that he had done it, or something like it. Something that cost them time or money they could ill afford. Like buying a new, unnecessary truck to the tune of one hundred and twenty-five thousand dollars. Or putting money down on an adjoining piece of property for an expansion they were nowhere near ready for. Or promising deliveries that were far over and above the plant's already filled capacity.

Ever since their mother had become too ill to work and Nicki had begun to spend more time with her than at the plant or the pit, Richard had, with a grand display of nobility, doubled his own time there. The work had to be done, and he wouldn't dream of taking Nicki away from home at a time like this. He would handle things, and they weren't to worry about anything. Which had made her worry all the more.

She sighed. Richard enjoyed playing the wealthy benefactor. He extended credit, he donated money, material and time—more often than not her time—to any cause that might get the Lockwood name in the papers. He played the successful, generous businessman to the hilt, and refused to listen to her warnings that if he kept it up, there wouldn't *be* any business.

She nearly laughed. As of yesterday, there was no business, at least not for them. Why? she asked herself for the thousandth time. Why had her mother done this insane thing? For the person responsible for her beloved husband's death? Had Travis truly wormed himself so fully into her mother's heart fifteen years ago that she had left half of the company she and Robert Lockwood had built up from nothing to him, to the exclusion of her own children?

She knew Emily had seen something in Travis, even as a teenager with a wild reputation as the son of the ludicrous town drunk, something that she had never seen in her own son. She had more than once told Nicki that she wished Richard had half the brains and gumption of Travis Halloran. Silently, although she felt slightly disloyal to her brother, Nicki had agreed. Even at fourteen, she had sensed the tremendous difference between the two; it was what had drawn her to Travis—

Stop it, she told herself sharply. Concentrate on this mess.

Her mother had been proven right too many times to count in the years since her father had been killed. Richard had absolutely no head for business, and it had taken both her and her mother to undo the damage he seemed to inflict so easily.

In the past six months, Nicki had had little time left for the day-to-day business operations; she'd spent every possible moment with her rapidly failing mother. And she was only now finding out what six months in Richard's hands had done to their financial situation. She hadn't had a chance to go through everything yet, but perhaps Travis wouldn't be getting such a prize after all.

And why, she thought suddenly, was she bothering with this? He was half owner now, let him straighten it out. She smiled icily. Whatever Travis Halloran had been doing all these years, she doubted it ran to solving problems of this kind or size.

The smile faded as she remembered his words, flung at her under the tree that had sheltered so many of their quiet, heartfelt talks. A superior bitch. Had she really become that? That last thought had been decidedly arrogant, she admitted. Who knows what he'd been doing? And on the heels of that thought came a quick, vivid memory of a gleaming Mercedes sitting in their driveway. The expensive car shook all her disdainful assumptions, she admitted ruefully. For all she knew, he was—

He was standing in her doorway. One shoulder against the doorjamb, he stood with ankles crossed, as nonchalantly as if he— She nearly laughed at herself as she realized her next thought would have been "as if he owned the place."

"Somehow I don't think that smile is for me."

"Oh, it was. Indirectly." She managed to keep her voice cool despite the sudden hammering of her heart. In the hours she'd spent with him as a girl suffering from a severe case of puppy love she'd tried to hide, she'd often fantasized about what he would look like years ahead. Nothing, she'd thought then, could surpass those dark good looks, that air of reckless energy. But the boy had become a man, and he was more devastating than she had ever imagined.

He wore jeans today, faded and snug, but whole. A sudden vision of the first time she'd seen him flashed through her mind, a memory of sitting in a heap at his feet, expecting him to laugh at her because all of Richard's friends did.

But he didn't. And she'd known instinctively that this one was different, this one was special.

She hated the fact that he was able to affect her like this, and she narrowed her gaze. The jeans were faded, but the leather sport shoes were new, and the gray sweater he wore looked like some kind of linen blend. And expensive. As was the soft gray, suede bomber-style jacket he wore, she realized. And the thin gold watch that banded his right wrist.

Only now did she remember that at the funeral he had been wearing an exquisitely cut suit that bore the unmistakable stamp of an Italian designer. And, she thought as the pictures played back in her mind, a silk tie. The Mercedes, she thought again suddenly. She'd known he was mocking them when he'd made the crack about stealing it, but she'd wondered if perhaps he'd rented it in an effort to impress them. Maybe it *was* his, she thought now. And despite having spent a great portion of a sleepless night telling herself she didn't care, she wondered what he'd done all these years.

"Taking inventory?"

There was a touch of asperity in his voice, and she snapped upright.

"Why not? Isn't that what you're here for?"

"Sure. Why not?"

"Why not, indeed," she said tightly. "So tell me, Mr. Halloran, where would you like to start in surveying your new kingdom?"

The only visible reaction to her tone was in the slightest chilling of already cool gray eyes. "Why not right here?" he said, his tone carefully level.

"Here?"

"I've heard if I want to know what's really going on around here, I should come see you."

"Richard is the—"

"Figurehead. You're the brains." She flushed, then was furious when he added, "Not my opinion, of course. But the guys out in the yard say you do all the work."

"Then let me do it. I have too much to do to—"

"Besides," Travis interrupted smoothly, "Richard and I are hardly on speaking terms."

"What," she grated, "makes you think that we are?"

"We're talking, aren't we?"

"You're talking. I'm trying to work."

"I always knew you'd wind up running the place."

"I didn't. But then I never knew you'd end up owning the place, either."

"Half."

"A half that makes it impossible for us to function."

"Then you're admitting there is an 'us'?" His tone was sweetly even.

"By 'us,' I meant Lockwood, Incorporated." The words nearly hissed through her clenched teeth.

"And heaven forbid a non-Lockwood should be part of that."

"If heaven could forbid it, you wouldn't be here."

"Is it that, or is it just me?" he asked softly.

"Both," she said flatly.

"You hate me that much?"

"What did you expect? To be welcomed with open arms?"

"I was, once."

"Get out."

A dark brown shot upward. "Orders, Ms. Lockwood?"

"You may own half of this place for now, but this is still my office. Get out."

"My, you do that well," he said, that casual nonchalant tone back in his tone. "That imperious, nose-in-the-air Lockwood glare. You do it almost as well as your mother did."

She stood up suddenly behind the wide desk. "You bastard," she snapped.

"Oh, no. I'm many things, but not that. My parents may not have been much by the exalted Lockwood standards, but they were married."

Her cheeks flamed. She felt it, hating her telltale fair complexion. "Those 'exalted Lockwood standards' seemed attractive enough to you, once."

"And unattractive to you, as I remember. You called them ... arrogant, I think was the word."

A chill swept her as he called up more of the memories she was trying so hard to suppress. "Perhaps," she said, struggling to retain a fragile control over her voice and emotions, "I was too young to realize the importance of standards, then."

He didn't miss the implication that if she had, she wouldn't have spent so much time with him. "But you're older now," he said coolly.

"And wiser. Enough to know that standards are what give us integrity and principles."

"Well, since obviously I can't offend your mother's standards anymore, it must be your personal version. It goes against them to let in an outsider?"

"No." The memories were stinging inside her, pushing her to the edge of tears that she swore she would not give in to, and she struck back in the only way she was sure would hurt him. "It goes against them to let in an ex-con."

Chapter 3

She'd meant it to hurt, but she hadn't expected to cringe inwardly at the flash of pain in his eyes. And she certainly hadn't expected that the look of stone-faced resignation that replaced the instant of pain would somehow strike a blow to her as deep and harsh as the one she'd delivered.

She didn't understand it. She should be exulting in the knowledge that she could hurt him as he'd hurt her. She hadn't forgotten the nights of agony, endless hours of wrestling with the pain of her father's death. And the pain of betrayal. So why did the sight of his eyes turning to the cold, bleak gray of granite stab at her so?

"Well, Ms. Lockwood," he said, his voice cold, "I'm afraid you're stuck with...this ex-con."

"I know."

Much of the heat had gone out of her voice, and he looked at her a little oddly. But his voice was still cool, still rigidly even when he said, "In that case, you won't mind if I take a look at the books?"

One delicate brow arched. "The books? Don't you want to look at the plant?"

"I've seen it."

"That was . . . a long time ago."

He never even blinked at her reference to the times when Richard, eager to impress his rescuer with the true extent of his family's wealth, had brought Travis here to show the place off. He'd bragged proudly of the day when it would all be his, when he would be the Lockwood of Lockwood, Incorporated. Travis had guessed then, as he'd watched the men of the plant scowl at Richard behind his back, and smile at Nicki as she darted around and asked her quick, clever questions, how it would turn out in the end.

"I meant today." He leaned casually against the edge of her desk. "I've been here for a couple of hours."

No wonder she hadn't been able to concentrate, Nicki thought wearily. She'd always seemed to have some sixth sense when it came to him; she'd often known he was in the house before she'd ever seen him, coming downstairs or in from outside unerringly within moments after he'd arrived. He'd always laughed, teasing her about her "radar," but she'd known he wasn't laughing at her. That radar still seemed in working order.

"The books?" he prompted.

"All right." She shoved the memories back again; the effort sharpened her voice once more. "I'll set them up for you. But if you're expecting me to sit here and explain everything to you—"

"I don't expect anything from you, Ms. Lockwood."

The words, and the formal title dug a little deeper into the wound caused by that look in his eyes.

"Travis—"

"I wouldn't think of keeping you from your work. If you'll just point me in the right direction, I'll . . . struggle through."

Swearing inwardly at her chaotic emotions, she covered her agitation with a quick, jerky movement for the power switch of the computer terminal on her desk. She flipped it on with an angry flick of her wrist.

"Nothing's been entered in the past few weeks," she said shortly, with no attempt at justification as the machine ran through all the system checks and loaded the accounting software. She'd been much too wrapped up in the grim knowledge that her mother was slipping away from her so quickly to worry about this; thus the monumental pile of paperwork on her desk.

Travis merely nodded, not asking for an explanation. She straightened then, looking at him.

"The program is pretty self-explanatory. F1 is your help key. You just—"

She broke off, doubt showing in her eyes. Travis read her look and said dryly, "Believe it or not, I can find my way around a keyboard." He chuckled mirthlessly. "I may be an ex-con, but I'm not an idiot."

"I never thought you were. I know better. I just didn't know what you'd been . . . if you'd ever . . ."

She stopped, floundering, her color deepening. Hastily she gathered up the stack of papers and stepped out from behind her desk.

"I'll do these down in Mother's office . . ."

Travis heard the strained note in her voice, but couldn't stop himself. "Wouldn't it be easier for me to move?"

"No!"

His slow smile was a joyless one. "Sacred territory? Not to be soiled by the presence of an ex-con? What if I decide it comes with my share of the business? She did leave it to me, after all."

Nicki paled. Her hands tightened around the pile of papers, and without another word she walked out of the office. Travis knew that if he'd wanted revenge for her remark, he'd gotten it in spades.

With a smothered sigh he sat down at the desk and tugged the keyboard toward him. His mouth twisted into a wry smile as he looked at the screen glowing with the familiar logo. Ironic that they used the same program. Quickly he tapped a few keys, made a selection, and sat back to read.

By the time a sound at the door broke his concentration, the picture was gloomily clear. Lockwood, Incorporated was on the edge of real trouble. And for senseless, illogical reasons he didn't understand. What the hell had been going on here, anyway?

He looked up in time to see Nicki cross the office to a bank of file cabinets and silently file away several papers. Then she left the room again, only to return in less than a minute with a large cardboard box. She walked past him to set it on the credenza behind her desk, then, at last, turned to face him.

"I've cleared out some things." Her voice was carefully neutral. "If you don't like…that office, then as half owner, I'm sure everyone will understand if you pick whatever one you do like."

He studied her for a moment, regretting his earlier words for reasons he didn't quite understand. Lord knows, she'd fired the first salvo in this skirmish. Yet he couldn't seem to rid himself of the instinctive reaction he had to her pain. Couldn't break the old habit of wanting to protect her. When he spoke, his voice was soft.

"I don't want your mother's office."

"Fine. Take whatever you want."

The inference that he would with or without her okay was clear in the slight edge that had crept into her voice. He tightened his grip on his temper; since he'd already known how much worse that belief was coming from her, he should have been prepared. He kept his tone quiet.

"You haven't asked why I changed my mind."

She gave him a look that told him exactly why she thought he'd changed his mind.

"I still don't want it. But I want to know what your mother expected me to do with it."

"Don't ask me. I don't understand why she did it at all."

"Don't you?"

It came out as nearly a whisper through his suddenly tight throat, and Nicki's head shot up. She stared at him for a moment, and he could read in her face that this was familiar territory for her.

"No. But you do, don't you? She told you. In that letter."

Travis stiffened. Then he made himself relax, and shrugged without speaking.

"Why? Tell me why!"

"Think about it," he urged softly.

"Do you think I haven't?" It broke from her on a cry, and she looked away. When she spoke again, her voice was lower, if not calmer. "I know she...cared a great deal about you...once. But to do this..."

She trailed off, her incomprehension apparently too deep for words.

"Looks like you've got two choices, then. Either your mother was crazy, or she had another reason."

"She wasn't crazy! She was lucid almost to the end."

Travis raised an eyebrow, waiting for her to acknowledge the alternative. Instead, her voice becoming heated, she turned on him.

"I don't know why she did what she did. I don't care what she wrote to you. And I don't know what kind of hold you had on her, or how you managed it, but we're going to see that you don't keep it. This is Lockwood property, and it's going to stay that way."

He forced himself not to react to the not-so-thinly veiled accusations, and merely raised an eyebrow. "We?"

She looked a little surprised. "Richard and I."

"Oh." He gave her a one-shouldered shrug. "Sorry, I'm too familiar with Richie's kind of help to believe that he'll be of much use to you."

She went stiff. "I will not discuss my brother with you. You've already tried to hurt him enough." She moved forward, looking pointedly at her desk. "I've cleared out an office for you. Please use it. Now."

Give it up, Travis told himself. She'd had fifteen years to think about it, and it hadn't made the slightest dent in that Lockwood certainty. Without a word, he gathered up the notes he'd made and started toward the door. At the last minute, he turned back.

"Is it the brother we're not discussing who's been running this place lately?"

"I said I won't—"

"I know. I just wondered who'd been making all the bonehead decisions around here. Somehow I don't think it's you."

Nicki glared at him, yet there was an odd glow in her eyes, and he guessed that while she was angry at his criticism of the way the company was being run, she hadn't missed the implied compliment. Perhaps she was even pleased by it, which, he realized ruefully, would make her even angrier.

He saw her soft, full lips tighten, and guessed she was battling to hold back some sharp remark. He left before she lost the fight.

"So you've decided? You'll accept the inheritance?"

Travis paced the lawyer's office, stopping before a wall of books. "For now. Something's wrong in that company, and I want to know what it is."

And the fact that he was virtually certain the something wrong was Richard didn't hurt matters, either. He'd thought he'd outgrown the need for revenge, but perhaps he hadn't after all; he wouldn't mind finding out Richard had been the failure.

John Langley's silence caught his attention, and he turned around. The attorney was carefully setting out several papers on his desk, facing the side where Travis had been seated before he'd begun his pacing.

"If you'll just sign these, then . . ."

Travis raised an eyebrow at the carefully level tone, but walked over to the chair before the desk and sat down again. He scanned the papers, then lifted his gaze across the desk to the thin man.

"What about the other arrangements we discussed?"

Langley picked up a folder from beneath his left elbow. He held it out across the desk. "Right here. I think this will accomplish what you want."

Travis took the folder and started to open it. Then he stopped. He lifted his head and looked at Langley. The man's expression was the same as always, carefully neutral, but something in his eyes gave Travis the clue. He closed the folder.

"I see the San Remo grapevine is as effective as ever."

Langley sat back in his chair. "If you mean have I heard the town's version of what happened fifteen years ago, then yes." He smiled rather wryly. "A great many people took great pains to make sure I heard all about it."

Travis lifted a brow. "The town's version?"

Langley propped his elbows on the arms of his chair and laced his fingers in front of him. "If I have learned anything in my limited time here, it is that anything involving the Lockwoods is news."

Travis smiled, a little grimly. "Headline news."

"Yes. And the Lockwood interpretation of events is what is usually accepted as fact."

"Usually?" Travis met the man's steady gaze. "Meaning you're the ... exception?"

"I have," Langley said, "a very logical mind. I do not know the people involved, except superficially. I have no preconceived ideas, nor am I emotionally involved. I prepared Mrs. Lockwood's will, and listened to what little she said. There is only one conclusion I can draw."

"Oh?"

"Arthur Conan Doyle said, through Sherlock Holmes, 'When you have eliminated the impossible, what remains, however improbable, must be the truth.' I found it impossible to reconcile the given fact of Mrs. Lockwood's words and actions with what I was told about the events surrounding her husband's death. Therefore ..."

He shrugged, as if his conclusion was only an exercise in logic and not a flaunting of an entire town's beliefs. Travis sucked in a deep breath, then blinked, a little stunned by the strength of his own reaction. He didn't even know this man, why should it matter what he believed?

Because he's the only person in this damned town who doesn't believe the Lockwood version, he told himself. And probably only because of that very thing: Langley didn't know him. If he did, if he'd grown up here, hearing all his life about Travis Halloran, perhaps his logic wouldn't have been quite so crystal clear.

The why didn't matter, Travis realized suddenly. Only the fact that this man had done what no one else had; looked at the facts and reached a decision that wasn't based on the unsavory reputation of a wild, reckless boy, and the fact that he was the son of the town's drunken nuisance.

"Thank you," he said quietly.

Langley looked surprised. "For what? I merely reached the only possible, logical conclusion."

Travis let out a mirthless chuckle. "For being the only one in this town capable of doing just that."

And as he signed the papers Langley had drawn up, he tried not to think of the one person in this town who should have been able to do it, who should have known him well enough to know that what they said was impossible. But she hadn't known it then, when she'd had all the faith of a young girl's heart in him, and she certainly didn't now, when there was nothing of that young girl left.

It didn't matter that he knew, deep down, that he was asking too much. It didn't matter that he knew he was being unreasonable to want her to turn her back on her own family for him; with Nicole he'd always led with his heart, and his heart didn't want to listen to reason. Not fifteen years ago, and not now.

Nicki tapped her pencil on the yellow legal pad on her lap, pondering the list she'd begun. With her chair turned away from her desk, she had her feet up on the credenza, staring out the rather grimy window into the yard.

It was much worse than she'd feared. They were in trouble, much more trouble than she'd realized, until Travis's words had made her take a much closer look. She'd been aghast at what she'd found.

It was going to take a minor miracle to get them out. She had to restrain herself from tracking down Richard and asking him what the hell he thought he'd been doing while their mother lay dying, but she knew if she confronted him now, she would say things she might regret later. She might be furious at him, he might be the biggest bonehead in the entire world when it came to business, but he was still her brother.

Bonehead. That's what Travis had said. Bonehead decisions. Well, as much as she hated to admit it, he was right. But then, Travis had never been stupid, no matter what the general opinion of the gossips in town had been.

She remembered one day when he'd arrived at the house, pulling up in his battered old Mustang and parking it in front of the door as if he had every right, just as he had all year. She'd seen him from her window, and despite being sick and feverish from a nasty early summer cold, she'd run down the stairs to greet him, skidding across the marble floor at the bottom.

"Hey, slow down!" he'd said, stopping, his brows furrowing as he took in her pajamas and robe. "What's wrong, Nicole?"

He was the only one, besides her mother, who used her real name. It made her blush, because every time he did she remembered what he'd said when she'd asked him why.

"Because you're going to be a beautiful woman some day. Nicole will suit you then. Just like Nicki does now."

She hoped her feverish face hid the rise of color in her cheeks; it must have, because he reached out one hand to touch her forehead.

"I've got—" she had to break off for the sneeze that shook her.

"A rotten cold," he finished. "And you're burning up. You should be in bed. And not," he added with a sternness that somehow didn't seem odd from the by then seventeen-year-old Travis to the fourteen-year-old Nicki, "running around with bare feet. Scoot back upstairs."

"But I—"

"Do as he says, Nicole," her mother directed from the door of the library. She sounded so odd, Nicki thought, and she was staring at Travis with such a strange look in her eyes ... "Go on."

"But I want to talk to Travis—"

"Now."

"Mom—"

"Go on, Nicole. I have to ... talk to your mother for a minute. But I'll come up and see you before I go." His eyes flicked to her mother. "If it's all right."

Her mother nodded, and Nicki reluctantly started up the stairs. But when Travis followed her mother into the library, curiosity overcame her and she tiptoed back down and crept over to the door.

"You wanted to see me?"

Her mother's voice held that odd note of animation she recognized; she heard it whenever she'd done something her mother thought exceptionally clever. And she heard it almost every time her mother talked to Travis, she realized suddenly. Odd that she'd never noticed before; perhaps it was because she couldn't see but could only listen from her spot outside the door.

"I thought ... you might want to see this."

There was a rustle of paper, and then a small exclamation from her mother.

"A's and B's!"

A report card, Nicki realized. And he'd done well, she thought with a rush of pride in him. He'd told her once he'd always done just enough to slide through with Cs, more often Ds. Or, at least, he had until her mother had gotten hold of him. Emily Lockwood had pushed and demanded, and Travis had responded first with anger, then disbelief, and finally, this year, with results.

And sitting there, crouched outside the library doors, Nicki had remembered the first time Travis had ever talked to her about what her mother was doing. It had been six months after he'd started coming to the house regularly, and he was still in the disbelief stage.

"I don't know what the he—" He'd broken off, giving her a sideways look.

"Oh, please," Nicki had said scornfully, "Richard swears in front of me all the time."

"Well, he shouldn't."

"I'm not a child, you know," she'd said with all the superiority a fourteen-year-old could muster. "You don't know what?"

It seemed to take him a moment to remember what he'd begun to say. When he did, much of the earlier heat was gone. "I don't know what your mother's up to."

"What do you mean, 'up to'?"

"Why she's spending all this time nagging me about school and reading and learning."

"She thinks you're smart." Nicki had shrugged. "She does the same thing to me."

"She doesn't nag Richie."

Nicki had grinned; she knew her brother hated the nickname, but she couldn't help it. "Because he isn't smart. He doesn't have the brains, the drive, or the potential you do, that's what mother says."

Travis had stared at her. "Why? Why does she care?"

"Why not?"

"I'm not— She doesn't— Hell," he'd spat out, his earlier words apparently forgotten, "my own father doesn't give a damn, why should she?"

Nicki had bit her lip, his bitter words hurting her somewhere deep inside; she knew enough about his home life now to know what Travis had just said was quite probably true.

"Maybe *because* Richard doesn't have the brains, the drive, or the potential," she'd said with the sometimes devastating acumen of the young.

"Well, if she thinks she's going to reform me or something, she's crazy." His voice had taken on that stubborn tone she'd come to know.

"Oh, quit," she'd said, hating it when he got like that. "Besides, why would she want to reform you if she thinks you're so great the way you are?"

He'd stared at her, as if still startled by the way this irrepressible girl with the upturned nose faced him down without a qualm. Then he'd grinned.

"You always manage to turn it around on me, don't you?"

She'd smiled at him. "You know it's just an act. You try to sound tough, and act like you don't care, but I know better."

"You," he'd said, reaching out to tap her nose, "know too darned much."

But he was smiling when he'd said it, and she'd seen that warmth in his eyes that she somehow knew shone only for her. And maybe, like now, when he showed her the results of her efforts, for her mother.

"I told you that you could do it," her mother said in a triumphant tone that had startled Nicki out of her daydream. "And in only a year!"

"I know." Travis sounded strange, as if his throat was tight, so that it hurt him to speak. "I... No one ever believed in me like that before..."

"Ah, Travis, don't ever let anyone tell you you can't do anything you want to. You have it all. Everything I wish Richard—"

She stopped abruptly, and Nicki knew why. She herself had suffered from that feeling of disloyalty when comparing Richard to Travis and finding her brother so wanting.

And she knew now why Richard wasn't home yet; she doubted that his report card would measure up to Travis's. But then she had found herself scrambling away and up the stairs to avoid being caught eavesdropping.

And two months later, her father was dead because of Travis.

Nicki's mind, recoiling from that painful memory, sent her careening back to the present. A truck was rumbling past the window, vibrating the glass. She glanced out, seeing the full mixer pull out of sight around the corner of the building.

And then, suddenly, she became aware of something else, a disquieting, shivery feeling of being watched. Only then did she remember that, somewhere near the end of her reverie, she had vaguely registered her office door opening.

She glanced over her shoulder toward that door, and smothered a small sound of dismay when she saw Carl Weller standing there, an expression that could only be described as lurid on his unshaven face.

In the privacy of her closed office, preferring the comfort of having her feet up, she hadn't been particularly cautious about her position; Weller's avid gaze on the long, bared length of her legs made her wish she'd worn something other than a dress. It was hardly practical for a cement plant anyway, a dirty, dusty place at best, but she'd had a meeting this morning and hadn't had time to change.

Then anger spurted through her; she'd be damned if anyone was going to control what she wore or how she sat in her own office. Carefully, giving no evidence at all of haste, she lowered her feet to the floor. She stood up slowly, glaring at the man across the desk. He was about her own height, thin except for a noticeable beer belly, and his eyes were a dull, cold brown that had always bothered her.

"Have you ever heard of knocking, Mr. Weller?"

"Hey, I did!" the man cried defensively. "You didn't answer!"

"Do you know what a closed door means? Did it ever occur to you that there might have been a reason I didn't answer? That perhaps I didn't want to be interrupted?"

"Hell, you weren't doing anything but staring out the window!"

Nicki slapped down the legal pad she'd been holding, her anger ballooning. "If I spent half my day like that, I'd still accomplish more than you," she snapped.

Weller smirked. "Well, I guess it's a good thing I work for your brother instead of you, honey."

Nicki's blue eyes went icy. "Mr. Weller," she said sweetly, "you call me that again and there won't be enough of you left to be fired."

Sensing he'd pushed too far, the man backpedaled hastily. "All right, take it easy. I only came to tell you that your brother wants to see you."

"Fine. He knows the way." She sat down and tugged the keyboard of the P.C. on her desk toward her.

Weller ran a hand over his thinning, mouse brown hair. "He meant in his office."

"I don't have time." She tapped a few keys. "If it's not important enough for him to come here, it's not important enough to bother me with."

Weller looked taken aback, then his lip curled nastily. "I'll tell him you said that, Your Highness."

Nicki didn't even look up. "You do that."

Weller turned on his heel and headed for the door. Then his footsteps came to an abrupt halt, and Nicki heard him grunt as if he'd run into something solid. She looked up, and saw Travis blocking the doorway of her office, Weller glaring up at him.

"Move it, con man."

Travis lifted an eyebrow as he looked at the grubbily clad man. "Interesting choice of words," he said mildly. "Been listening to Richie?"

With a snarled grunt, Weller tried to shove his way past Travis. It was like trying to move one of the trucks parked outside; he never budged. Then, with an elaborate bow, he stood aside and let the man pass. Straightening, he propped one shoulder against the doorjamb and crossed his arms casually.

Slowly, Nicki stood up, barely realizing she was doing so. "What are you doing here?"

"I heard you and your friend as I was passing by. I thought I'd stop and see if you needed any...pest control."

So he'd been listening, she thought, wondering how much he'd heard. Or seen. Then she saw his gaze flick from her dress to the credenza she'd had her legs propped on, and she knew he'd seen and heard more than enough. Her chin came up.

"I don't need any help from you."

"I can see that. You handled him fine. What I don't see is why the jerk still works here."

"He's a friend of Richard's. He's been here for years."

"Oh?" He straightened up and walked into her office. "Richard managed to keep a friend for years?"

"Yes," she said stiffly. "Something you wouldn't know about."

His expression never wavered. "You're right. I don't know anything about the kind of friendship that lets you be an ass—a jerk to a friend's sister. Not to mention one of your bosses."

He sat on the edge of her desk, one foot braced on the floor, the other casually swinging free. Nicki opened her mouth to retort sharply that she knew exactly what kind of friendship he knew about, the kind that let him try to blame a friend for his own deadly mistake. But the words wouldn't come, and she wound up just standing there, glaring at him as she resisted the urge to back away.

Strangely, he looked at her as if he knew exactly what she was thinking, exactly what she wanted to say. As if he still had that instinct that, years ago, had allowed him to coax her deepest thoughts and dreams out into the open. But he only said, "Is he always like that?"

Nicki sighed. "Yes. A jerk." The words came easily now, as if she'd never suffered that temporary muteness. She sat back down, some of her anger at Weller returning. "I'd fire him in a minute," she admitted, "if it was up to me."

Travis ran a finger along the edge of the calendar on her desk, riffling the edges of the pages. "I get the feeling it wouldn't be for just his . . . attitude."

"No. He's lazy, incompetent and a pig."

He lifted his head. "But you keep him. Because he's Richard's friend."

"Yes."

He studied her for a moment, an odd expression in his eyes, then let out a short, compressed breath. "Loyalty," he said softly. And Nicki knew he wasn't talking about Weller. Or Richard.

"And I suppose," she said, her voice icy as anger rose in her again, "you feel you deserved loyalty, even after what you did?"

That odd expression in the gray eyes vanished. "Me? Of course not." He stood up abruptly. "You made it quite clear that I didn't deserve even the loyalty you give to . . . lazy, incompetent, piggish jerks."

Despite herself, Nicki winced. She hated the fact that she could still hurt for him, and instinctively struck back. "At least Carl never killed anyone."

His jaw tightened. Nicki could almost see him fight down the denial that rose to his lips. It surprised her. Was he, at last, going to stop denying it, going to start taking responsibility for the tragedy he'd caused?

If only he would, she thought suddenly. If he had, in the beginning, it would have made so much difference. He'd been a kid then, a little wild and reckless. It had been an accident, that night his reckless driving had shattered her world. But she could have, she'd realized, forgiven him. In time. But he'd tried to dodge it, to sidestep the blame in the worst possible way, by passing the buck to a friend, and for that she could never forgive him. Especially since that friend had been—

"Damn it, Nicki, I said I needed to see you now!"

Richard was already shouting as he burst in the door. Then he spotted Travis and whirled on him.

"What the hell are you doing in here?"

"Discussing . . . personnel," Travis said mildly, that emotionless mask that had slipped for a moment when confronted by Nicki carefully back in place.

"Personnel?" He tugged at his hair. "That's my department, Halloran. You keep your nose out of it." He seemed to remember then what he'd been yelling about when he'd come in, and turned back to his sister. "Why didn't you come when I sent for you? I have to talk to you—"

"The next time you need to talk to me," Nicki interrupted coolly, "I suggest you pick yourself up and walk over here. If that thirty feet is too much for you, use the phone. Or write a memo. But don't *ever* send that man in here again."

"Aw, Carl's okay, you just never have liked him."

She ignored his suddenly cajoling tone, and his words. *"Ever,"* she repeated. "You do, and he's gone, friend of yours or not."

Richard's temper flashed again. "Look, Miss High and Mighty, you don't fire anybody around here without my say-so. I run—"

"Nothing."

It was only one word, delivered with deadly calm, but it stopped Richard in mid-tirade. He whirled back to Travis, gaping.

"You seem to forget," Travis went on levelly, "that you don't have a controlling interest in anything here." His gaze flicked to Nicki. "If she wants to fire the . . . jerk, she's got my vote."

"I told you I don't need your help!" Nicki put in furiously.

"Your vote? Your help?" Richard almost screeched.

"If she wants it."

Richard spun awkwardly back to Nicki. "What the hell have you been up to? What's he done? What's he talked you into? I know you want to run this place all by yourself, but would you really throw in with Dad's murderer to do it, you disloyal little—"

"Knock it off, Richie," Travis warned.

"Stop it!" Nicki shouted, and she wasn't sure at which one of them. "I don't need you to defend me," she ground out to Travis, then glared at her brother. "And I've had enough of your silly, childish tantrums! Both of you, get out of my office!"

"But—" Richard began.

"Now!"

Cowed by her wrath, Richard shuffled toward the door. Travis let him pass, then followed, only to stop and look back over his shoulder. There was something oddly akin to a salute in his eyes as he glanced at her, and one corner of his mouth quirked upward before he went out and pulled the door quietly shut behind him.

Nicki sank down into her chair, wrapping her arms around herself. She was so upset that she was shaking a little, angry at Travis for putting her in the position of looking like she was aligning herself with him against her brother, furious with her brother for his vicious accusation, and, above all, frightened at the warm, proud feeling that look in Travis Halloran's eyes had given her.

Chapter 4

She shouldn't have yelled at Richard like that.

Nicki sighed and put down the lengthy list of things to do she had finally finished. Whatever his faults, he was her brother, and all she had left of family now.

What did it matter if he had a blind spot about Carl Weller? They'd been friends for years, and she had to admit Travis had been right; Carl was about the only friend Richard had kept that long. She shouldn't complain if Richard kept him on out of loyalty, even though—

Loyalty. The word echoed in her mind, soft and intense, as it had sounded when Travis had whispered it. Whispered it in a voice that clawed at her inside, that made her once again get the feeling that he'd somehow been the victim. It was crazy, she insisted silently. She'd given him her loyalty once, all of it, and it had brought her nothing but pain.

No, she corrected herself, not just pain. It had given her strength, as well. When her school friends had stared in shocked awe when she spoke of Travis's visits, she had responded with all the strength and loyalty of her young heart, as if she alone could convince them he wasn't really the cold,

tough guy they thought he was, that what fascinated them
so was only a front put on to hide the real person beneath.
With the memory of those quiet talks beneath the willow to
bolster her, she was unshakable.

"But Travis Halloran, Nicki!" This had been from Cyndy
Alexander who, for reasons Nicki couldn't comprehend,
seemed to think Richard was the man of her dreams. "He's
nothing but trouble, everyone says so."

"He is not!"

"Well, he is gorgeous," Melissa Morton put in, "I
wouldn't mind having him come around *my* house, but my
mother would have a fit."

"My mother likes him," Nicki said staunchly.

Melissa lifted a brow. "Doesn't she think he's too old?
He's nearly seventeen, isn't he?"

"Too old for what?" Nicki asked, genuinely puzzled.
"To be my friend?"

"Oh, Nicki, grow up," put in Lisa Corliss, Nicki's closest friend and supporter. Except in this. "I mean," she
added with a worldliness beyond her fourteen years, "he *is*
gorgeous and sexy, with those go-to-hell eyes, but not for
you. He's...experienced. I mean, he's been around, with a
lot of girls, and you're just..." She waved a hand vaguely.

"It's not like that," Nicki protested, embarrassed by
Lisa's precocious observations.

She meant it; she supposed she did have a crush on Travis,
as much as a girl just discovering boys could. But the
friendship she'd found with him, the fact that he was the
only person who really listened to her, the only person who
heard her, was so precious she'd kept it hidden, afraid if she
let it show he'd go away to avoid being embarrassed by the
unwanted romantic fantasizing of a fourteen-year-old. And
no matter what her friends thought, she didn't want him to
go away, for any reason.

And if her mother stood up for him, the least she could
do was be as strong. She had been proud when, faced with
a group of San Remo matrons who sat gaping as the town
bad boy sauntered out of the Lockwood library and through

the parlor as if he lived there, her mother had calmly introduced him as if he were an honored guest, using the power of her position in the local society to force their acceptance.

Travis had gone along with it, only the wicked glint in his eyes showing that he knew perfectly well what they were thinking. As coolly as if he'd been dressed in clothes to match their expensive dresses instead of ragged jeans and a torn sweatshirt, he acknowledged the stiff greetings with impeccable politeness.

But he hadn't been able to resist a broad wink and a grin at Nicki, who sat suffering through the impossibly boring conversations at her mother's orders. And as he went past her chair and out the door, she heard him laugh, just loudly enough to be heard.

As she sat listening to the horrified exclamations, and her mother's regal dismissal of them, she was more aware than ever of the social gulf between them.

"Why?" she asked him when she'd been able to break free and meet him beneath the willow. "How can they treat you like that?"

He shrugged, the casual movement of someone long used to such treatment. "Why do they treat you the way they do?"

"But that's different. They don't even know you."

His casualness gave way to a sudden intensity. "Do they know you? Really know you? Or do they just know you're a Lockwood and treat you that way?"

She stared at him, stunned. It was a concept she hadn't confronted yet in her young life. Wherever she went, the mere mention of the Lockwood name guaranteed her respect. Wherever Travis went, his name—and the reputation that went with it—guaranteed him at the least wariness, more usually distaste or outright dislike. And she wondered if the gulf between them was so wide after all.

"You're right," she whispered after a moment. "They don't know me. They ask me all these dumb questions, but they don't listen to the answers. They don't really care. They only do it because I'm a Lockwood and they think they have to.''

Travis had looked at her wide eyes, and at the harsh realization in them. She looked away. "Sorry, Nicole," he said gruffly, putting an arm around her shoulders. "I didn't mean to—''

"No." She cut him off. "I should have known." She looked back at him with troubled eyes. "But at least they're nice to me...even if it is just because I'm a Lockwood. But you ... they ...''

"Would like me removed from their pretty little world. Yeah, I know." He grinned, as if to show he didn't care, but Nicki saw it was a little crooked, a little off center.

"Why do you encourage it? Why do you act like...like they're right about you?''

"I just give them what they expect.''

"But why?''

"They're gonna believe it anyway.''

"But wh—''

"Damn—'' he said in affectionate exasperation, "don't you ever run out of questions?''

"How else will I learn? Besides, you're the only one who tells me the truth.''

He opened his mouth and then shut it, not knowing what to say to that.

"So, why?''

He sighed. "Nicole, my father runs a bar, a dive that nobody you know would be caught dead in. The city's been trying to get rid of it for years. They want to clean up that part of town, but he won't budge, and it makes them mad. If there's a fight there, my old man's more likely to jump in and join it than break it up. The cops are always out there. It barely breaks even because he drinks up the profits.''

"So? That's your father, not you.''

He chuckled ruefully. "I wish the rest of this town could separate the two. To them I'm as tied to him as you are to the Lockwood name.''

"But that's not fair! Why should you get blamed because your father's a—"

His jaw tightened when she broke off, and a look came into his eyes that frightened Nicki; he looked so very old, and so very angry. As he looked at her, the anger faded. He ran a hand through his shaggy hair. Then he sighed.

"A drunk? The town clown? And troublemaker? Who's always starting a fight, or mouthing off about this town trying to break him, and that they'll pay for it?" She saw him try to hide a shudder of distaste. "And then he starts whining. Tries to get them to feel sorry for him..."

Something in his eyes answered her original question for her. "That's it, isn't it?" she breathed. "You'd rather have them dislike you, rather have them mad at you, than feel sorry for you because of your father. So you go out of your way to make sure of it."

He shrugged, looking away, but the pain in his eyes before he did made her almost glad he hadn't answered.

After a while, she asked softly, "What about your mother, Travis? You never talk about her."

"She's dead."

"I know, but—"

"She's been dead for eight years. I barely remember her anymore."

"Maybe that's... why your father drinks. Because she died."

He laughed harshly. "I doubt it. They were...quite a pair. He'd get drunk, then beat her up. And then she got drunk herself, to take away the pain. Finally it killed her."

Nicki stared at him in horror, but it had little to do with the grim words he'd said and everything to do with the realization that had just struck her.

"That's why you... When you... Those cuts and bruises, and that black eye..."

He looked away quickly, but not before she caught the expression that flitted over his face.

"It was your father, wasn't it? All those times when you were hurt, and everybody said you'd just gotten in another fight, it was your father..." She faltered, a sob rising in her throat.

"Don't." His voice was husky, thick. "Don't cry. Not for me, Nicole."

"But you let them think you're always in trouble, always fighting, beating people up..."

"It doesn't matter."

"But it does!"

"Damn it, don't feel sorry for me. I can't stand that. Not from you."

"But if you told them—"

"Told them what?" he snapped. "That my own father hates my guts? What would that do except tell them they're right? What kind of kid has a father who hates him, except the kind they already think I am?"

"Stop it!" Nicki scrambled to her knees in front of him, tears staining her cheeks, her eyes wide and filled with pain. "Just stop it!"

"Nicki—"

"You're not like that, you're not like they say! But you make sure nobody can see it."

Travis sighed wearily. "People see what they want to see."

"What do you expect? Other people won't stop putting you down until you stop putting yourself down."

He stared at her for a long, silent moment, then reached out a hand to tug at the long, fiery braid of her hair. "Are you sure you're only fourteen?"

Nicki blushed, but shot back, "Are you sure you're not about a hundred?"

His mouth quirked sideways. "Sometimes," he muttered under his breath, "you make me feel that way."

Nicki's brow furrowed. "What?"

"Nothing. Never mind. And don't worry about me. I'm a survivor."

A survivor. The word rang in her head now, bringing an end to the chain of memories and bringing back the quandary she'd been mired in. He'd had to be survivor, to get through his life with his father, and she couldn't help the compassion that still tugged at her at the recollection of all the times he'd shrugged off the black eye, or the split lip.

But that compassion was at war with the knowledge that he had once been a survivor at the cost of her father's life. He had died, if not at Travis's hands then certainly as a direct result of his recklessness. He had—

A sudden commotion broke in on her thoughts. Shouts, curses, then warnings. Outside. Near the chemical drums. Jumping to her feet, she whirled to look out the window, peering through the pervasive grime of cement dust.

Men were clustered around the grouping of chemical barrels, one of which had an ominous, spreading pool of liquid beneath it. For a split second she just stared, but when no one seemed to be doing anything, she spun away from the window and headed down the hall toward the dispatch center at a run.

She glanced around incredulously at the normal look of the busy room; they didn't know.

"Hit the water switch," she shouted, "the hydrochloric tank is leaking!"

There was a frozen moment of motionlessness as everyone stared at her, then, as she started toward the switch herself, someone finally moved and did it. Nicki ran to the window that gave a narrow view of the backside of cement plant number one, and to her relief she saw the gush of water flowing into the yard to neutralize the burning acid they used to clean the trucks.

"What happened?"

"I don't know," she said grimly, watching the flurry of activity below, "but I intend to find out. Now."

Only when she turned to go did she realize who had asked the question.

"What are you doing in here?"

Travis shrugged. "Trying to learn. Any objections?"

"You're the boss." Irony laced her voice. "Do what you want."

Travis looked at her, an odd light in his eyes. "What I want . . ." he began, then stopped.

She shrugged and began to walk to the door. He followed.

"This is quite an operation you have here." He gestured at the big room with the angled glass windows that gave a clear view of nearly all the traffic in and out of the busy yard. "Like a control tower."

She didn't look at him. "Essentially, that's what it is."

"Is everything done by computer?"

"Mostly." She pulled open the outer door and started down the steps. "They track the contents of the bunkers and silos, and the slurry tank. And do the figuring of the weights of rock, sand, cement, and water for the load, depending on the slump."

"Oh."

She gave him a sideways look as they reached the bottom of the stairs. "That means how wet—or runny—the concrete is. A one slump is—"

"Dry. Five is wet. I know."

Surprised, she raised a brow. "Been asking questions?"

"All my life."

Something in his tone made her look at him sharply, but his face was expressionless as they walked around the building. They made their way past the two cement plants, each with its huge bunkers full of raw materials towering overhead, and walked toward the small group of men clustered in the now flooded yard. As they neared the scene, Travis eyed Nicki dubiously.

"If acid leaked, should you be out here like that?"

She glanced down at her expensive heels and nylon-clad legs. "These shoes aren't nearly as important as finding out what happened here. Besides, the water will have neutralized the acid anyway."

He looked at the flood. "Where did it all come from? Pressure hoses?"

"Better. The slurry tank."

Travis glanced toward the huge, tall silo that held both fresh water and the water reclaimed from the remnants of loads that were returned to the plant after a job. Nicki noticed that he didn't have to ask what she meant; he had indeed, apparently, been asking questions. Or, she thought suddenly, not sure why, he'd already known. What *had* he been doing all these years?

"You just open it?"

She nodded.

"Then what?" he asked, looking at the huge pool of water that was now lapping at their feet.

She gestured toward the lowest corner of the yard, where the water stood the deepest. "There's a pump over there. It pumps it back to the tank."

Travis raised an eyebrow. "Slick."

"It works."

"When somebody remembers to do it?"

Her head snapped around. "Our people know their jobs."

"Then why did you have to do it?"

"That," she said as they skirted the edge of the water and approached the group of men, "I intend to find out."

"Son of a—" The tall, lanky man broke off as one of the others coughed violently. He looked up to see Nicki, and said quickly, "Sorry, Miss Lockwood."

"It's all right, Max. What happened?"

After a brief, suspicious glance at Travis, the bearded man turned his attention back to Nicki. "Damned if I know. The valve's broken clean off."

"Somebody hit it?"

"Couldn't be," one of the others chimed in. "I was here after the last truck left, and it was fine."

"He's right," Max said. "Besides, it's not bent, or anything, like it would be if one of the trucks backed into it. The valve handle's just broken clean off, like somebody hit it with a hammer."

Nicki's brow creased. Her eyes flicked over the half dozen men gathered there. "And no one saw anything?"

A chorus of negative shakes of the head was her answer.

"Why didn't you call dispatch?"

Max looked blank.

"For the water," she said patiently. "If I hadn't heard you yelling and looked out, they never would have known to hit the switch."

"But Carl said . . ."

Max trailed off, but Nicki hadn't missed his words. "Carl said what?"

"Aw, nothing. I must'a misunderstood him."

"Max, somebody could have gotten hurt here, at the least badly burned. Don't protect someone who endangered all of you."

Max shifted his feet uncomfortably. Nick understood, knew that he was well aware of Carl's favored status as a friend of Richard's.

"Hey, the guy hung us all out to dry," the short, wiry man who had spoken before broke in; he was new, Nicki noted, and perhaps not as impressed by Carl and the way he lorded his "in" with the boss over the others. "He said he was going to turn in the alarm."

Fury rose in her. She clenched her teeth determinedly. She wanted to vent her anger, but realized that in front of the men was neither the time nor the place. She was going to find Richard, right now, and have it out with him about Carl Weller. She'd had enough—

Nicki jumped as someone sloshed through the water behind her, splattering her legs. She whirled around so quickly to see who the idiot was that she slipped on the wet asphalt; only Travis's quick, strong arm grabbing her kept her from going down.

"Are you okay?" Travis glanced quickly at the leaky tank with its hazard symbol, then back at her spattered legs and clothes. "Are you sure that stuff is all right now?"

"Yes. I'm fine."

She tried to pull away, but his arm was like a steel band around her waist, unyielding. His touch disconcerted her, which added to her anger when she saw who had splashed her.

"Hey," Carl said with a broad, casual grin as he came to a stop in the puddle, "good, the water came on."

"No thanks to you," Nicki grated, only able to speak at all because Travis had at last released her.

"I was going to call it in," he said, unperturbed, "but I had to take an emergency phone call first. I figured somebody else'd do it."

"Of course," Nicki said, seething. "You always figure someone else will do it."

Carl shrugged blithely, gesturing at the water. "And somebody did, didn't they?"

"And somebody could have gotten hurt in the meantime!"

"Nobody did." The hard brown eyes went over her slender body in a way that made her feel dirtier than the grubby water he'd spattered her with did. "Except you got a little wet. But you're a tough lady, aren't you, Miss Lockwood? You know if you're going to play with the boys, you're going to get dirty."

She felt Travis tense beside her. She let her fingers brush his arm, hoping he'd get the signal to do nothing, although she wasn't sure why she thought he might do as she wished. Amazingly, he did.

"If you mean," she said icily, "can I fight dirty like the *boys*—not the *men*—here, then you'd better believe I can."

"Uh-oh," Carl said in mock terror, "I think I made the boss lady mad!"

"What was the phone call about?"

Carl gaped, and Nicki turned to stare at Travis.

"Huh?"

Travis arched a brow at Weller's confusion. "Your emergency phone call. What was it about?"

"Oh, uh, it was... Er..." Color flared in Weller's unshaven face. "Hey, I don't have to explain anything to you! None of us do!" He looked at the other men, as if seeking support. "He's going to be out of here as soon as Richard gets that stupid will his mother left straightened out. Don't tell him anything."

The faces that met his outburst were hard; any one of them could have been injured through his neglect, and they all knew it.

"Hey, don't look at me like that, man! *He's* the enemy, not me!"

"Carl," Max said angrily, "go find someplace else to screw up."

Swearing, Weller swiped at the water with his foot as he turned and stalked off. It rose in a sheet, drenching Nicki from feet to mid-thigh. She felt Travis tense as if to go after the departing Weller, but he stopped when she muttered, "Never mind."

He looked at her. Her chin came up. "I was already wet. A little more doesn't matter."

"A little more?" He looked at her limp dress, and the way his eyes lingered over the way it clung to her legs made Nicki feel oddly warm despite the chill of the wet cloth. As did the strangely thick sound of his voice when he added, "You need to go home and get out of... I mean, get into some dry clothes."

The odd break in his words sent a shiver up her spine that was at odds with the warmth he'd kindled, and she turned away with a jerky little motion so he wouldn't see.

"There's something I have to do, first." Her confusion over her conflicting emotions made her voice tight as she started back toward the offices.

"What's more important than not catching pneumonia?"

Her anger was returning, helping her to shove the turmoil Travis seemed to inflict on her so easily out of her mind. Her steps hastened, but Travis kept up easily with his smooth, long-legged strides.

"Getting rid of Carl Weller," she snapped. "He's lazy, useless and obnoxious, and I've had it."

"He's worse than that," Travis said. "He's dangerous."

Nicki stopped suddenly, a little startled by the grimness of his tone.

"Dangerous? I know he's careless, but isn't that a bit extreme?"

"No." It was flat, uncompromising.

"How can you know?" Nicki was irritated to find herself in the position of practically defending the likes of Carl Weller, but Travis was being so arbitrary about it... "You never even knew the man a week ago."

"I know his kind. A sneak with a mouth bigger than his brain, and probably a knife to make up the difference."

"Carl?" Her voice rang with disbelief; she'd never liked the man, despised him, in fact, but she'd never considered him particularly dangerous. "If anything, he's a coward."

"Exactly. That's why he's dangerous. A man will come out front and fight you clean. A coward slinks around behind you and then slits your throat. And believe me, he's got the look."

Nicki caught her breath. He saw her staring at him and smiled, a thin, bleak curving of his lips.

"You learn a lot in jail," he said, confirming the guess he'd read in her eyes, "or you don't come out alive."

Nicki turned away abruptly, starting toward the building again as fast as she could manage in heels over the uneven pavement. She'd always put that part of what had happened out of her mind, unable to even imagine Travis in jail. He'd always been so wild, so reckless, that the thought of him caged, trapped, had been inconceivable to her young mind.

He'd had the same wanderlust she'd had as a girl, a longing for the far away, the exotic, the unknown. During those idyllic months together, when he'd finished his sessions with her mother, they'd spent many an hour in the seclusion of that willow-shaded spot, talking of their plans, of how they would someday see the world.

It had been the first time in her life that she had ever really felt guilty about her family's wealth. He wanted it as badly as she did, perhaps more, since the life he'd known until now had been so much more miserable than her own. Yet she was the one who would have her dream; her father had already promised her a trip to wherever she wanted to go when she graduated college.

"I'll get there," Travis insisted. "Somehow."

"You could join the Navy," Nicki said, some slogan about seeing the world coming vaguely to mind.

Travis laughed. "Yeah, sure. Can you see me in one of those stupid hats?"

Privately, Nicki thought he'd look fantastic in a dress white uniform, but she kept that, as she did all other such thoughts, to herself. "But at least you'd get to go places."

"And put up with all those rules and regs? No, thanks. I couldn't handle that."

"You could wait and come with me," Nicki said innocently.

Travis seemed to stop breathing for a second before he said flippantly, "Sorry, can't afford first class."

"I can. For both of us."

Nicki wondered if he'd felt a cool breeze she'd missed, because he seemed to shiver. "You really would do that, wouldn't you?"

"Of course," she said simply. "I'd rather go with you than anybody else, anyway."

He groaned. "Damn, don't say things like that."

"Why not? It's the truth."

He looked at her for a long, silent moment, then sighed wearily. "You know, Nicole Lockwood," he said softly, "sometimes you make me feel . . ."

"Feel what?" she prompted when he trailed off.

"Never mind."

She made a disgusted sound. "I hate it when you do that!"

"I know."

"So what will you do?"

He shrugged, then laughed as if to shake off the serious mood that had overtaken them. "I don't know. Ship out on a freighter, maybe."

Nicki's eyes widened. "Really?"

"Nah," he said with another laugh. "I couldn't hack being at sea for months, with no way to get off the ship. I'd feel too trapped."

And less than a year later, Nicki thought grimly as they started up the stairs to the office, he'd been in the tightest trap of all. She stifled a shudder. She'd always buried any disquiet about what had happened to him beneath her anger and grief over her father; now, for the first time, she wondered how he'd stood it.

"Something bothering you?"

It wasn't so much the words as the tone of his voice that made her look at him sharply. The moment she saw his eyes, she knew that he had guessed her last thought.

"No," she began, but when he kept looking at her steadily, she couldn't seem to go on with the lie. She'd never been able to lie to him; she didn't know what had possessed her to think she could start now.

"It was hell," he said softly, as if she'd answered with the truth. "Two years of hell."

Nicki's eyes stung at the pain in his voice. "It was . . . a long time ago," she said inanely.

"It was yesterday."

His voice was bitter, harsh, and that unexpected tide of guilt rose in her again. Furious at herself for letting him get to her again, as they stepped inside she turned on him, and struck back in a voice equally bitter and harsh.

"You put yourself there."

He laughed, a short, rough burst of sound. "Did I?"

"Don't start that again."

"Right. I forgot. When a Lockwood's involved, there's only one side to the story."

"There's only one truth, you mean."

He looked at her for a long moment. "That's exactly what I mean."

"Why, Travis?" Her anguish broke free. "Why do you have to lie about it? Maybe you were driving crazy, but it was an accident. Can't you just admit it and stop this . . . this charade?"

He stopped their progress down the hall by gripping her shoulders and turning her to face him. "I'll be the first to admit I'm no angel," he said, "but there's one thing I've never done. I've never lied to you, Nicole."

It was the first time he'd used that name since he'd been back, and it sent a quiver through her just as it had fifteen years ago. She stared at him, searching his face as if it held all the answers she'd never had.

"Travis—"

"Get your hands off my sister!"

Nicki jumped, but Travis never moved. Nor did he remove his hands from her shoulders; he merely turned his head to watch Richard storm furiously down the hall toward them.

"I said let go of her!"

Travis turned his head away from Richard without a word, his gaze going back to Nicki questioningly.

"Please," she whispered. After a second Travis nodded, and released her. But he didn't step away, only turned unhurriedly to face Richard.

"Got a problem, Richie?"

"My problem is you, Halloran!"

"Don't hurt yourself," he drawled, looking at Richard's flushed face. "Your sister and I were just having a little . . . historical discussion."

"I don't care about that—"

"Somehow I didn't think you did." His eyes flicked to Nicki as he cut her brother off; her face showed clearly that she knew her brother's bluster had been more out of habit than any desire to defend her.

Richard seemed thrown off track, and it took him a moment to regain his momentum; even to Nicki it seemed studied, planned. "I don't know what kind of stunt you're trying to pull here, but it's not going to work!"

"Stunt?"

"You know damned well what I mean." He tugged at a thin lock of hair.

"'Fraid not, Richie."

"I'm talking about that so-called accident we just had!"

Travis merely raised an eyebrow; Nicki turned to stare at her brother.

"What are you talking about?"

"Don't tell me it didn't occur to you to wonder why we suddenly had an accident with one of those chemical drums? We've never had any trouble like that—"

"I know that. What's that got to do with Travis?"

"You're such a fool," Richard told her scornfully. "You never could see past the end of your nose when it came to him, until we made you."

Nicki flushed. "Stop it, Richard."

"Well, it's the truth. You followed him around like a love-struck puppy, and you're still doing it."

"I am not!" She was blushing furiously now, and she didn't dare look at Travis, hating the fact that he was witnessing her humiliation.

"He killed our father, damn it! Doesn't that mean anything to you?"

"You know it does. But what has that got to do with the acid spill?"

"I should have known you'd be too blind to see it. You always were blind around him."

"Damn it, Richard." He looked startled when she swore. "Quit beating around the bush and say what you're trying to say."

"What he's trying to say," Travis cut in, his voice cold and hard, "is that I'm somehow responsible for what happened out there."

Nicki's eyes widened. Her gaze swiveled to Travis, stunned. Of all the possibilities, that had never occurred to her.

Could it be? she wondered. Was she really that blind? Did just his presence make it impossible for her to see the truth? Could she see nothing else when pinned by those gray eyes?

But why would he do such a thing? Why would he purposely damage the business he now owned a large piece of? Her confusion showed clearly in her eyes, and she saw

Travis's face set in those expressionless, masklike lines once more. It hadn't changed since all those years ago, when he'd presented it to all the world. Except for her.

"Travis," she said urgently, "you didn't, did you?"

"If you have to ask, it wouldn't do me any good to deny it." His jaw tightened, and she saw the pulse beating at his temple. "Just like that. Again. Signed, sealed and the Lockwood verdict delivered."

"I knew he couldn't deny it!" Richard crowed.

Travis looked at the gloating man who had once, he'd thought, been his friend.

"I learned the hard way when not to waste my energy. Just like I learned the hard way who my friends really were, Richie."

With a glance at Nicki that made that odd feeling of compunction flood her again, he turned and walked away, leaving her staring after him, wide-eyed and confused.

Chapter 5

Travis walked up the street slowly, hands jammed deep into the pockets of his jeans, aware of but ignoring the stares that met him every step of the way. He told himself they couldn't possibly all recognize him. Some of them were too young to have known about him. Some, he thought with a wry inward smile, probably hadn't even been born when he'd left under the proverbial cloud.

But they looked anyway, and he wondered, as he had years ago, what it was about him that made people look twice.

Back then it had been understandable, he supposed. He'd gone out of his way to cultivate that rough look, that impression of being always on the edge of trouble. Not that he'd had much choice; when your wardrobe was limited to three pairs of ragged jeans and a few T-shirts, it was hard to do much else.

The leather jacket he'd worn back then had been from a secondhand store whose owner had been willing to accept the construction of some shelving in his storeroom as payment. Coupled with the shaggy hair he couldn't afford to get cut anyway, and the frequent marks from when he hadn't been able to move quickly enough to dodge his father's raging swings, he looked more than a little wild.

It hadn't, he thought, been because he'd wanted to draw attention to himself. The opposite, if anything. He didn't want anyone getting close, anyone who might find out. As Nicki had once guessed, he'd decided back then that he'd rather have everybody in town mad at him than have them look at him with the contemptuous scorn they turned on his father. His appearance, and the attitude he had cultivated then was all for a reason. And it had done what he'd wanted—kept people at arm's length, so that no one found out how scared he was underneath.

No one except Nicki. She knew. She'd always known, always sensed it somehow. And hadn't thought any the less of him for it.

But now, he thought in puzzlement, it was the same. He dressed respectably, even well when the occasion demanded it. He got his hair cut, and shaved, with some regularity. The ragged, belligerent kid was gone; there was nothing he could see on the surface that would make people take that second glance.

If he had any sort of inflated ego, he might have thought the women looked twice because they liked what they saw; their expressions certainly seemed to say so. But he'd had too much bitter experience with that expression to believe it.

And men looked, too, with a kind of wariness that he remembered. He'd seen it often enough in the faces of the straighter, richer high school crowd, even when they'd been looking down their noses at him. They seemed to consider him some kind of threat, but since he generally steered clear of their kind, he'd never quite been able to understand why.

Nicki had told him once, in one of their long sessions beneath the willow tree, that it was because he made them feel trapped, caught in their narrow existence, afraid of any kind of danger, and doomed to spend their lives without a single taste of adventure.

He'd laughed, dubbed her an amateur shrink, but the words had once again been wise beyond her years, and made him wonder. Enough to ask her something else, wanting to hear her answer.

"How about the girls, then? Got an answer for them, too?"

She'd flushed a little, but held his gaze and answered. "It's the same thing. Only you're that taste of adventure they're too chicken to try."

He'd laughed again, thinking it absurd. It had been a long time before he realized that she'd been exactly right, that women were strangely attracted to the threat, the sense of danger they attached to him. They were drawn to the image, the only thing he showed them, as if it gave them some vicarious thrill. As if they were proving something by being seen with him. Or fulfilling a dare made with their rich friends.

They used him and cared less than nothing about him personally. It had been a hard lesson to learn, but one he remembered now, any time he caught those furtive glances from women who seemed intrigued by him.

Was there still some of that old aura clinging to him? Was that why they looked at him? Or was it just that he so obviously didn't belong in this town that had so thoroughly cast him out?

Maybe, he mused, it was some kind of cosmic quirk, that of all the towns he'd ever been in, this was the one where he stood out for some unknown reason, the one where heads turned when he walked down the street, where people he didn't even know gawked at him.

He didn't know and firmly decided he didn't care. He didn't care what anyone in San Remo thought of him, or if they thought of him at all. Except for Nicki. And he knew she thought of him; sometimes he'd swear he could feel it. He only wished that he could hang onto any belief that it wasn't always with hatred.

His steps slowed as he turned the corner he'd been headed for. He'd parked a couple of blocks away, not wanting to draw any attention to this pilgrimage he wasn't sure why he was making. He came to a halt, staring.

It was gone. In the place of the small, shabby, window-less wall that had been the front of Halloran's Tavern, was a bright, cheerful, glass-walled pub, chairs neatly placed upside-down atop the tables as someone swept the floor. It appeared spotless, a far cry from the dark, dingy hole he remembered, with several of the local drunks perched pre-cariously on dilapidated bar stools, beginning even at this morning hour their daily drinking.

The sight of it then had made him shudder. Now it was merely a genial and apparently successful gathering place with an atmosphere of warmth and cheer that made his memories of the old place seem even bleaker.

The whole area was cleaner, several of the shops and businesses had been remodeled, and he had a sudden vision of the city council rejoicing as they began their renovating, now that they'd gotten rid of the last of the dreaded Hal-lorans.

He turned abruptly and started back the way he'd come. He'd been a fool to come here. He hadn't come back when his father had died, not even to make the arrangements to ship his body back to Minnesota for burial; he'd done it over the phone. So why now? And why had he come here, to the bar he'd hated so much?

He didn't know what he'd been looking for, anyway. He was glad to see it gone. He only wished this town would forget the name Halloran as easily as they had probably forgotten the saloon that had borne it.

He hurried back to his car before he could get swept up into that old folly of regret, of wondering if there hadn't been something he could have done, somehow, to change things. Something he could have said that would have made his father, or his mother, stop drinking before it had killed them both. He knew better now, and told himself so re-peatedly, but here, in this place that was so familiar yet so changed, he was finding it hard to remember.

So much for memory lane, he thought as he unlocked the door of the Mercedes. He should have known it was a rotten idea. Never again, he told himself. Yet when he started the car and pulled away from the curb, it was to head toward the other place he'd sworn not to go.

"My God, Nicki, is it true?"

Nicki smiled wryly at the pretty blonde who had cornered her the moment she stepped out of Frank Hartford's office.

"Hi, Lisa. How are you? How was your trip?"

"Fine," the tall, lushly rounded woman said, not at all diverted. "Well?"

"How long have you been back?" Nicki's question was purely rhetorical; she knew any number of people who would have made certain her friend had heard the news the instant she set foot back in town.

"Never mind that," Lisa said impatiently. "Is it true? Did your mother really—"

"Yes."

She didn't want to talk about it, but she knew her friend well enough to know she wasn't going to drop it. When Lisa stayed close on her heels as she walked to her car, she knew she was right. Her mouth twisted wryly again.

"It's true, she did it, and I don't know why."

Lisa's eyes flicked to the door of the office Nicki had just left.

"Is that why you're here? You're fighting it?"

"We're trying. Frank doesn't hold out much hope. Everything appears watertight."

"I heard your mother went to some other lawyer to do it. Why?"

"It seems you heard everything." Nicki sighed. "I don't know why. Neither does Frank, except that he would have tried to talk her out of it, no matter what her reasons were. He didn't know anything about it. We were all surprised when the will showed up."

"But I don't understand. I mean, my God, he killed your father. Why on earth would she do it?"

Nicki unlocked her car door, then paused to look at Lisa again, recognizing her perplexed look as one she'd seen quite often in her own mirror lately. She gave a soft, rueful laugh.

"I don't know," she repeated. "I wish I did. Can we please drop it now? How was Hawaii?"

Lisa hesitated, as if loathe to let the subject go, but something in Nicki's flat tone got through to her. "Oh, it was wonderful." Her eyes began to sparkle. "I met the most marvelous man."

"You always do."

"Oh, quit. You've let that dirty cement plant take over your life. It's all you think about. You don't even have a social life."

I haven't been married and divorced twice, either, Nicki thought, but she kept the thought to herself. Despite her sometimes flighty actions around men, and the shallow image she presented, Lisa was her friend and she would never hurt her feelings.

"I don't have time." She opened the door of her car and tossed her purse inside. "I'd love to hear all about your Hawaiian fling, but I have to get to that other dirty place, the gravel pit, before I go to the plant."

"Good," Lisa said, dimpling as she grinned, "You can take me home in between, since it's on the way. I need a ride."

"Where's your car?"

"Oh, I traded it in. My new one's not here yet. Wait till you see it, it's the cutest little red convertible. So what are we waiting for?"

"I may have to spend an hour or so at the pit," Nicki warned.

"No problem," Lisa said blithely. "We can catch up."

Had she ever had that much energy? Nicki wondered as she wheeled her rather staid, dark blue coupe into the flow of traffic. If she ever had, she couldn't remember when. It seemed as if she'd been tired forever.

"Are you all right?" Lisa asked, concern taking all the buoyancy out of her voice.

"Fine. Just tired."

"I should have stayed here," the blonde fretted. "You needed me to talk to."

The cloudy look of an ever-present grief shadowed Nicki's bright blue eyes. Then it faded, and she reassured her friend.

"I told you to go ahead and go. You'd been planning on it for weeks. It was enough that you cut it short to stay for the funeral."

"But your mother—"

"We knew it was coming."

"Still, I know it was hard on you. You must miss her terribly."

"Yes. I do."

It was true. Her mother had been an austere woman, not the friendly, cozy mother she'd sometimes longed for, but she had never doubted her love, had always had her support, and wished daily that she was here to offer some of her discerning common sense. And to explain why she had done this thing that had thrown her life into chaos.

"I'm sorry, Nicki. And then this on top of it."

"It's been . . . an interesting two weeks."

Lisa eyed her speculatively. "Have you . . . Has he . . ."

Nicki smiled wryly again. It wasn't like Lisa not to just blurt out whatever she was thinking.

"I mean, I saw him at the funeral, I know he's still gorgeous, but he looked . . . different."

"He is. And isn't." She shrugged. "It's been years. We've all changed."

"Not like that. I mean, he was always a little tough looking, but not so . . . hard."

"He spent two long years in jail, Lisa. What do you expect?"

Lisa raised a brow. "You used to say that wasn't enough for what he'd done. Now you sound like you feel sorry for him."

Nicki gritted her teeth, concentrating on her driving a little more than she truly needed to.

"Nicki?"

"Whatever I feel for Travis Halloran, it's not pity."

"Then what is it?"

"I don't know." She hadn't meant to say it, but the words had slipped out before she could stop them.

"Oh, Nicki, no! He's not getting to you?"

"No!"

Lisa's brow rose once more at her emphatic tone. "Are you sure? You sound awfully tense about it."

"I'm sure. Now tell me about this wonderful man of yours."

After a moment, Lisa accepted the red herring gracefully and began to talk of her trip. She chattered on cheerfully as Nicki listened in amusement; Lisa's adventures all started to sound alike after a while.

"Are you sure this one isn't married?" Nicki asked as she made the turn off of the main street onto the older road that led to the pit.

"Of course. I learned my lesson about that. He's absolutely charming, Nicki. He's handsome, dresses like the cover of *GQ,* and drives a gorgeous Mercedes."

"Of course."

"Well, I know that kind of thing doesn't mean anything to you, but I— There," she cried suddenly, "a Mercedes just like that one."

Nicki glanced in the direction her friend was pointing, and nearly drove off the road.

"What on earth is *that* car doing parked at a dump like that?" Lisa asked.

Nicki jerked her gaze back to the narrow, winding road. She knew the answer to Lisa's question, but if the blonde hadn't seen the lean, dark-haired figure sitting on the steps of the ramshackle house, she wasn't about to point him out and bring on another rash of unwelcome questions and speculation.

She hadn't seen him for nearly a week, not since that day Richard had virtually accused him of being behind the acid spill. She'd wondered, with the feeling of a person waiting for the other shoe to drop, where he'd gone to, and what he would do now. While she had never thought that he'd given up and gone, she had never expected that he would be here.

She'd grown used to driving past the house every time she went to the pit. She'd gotten very good at ignoring it, although it had taken a long time to break the habit of glancing at it as she went by. It had been standing empty, amid a scraggly lawn of mostly weeds, for nearly five years now, ever since Jim Halloran had finally succumbed to the ravages of years of heavy drinking.

Not, she thought, that it had looked much better when he'd been alive. Or even when Travis had been there, although she knew he'd tried now and then to clean the place up. She wondered why he'd gone back; he couldn't have many happy memories of the place. She'd never seen him as wiredrawn as the one time she'd been there.

He'd given her a ride home from school one day when Richard had, as he was often wont to do, forgotten her. He'd had to go by his house to pick up his uniform before going to the part-time job he had at a gas station in San Clemente, just down the freeway a few miles.

The job, she had realized, that no one else knew he had, and had had for over a year. Even the rather rowdy, scruffy bunch of his friends, kids who got themselves talked about nearly as much as he did, didn't know. They all thought he was out somewhere, up to no good, and he let them think it. Along with everyone else in town.

"I don't care what they think," he told her, "so don't go spreading it around, all right?"

She didn't understand, it seemed so unfair, but as she sat in the car waiting for him, she knew that she wouldn't go against his bidding.

He'd looked at her rather oddly, almost defiantly when they pulled up in front of the small, old house. She didn't understand until he said tightly, "Sure you want to be seen in this neighborhood?"

It hit her then, and she made a face at him. "Are you calling me a snob?"

He'd looked a little taken aback, then sheepish. "I guess I was. Sorry, Miss Lockwood."

"You're the one who's so touchy about it. Maybe you're the snob."

He chuckled. "Maybe you're right," he agreed, and got out of the car.

She remembered the moment when she suddenly realized he'd been gone a very long time, especially since he'd been in a hurry to get going so he could drop her off and not be late. She waited a little longer, then got out of the car and started up to the house.

She stopped in the doorway, stunned. Never in her young, protected life had she encountered anything like this. The odor of an unwashed body combined with the unmistakable stench of the regurgitated contents of a rebellious, alcohol-drenched stomach almost overwhelmed her. She fought back a wave of nausea.

After the bright sunlight she couldn't see much in the dim room, but she could hear. And she heard Travis, his voice soft, coaxing, yet incredibly weary.

"Come on, Dad. Just a couple of more steps. You can do it. Then you can sleep."

She heard a sound that could have been a snarl or a moan, and an odd thumping noise.

"Don't pass out yet, Dad. I can't carry you."

Yet he nearly was carrying him, Nicki realized as her eyes adjusted and she could make out the shadowy shapes across the room. Travis's tall, lean body bent with the effort of keeping the older, much heavier man upright. Half dragging him by the arm that was pulled over his shoulders, Travis worked his way toward the darker shadow of a hallway entrance.

"Leggoame!"

The angry shout came suddenly, as did the wild swipe of a beefy arm. Travis dodged agilely, away from the blow that was clearly meant for the side of his head.

"Sonovabitch! Useless, jus' like your mother was."

The drunken man swung again, fist clenched this time, and Travis had to duck quickly to avoid what surely would have been another split lip. The movement turned him toward the door, and he saw Nicki standing there.

He went rigid, and even in the gloom she saw the color flood his face. He swore, low and strained.

"I told you to wait outside!"

The words were sharp, harsh, but Nicki heard only the humiliation that laced through them.

"I'm sorry," she whispered, and turned to run back to the car.

Several minutes passed before Travis came out, carrying the dark blue gas station uniform. He climbed into the car and started it without looking at her. His face was so set and rigid it frightened her. He said nothing, and she was too dismayed to speak. She just sat in silence, the ugly scene replaying over and over in her mind.

This was what he lived with, this was what he came home to. So many things made sense now, his attitude, the bitterness, the rough edges. She suppressed a shudder, knowing that although he wasn't looking at her, he was tautly aware of her every move.

He drove slowly, with intense concentration; he always slowed his usual reckless pace whenever she was in the car with him. She didn't know why she'd thought of that now, except that maybe it kept her from thinking about what she'd just seen.

He pulled the battered but smooth-running Mustang to a halt in front of her house. He sat silently for a long moment, staring at the steering wheel. Nicki wanted to get out, to spare him from having to say anything, but she couldn't seem to move. She could only watch as he picked at a thread from the rip in the knee of his jeans. At last he spoke, his voice low and taut.

"I'm sorry you . . . had to see that."

"Trav . . ." She trailed off, unable to think of a thing to say.

"He's . . . not usually that bad . . . this early."

Nicki winced. What must it feel like, to have to apologize for your own father?

"I try to get him to stop . . . so did my mother . . ."

"And that's when he hits you," Nicki said in sudden understanding.

He lifted one shoulder in dismissal. "He just gets . . . mad at me sometimes. He wants me to help him at the bar instead of working at the station."

"But you . . . don't want to?"

"I can't!"

It burst from him in a rush, and she turned in her seat so she could see his face. "Why, Travis? Why does it make you sound like that?"

"I can't work there, for him. Don't you see? He's a drunk, my mother was a drunk, half his customers are drunks, too, and I—"

He broke off, the thread he'd been tugging on giving way under the sudden increase in tension. He looked away from her, but not before she'd seen the fear in his eyes. It took her a moment to put it together with his words and make sense of it.

"You think if you work there, it will happen to you? No, Trav, you wouldn't, not you."

"It could." There was a small, ripping sound as the already torn denim gave a little more under the pressure of his rigid fingers. "Maybe it's . . . hereditary or something. Maybe . . ."

"Travis, no. Don't think that."

"I don't want to end up like that! Like . . . him."

"Then you won't," she said with all the confidence of her faith in him. "You won't let it happen. You're stronger than he is, I know you are."

He looked at her then, that strange expression she saw so often lighting his eyes. Then he said softly, "When you look at me like that, I can almost believe it."

"Believe it," she'd told him earnestly, "You have to believe it."

She'd never gone back to that house. Even later, when it shouldn't have mattered anymore, she had driven out of her way to take the back road so she wouldn't have to go past it and face the way it made her feel. Telling herself she hated him, and that what happened there didn't matter anymore, that nothing could ameliorate what he'd done, she'd made herself go back to the direct route.

And she wished now she never had. Everywhere she turned it seemed he was there, and the memories rose up to torment her. And the questions.

"...even listening?"

"Of course," Nicki answered as she drove through the chain-link gate into the quarry, although she hadn't heard anything Lisa had said since she'd seen that solitary figure on the porch steps. He'd always seemed that way, alone, even all those years ago, even at the head of the rough crowd he'd run with.

"So what do you think? Should I invite him here?"

"What I think," Nicki said, knowing that no matter what she'd missed, it was a safe answer, "is that you should do what you want. You will anyway."

Lisa grinned. "That's what I love about you, Nicki. You know the worst about me, but you're still my friend. You don't try and change me."

"It's hopeless," Nicki said, teasing. The woman had been her friend since elementary school, had been a rock of support in the dark days after her father's death, and had been the only one who truly seemed to understand the grief and betrayal she'd felt. Others might dismiss Lisa as a shallow socialite, skating along on the surface of life, but Nicki knew there was a loyal core to her that few saw.

"I'll just wait here," the blonde said, looking around with a wrinkled nose at the piles of dirt, rock and gravel, and the dust that floated in the air. "I'll do my nails or something."

"Okay." Nicki gathered up the papers she'd brought, got out of the car and headed toward the office.

"Afternoon, Miss Lockwood."

Nicki turned to see Paul Malone, a long-time heavy equipment operator for the quarry. "Hello, Paul. How are you? How's the new baby?"

A grin creased the dusty face. "Just fine. Prettiest little girl you've ever seen. Don't feel like I'm old enough to be a grandpa, though."

"You don't look it, either."

"Now, I know better than that. Anyway, I'm off to see her now, since my loader broke down, too."

"Too?"

"Yeah. Didn't you know? That's the third one since last Tuesday. First Lenny's, then Tim's on Thursday, and now mine. Can't figure it out."

"What's going wrong?"

"Different on each one. Hydraulics, brakes, gear box... Just a run of bad luck, I reckon. Weird that it all happened at once, though."

"Yes." She'd have to ask about it, she thought. "Do you know where Esteban is?"

"Scale house," Paul said.

Nicki nodded, exchanged a few more words, then headed for the small building to find the plant superintendent, a man who had also worked for the Lockwoods for years.

"Nicki, hello!"

Esteban Montero greeted her ebulliently, as if she hadn't been here just last week.

"Hello, Esteban. I brought those projections you wanted."

"Good, good. I want to finish my flowchart. We are running a little behind, and I may have to make some adjustments."

"I ran into Paul outside. What's this about equipment problems?"

Montero rubbed a hand over his jaw, his dark brown eyes looking troubled. "I don't know. We have had many little things go wrong this past week." He echoed Paul's list, then added, "And two trucks are broken down, as well. Vandals, we think."

"Vandals?"

"Yes, it looks that way. Teenagers, perhaps. Although the night watchman is very diligent. He saw no one around, and only our people have come in and out. They must have come over the fence, although no one saw anything."

"What happened to the trucks?"

"Sand."

Nicki's brow furrowed deeper. "Sand?"

"In the gas tanks." Montero shook his head. "And it appears that three of our loaders have been tampered with, as well."

"Tampered with?"

He nodded, his expression somber. "Lines cut, fluid drained out." He shook his head again. "If we were on strike here, this is the kind of thing I would expect. Little things, but enough to be a great nuisance."

"Any idea why?"

Montero shrugged. "Who can say?"

"No one with a grudge? We haven't fired anyone lately, have we?"

The man grinned, white teeth shining in his brown face. "No one, you know that. We have good people here."

"I know. Just checking."

"Speaking of good people, that new man seems very smart. He is learning our operation here very quickly."

"New man?"

"Yes. The one you sent the memo about, that we should tell him whatever he wanted to know."

Nicki's brows shot upward. "Trav—Mr. Halloran?"

Montero nodded. "It is . . . different to have a man in his position ask simply to learn. I respect that."

She had resolved to put the rumor mill to rest, and the memo she'd sent to all the foremen and superintendents had been explicit in its explanation of Travis Halloran's status. It had been met with reactions ranging from anger to disbelief; everyone, it seemed, either remembered or had been told the story of Robert Lockwood's death.

Yet wherever he had gone, whoever he had approached for information or knowledge, the opinion seemed to have changed. With the exception of close associates of Richard's, everyone had responded much as Esteban Montero had—with eventual respect, albeit sometimes grudging. The men in the yard at the plant, the people in dispatch, the drivers, all of them admitted that he hadn't been what they'd expected.

"What did he want to learn?"

"Many things." The man grinned again. "Although I believe he knows even more than he lets on. Certainly no one needed to teach him to run a 'dozer. He asked if he could try, and he wheeled that big thing around like it was a sports car."

"He . . . did?"

"He would only say he'd learned to run one years ago. I would say he hasn't forgotten much. The men were quite impressed."

"Oh."

Once again she wondered what he'd been doing all these years, where he'd picked up this unexpected knowledge, and once again she smothered her curiosity; she didn't care, she told herself. And she wasn't about to let anyone else think she did. Especially Travis.

"So, what else did he want?"

"He asked many questions. Not foolish ones, but good ones. He knew the basics already, but he wants more. And he is spending many hours learning."

"Is? How long has he been coming here?"

"Oh, several days now. He first came last Tuesday. He was very polite, not at all what we expected. No one was happy he was here at first, but now, no one minds. They have come to believe he is sincere."

Last Tuesday. The last time, until that glimpse today on the steps of his old house, that she'd seen him. The day after he'd walked out on her and Richard. Walked out without denying what her brother had said. Without a response to her plea that he deny it, a plea she had tried but been unable to suppress.

She'd wondered where he'd gone. Well, now she knew. He hadn't beat a strategic retreat, he'd merely shifted his field of battle.

"Is there a problem, Nicki? Your memo said—"

"I know, Esteban. No, there's no problem. I'm just... surprised."

"That he came at all? Or that the men have come to like him?"

The dark brown eyes were fastened on her keenly, and she didn't bother to dissemble. She had a great deal of respect for this man who had charmed her as a child with his old-world courtliness, and she refused to insult him by pretending she didn't understand.

"Both," she said frankly.

"I understand," Montero said quietly. "This must be very difficult for you. Your lovely mother passing, and then finding she had left all this to the man you hold responsible for your father's death."

"*I* hold him responsible? He *is* responsible."

Montero hesitated for a moment, then sighed. "Yes, Nicki. I know. It is just...I find it hard to believe of the man I have come to know in these past few days."

Days, Nicki thought numbly. Only days, and he had turned the entire crew of the pit around. Then she wondered why she was surprised. He'd had her so confused the first day that she was still reeling, so a week was plenty of time for him to pull it off here. Not even a week, really, in working days. Four days, since Tuesday.

Tuesday.

It hit her then with the force of a blow. Tuesday. Travis had first shown up here on Tuesday. Which just happened to be the day the trouble here had begun.

Chapter 6

Nicki heard the shouting even before she got inside.

"....think you are?"

Richard again, she thought with a sigh. And she could just guess who he was yelling at in that tone that grated so on her nerves. Travis was back.

She didn't need this, she thought wearily. Not now. She'd just had another run-in with Carl Weller, and she was in no mood to deal with one of her brother's tantrums. Or with Travis.

She'd forced her suspicions about the incidents at the pit to the back of her mind. Not that she didn't think Travis capable of such things; if she had to believe he'd killed her father, what was a little carefully engineered sabotage? What held her back was the lack of proof. And a motive. This was his business now, half of it, anyway. What reason could he have to damage it?

Richard insisted he wanted revenge, but Nicki didn't understand that, either. He had no reason, unless he blamed them for what had happened to him years ago. But all they'd done was tell the sheriff the truth. How could he blame them for that? And even if he had, if he truly wanted revenge, he would have done something long ago, not waited fifteen years, she told herself.

Besides, the Travis she'd known wasn't like that, or he would have retaliated against his father long ago. But he never had, despite the beatings. So why would he come after them now? Could those two years in the custody of the California Youth Authority really have been so much worse than the hell he'd lived with at home?

She couldn't deal with it now, she thought, and quashed the thoughts once more as she headed down the hall toward that raised voice. She paused just outside the door to her brother's office.

"You can't talk to me like that!"

"You don't want people to talk to you like you're an idiot, then quit making idiotic decisions."

Travis's voice was low, derisive and utterly calm. And there was nothing more guaranteed to make Richard even angrier than staying calm while he lost his cool; she knew that from rueful, firsthand experience. She stepped into the room.

"You don't know a damned thing about the cement business, so where do you get off—"

"I don't need to know sand from pea gravel to see that you're digging a financial hole here you may not be able to get out of."

"What do you know about finances? You're nothing but a lousy—"

"Easy, Richie. Don't say anything I might have to belt you for."

Nicki saw her brother back up warily, and heard Travis chuckle. His back was to her, but she knew the sound; it was how he'd always laughed when he knew someone had fallen for the image. It was how he'd laughed the day he'd left their parlor in the wake of the shocked gasps of the local matrons.

"What have you done now, Richard?"

Richard jumped, but Travis only moved aside to let her pass, as if, despite his back being to her, he'd known the moment she had arrived. He was dressed in trim, tailored gray slacks and a pale gray shirt with the sleeves rolled up over muscular forearms. Expensive clothes, she registered once more, and the questions about the past fifteen years rose again. And she smothered them again.

"What, Richard?"

"Nothing," her brother said defensively.

"Only sent eighty yards out to the Bell-Hornung project this morning," Travis said dryly.

"What?" Nick's gaze flicked from Travis to her brother in astonishment. "They're already two months behind. They owe us over twenty thousand dollars!"

"And," Travis added, "shorted the Shelby job by a full load."

"Damn it, Richard!" Nicki exploded. "Sam Shelby is our best customer!"

"Bell-Hornung is a good project," Richard protested. "High visibility."

"Visibility doesn't pay the bills," Nicki snapped.

"George Hornung is a prestigious man in this state. Being in on one of his projects is good P.R."

"He's a big talker who doesn't pay his bills."

"You never look at the big picture—"

"You keep this up, and a picture is all you're going to have to look at, because this place will be gone!"

"You're exaggerating." Richard shifted uncomfortably. "You keep saying we're in trouble, but we're still here."

"Because I'm breaking my neck to save us," Nicki said furiously. "I'll have to call Sam and apologize. And figure out where we'll come up with that extra load, when we're already maxed out today."

She started toward Richard's desk and the phone, then whirled back on him.

"And another thing! I've had it with Weller. I want him out of here."

An odd look flitted across Richard's soft features, gone so quickly Nicki couldn't quite describe it. Then, to her amazement, Richard said firmly, "No."

She stared at him. "What?"

"I said no."

"I heard you. I just don't quite believe it."

"Me, either. Had a backbone transplant, Richie?"

Richard glared at Travis. "Keep out of this."

"No. The man's a menace."

"Not to mention offensive and useless," Nicki said, glad of the support despite its source. "I don't want him on this property another minute."

"He's union. You can't just fire him."

"Watch me," Nicki said. "I've got enough on him to make even the teamsters sit up and take notice."

Richard paled a little, but shook his head.

"I know an attorney," Travis said casually, "who specializes in union firings. If you've got the documentation, he can make it stick."

"I told you to stay out of this, you—"

Travis did nothing but lift his head, turning his gaze from Nicki to her brother, but Richard instantly fell silent.

"What's the name of that attorney?" Nicki asked, eyeing her chastened brother in disgust. He'd never had any spine at all, she thought. Why he'd suddenly found some gumption now was beyond her. As was why Travis would know a lawyer who specialized in unions.

"I'll get his number for you."

"All right, all right," Richard said, his tone wheedling now. "I'll talk to Carl, tell him to back off, stay out of your way."

"Not good enough, Richard."

"Okay, I'll fine him or something."

"I doubt if even that will get his attention."

"C'mon, Sis. He'll behave, I promise."

Nicki hesitated.

"He's my friend, Nicki."

"Then teach your friend some manners," she said, capitulating. She supposed Carl Weller was one of her smaller problems at the moment.

"Easier to teach manners to a rattlesnake," Travis muttered.

"Get out," Richard spat, "you've caused enough trouble already!"

"Still blaming everybody but yourself, aren't you, Richie?"

"Get out!" Richard shouted.

He looks frightened, Nicki thought as she decided to make her call from the relative peace of her own office. Then she dismissed the thought as the more important matter of how to placate Sam Shelby took precedence in her mind.

"You're right, you know."

She hadn't realized Travis had come out of the office with her. "About what?"

"Hornung. He's a windbag."

"I know." She yanked open the door of her office, then stopped as something occurred to her. "But how do you?"

He shrugged. "I heard it around. Heard he's having money trouble, too. I wouldn't count on that twenty thousand, if I were you."

Nicki tossed her purse onto her desk. He had followed her in without invitation, but she couldn't seem to find the energy to protest. She sat on the edge of her desk, resisting the urge to rub at eyes that were already weary even this early in the morning.

"Or the five thousand more they'll owe us for my brother's brilliant move today?"

"Or that."

"And just how did you become so well informed?"

"Does it matter?"

Nicki sighed. She wanted to say no, it didn't matter, that nothing he knew or did or said mattered. But somehow she knew that if she opened her mouth, *yes* was going to come out. Yes it mattered, yes she wanted to know how he knew all the things he knew, including about the cement business, where he'd learned them, where he'd been, what he'd done. She knew it, so she kept her mouth shut.

She got up to walk around to her desk chair, inadvertently knocking her calendar to the floor. She bent for it at the same moment Travis did. His left forearm, bare below the rolled shirt sleeve, was tanned and strong.

And scarred.

She stared at the wicked, curved mark that began at his wrist and curved up the inner side of his arm nearly to the elbow. It was a thin line, puckered slightly here and there, with the paleness of an old injury. But no matter how old it was, it had obviously been a nasty wound, and the thought made her shudder.

"My God, Travis, what did that to your arm?"

He straightened, carefully set the calendar back on the desk, then let his gaze go to her face. After a moment he said flatly, "A knife."

She stared at him. She knew this hadn't happened after he'd started coming to the house, and she didn't remember ever seeing it before. Unlike some of the others in his crowd, he'd never carried a knife that she knew of, or else he had stopped when he'd begun to come to the house. He relied on his reputation to keep any potential opponents at bay, he'd told her, and he didn't want to get caught carrying a weapon at school. She'd smiled, knowing that a few months before, he couldn't have cared less about getting suspended or expelled.

"But you never carried..." she began, then stopped at his chilling look.

"I did a lot of things in jail that I'd never done before."

Her gaze flicked to the scar once more, then back to his face. "That happened . . . there?"

"In jail, Miss Lockwood. Sorry if you don't like the word."

She flushed. "I . . . It's just . . . Who had a knife in—in jail?"

Travis laughed harshly. "A muscle-bound weight lifter who had designs on my cute little backside, as he put it."

Nicki looked at him, puzzled. Then her eyes widened in shock and she went pale as she realized what he'd meant. "Oh, God, Travis..."

"What did you think C.Y.A. was, summer camp?" His voice was scornful.

"No, but..."

"Oh, don't worry, I saved my...virtue." He flexed his left hand forward; the scar rippled as the muscle bunched. "He was set up on my right side. Didn't expect me to lead with my left hand. I figured I got off cheap. He never tried it again. On anybody."

She went even paler. "Did you...?"

His eyes narrowed as he looked at her. "Kill him? Is that what you want to know?"

"No, I—"

"I'm surprised you have any doubts. After all, you already think I'm a killer anyway."

"I didn't mean—"

"You just believe what you want. You will anyway. It seems to be a Lockwood trait."

"All I wanted to say is that I hope you hurt him back."

Travis stared at her, stunned. "What?"

"I..."

She faltered, turning away as if she wished she hadn't let the words slip out. She walked over to the window and stared out, watching the sun glisten on one of the silver pneumatic trailers that had pulled up to the cement silo and was off-loading up the four-inch pipe. Fifteen pounds of pressure, she thought automatically. All it took to fluff up the fine, powdery cement enough for it to travel up the eighty-five foot pipe to the top of the silo.

"Nicki... Did you mean that?"

The tight, strained words yanked her mind away from its desperate effort to think about anything except the impulse that had driven her to say those foolish words.

"I don't know."

She kept staring out the window, watching as the first trailer emptied and the driver moved the truck up so the second could be hooked up to the pipe.

"I never... thought about it, really. I mean, I knew that you were... in jail. I was so angry at you, so hurt, that I wished it on you, a hundred times, without ever thinking about what it really meant."

"Would it have made a difference?" He sounded like a man testing waters he suspected were full of sharks.

She turned then and saw a look in his eyes that made her heart take a funny little leap and her stomach knot. "I don't know," she whispered. "I hated you so much..."

"I know." A shiver rippled through him. "Nicole, I—"

"Please, Travis. Not now. I...need to think. And I can't with you in here."

"Why?" he asked softly.

Her chin came up. "Because you upset me. Is that what you wanted to hear?"

"No. But it's a start."

Nicki wondered, as he turned and left without another word, why he had been so content to leave. Just as she wondered about the odd look that had been in his eyes. It wasn't until several minutes later, as she tried to concentrate on how she was going to carry out the promises she'd made to Sam Shelby, that she realized she had spoken of hating him in the past tense, and that the look in his eyes had been one of hope.

The hallway was dark when Nicki finally gave up for the day. She wasn't finished, but she was exhausted, and after she'd read the same bid proposal three times over and still wasn't sure if it was right, she knew it was time to quit. It was to one of the bigger development companies in southern California, and too important to mess up. Although, she thought wearily, it probably wouldn't matter; thanks to Richard overextending their production, the bid would have to be too high anyway.

A twinge of anger at her brother surfaced anew; she would have liked to have been involved in that marina project. It had been the development company's idea, she'd read, to design a youth dock where kids could go to learn to sail, wind surf, or row. And they were footing most of the bill for it. And insisting that the small area of wetlands that was a habitat for several species of coastal birds be left intact. Those were the kind of people she liked to deal with. But Willow Tree would take one look at her figures and laugh themselves sick.

She stood for a moment outside her office door, waiting for her eyes to adjust so she wouldn't have to turn on any lights on her way out. When she could see well enough, she started toward the outer door, stopping only when she saw the sliver of light showing beneath the door to the office that had been her mother's. Since it was the only empty office, he'd wound up reluctantly taking it.

She started to go on, telling herself it was nothing to her if he stayed here all night. She made it two steps past the door before she turned back.

When she tapped on the door it swung open. The light she'd seen had been cast by the desk lamp; the rest of the room was in darkness. From behind the big desk that her mother had found at an exclusive antique shop, Travis raised his eyes from the paper he held and looked at her, then glanced at his watch.

"Yes," she said, "I know it's late."

"And you're still here."

"So are you."

He smiled crookedly. "I'm trying to learn the concrete business from the sand up, so to speak, in a few days."

"So I've heard."

He raised one dark brow. "Oh?"

She shrugged. "People talk."

"Especially to the boss."

"Yes." He hadn't sounded sarcastic, so she didn't bother to deny it. They both knew it was true.

"Your people have a lot of respect for you."

"They're starting to have respect for you, too." She looked at him curiously. "They say you know more than they expected. And where did you learn to handle a bulldozer?"

He grinned. "You heard about that, huh?"

"Esteban was impressed, and he's not a man easily impressed."

"I admit, I was showing off a little. It was the first time in days that I'd run into something I knew all about."

"From what I've heard, you're learning about everything fast." Or, she thought again, unable to suppress the suspicion, you already know much more than you're letting on.

"They really do report to you, don't they?" He saw her tense. "Easy, Nicole," he said softly, "they did exactly what they should have done. I'm the outsider. I'd have been worried if they hadn't reported to you."

The outsider. He'd always felt that way, called himself that. The word knifed through her, reaching some deep, protected place and slicing through the hard, bitter shell that surrounded it. A tiny sound broke from her lips, and she pressed her hand to her mouth. Travis stood up, his gaze fastened on her, his eyes lit with intensity.

"You look as tired and hungry as I am. Let's get out of here and get something to eat."

She shook her head mutely, unable to speak; the battle between the mind that firmly said no and the emotions that were saying yes was etched on her face.

"You're not hungry?"

"Yes," she managed, "but—"

"Let's go, then."

He folded the paper he'd been holding and tucked it into his pocket, then turned and pulled his jacket off the back of the chair. That same gray suede jacket, she thought, the one that turned his eyes the soft gray of a dove. So much warmer, so much more forgiving than the icy gray of granite...

Why was she always thinking like that, as if she were the one who had to ask forgiveness of him? It wasn't a new feeling, although it had grown much stronger since he'd returned; she'd always had it, ever since she'd been told that he'd been turned over to the California Youth Authority and was really going to jail.

It was no less than he'd deserved for what he'd done, she'd told herself over and over, and more than once she'd been furious with herself because the idea hurt so much. She didn't know why she couldn't drop it. And why she couldn't just forget him and go on with her life. And why was she thinking about the color of his eyes anyway, when what she should be doing is saying no to him?

But by the time she had come to her senses they were outside, and she found herself waiting while he opened the passenger door of his car, then getting in without a word of protest. She should go, she told herself. It might be a chance to find out if he knew anything about the problems at the pit. Not that he'd admit it if he was responsible, but he might give himself away somehow.

"Nice car," she murmured when he slid into the driver's seat.

"Yes." When she looked at him, speculation in her eyes, he said casually, "It's a company car, actually."

"Company car?"

"I'm . . . using it for the trip here."

So that explained it, Nicki thought, the speculation fading as he started the motor. As if he'd read her mind, his mouth twisted ruefully.

"You never really thought it was mine, did you?"

"I wondered." And she wondered at his tone, which made the words more a statement of fact than a question. She ran a finger over the rich leather of the seat. "You must have a nice boss, if he just loans out cars like this."

He chuckled, and Nicki got the oddest feeling that it was at some joke she didn't see. He wheeled the car out onto the street before he said, "He's . . . a lot of things, but I don't know if nice is one of them."

"What kind of company is it?"

The words were out before she remembered she'd sworn she didn't care, didn't want to know anything about him. Travis glanced at her, giving her that uncanny feeling that he knew what she was thinking as well as he ever had.

"Do you really want to know?"

She caught her breath. When everyone else had been saying she was impossible to understand, Travis Halloran had understood her perfectly. It seemed he still did.

"Yes," she said perversely, ignoring the fact that he had given her the perfect chance to retreat, "or I wouldn't have asked."

The moment she said it she knew it was true; she did want to know.

"Construction, mostly," he answered easily as he accelerated up the freeway ramp.

"Your boss is a contractor?" So he *did* know more about the concrete business than he let on.

"Of sorts."

"He must be doing well," she said, looking again at the luxurious interior of the car.

"He's getting by."

"Construction... You run a bulldozer?" she guessed.

There was a half second's hesitation before the answer came. "Sometimes. Sometimes I do... other things."

"Oh."

She left it at that, but she didn't understand. That kind of rough work didn't jive with the expensive clothes he wore, unless he spent everything he made on them. It didn't seem likely; he'd never been that way, as some of Richard's friends had been, and as Richard had been. Not that all the expensive clothes in the world could ever give Richard the kind of negligent, throwaway ease Travis had. Even when all Travis had had were ragged jeans and T-shirts he made Richard look like a stiff, overdressed Ken doll.

Maybe that was it, she thought. Maybe he bought nice clothes now because he'd never had any then. He hadn't seemed to mind, and she'd always thought he looked wonderful no matter what, so she'd never asked. Perhaps it had bothered him more than she had ever realized.

She remembered then, with nauseating clarity, the time she'd overheard Richard's friends teasing him about his "charity case."

"He's trash," one of them had said, "just like his father. And you can't change that, even with Lockwood money."

"Don't tell me, tell my mother," Richard had retorted. "She's the one who's doing it. I dumped the jerk a long time ago. And I only invited him over the first time because he helped me out once. Not that I needed it, of course."

She'd forgotten that until now, forgotten how angry she'd been at Richard for deserting Travis at the first sign of pressure from his smug friends. She'd wanted to storm into the room and tell them all off, but she knew they'd just laugh at her, as all Richard's friends did. Except Travis. Who wasn't really Richard's friend at all. *I don't know anything about the kind of friendship that lets you be a jerk to a friend's sister.*

His words came to her, their truth and accuracy ringing in her mind. He'd never been like the rest of them. And he would never desert a friend so easily. But he had, she thought. He'd deserted Richard, at the most horrible time possible. But she'd just admitted that Richard hadn't really been his friend. Why should he have stuck by Richard when she knew that if the positions had been reversed, Richard would have done the same thing Travis had done?

"Are you all right?"

In her confusion she must have made some small sound, for Travis was looking at her with concern.

"I . . . Yes. I'm fine."

For the first time since she'd been once more caught up in memories, she looked out the window. And saw the ocean sparkling in the moonlight.

"Where are we?"

"San Clemente. I thought we'd eat at that place on the pier." He pointed toward the low building as he parked the car in the public lot just above it. "I was there the other night. It's pretty good."

"You... were?"

She barely managed the words, so stunned was she at her own reaction to the thought that he might have had a date for dinner. It made her gasp inwardly as her stomach recoiled, as if she'd been struck.

"It's handy. I'm staying in a house just a few blocks south of here. It's a nice walk."

Nicki stared at him. She knew that area, above T-Street beach, famous among local surfers. It was one of the most sought after parts of this small, seaside community, and houses there didn't come cheap.

"Your boss?" she hazarded as they got out of the car.

"No. One of his... V.P.'s."

One delicate brow arched; she hadn't suspected the company was big enough to have a vice president, let alone more than one. And generous, apparently. As was the president—cars and houses, loaned to an employee.

"What's wrong?" An edge had crept into his voice. "Doesn't match your preconceptions?"

Nicki flushed, caught. "I suppose. I never claimed not to have them."

A little taken aback by her honest admission, Travis didn't speak for a moment. Then, quietly, "Sorry. I didn't mean to snap at you."

"It's okay. I didn't mean..." She trailed off.

"Didn't mean what?"

"I don't know. I don't seem to know anything anymore."

They had a quiet, pleasant dinner, the conversation about nothing more consequential than the weather and the scenery. She thought often of directing the talk toward the pit and what had happened there, but she couldn't bring herself to do it. And later, when she found herself agreeing to a walk on the beach, she didn't want to talk about work.

As a girl on the edge of womanhood, she'd often fantasized about walking in the moonlight with Travis. Not as they had, on occasion, when their talks under the big willow had lasted into the evening and he had walked her back to the house. Not that she hadn't treasured those moments, as she had all the time she'd spent with him, even as she was surprised by his unswerving adherence to her mother's rules about what time she had to be inside. She had treasured them, and they were enough for her, then.

But what she'd dreamed about was being alone together, at some vague time in the future, on a beach like this, when he would see her as a woman, not a girl.

"I used to think about this," she said softly, not meaning to say the words aloud but unable to stop them once she'd begun, "years ago. Being someplace like this, with you, when I was old enough."

She heard him suck in a breath. "You...never said."

"I was afraid to. I was just a kid, and you were... I was afraid you'd laugh."

"Did I ever laugh at you?"

"No. You never did." She stopped, looking up at him, at his face shadowed by the moonlight. "Even when your friends laughed at you about me."

He went still. "You knew that?"

"That they laughed about your little shadow? Yes."

"I'm sorry. They just didn't understand."

"No one did."

"Except us."

She lowered her eyes. "Except us."

"Nicole..."

He lifted her chin with a gentle finger. For a long, silent moment he just looked at her, and she could see the silver light of the moon flashing in his eyes. His lips parted, as if he were having trouble drawing in enough air, and she found herself doing the same.

"Did you think about this, too? Back then?" he asked huskily.

"Yes," she breathed, knowing without the words what he meant. Then he was doing it, his head lowering, his mouth coming down soft and warm on hers.

The protest of her mind, the crying out that this was the man she'd hated for fifteen years, died in the first split second of flashing, blazing heat. The years between fell away in a puff of ash. This was Travis, her Travis, and it was happening just as she'd dreamed it would.

Well, not quite. She'd never dreamed of this heat, this instant conflagration, sending ripples of fire along nerves she'd never known she had. She'd never known sensations like this existed. Not at fourteen, and not through all the years since, had she ever felt anything like this.

His fingers threaded through her hair, and felt strong and warm as he cradled her head. His mouth urged, coaxed, then she felt the searing flick of his tongue over her lips. She gasped at the unexpected pleasure of it, and as her lips parted on the sharp breath, his tongue darted between them.

He did nothing more than stroke the sensitive inner surface, then she felt him shudder and draw back. A tiny moan of protest escaped her at the loss of his heat, and she heard him groan as he pulled her tightly to him.

"Damn," he muttered, his chin coming to rest gently on her hair. "I should have known."

She sagged against him, wondering where all her strength had gone. "Known?" Her voice was shaky.

"That it would...be like that. God knows I thought about it often enough."

She quivered at the impact of the words. "You...thought about it, too?"

He laughed, a little roughly. "Hell, I spent half my time feeling like some kind of pervert because the only girl I could talk to was you. I used to wish the time away, thinking that in four years you'd be eighteen and I'd be twenty-one, and it wouldn't matter..." She stared up at him, steadying herself with a hand against his chest. She could feel his heart hammering beneath her palm; it helped somehow to know his was racing just as hers was.

"But you... I heard... all those girls..."

His laugh was jagged sounding, sharp, like broken glass. "Believe me, the kind of girls who hung around with me then weren't the kind you talked to." Bitterness tinged his voice. "Except for the ones who went slumming, of course. For them, I was good enough to...give them a thrill or two, maybe a quick fumble behind the bleachers, but in the light of day, in front of their friends, I was back to dirt under their feet again."

"Oh, Trav..."

"Except you. You were the only one who ever knew... who I was. Who ever looked past *what* I was."

"It wasn't fair," she whispered. "They all judged you by your father."

"Except you."

He lifted one hand to smooth back a strand of her hair that had been tossed by the wind across her cheek. The fractional hesitation told her that was all he'd intended to do, but then his fingers were caressing the soft skin of her cheek, moving until he had cupped her face with his palm.

This time she met him eagerly, lifting her lips to his without hesitation. Her willingness fired him, and he took her mouth fiercely, urgently. Her lips parted for him and he thrust his tongue deep, savoring the honeyed warmth. His arms went around her, to pull her even closer; she bent to him as if she had no will left to do otherwise.

Nicki shivered, even though wave after wave of heat was rippling through her. His mouth was soft and hot, his chest solid and hot, arms strong and hot around her. When she tentatively moved her tongue to brush over his, she heard him groan and felt a shudder go through him. His response renewed hers, and she trembled in his arms. She moved her tongue again, wanting more, savoring the taste of him, craving the little sparks that shot through her as she'd never craved anything before.

When at last he broke away, his breath left him in a long, shaky sigh. She echoed it, sagging against him again as her mind whirled from the wonder of it. She buried her face against his shirt, the cool breeze off the ocean nothing in the face of his heat. She heard his heart slamming in her ear pressed to his chest, heard his quickened breathing that matched her own.

"I thought I knew...I fantasized so much...about what it would be like. I never came close," she whispered. "I didn't know..."

"You make me feel like I don't know anything," Travis said hoarsely. "Oh, God, Nicole. What do we do now?"

It was a question she had no answer for.

Nicki wondered if she would ever get back to normal. She remembered the days when she'd ended each day satisfied with the amount of work she'd accomplished, when she'd been able to keep on top of things, even the dual load of running the plant and the pit. Now it was all she could do to stay within sight of even.

She yawned; she'd slept little last night, her mind, full of the evening's events, had not let her rest until the early hours of morning. She'd never asked Travis anything about the time he'd spent at the pit; face to face with him she'd found it impossible to believe he was behind the string of problems. In the grim light of dawn, she found it impossible to regain that certainty.

She had found herself constantly touching her lips, remembering the feel of his mouth on hers, thinking she was mistaken, she couldn't have really caught fire like that. Even now her fingers stole upward to touch the soft fullness of her lower lip, remembering the flame that had sizzled through her at the touch of his tongue on that sensitive flesh. Her body still tingled, as if it remembered the hard, solid heat of him as he'd held her close.

The phone shrilled, and with a sigh she picked it up.

"Nicki Lockwood."

"This is Max, Miss Lockwood."

"Yes, Max. What is it?"

"We've got a problem. Belt on the main conveyer motor broke. We lost half the load of sand on it, and it's really a mess. And we don't have a replacement in stock."

"Great," Nicki muttered. "Any other damage?"

"The motor seems okay. We're lucky it didn't burn out."

"That's something, I guess." Her brow furrowed. "Didn't we just replace that belt?"

"Yep. Last week. That's why we don't have another one."

"Well, order one, then."

"Yes, Miss Lockwood."

"What happened, Max? If that belt was new..."

"I know. I can't rightly see how it happened. I saw that belt just last night, before I left. It was fine then."

Nicki sat up straight, her fingers tightening around the receiver. "Meaning?"

"That there's no way it could have just broken. It could have been defective, I guess, but I checked it out pretty carefully before we put it on."

"You think...it was tampered with? Last night?"

"Well, I've looked at it real close. It *could* have been cut partway, but I can't be sure. All I know is, it was fine when I saw it before I left last night."

"When was that?"

"Five-forty. I know that for sure, because I'd just shown it to Mr. Halloran. He wanted to know all about it."

Chapter 7

Nicki knew she was doing what she despised most, running and hiding, but she couldn't seem to help it. She had to think, and she couldn't do it in her office.

She had barely managed to escape Richard, dodging into the dispatch office when she heard his voice in the hallway. Her mother's office had been empty as she passed, and she had wondered where Travis was. And, with a touch of bitterness, she also wondered if his absence meant there would be no little disasters this morning.

No, she thought as she paced the floor of the library. She'd come straight home to this room and locked the doors, and had been crisscrossing the floor ever since. No, she just couldn't do it. She couldn't believe that the man who had kissed her so sweetly, so urgently last night was responsible for this string of mishaps.

Fool, she told herself. A little moonlight, a kiss or two, and you're right back where you were fifteen years ago. You didn't want to believe he was responsible for Dad's death, either. True, in the strictest sense of the word she supposed it had been an accident, but it had been brought about by one person's reckless act, the "gross negligence" the juvenile court had cited. And that person was Travis Halloran. It was Travis who had been behind the wheel of Richard's car. It was Travis, driving too fast, who had forced her father off the road leading to their house. And, most damning of all, it was Travis who had tried to shift the blame, to evade the responsibility for what he'd done.

But why would he be doing this now? Did he truly want revenge, badly enough to destroy the prize her mother had inexplicably left him? And if that was what he wanted, why was he putting in so many hours, working so hard at learning the business? So he would know where best to strike at it?

That didn't make sense, either; he didn't have to know, as he'd put it, sand from pea gravel to figure out how to undermine them. And why would he call Richard on his bonehead decisions, when all he had to do was sit back and let her brother run them into the ground, if that's what he wanted?

Besides, it didn't fit him. Travis would never resort to piddling little tricks like those. He might, she thought wryly, blow the place sky high, but this kind of thing was too petty for him. That this certainty was a paradox in view of what else she believed of him was something she couldn't deal with at the moment.

She came to a halt before the desk that had been her father's. She ran a finger along the edge of the polished oak top, remembering all the times she'd snuck in here to watch him work.

She'd been smugly pleased that he let her stay; Richard always got kicked out. Of course Richard had always gotten bored and restless easily, while she had curled up in the overstuffed recliner opposite her father's chair and read quietly, glad just to be there.

She turned and walked to that chair now, kicking off her shoes and curling her legs up under her. This was where Travis had often sat, too, reading, before her mother had come in to quiz him, to buffet him with the questions that sometimes made him angry, sometimes frustrated, but always made him think. She knew, because she'd undergone it enough times herself.

Her eyes drifted to the desk once more. Her father had looked upon his wife's efforts with Travis with an indulgence that was tinged with a sort of regret. It was the regret that took Nicki a long time to figure out. Then one day he'd said something that made sense of it for her.

"If we're going to keep Lockwood in the family, it's going to be up to you, Nicki. You've got the head for it, not your brother."

It was then that she'd realized that her father saw Richard as clearly as her mother did. And knew as well as his wife did that what Richard lacked, Travis had twice over. Knew it well enough to consider making an impossible dream possible.

She sat up straight in the chair. She'd forgotten that. Had forgotten the quiet discussion she hadn't been meant to hear, her mother and father here in this room, talking of sending Travis to college.

"He's got the brains, there's no doubt about that," her father had said. "But would he do it?"

"He would," Emily Lockwood had said firmly. "He won't admit it, but he'd do just about anything to go to college. And he'd do well. He's too stubborn not to."

Nicki hadn't been so sure; Travis was stubborn, but he was also too proud to take what he would consider charity. Just as she thought it, her mother confirmed it.

"Of course," she'd said with a smile softening her face, "he'd insist on paying us back."

"By working at Lockwood?" Her father's voice had echoed with amusement.

"Perhaps," her mother had said lightly, and they had both laughed.

She wondered if her mother had ever mentioned it to him, if Travis had ever known about the chance they'd wanted to give him. Unexpectedly she found herself hoping not; going to jail had been bad enough—knowing what else he'd lost would be unbearable.

She caught herself in the middle of that thought. Why did she care if Travis hurt? No matter what had happened to him, he was alive and her father was dead. And a couple of kisses in the moonlight, no matter how sweet, no matter how hot, didn't change that.

She felt a sudden burst of shame, shame that she had let him kiss her at all, that she had been so weak as to succumb to the old memories, that she had given in to the temptation to find out if it could be as good as she'd imagined. And she'd found out it was more than good, much more. More than she'd ever thought a simple kiss could be.

The memories of those kisses rose up like bright, sweet fire, searing her shame to ashes and sending undulations of remembered heat through her. And his poignant question echoed in her ears—*What do we do now?*

"I don't know," she whispered into the quiet room.

The knock on the door made her jump, so lost was she in her emotional dilemma. Automatically she glanced at her watch; no one they knew would expect anyone to be home at this hour. She started toward it, then stopped a moment to wipe her cheeks when she realized they were damp. Sometimes it seemed the only thing she did consistently anymore was cry, she thought despairingly.

The moment she opened the door and saw Travis there, she knew she'd guessed it might be him. She just stood there, unable to speak. He started to say something, but the words died unspoken when his gaze met her still damp eyes. Pain twisted his face.

"Oh, Nicole…" He swallowed tightly. "It's been hell for you, hasn't it?"

Absurdly, Nicki wanted to go to him, to huddle in his arms, to have him protect her. Absurd because, if she had any sense, she'd admit he was the one she needed protection from. Determined not to weaken again, she steadied herself. Her chin came up.

"What do you want?"

As if he'd seen only that moment of wavering, and not heard at all the sharpness of her voice, he said quietly, "You didn't come to the office. I was worried."

"About what?"

"You. After last night, I—"

"Last night was a mistake."

He drew back and studied her face carefully. "Was it?"

"Yes."

She turned away. Travis followed her inside before she could close the door.

"Why?"

"It should never have happened."

"Dinner? We had to eat."

She flushed. "You know what I mean."

"Yes. You mean when I kissed you."

She lowered her eyes.

"So what part was a mistake? That I did it, or that it was so...good?"

"That I let you."

"I got the distinct impression that you did more than just 'let' me."

"Ye—" Her voice broke. "Yes! And that was the biggest mistake of all!"

"Why? Because it shook the hate you've been nursing all these years? Because you liked it?" His voice dropped, went soft and husky. "And don't tell me you didn't, Nicole. I know better."

She shivered, that undertone in his voice bringing back all the sweet, stinging memories and sending a frisson of sensation feathering up her spine.

"No," she whispered, protesting the feelings he roused in her, feelings that she couldn't seem to fight.

All Travis heard was the denial, and anger flicked at him like the tip of a lash. She might deny everything else, but he wasn't going to let her deny this. He reached for her quickly, before she could dodge away, his hands going to grip her shoulders. He felt her tremble and tightened his grip, more to steady her than to control her. The moment he did she stopped, looking up at him, wide-eyed.

"Travis," she breathed, unable to say anything else. The sight of her lips parting for his name sent a shaft of heat lancing through him. He pulled her close, his head darting downward quickly, his lips closing on hers.

The fire flared as before, with a fierce swiftness that made them both gasp. All her thoughts of denying this sweetness fled before the onslaught. His tongue stroked, caressed, invaded her sweet warmth, and she felt an answering warmth building somewhere deep inside her. She opened for him, luring him on, not satisfied until she heard him groan low in his throat.

Her arms encircled his neck, her fingers threading through his hair. Her hands stilled; this, too, was more than she'd ever dreamed, this feeling of the thick, heavy silk of his hair sliding over her skin. Her fingers flexed then, savoring it.

His mouth moved on hers, harder, deeper. He was drinking her in, absorbing her, like a man too long in the desert faced with the sweetness of crystal water. She let him, unwilling, unable to fight this. Thinking that it couldn't be fought, not when it was so strong, not when it was so right. Not when it was Travis.

The small sound of protest she made when his mouth left hers changed to a quick gasp of pleasure as his lips moved along her delicate jaw and down her slender throat, nibbling, kissing, leaving a trail of fire that made her quiver.

He lingered in the hollow of her throat, tasting, and the feel of the rough, wet velvet of his tongue against her skin sent a shudder through her. She was shivering, yet aflame at the same time, and she thought inanely how appropriate that was; she'd been confused since the moment he'd come back into her life.

His hands slipped to the back of her head, tilting it so he could begin again that searing kiss that she was already feeling in parts of her she hadn't known existed. She moved as if she were made of wax, softened by his lips for his hands to mold as they willed.

His hands moved, sliding down over her shoulders as his tongue thrust, probed, sending little darts of heat and pleasure through her. She began to feel oddly heavy in that place deep inside that he had stirred to life, and in the tender flesh of her breasts. She was seized with a need she'd never known, a need for his touch in all those deep, private places, a need she instinctively knew only he could assuage.

And then she knew it would take much more than just his touch, for he was stroking the outer curve of her breasts, adding to their heat with his own, and it only made the need worse, sharper, more desperate.

The intensity of it frightened her, and she tried to pull away. When she did, her hips moved against him and she felt the hot, hard ridge of male flesh at the same moment she heard him gasp. Somehow it reassured her, eased the fright; she was not alone, careening out of control, he was with her, and as aroused as she was.

But Travis had felt the change in her, sensed her moment of panic. With hands that were shaking, and a grip that was nearly painful, he set her away from him. He stared down at her, with eyes still hot, and his pulse leaping visibly at the base of his throat.

Slowly the heat faded from his eyes, replaced by a tenderness so strong it took her breath away. He lifted a hand to gently brush the backs of his fingers across her cheek.

"I'm sorry, Nicole," he said softly. "I had no right to push that hard when you're so vulnerable right now."

"I'm just so... confused," she said miserably.

"I know." His voice got a little gruffer. "Just don't be confused about this, Nicole. Denying it won't change it."

"I can't deny it. I don't even know what it is." Her voice shook, laced with equal parts of bewilderment and agitation.

"You will," he promised solemnly, with a fierce determination that made her stare at him, unable to rid herself of the idea that he meant so much more than what had just occurred between them.

"Travis, I—"

"No." He cut her off gently but firmly. "Not now. Neither one of us is thinking very straight."

He grinned suddenly, that flashing, lopsided grin that had once sent her heart racing and made her breath catch. It still did.

"How about some lunch, Ms. Lockwood? I noticed the McDonald's is still in the same old place. Still addicted to their fries?"

The abrupt shattering of the tension left her a little dazed, but in the face of that wicked grin she could do nothing but what she'd always done; smile back and acquiesce to whatever he'd said.

"Good. Let's go." He took her arm, not giving her a chance to refuse. "Only one ground rule. No shoptalk."

His enthusiasm was infectious, and irresistible. She was seated in the car and they were halfway down the long driveway before she realized that she'd tacitly agreed not to discuss the topic foremost in her mind; the accidents at the plant and the pit.

The sense of relief that filled her told her much about her state of mind. Coward, she berated herself inwardly. You don't want to ask because you're afraid of the answer you might get. Afraid that he'll deny it, just like he did all those years ago.

Catch-22, she thought suddenly. He wouldn't admit it if he were guilty, but if he denied it, she'd assume he was only hiding his guilt. No matter what he said, her reaction would be the same.

If you have to ask, it wouldn't do me any good to deny it. He'd said that when Richard had flung that accusation at him, but only now did Nicki realize exactly what he'd meant. And how true it was.

No matter what the emotional basis, she couldn't deny the unfairness of it. And she'd found too much built-in unfairness already in life. But the alternative, believing he was innocent, left her two choices: she had to accept that the string of accidents were just that, accidents, or that someone else was behind them. She wasn't sure which she found hardest to believe.

"Hey." He reached over and nudged her gently beneath the chin. "No serious thoughts. Put 'em on hold." He grimaced wryly. "Believe me, they won't go away."

A sigh escaped her unaware. Travis said nothing until they pulled into the parking lot of the fast-food restaurant. Then he turned in his seat to look at her solemnly.

"Do you want to go back?"

"No." She was surprised at how quickly the answer came. "It's just—" She broke off. "Sorry. You said no shop-talk."

"We can find something else to talk about, can't we?" he said with a smile, a wistful smile of reminiscence touched by sadness. It was a heartbreaking smile, and Nicki felt hers quiver.

"We always could," she said softly.

"Yes." The sadness vanished in the renewed flaring of that bright, hot hope. "We always could."

It was like slipping back in time, sitting there with him. He'd brought her here a few times then, this being the best he could afford, and they'd sat and talked over the French fries and a soda she always ordered. He'd often accused her of purposely ordering nothing else because she thought he couldn't afford it, but he'd finally had to accept that it was simply her favorite meal.

"I remember," she said softly as she sat down with that same order of fries and a soda, "when we used to sit here and talk about seeing the world..."

"So do I." He stole one of her fries, just as he'd always done then. "So tell me, what was your trip like? Paris, London, Amsterdam, you must have hit them all."

"No."

He looked at her quizzically, the purloined fry halfway to his mouth.

"No, what?"

"I didn't hit them all. I didn't hit any of them."

He lowered the fry to his napkin. "You never went?"

"I never left San Remo. I... couldn't. When I finished high school, I had to go straight to college. Mother needed me at the plant as soon as possible. Richard wasn't doing very well, and she needed the help."

She didn't say why. She didn't have to; they both knew it. Because of her father's death, she had lost the fondest dream of her childhood.

"I'm sorry," he said lowly, his expression showing that he wondered if she held him responsible for this, too.

"It was a silly dream," she said a little tightly.

"No. No, it wasn't. I'm sorry you... lost that dream."

"So did you."

He shrugged. "Oh, I've been a place or two. Alaska, Canada, Mexico, South America. Even worked a job in Saudi Arabia, once."

Her eyes widened. "You built things in all those places?"

That crooked grin flashed, sending her stomach on a flip-flopping little roll. "Not single-handedly."

"Tell me, what was it like?"

He couldn't resist the fervent plea, besides, it was a safe topic. So between bites of the hamburger he'd ordered, he told her of the dam in South America, the school in Mexico, and all the other projects that had taken him some of the places they'd talked about as kids.

Nicki drank it in, her eyes alight. Twice he seemed to catch himself before letting slip something he didn't want to tell her, and she could almost see him tighten his guard. At last he stopped, and only then did Nicki become aware of the stares they were getting.

Just like old times, she thought again. Then, they had been the center of attention, the target of glances and outright stares that ranged from curious to speculative to aghast. She'd ignored them, her chin high, and been rewarded with one of Travis's lopsided grins of salute.

She knew why they had stared, knew that it wasn't just because he was older than she, and she just on the edge of womanhood. No, it was because everyone in this town knew who she was, who he was, and the combination of a Lockwood and the Halloran boy was enough to set the tongues twitching for miles.

Not, she thought, that they weren't getting as much attention now. But there were differences now, the flurry involved only the older patrons in the place; the younger ones were too caught up in themselves to notice them. But the others, the ones who recognized them, were making up for it; the whispers that traced around the dining area were ominously apparent, like the hissing of a snake.

Travis seemed to become aware of it at the same moment. "Sometimes I wonder what this town would have done for entertainment if I hadn't been around," he muttered.

"They would have picked on someone else," Nicki said, bitterness lacing her voice. "They have to have something to keep their little minds occupied."

Travis lifted a brow at her tone, but he only said, "Makes a good case for living in a big city, someplace where everybody's too busy to mind anyone's business but their own."

"Is that . . . where you live now? In a big city?"

If he was surprised by the question after her concentrated efforts at disinterest, he didn't show it. "San Diego."

"Oh."

She didn't know what else to say. She bit at another fry, took a tiny sip of soda, then watched as he took another bite of his hamburger. As he did, she caught a glimpse of the scar, and at the thought of how painful it must have been, her stomach nearly returned what she'd eaten so far. Travis saw her glance, saw the pained grimace that crossed her face.

"Don't, Nicole. It was a long time ago. I shouldn't have been so rough on you about it."

"I can't . . . You . . . It must have been horrible," she ended in a rush, shuddering.

"Forget it."

She turned troubled eyes on him. "Have you?"

"I know it must not seem like it, but I really don't think about it much anymore." His mouth twisted wryly. "It's just that the memories seem to be stirring lately."

Nicki gave a low, rueful chuckle. "Don't they, though."

He watched her for a moment. "Are they all bad?" he asked quietly. "Don't you remember any of the good ones?"

"I remember." She lowered her eyes, picking at another fry. "I've always remembered. All of it. That's what made it so hard."

She heard him take a quick, deep breath. "Nicole, listen, I—"

He broke off, and she looked up in time to see him clench his jaw and look away from her. Whatever it had been, it was clear from the effort it took him to stop that it was something he badly wanted to say.

"What?"

"Nothing."

"Travis—"

He shook his head.

"You keep doing that. What is it?"

"I . . . can't."

"Why? Why won't you tell me?"

"Some things you can't tell people. They have to see for themselves."

"See what?"

He sighed. "I'm not making any sense." His mouth quirked. "All those stirring memories."

He was obviously determined, and she had to let it go. They ate in silence then, Nicki finishing first and glancing once more around the busy room.

She caught more than one surreptitious watcher red-handed, but it was no surprise; she'd known they hadn't stopped looking since she and Travis had come in. That didn't bother her as much as the furtive way they jerked their eyes away, as if they could hide their nosiness by looking somewhere else. Curiosity she could tolerate; sneakiness made her angry.

"Can we leave?" she said suddenly, sharply, as soon as he'd finished.

Travis looked at her a little oddly, but got to his feet. Nicki didn't look at anyone, but still sensed the heads turning as they walked out. She remained tautly silent until, in the car, Travis said mildly, "Where to?"

"Anywhere."

It was low and harsh, and stopped him from asking any more questions. Without a word he started the car and drove out of the lot. She lapsed once more into silence, seemingly oblivious to her surroundings. When at last he pulled over and parked, she looked around in surprise. He'd brought her home.

"I thought we could . . . talk, here."

She followed the direction of his gaze, toward the graceful green sweep of the willow tree. Her mind cried out *no,* that it would be too painful there in the place full of so many memories, but her heart blocked the word. Slowly she nodded.

Almost without thought they took up their old, familiar positions, Nicki sitting cross-legged on the soft grass, Travis stretched out on his side and propped up on one elbow, his long legs crossed at the ankles.

"Are you all right?" he asked after a moment. "You seemed in an awfully big hurry to get out of there."

"I was." She plucked at a blade of grass. "They were horrible."

"No more than usual."

"That's what I mean," she muttered. "No wonder you never came back."

"You think I let them stop me?"

Her brow furrowed. "Then what did?"

"You."

"Me?" She looked startled. "How?"

"You made it pretty clear how you felt."

"I was upset. That night . . . my father . . ."

"I know. I meant later."

"What do you mean?"

"The letters." He plucked a long blade of grass and caught it between his teeth.

"What?"

"When the first one came back, I figured you were still mad, so I waited." His teeth clenched on the piece of grass. "I thought, after a while, you might stop hating me long enough to..." He trailed off, then said gruffly, "But when the last one came back with that note, I gave up."

"You...wrote to me?"

"Only four or five times." His smile was crooked. "It took me a while to get the hint. I—"

Her words and expression got through to him then; his eyes narrowed as he looked at her.

"You didn't get them?"

Eyes wide, she shook her head mutely.

"But the note you sent..."

"I didn't. I never even knew you'd written."

"It was in your handwriting."

"I didn't," she insisted, mystified. "What did it say?"

He smiled, a little grimly. "I think the exact words were 'Get lost, scum. I hate you.'"

Nicki's eyes widened. "I didn't," she said a third time, but something flickered in her memory.

"I remember it, Nicki. Getting something like that from you is not something I'm likely to forget. For weeks I saw those big red letters in my sleep."

She gasped as the flickering, elusive memory leapt to life. "Red?"

"As blood." He saw the knowledge in her eyes, along with a stunned, pained shock. "It's okay. I understand how you must have felt—"

"Travis, no! I mean, I wrote it, I remember it now, but not to you! It was never for you." His brow furrowed, and she rushed on. "It was for Scott."

"Scott?"

"Scott Ellis. A boy in my class, and he was always bothering me. He used to call me names...because of you. I was going to leave that note on his desk at school, but I lost it..."

He looked at her for a long moment, considering, and Nicki had a sudden flash of insight about how it must feel when no one believed you.

"I didn't send it," she whispered. "I don't know who..."

"Your mother used to get the mail, didn't she?"

"No! I mean yes, but she wouldn't do that," Nicki protested.

"Oh?" There was a world of irony in his voice.

"She wouldn't! In fact she said once, when I was so miserable from missing you, that maybe someday you'd... contact me..."

"You... missed me?"

"Horribly. I didn't want to, but I did. Then I'd think about my dad, and feel so damned guilty..."

"Oh, Nicole, you really went through hell, didn't you?"

"I hated myself for even thinking about you, and I hated my dad for dying. But most of all I—"

"Hated me," Travis supplied softly when she stopped.

She turned haunted blue eyes on him. "Yes!"

"I know. Anyone would feel that way if they thought... what you did."

"It wasn't that!" Her vehemence startled him. "I mean, I was angry about Dad, but I think I could have forgiven that, eventually. It was stupid and careless and reckless... and... and..."

"Grossly negligent," he prodded grimly.

"Yes! But it wasn't—" She stopped for a gulping breath. "It wasn't..."

"Murder?"

"No."

"Well, that's something, I guess," he said flippantly. "The court called it involuntary manslaughter, but I never thought I'd hear even that much of a concession from a Lockwood."

"I know it really wasn't murder," she whispered. "But why did you have to say those things? Why did you have to lie?"

He stiffened. "I told you I never—"

He stopped abruptly. The urge to say it all again, to tell her, make her realize the truth, rose up in him. But what could he say? She'd never believe that he hadn't been driving that night. She'd believe, as she always had, that he'd only been trying to blame Richard to keep himself out of trouble. If she hadn't believed him then, with more than a year of closeness and trust between them, she certainly wouldn't now, with fifteen years of distance separating them.

"Never mind. If you don't already know, there's nothing I can say to convince you."

"But—"

"No, Nicole. That's the one thing I won't discuss."

Stung a little by his coldness, she snapped, "I thought your father was the one thing you wouldn't discuss."

"That doesn't matter anymore. He's dead."

"I know." Her anger faded before his bleak expression. "I thought that you might . . . come back, then."

"Why? There was nothing for either of us here. I took him back to Minnesota. It was the only place I ever remember him saying he'd been happy."

It was one of the most desolate statements she'd ever heard, but the flat, unemotional tone of his voice told her he had no interest in or desire for her sympathy.

"He must have been a very unhappy man."

"I suppose."

"I'm sorry he took it out on you."

"It doesn't matter anymore," he said again.

"Does something like that ever not matter anymore?"

"I don't know," he said, looking at her pointedly. "Does it?"

She knew what he meant, and she had no answer for him. She ran her hand over the lush grass, feeling it bend against her fingers, and remembering how the dark silk of his hair had felt against her skin.

"Travis?"

"What?"

"Those letters . . . what did they say?"

He went still. "Nothing you were ready to hear. It's probably just as well you didn't get them."

"I still don't understand. My mother wouldn't do that, honestly. And she wouldn't have sent that note."

He sighed. "Probably not. Sounds more like Richie to me, anyway."

After a moment she said softly, "Mother used to tell me, when I would get so angry at you, not to judge you too harshly. That she didn't ... hate you for what happened."

Travis laughed, unable to hide the bitterness of the rough sound. "Now that," he muttered, "is a piece of irony I could do without."

"But—"

The sound of a racing engine and the squeal of protesting tires jerked both their heads around in time to see Richard's long, white convertible roar up the drive. They watched as he stopped and got out to stare at the gleaming Mercedes.

Even from beneath the tree they could see his face contort with anger, and then, with a sudden, vicious movement, he struck out with one foot and kicked the door of the black car.

Nicki's eyes widened; Travis merely let out a half-amused, half-disgusted exclamation.

Nicki turned to Travis. "What did he do that for?"

"Haven't you figured that out yet?"

"I know he's angry about you being here—"

"It's a lot more than just that. He's afraid of me."

"Afraid?" She looked at him. "Why?"

"Think about it."

"I don't understand. Kicking your car is ..."

"Juvenile? Immature? Or just plain Richard?"

She couldn't think of a thing to say; she'd thought the same thing too many times herself. But why would Richard be afraid of Travis?

She watched her brother as, spotting them, he strode toward the willow tree.

"Well, isn't this sweet! Reliving old times?"

Travis never even blinked at the biting sarcasm. "Hi, Richie."

"Get out of here."

Travis raised a brow, but didn't speak.

"My sister may be fool enough to believe whatever line you're feeding her, but I'm not. You're trespassing. Get off this property."

"Richard—" Nicki began, but her brother cut her off.

"I don't want to hear anything from you. What the hell do you think you're doing, hanging around with the enemy? Dad would be turning over in his grave if he knew."

Nicki blinked, a little stunned by his choice of words. Yet instead of being hurt, all she could do was think of what Travis had said. Richard was acting exactly as he always did when he was afraid; striking out at anyone within reach. Anyone who couldn't—or wouldn't—strike back.

"Knock it off, Richie. Your problem's with me, not her."

"She's my sister, I'll talk to her any way I want."

"The hell you will."

Travis didn't even move, but something in his voice made Richard back up a step.

"Defending her honor?" Richard sneered. "How touching."

"Shut up, Richard," Nicki said wearily.

"Tell me, Richie, who's minding the store? How are they surviving without you?"

"None of your business!"

"I'd say it's exactly that."

"Look, she may buy all this phony concern, but I know better. I know what you're up to."

"Oh, really? What am I up to, Richie?"

"You're trying to get her to side with you, to give you control of the company."

"What makes you think I want control?" Travis asked lazily. "Maybe all I want is to keep you from having it."

Richard flushed. Then something strange flashed in his eyes, something Nicki thought was oddly furtive. Travis caught it, too; Nicki sensed his sudden intentness.

"Something else you want to say, Richie?"

"So I was right," Richard said. Nicki heard a strange note in his voice that matched that look that had glinted in his eyes.

"I suppose," Travis drawled, "even you are right now and then."

Richard's voice went haughty. "I didn't want to believe it, of course."

"Never stopped you before," Travis said mildly.

"Well, if you think you're hurting us, you're not."

"Richard," Nicki said in exasperation, "what are you talking about?"

"All those things that have gone wrong at the plant lately."

Nicki sucked in a quick breath, her glance flicking to Travis.

"Don't forget the ones at the pit," Travis said.

Richard gaped at him, startled into silence.

"Go ahead, Richie. Don't lose your nerve now," Travis tilted the blade of grass upward with his teeth.

Nicki was staring at Travis, barely breathing. The subject she'd been avoiding all day was here, huge, hovering, and unavoidable. Travis merely lolled back on his elbows as Richard gawked at him, his mouth opening and then shutting like an oxygen-starved fish. His thin lips pursed, and he pulled at a strand of hair as suspicion lit his pale, watery blue eyes, and his words were warily spoken.

"You know about the accidents at the pit?"

"I'd have to, wouldn't I, Richie-boy, if I'm responsible for them?"

Chapter 8

Richard's jaw dropped as Nicki gasped.

"That *is* what you were about to accuse me of, isn't it?" Travis asked as casually as if discussing the weather.

Oh, God, Nicki thought. Was he going to admit it? Was he going to confess to being the one who'd caused those accidents, the one who had cost them countless dollars and even more precious time? Was he really out for some twisted kind of revenge, or, as he'd said, just to keep Richard from controlling the company?

Not, she admitted with pained honesty, that the thought of Richard in control didn't scare her senseless. But he was her brother, the Lockwood son. He had a right, didn't he?

Richard seemed to recover himself. He drew himself up straight, the effect spoiled by the paunch that hung over his belt. "It's obvious, isn't it, since they started the moment you showed up?"

Nicki caught her breath; she'd been tortured by the same thoughts ever since Richard had first accused him, but somehow, hearing Richard saying it again now was even more awful. But Travis just looked at Richard, nothing disturbing the emotionless mask of his face, or the even tone of his tone.

"Actually, there probably is a connection there."

"Travis, no!" The protesting cry broke from her against her will, and drew her a startled, then assessing look from Travis.

"God, Nicki, you're such a fool!" Richard looked at her scornfully. "You're acting like you did when you were a kid, hanging around this...this...jailbird all the time."

On the word jailbird, Nicki's eyes darted to Travis, but he didn't even react. She wondered why it didn't seem to disturb him, especially when she remembered the searing flash of pain that had flared in his eyes when she had called him an ex-con.

"I'm sorry, Nicole," Travis said softly.

It took her a moment to understand what he meant. When she realized that he was apologizing for Richard's insult, it made her throat tighten unbearably.

"'I'm sorry, Nicole'," Richard mimicked sarcastically. "Nicole. Like you were something special, when you're just my dumb little sister. So dumb you can't even see through this con man."

Color flooded Nicki's cheeks. "Stop it, Richard."

"Can't you see what he's up to? That he wants to destroy Lockwood?"

"Why would he do that, when it's partly his now—"

"You really are blind!" Richard's lips tightened as he glared at her, but his eyes held a touch of apprehension as his gaze flicked to Travis, as if he were a man poking at a wolf with a stick he wasn't positive was long enough. "I told you, he wants revenge, of course. Against me, because I know what he is, even if you won't admit it. Because I wouldn't let him blame me for what he did. He's too much of a coward to go after me, so he's trying to ruin the company."

Nicki felt Travis tense. Or thought she did; when she glanced at him, he looked the same, casually propped on his elbows, his expression bland as he watched them, waiting.

"But he couldn't, even if he wanted to," Nicki protested. "He only has fifty percent—"

"I suppose you believe he's spending all this time with you because he wants to, don't you?" Richard said, cutting her off again. "You're supposed to be so smart, but you're a dunce when it comes to him. Haven't you figured it out yet? He's only trying to keep you in line. He doesn't want you, he wants your twenty-five percent to go with his fifty. He—"

"That's enough." Travis didn't move, but at his quiet words Richard stopped as if he'd pounced. He swallowed nervously, eyeing Travis before going on.

"Can't stand the truth, Halloran?"

"Shut up, Rich."

Richard's pudgy hands curled into fists, but, eyeing Travis's lounging, well-muscled body, he didn't move. "I wonder if you'd be such a wise guy in front of the cops, Halloran."

"Richard, stop it." Nicki's voice was strained; she could still sense the tension building in Travis.

"What's wrong, Sis?" Richard turned on her. "Don't want to see your boyfriend carted away in handcuffs again?"

Nicki paled, fighting the memories that flashed through her mind at his words, memories she'd fought for years to keep buried so deeply they would never surface. She sensed rather than saw Travis move; he uncoiled from the grass with a speed that made Richard back up once more.

"I warned you, Richie. Your problem is with me, not your sister. You take it out on her one more time, and you'll answer to me."

"You go to hell!"

"Been there. It's overrated."

Richard glared, started to take a step forward, but then something about Travis's ready posture and the steady stare of granite-gray eyes made him hesitate. He switched his glare to Nicki.

"All right, but don't say I didn't warn you! Don't come crying to me when you find out I'm right—"

He ended with a curse, low and vicious, as he turned on his heel and stalked off. Travis took a step after him, his jaw set and rigid. Nicki quickly reached for his arm to hold him back; it was rock hard and taut beneath her fingers.

"No, Travis. Please."

"I told him what would happen if he talked to you like that again."

"He's just...upset."

"He's a spoiled brat."

"I know."

That stopped him. He turned to look at her. "How have you kept from throttling him?"

Nicki shrugged. "He's my brother."

"That doesn't give him the right to abuse you."

"He doesn't mean to." She lowered her eyes. "Besides," she added in a whisper, "he's all I've got, now."

Pain flashed across Travis's face, but Nicki didn't see it as she lifted her head to watch her brother storm into the house.

"Travis?"

He made some sound, not a word but merely an acknowledgment that she'd spoken. It was such a taut, hard sound, so strained, that she wondered if he'd done it because he couldn't speak.

"When he called you a— That," she said after a moment, "why didn't it bother you?"

There was a pause, and Nicki turned back to him in time to see a wry expression flit across his face.

"It's true, isn't it?"

"Not that," she said impatiently. "I mean, it just seemed to roll right off of you, but I said virtually the same thing and you—"

She broke off at the look that came into his eyes. It was that same flashing stab of pain, but it was gone in an instant.

"Because," he said in a flat, even tone that belied that look of anguish, "I don't give a damn what Richard thinks of me."

Nicki caught her breath at the clear implication.

"And," Travis added solemnly, "I have absolutely no respect for his opinion."

This time she blushed. Flustered, she muttered something that was supposed to be appreciative, but came out merely confused. She wondered where the poise that allowed her to handle a crew of sometimes rowdy workers had gone. She had gotten compliments like this before, sometimes from that same rowdy crew, if only in the respect they accorded her. So why, she wondered, did it disconcert her so coming from Travis?

"He was always only an excuse, you know," Travis said softly. "So I could keep coming here to see you."

Those sweet, precious memories stirred again, and she was seized with a sudden need to put him at ease.

"He's just talking, you know. He won't really call the police."

He stiffened. "What's that? Reassurance?"

She looked puzzled. "I just wanted you to know—"

"Meaning you think I did it?"

"I didn't say that."

He studied her for a moment. "But you thought it, didn't you?"

Her chin came up; her eyes were troubled, but she faced him squarely. "I wondered. He's right about one thing. Those things, all those accidents, did start to happen right after you came."

"So naturally I must be guilty," he grated. "Damn, how many times can I get hung by coincidence?"

"Travis—"

"Never mind, Miss Lockwood. I should have known better than to expect anything else. Why didn't you call the police yourself?"

She was stung by his biting drawl of the formal name. She had wanted to tell him she hadn't told anyone of her suspicions because she couldn't make herself believe it was true. But his tone made it impossible.

"If you're innocent," she said coolly, "then you have nothing to worry about, do you?"

He laughed, a short, harsh, utterly grim sound. "You picked the wrong person to try and sell *that* bull to." He sucked in a breath. "I suppose you believe the rest, too? That I'm just using you? That what's happened between us is a lie, too?"

She couldn't speak; she wasn't sure what she believed anymore.

"Never mind," he said grimly. "I've had about all I can stand of the Lockwood beliefs for one day, anyway."

Nicki colored. "Then why don't you leave?"

"Good idea."

He started to walk past her, then stopped. "I'm not going to beg you to believe me. It didn't do me any good fifteen years ago, and I swore I'd never do it again. Of anybody. For anything."

He stood looking down at her, gray eyes hot with a mixture of anger and torment that frightened her somehow.

"But there's something else I'm not doing to do." His voice had dropped, becoming husky, as if making a vow. "I'm not going to let you forget this."

Before she could react he had hauled her up hard against him, his head darting downward, his mouth taking hers fiercely, swiftly, cutting off her yelp of protest. He held her fast, even her fit, taut strength no match for his. His mouth commanded, and to her dismay she found herself unable to do anything but comply as his heat flashed through her, setting her ablaze.

The moment she stopped fighting him his mouth gentled, his arms, while still holding her, became a support rather than a steel snare. His lips coaxed, his tongue sweetly probed, sending her blood singing through her veins in hot, pulsing beats.

Despite herself she moved, pressing her tingling breasts harder against his chest. She felt her nipples rise to his heat as if begging for it, skin to hot, satin skin, without the interference of clothing. The thought sent a shudder of fierce desire rippling through her, and she gave a little moan under its force.

At the sound his hands slid down her body, to grasp her slender hips and pull her against him. She felt him, the full, engorged length of him surging against her, and the same thought of naked skin against naked skin swept her again, the image weakening her knees.

She sagged against him. He broke the kiss to hold her up, supporting her with the same strong arms that had held her captive.

"Travis," she whispered, amazed that her swollen, tingling lips could even form the word.

"Don't forget this, Nicole," he said hoarsely. "It's not a lie, it's real, maybe the only real thing in this damned world. If you can't believe that . . ."

She could feel the words vibrating in his chest beneath her cheek. Over the pounding of his, she felt the hammer beats of her own heart gradually begin to slow, felt the heat of her blood subside to a simmering warmth, but any further words seemed beyond her; she had only enough strength to cling to him. When at last she spoke, it was to echo his own heartfelt question.

"What do we do now?"

His arms tightened around her; his head came down as his cheek rested on the tousled auburn silk of her hair.

"We do what we have to do. Just don't ever forget how right this is. It was meant to be, Nicole. From the start. We just had to grow into it."

A choking sound, a half sob, broke from her. "For fifteen years?"

He let out a compressed breath. "That," he said sourly, "wasn't my plan."

"Your plan?"

"I figured I'd wait, at least until you were eighteen, and see if you . . ."

"If I what?"

"Wanted me."

She shivered, her fingers tightening around the gray suede jacket. "I . . . always wanted you."

"I think I knew that. But you were so young, and you never said anything."

"I didn't dare. I knew you always had . . . girls hanging around you, even some my age . . ."

"The gigglers. I remember. They got their kicks out of pretending to like the town bad boy."

"I wanted to be . . . different. Not one of the ones who followed you around, but the one you came to, the one you talked to."

"You were. The only one. Even then."

A shiver gripped her again. "God, Travis, it should have been so easy. How did things get so messed up?"

"You know how."

She stiffened, but he soothed her, his left hand stroking the auburn silk of her hair.

"I know you don't like to think about it. Lord knows, neither do I. But it's time you did, Nicole. Think about it long and hard."

He backed away, but still held her shoulders until he saw she was steady enough to stand. She was looking at him with troubled eyes, the bright blue clouded with confusion and doubt.

"I know, Nicole. For years you've hidden it away. But if you don't bring it out, look at it again—" he reached out and gently caressed her still swollen lower lip with his thumb "—we'll lose this. And we've lost so damned much already."

He released her then, but Nicki felt as held by his darkened gray eyes as she had by his strong, supple hands. And then he was gone, leaving her staring after him from beneath the willow, her fingers at her lips as if his caress lingered, as if he'd branded her with his touch.

Travis hung up the phone, and stood there staring at it for a long moment. Things were backing up at home; he was going to have to make a trip back soon. Maybe this weekend, if he could manage it.

He picked up the mug of coffee he'd set down when the phone had rung, and walked over to the big, plate glass window at the front of the house. No wonder Martha had never been able to bring herself to sell it, he thought as he looked out over the blue Pacific sparkling in the early morning sun. When Martha had found out he was coming here, the dynamic vice-president of Willow Tree had practically ordered him to use her house.

He thought of how it had looked another time, glittering not beneath the flood of gold but the ethereal silver moonlight. And how Nicki had felt in his arms, how her mouth had felt beneath his, how she had turned to some soft, flowing thing and had taken him with her, robbing him of any last bit of will or strength.

He sighed, and took a sip of the coffee that was now barely lukewarm. Somehow, when he'd come here, he hadn't expected this. He'd thought about her every day of his life since she'd first tumbled off the banister at his feet, but always as the fiery-haired scamp of his memories. And so much time had passed, so much had changed, he had changed, he'd never expected this reaction to her. He'd thought the old, silly dreams long dead, beyond resurrection.

The moment he'd seen her at the funeral, tall and sleek and elegantly curved, more beautiful than even he'd dreamed she would become, the old dreams came back in a rush. And the thought of the old Nicki, the one who had shared his thoughts, his dreams, who had known his soul, combined with this beautiful, tempting woman, was shattering.

He'd always thought that it might be like this. That she might be the one to reach the part of him he'd never given to anyone. That she already held the key to the part he'd kept hidden and protected all these years. It figures, he thought. She'd owned his heart and soul and mind all those years ago, why should it surprise him that now, as a woman, she would own his body, as well?

But his wildest imaginings back then, he thought ruefully, still wouldn't have prepared him for this. He didn't think anything could have prepared him for the way he caught fire when he touched her, kissed her. And anything beyond that didn't bear thinking about. But he thought about it anyway, and shuddered under the impact of imagining them intimately entwined, her silken skin bare against his, her long, curved legs wrapped around him . . .

He slammed the mug down on the table before the window, swearing at himself for letting his fantasy get out of hand; all he'd done was torture himself with that rising, yearning ache that he'd been battling since he'd first seen her again. A burning ache that was compounded by the fact that she still didn't trust him.

Of course she doesn't, he told himself. She's spent the last fifteen years blaming you, hating you, for killing her father. You're not going to change that in fifteen days. But at least, he consoled himself, they were talking. They were communicating. And kissing . . .

"And just when," he muttered aloud, "did you turn into a masochist?"

Still shaking his head at himself, he went to get a towel to wipe up the coffee that had sloshed out of the cup when he'd slammed it down. Then he took the cup to the kitchen and washed it. He stood for a long time, staring at the sparkling ocean through the expansive bay window in the breakfast nook of the house. Then he turned abruptly on his heel, grabbed his jacket, and headed for the door.

Nicki stared at the copy of the forms she'd mailed out, knowing that although she'd trimmed all she could trim, the bid was still too high. With all of Richard's foolish maneuvering they would be lucky to meet the orders at all, and although she'd cut the profit margin to nearly nothing, she knew the end figures were above what other operations could offer.

She sighed, mentally giving up the idea of winning this bid on the marina project. No company would accept this when they could get their product so much cheaper. Not even to deal with Lockwood, who had the best reputation in the area for quality and service. At least they did for now, she amended sourly. If this kept up, that reputation would be crumbling quickly.

She leaned back in her chair, running a hand over her denim clad knee. She'd gone back to her usual uniform of jeans paired with soft silk shirts; the denim for practicality around the yard, the silk a touch of feminine luxury she needed in this place. Today it was a simple shirt in a deep teal, which gave her eyes a turquoise tint.

She tried desperately to keep her mind off Richard's accusations. Every time she thought of them, her own doubts rose up to taunt her. And her own harshest judge, her inner self, berated her for being more upset at the idea of Travis using her to gain total control of Lockwood than at the thought that he might be behind the sabotage.

God, maybe Richard was right. Maybe she did have a blind spot when it came to Travis. What else could explain why her mind always came up with explanations for everything when she was with him, rationalizations that soothed a doubting mind, only to have it torture her again when she was alone? Did his mere presence have such a power over her?

Stop it, she ordered herself. Get back to work. She forced her gaze back to the papers in her hand.

No, she thought, no company in their right mind would take this bid. And this company was most definitely in their right mind. Willow Tree had come out of nowhere six years ago to become one of the biggest in San Diego. She would have liked to have been in on the ground floor of their expansion into Orange County, but based on these figures, there wasn't much chance of that.

Her eyes strayed to the logo that graced the newspaper ad soliciting bids. With a wry smile she wondered how much of her attraction to this company was based on the appeal, to her at least, of their name. Lord, she thought, you're a soft touch. Just the name Willow Tree, and you're a goner. One slender finger reached out and traced the flowing lines of the simple design. The movement was interrupted when a small sound at the door made her look up.

"Good morning."

His voice was low and husky, and if he was feeling any lingering anger after she hadn't denied her suspicions, it wasn't showing now. The only thing in his face was that same soft, warm tenderness that had weakened her knees yesterday. It was lighting his eyes, and sent a shiver down her spine and all thoughts flying from her mind.

"You're here early." He came in quietly, pulling her office door closed behind him.

"I couldn't . . . I had some work to do."

"I couldn't sleep, either."

She colored, knowing it would do her no good to deny he was right; he knew it, and she knew he knew it. He crossed the room and sat on the edge of her desk.

"Watch the dust," she said, eyeing his dark slacks. "We had a pop-off this morning."

"A what?"

"Don't tell me you missed something in your brain picking."

He looked at her a little sharply, as if weighing her voice for any sarcasm. After a moment he shrugged. "Guess so. What's a pop-off?"

"It happens when they overfill the cement silo. It pops off the filter bags at the top and sends this—" she ran a slender finger over the polished surface of her desk and held it up; the tip was covered with a fine, grayish-white coat of dry cement "—everywhere."

He looked at her finger intently. She saw his left hand begin to move, as if he were going to reach for her, then he stopped. An odd, almost bitter smile flickered over his face.

"The cement equivalent of blowing a gasket?" he said wryly, in the tone of a man all too familiar with the feeling.

"Sort of. It's a nuisance, but harmless, as long as you get this—" she gestured at her computer "—covered in time."

Instinctively he followed the movement of her arm, and saw the newspaper clipping that sat on her desk. His gaze snapped quickly to her face, as if startled.

"You're making a bid on the marina project?"

She nodded.

"I didn't see the figures in the records anywhere."

With a sigh, she nodded again. "I know. I didn't really want to keep a record of them. They're pretty grim."

He lifted a brow. "You don't sound very confident."

"I'm not. My minimums are way too high."

He reached out for the papers. She hesitated, then realized that what they held would come as no surprise to him. He knew where they stood. And, she thought, he knew why. An odd feeling of assurance filled her; she didn't have to explain, he knew it wasn't her fault. She handed him the bid copy.

She watched him as he read it, saw his eyes dart quickly over the pages, scanning columns, zeroing in on totals. He read it, she realized, as if he'd read hundreds of them before. Her brow creased, but before she could speak he was looking at her, a low whistle escaping him.

"Whew."

"It's the best I could do. We'd have to run double shifts to do it."

"It's not that. Your figures are a bit high, but not outrageous. But you really pared this down to the bone, didn't you?"

She smiled wryly. "I ran out of places to trim."

"I can see that. Your profit margin is down to practically nil."

She shrugged. "It was the only way I could come close to being feasible."

He set down the papers. He looked at her for a moment. "Why?"

She looked blank. "Why what?"

"Why are you trying so hard? You wouldn't be making any money on it, even if you got the contract."

She flushed. "Look," she began defensively, "I know what our financial position is—"

"Take it easy. I just wanted to know why this project is worth it."

"It's a big contract."

"That you'll barely break even on."

"It's a good project. Good exposure."

"You sound like Richard."

She bristled. "This is entirely different. They're a good, honest company, not a political stepping stone. They do quality projects. They have an excellent reputation in San Diego, and... and..."

Something about the way he was looking at her made her falter, her words trailing off.

"You seem to have done your homework."

Why was he staring at her like that, almost warily? "I try to find out about companies I deal with."

"What... else do you know about them?"

Her brow creased. "That this is their first project here. And I'd like for Lockwood to be part of it."

"Why?"

"It's good business."

His eyes flicked to the bid papers, then back to her face.

Nicki gave a disgusted sigh. "All right, all right. I can't explain it. I just like the way they work. Everything I've read about them, I like. This project, and the way they made the planners accept the expansion to include the youth dock and facilities. And they built an office complex in San Diego where they added a day care center, and footed most of the bill for it. And it's not for anyone's personal gain, either. I couldn't even find out who the president is. He keeps a very low profile, they say."

He looked away, quickly, and Nicki got the oddest feeling he was embarrassed. "You *have* done your homework."

"They're the kind of people I'd like to do business with. It would be worth the narrow margin on this project, if we can get a foot in the door. Then we might have an edge on future projects with them." She sighed. "But there's not much chance of that. We may have the best product, but those numbers aren't going to help."

"The best product." He gave her a crooked smile. "That old Lockwood superiority again."

"It is not," she said instantly. "It's the truth. Our sand is the purest, and Capistrano rock—"

"—is the hardest, densest rock in southern California, and makes the best cement. I know."

"Well, then you—" She caught the glint in his eyes. She flushed, then smiled reluctantly. "Darn you, Travis Halloran! You know that always gets me on my soapbox."

His gaze softened for a reason she didn't quite understand. "It always used to. I didn't know if it still did."

"It does," she admitted. Then, "Why are you looking at me like that?"

"I was just thinking that 'Darn you, Travis Halloran' sounds a hell of a lot better than 'Damn you,'" he said softly.

She blushed. "Small difference."

"It's a step." He smiled ruefully. "I've learned to take great comfort out of small crumbs."

She lowered her eyes, that undertone in his voice causing a sharp little stab of pain.

"But then," he went on, in a low, soft tone that was nearly a caress, "a crumb from you always was worth more than the whole loaf from anybody else."

Her gaze shot up to his face. That tenderness was there, warming the granite of his eyes, softening the lines of his face that had seemed so harsh, so severe to her when she'd first seen him after all the years he'd been gone.

The thought of how long it had been brought back what she had wondered earlier.

"It looks like you've read a few of these before," she said, lifting the bid papers.

He shrugged. "I've looked at a couple."

Enough to accurately judge this one. He *did* know a lot more than he was letting on. And he had already learned enough about their individual operation to recognize how close she had cut their profit margin. He was proving, if she'd had any doubts, just how right her mother had been about him. And she wondered where they might be today if they'd had Travis instead of Richard to help them run the place.

That old pang of guilt at her disloyalty dug at her. Her brother, who was the only family she had left. The only Lockwood left, other than herself. Again she tried to convince herself that for that reason, if no other, she should give him her allegiance. They should stand together, as the Lockwood heirs, the last of the Lockwood family. But Richard could be so... so exasperating. He was immature, and such a braggart, and at times made her so furious she could barely function.

And Travis Halloran still had twice the brain, the drive, and the potential that her brother had. She could see it as clearly now as she had then, and it tugged at her raw emotions to think what he might have become had it not been for one wild, careless moment.

It would be so easy, she thought, if it were merely an analytical, logical decision. Richard was an arrogant bumbler, Travis was quick, sharp and competent in a way Richard could only fake. There was no doubt about who, logically, was the best man for the business. Yet Richard was a Lockwood and her brother. And Travis was the man who'd killed her father, accident or not.

And quite possibly, he was the man out to sabotage the company she loved. And the man who might be using her to do it. The thought sent a shiver through her.

Travis stood up so suddenly her desk shook with the strength of his movement. She looked up, startled.

"Damn it," he swore under his breath, through teeth clenched so tightly she knew she hadn't been meant to hear it. She stood up, staring at him.

"What's wrong?"

"Damn it," he said again, "can't you—" He stopped abruptly, his jaw clenching again as he looked away from her. When he spoke again, the words were low and tightly controlled. "No. After fifteen years, of course you can't."

"Can't what?" She shook her head in mystification. And trepidation. He looked as he had at the funeral, his face carved into rigid, forbidding lines, as if he'd walled himself away so completely there was no way out.

Or in. She wondered why that thought bothered her most. He looked so grim she came around her desk, almost frightened for him.

"Travis..."

"Never mind," he said at last, calmer.

"I hate it when you do that!"

It was a reflex, the answer she'd always given him when he used to try to end a conversation that way. It startled him out of that rigidity. In his eyes she saw the memories come alive once more, just as she felt them flooding her until she felt she couldn't hold them anymore.

She tried to speak, but no words would come past her suddenly dry lips. Her tongue crept out to wet them, to try again, but the low groan that broke from him stopped her.

"God, Nicole..."

She knew before he reached for her that he was going to do it. And knew, with a burst of fierce honesty, that she wanted him to. Wanted him to touch her, kiss her again, wanted to know, had to know if it was as sweet as she remembered, as hot, as melting.

He pulled her hard against him, and fire leapt between them like a lightning strike. She gasped, stunned by the tingling of her body as it pressed against the hard, muscled length of his. The sound was cut off by his mouth taking hers, his lips urgent and demanding yet somehow pleading at the same time.

He backed her up against the desk, trapping her with his legs and arms, as if he feared she might try to escape. She couldn't find the breath to tell him she wasn't going anywhere; she couldn't do anything while he was kissing her like that, anything except turn to some hot, flowing mass of feeling beneath his mouth.

His hands came up to cup her head, to tilt it back as he probed deeper with his tongue. She felt his wet heat, dancing over her lips, then inside, stroking the soft, sensitive surfaces. He traced the even ridge of her teeth, then dove past them to flick at her tongue with his.

Nicki's hands went around his neck, whether to pull him closer or because she needed the support she wasn't certain. She just knew that his solid, taut body was the only anchor she had, the only thing that kept her from flying away on the updraft of the inferno he'd created in her.

His tongue flicked over hers again, then drew back. A tiny moan of protest rose in her throat at the loss. He did it again, deeper, sweeter, and again drew back.

More, she thought hazily. She wanted more. But he was gone, that hot, rough velvet was gone, and she felt bereft. But his lips were there, soft and warm and coaxing, rocking on hers gently. Then, through the dizzying waves of sensation, it occurred to her that she could get what she wanted, so easily.

Tentatively she tried it, the tip of her tongue brushing lightly over his lips. She felt him go still, felt the little shiver that rippled through him. It pleased her somehow, to know that she had done that, and she ran her tongue over his lower lip again. He tasted hot and sweet and male, and she quickly found that a taste was not enough. Especially when he groaned like that, low and gruff and deep in his chest, as if she had stroked someplace deep inside him. If this was an act, it was the most convincing one she'd ever seen.

She probed deeper, as he had done, seeking the same spots he had discovered in her, the places that sent fiery little bursts of heat shooting through her like a rain of sparks.

"God, Nicole," he gasped at last, wrenching his mouth away.

He stared down at her, his eyes as dark as charcoal. And as hot as charcoal could get, she thought, a little dazedly.

And she needed that heat. Needed it like she had never needed anything before in her life.

She lifted her hands to cup his face, having to order her passion-drugged muscles to obey, not realizing the sensuous grace the slowness of the movement gave her. With one slender finger she traced the line of his mouth, wondering why she had never known that a kiss could give such pleasure, why she had never felt this leaping fire before.

"Travis," she whispered, and knew that it was the answer.

As if he'd read her thoughts, as he'd always seemed able to, he groaned hoarsely and closed his eyes. When she gently stroked his lips again, his arms tightened suddenly, fiercely. His mouth came down on hers again, his tongue driving, thrusting; she welcomed him with a glad little cry.

He moved, nudging her knees apart with one strong thigh as he pressed her back against the edge of the desk. She never thought to deny him; the need to have him closer was much too strong. His hips came up hard against her, and she felt the pressure of aroused male flesh at the same moment his left hand slid down to cup the outer curve of her breast.

She twisted sinuously, not to get away from that searing touch but to bring it closer to the tingling peak of flesh that was crying out for his heat. And then his hand moved, his palm cradling that feminine curve tenderly, as if savoring the soft weight. His thumb flicked quickly, fleetingly over her nipple, sending a blast of flame rocketing through her.

She gasped, instinctively arching her back, thrusting herself against his hand. It stunned her even as she did it; she didn't know this creature she'd become, couldn't find the self she'd always known in this body that craved nothing more than his hands on her in ways she'd never dreamed of before.

She heard him make a sound, a low, husky whisper of her name that was nearly a growl. Then he stroked that begging crest again, and a little cry broke from her. She felt the caress in every part of her, felt the hardening of her own flesh beneath his touch as if the fragile silk of her shirt had melted away.

But most of all she felt that need again, that need for more, so much more. She had to have more. More of his kiss, more of his touch, more of things she'd never really believed possible. She had to believe it now. She had no choice. Travis had shown her it was possible. That with him, anything was possible. She could soar, she could fly, she—

The sudden clamor of the phone at her elbow made her jump and Travis stiffen. The spell broken, his head dropped to nestle in the curve of her neck. She could hear his quickened breathing, echoing her own. Her hand crept up to rest on the nape of his neck, her fingers threading through the heavy silk of his hair as she pressed his head to her.

"You gonna answer that," he asked thickly, "or shall I yank it out of the wall?"

What she wanted to say was yes, shut off the damned phone and go right back to what you were doing. What she did, after a little shiver, was pick up the receiver. As she answered, Travis, with a great effort, straightened up and released her.

Nicki found it difficult to concentrate with his eyes on her so hotly, still dark with passion. Her own breathing was only now slowing, the pace of her heart easing, but what she was hearing began to get through.

"What?"

Travis's brow furrowed at the sharpness of her tone. The heat began to fade from his eyes.

"How?"

She was gripping the phone tightly, and Travis frowned. She listened a little longer, then expelled an angry breath.

"All right. I'll be right there."

She hung up sharply. She just stood there, staring at the phone. Travis waited. At last she lifted her head to look at him.

"We seem to have had another...mishap."

Her voice was carefully even, without a trace of accusation, but he knew her too well to be fooled. Knew that look of doubt that shadowed her blue eyes.

He drew back as if she'd slapped him. And without a word, he turned and walked out.

Chapter 9

Nicki stared up at the towering slurry water tank. The sides were still wet with the overflow that was streaming down the sides.

"It's my fault, Miss Lockwood," Max said glumly. "I checked that the motor was running last night as usual, but I never thought to check the valve."

"Has it ever stuck before?"

"No." Max frowned. "In fact, it's not stuck now." He reached out and squeezed the ratchet handle; the ten-inch butterfly valve that controlled the flow of water through the tank moved easily. "It's working perfectly."

"Yes," Nicki said grimly, "it is, isn't it?"

And if it was working perfectly now, chances were it had been last night. Yet it had been closed, preventing the essential movement of the water in the tank that kept the residue of cement from settling to the bottom. And this morning, when they had begun to refill the tank, the overflow told them immediately what had happened; the sediment had settled and filled the bottom of the tank.

"That's why the function light didn't go off in dispatch," Max said. "It only registers whether the pump is running or not."

"I know."

Nicki's voice was tense with the effort of shoving her suspicions to the back of her mind. Deal with this now, she told herself, and think about how it happened later.

"Get a crew together to clean it out." She eyed the lowest hatch that gave access to the tank. "Let's hope it's below that level."

Max nodded. "Otherwise we'll be here for days."

Nicki stared at the valve handle. It would be easy, she thought. Just walk by, squeeze the ratchet and turn. You'd barely have to break stride, and chances were nobody would even notice. Anyone could have done it. Anyone.

"Miss Lockwood?"

She lifted her gaze to Max's face. He looked troubled, his graying brows furrowed.

"What's going on?" he asked. "We've had so many things like this happen lately."

"I know."

Max scratched his chin. "Some of the guys... Well, they've been saying..." He looked uncomfortable.

"Saying what, Max?"

"That all this started when Mr. Halloran showed up."

Nicki kept her expression even. "Who's been saying that, Max?"

He coughed. "Well, Carl, mostly."

"And you believe him?"

Max looked perplexed. "Well, I don't generally put much stock in what he says..."

"So why are you now?"

Max eyed her levelly. "Because he said you think so, too."

Nicki's eyes widened. "He said that? That I think...Mr. Halloran is responsible?"

"You and Richard both."

Nicki noted the absence of the respectful title that was always present when he spoke to her, or Travis, when Max spoke of her brother, but she didn't say anything. She was too busy trying to control the sick, roiling feeling that had risen in her stomach. She had admitted her suspicions to herself, why did it hurt so badly to hear?

God, she was so confused. Did she feel sick because she didn't want to believe the man who could kiss her senseless was capable of this kind of thing? Or because she let the man who might be responsible, the man who had caused her father's death, kiss her until she forgot where she was, who she was? And who he was?

But she couldn't help that, could she? Was it her fault all he had to do was touch her and she went up in flames? It didn't matter, she thought grimly. She couldn't control it, so it didn't matter whose fault it was. She couldn't—

"Miss Lockwood? Are you all right?"

She took in a deep breath and steadied herself. "I'm fine, Max. Sorry. What were you saying?"

"Just that it doesn't seem like Mr. Halloran would do something like this." Max looked embarrassed. "I mean, I remember what happened to your father and all, but..."

"I understand."

"'Sides, why would he? He owns half the company now, doesn't he? Why would he want to hurt it?"

"I don't know, Max."

"Problem is, I can't think of anyone else who'd want to, either."

Nicki couldn't, either, and only shrugged.

"So you don't think it's Mr. Halloran?"

"Even if I did," Nicki said, meeting his eyes, "I'm not going to make any accusations without proof."

Max pursed his lips thoughtfully. Then he nodded. "I should'a known better than to listen to that bag of wind. You're not the kind that goes around spreading dirt behind someone's back. If you really thought he did it, you'd come out and say it to his face."

Nicki colored slightly, not at all sure she deserved the compliment. Yes, she'd admitted her suspicions to herself, but she'd never truly confronted Travis with them, beyond that one desperate plea that he tell her hadn't broken the valve on the acid tank. Not, she thought ruefully, that she'd needed to; he knew what she'd been thinking as clearly as if she'd accused him openly, just as Richard had.

A sudden thought narrowed her eyes. Where had Richard, who, she'd admitted at last, was patently afraid of Travis, gotten the nerve to accuse him face to face? It was a note out of tune, as had been his unexpectedly spirited defense of Carl the other day. Had he just been striking back out of that fear she didn't understand? Or had he found some unexpected strength in an anger born out of Travis turning his own accusations around on him?

It was absurd, of course, to think that Richard might be behind all this. Whatever his faults, her brother loved this company. It was the one thing that gave him a sense of worth, and she knew he would never risk that. But if not him, or Travis, who? Why? And why now? She had no answers, but as she trudged back to her office the questions wouldn't go away.

But her office was no longer the refuge it had once been. She stopped just inside the door, staring at her desk. Her stapler was on its side, the blotter turned at an angle, the paper clip holder lying atop the pencil she'd dropped.

A vivid image leapt into her mind, an image of how they must have looked together, Travis standing between her parted thighs, pressing her back on her own desk, and her letting it happen, wanting it to happen, reveling in it.

God knows what would have happened if the phone hadn't rung when it had, she thought. She shuddered at the images that raced through her mind, and though she told herself it was with distaste, the sudden acceleration of her heart and the instant heating of her blood made the avowal a sham.

She crossed the room, walking as if barefoot on the three-quarter rock that filled the bunker outside the window. With controlled, careful movements she returned everything on the desk to its former place. It didn't help. The images were still intense in her mind.

And they stayed that way, never dulling as the days dragged past, flashing into her consciousness at unexpected moments, catching her at any unguarded moment and causing that tumbling free-fall of her senses and emotions.

The fact that Travis seemed to be avoiding her these days didn't make one bit of difference. He was ever present in her mind, and her senses remembered all too clearly every breath, every touch, every kiss.

She knew he was around, could feel that odd tingling of that old radar, but she saw little of him over the next week. She came face to face with him only once, after an angry phone call from Sam Shelby, when she had hurried to the dispatch office to find out what the mix-up had been.

"I swear, Miss Lockwood, the call came in last night, just as we were closing up!" Ed Hartman, the chief dispatcher, said earnestly. "They said they were running behind, and couldn't take the loads until tomorrow."

"Never mind that now. How fast can we get them rolling?"

"We're at capacity now. The Hornung job is taking—"

"Re-route them."

Hartman gaped at her. "What?"

"Pull the loads Shelby needs from the Hornung job."

"But I can't do that! Richard said—"

"I don't care what my brother said," she said flatly. "He shouldn't have promised it in the first place. Re-route the loads to the Shelby site."

"Yes, ma'am," Hartman said quickly, respectfully.

Nicki was aware that Travis was there, had known it since she'd come into the office. He was leaning against one of the desks, arms folded across his chest, watching her impassively. His eyes were that harsh, granite gray, and they chilled her as thoroughly as if she'd touched the cold stone itself.

She knew he would hear, knew exactly what he would think, but she had to ask. So when Hartman had finished relaying her instructions, she took a deep breath and forced out the words.

"Who called, Ed?"

"Sanders, one of their foremen."

"You know him?"

"Well, no..."

"But you've talked to him before?"

Hartman's brow furrowed. "Actually, it's usually Sandy in the office who calls us with any changes."

Nicki reached for the closest phone and quickly punched out a number.

"Sam? Nicki Lockwood. Do you have a foreman by the name of Sanders?" She waited, and then said grimly, "I was afraid of that." Another pause. "I know, Sam. I understand. The mixers will be there within an hour." She winced, then sighed. "I can't blame you. There's no excuse for such shoddy service."

When she hung up, Ed Hartman was staring at her, wide-eyed. "They don't have a foreman named Sanders?"

Nicki shook her head.

"Damn! I never questioned it, because he had all the details on the order."

Nicki looked at him sharply. "All the details?"

Hartman nodded. "The order numbers, the amounts, the dates—and that it was thirty-five hundred pound stress concrete instead of twenty-five."

Nicki's heart sank. It could mean only one thing: whoever had cancelled the run was on the inside, on one end or the other. And the way things had been going, there was little doubt about which end it was.

"I never thought that it might not be legit," Hartman said worriedly.

"I know, Ed. You had no way of knowing."

"But who the hell—"

"I don't know." She bit her lip before asking quietly, "Did you...recognize the voice, Ed?"

He looked startled. "Recognize it?"

"Yes. Was it...anyone you've talked to before?"

His brow furrowed again. "I don't know..." He trailed off, obviously thinking hard. Then he looked up at Nicki. "You know, now that you mention it, he did sound kind of familiar."

She tensed. "But you don't know who it was?"

"No. But now that I think about it, it seems like I'd talked to him before, you know? Maybe that's why I didn't ask any more questions about it."

Nicki sighed. "Maybe. Don't worry about it, Ed. You couldn't have known."

Hartman scratched his head. "Who would do something like that? Why?"

Her lips tightened; she didn't like thinking about the possibilities. Especially the most likely possibility.

"Could somebody be trying to mess up Shelby?"

"Or us," she muttered.

As she turned to go she felt Travis's gaze on her, and she couldn't help looking over at him. His eyes were icy, the planes of his face set in harsh, rigid lines; he'd heard her. And knew she was wondering yet again if he was the one. If he'd been that "kind of familiar" voice Hartman had heard.

He held her gaze for one long, cold moment, then turned his back on her, bending over the screen of the computer that monitored the storage levels in the bunkers and silos. Debby Manelli, the petite brunette who sat at that station, smiled up at him and went on with her explanations of the system.

Travis smiled back at her, and Nicki felt a ripple of queasiness go through her. He'd always had that effect, as if the sight of that flashing smile softening the grim lines of his face made every woman start thinking about what lay beneath the tough exterior. And thinking about being the one to reach it.

The queasiness settled in the pit of her stomach, and Nicki turned away. *Stop it*, she ordered herself fiercely as she hurried down the hall. *All he did was smile at you. It doesn't mean anything. Besides, Debby's happily married. And what have you got to say about it, anyway? He's...nothing* to you. Not anymore. So stop acting like she's poaching on your territory.

Your territory. She closed her office door behind her, leaning back against it. That was how she'd always thought of it, wasn't it? That special, vulnerable part of him, that deeply buried, gentle place he kept so hidden from the rest of the world, was hers, and only hers.

Or it had been. Then. And now? She wasn't even certain it existed anymore. Sometimes, when he would look at her with that tenderness that left her breathless, when he touched her so gently, she was sure that it did. And other times, like now, when he looked so grim and forbidding, she was certain that any softness in him had died long ago.

Or been killed. By the Lockwoods.

She fought off the traitorous thought. He'd brought it on himself, she told herself stubbornly, and wondered why she was having so much trouble hanging onto the convictions she'd held for fifteen years.

"I told you so!"

Nicki looked up at her brother, then at the sheaf of papers he was waving in front of her face.

"Now what, Richard?"

"You said I was wasting my time, wining and dining that guy. You said they didn't work that way." He waved the papers triumphantly. "Shows you what you know, little sister! Just leave the politicking to me from now on, you obviously don't understand how these things work."

"A fact for which I am eternally grateful," Nicki muttered under her breath. Then, aloud, "What is it you're gloating about?"

He thrust the papers at her again.

"I can't see it if you don't stop waving it like a flag, Richard."

With a smug smile, he dropped the papers onto her desk. The top sheet was a letter, and the logo on the top sheet caught her eye immediately. She scanned it hastily. Her eyes widened, and she read it again, more carefully, certain she had misunderstood.

"We . . . got it? Willow Tree?"

"We sure did," Richard crowed, "thanks to my influence. I told you you have to know how to treat those people."

"But the bid was way up—"

"Oh, Nicki, you're so naive. Don't you know the numbers don't mean anything? It's all in how you handle the people in charge of the bids."

"But—"

"That guy Howell is no different than anybody else. You show them a good time, spend a little money so they know you don't really need their business, and boom, they fall right into line."

Nicki looked at the acceptance letter with a sudden distaste. "I didn't think they were like that."

Richard looked at her pityingly. "That's your trouble. You're always looking for principles, and there aren't any in the business world. At least, not if you're going to be successful."

A condescendingly instructive tone came into his voice. "It's dog eat dog out there, and you have to bite before you get bitten. That's why you should leave this kind of thing to someone who knows how things are. Like me."

"Don't break your arm patting yourself on the back," she said wryly.

She looked at the letter again, wondering if the Chuck Howell who had signed it was truly as easily swayed as Richard was saying. She remembered the night after they had submitted the bid, when her brother had come home after taking the man out to the ritziest place in ritzy Newport Beach, just up the coast, muttering that he was the toughest nut he'd ever tried to crack.

"He acts like it doesn't mean a thing to him," Richard had complained. "Says I'm wasting my time, that he's only a vice president, and his boss has the final say."

"So why don't you take the president out instead," she'd said, tired of hearing about her brother's machinations.

"I tried. He won't go. Won't even talk." Richard's brow had creased. "Hell, I don't even know his name. Weird. Howell says he usually likes to know the people he deals with, but he turned this completely over to him."

If he's talked to his vice president, maybe he knows as much about you as he cares to, Nicki had thought glumly. And had consigned the hope of getting the marina contract to the slag heap.

And yet here she was, looking at the letter of acceptance she had never expected to see. Somehow she wasn't nearly as happy as she should have been.

"Well, don't you have anything to say?"

She looked up at him. "Like what?"

Richard flushed, then glared at her. "You're the one who wanted this job so bad. I did it for you."

She doubted that, then felt guilty for the thought. He was her brother, and the only blood relative she had left, she shouldn't immediately assume the worst. Perhaps he really had done it because he knew she wanted it so much. Perhaps.

"The least you could do is say thank you, or congratulations, or something," Richard grumbled.

She supposed he was right. They had gotten the contract. And she had wanted it. Did she have any right to quibble about the method?

"Of course, Richard. Congratulations." She smiled a little sadly. "I guess you were right."

"Well," Richard huffed, slightly mollified, "you could look a little happier about it."

"Sorry," she said automatically. "I am happy about it." *Just not nearly as happy as I thought I'd be.*

Richard stayed for several more minutes, boasting about his success. Nicki tried to tune him out, tried to ignore what it apparently meant. And for a long time after he'd finally gone, she stared at the letter in her hand.

His words echoed in her head. Was she naive, to expect any kind of principles from a big, successful business? She didn't want to think so, didn't want to believe that they were all like Richard said, but her faith in her own judgment was on somewhat shaky ground these days.

Her gaze went to the signature on the letter again. Had this Chuck Howell really been convinced by a couple of expensive dinners and Richard's endless patter to give Lockwood, Incorporated the contract? Had he sold the boss he'd said had the final say some bill of goods that had made him overlook the figures?

Or, she thought with a sudden qualm, had Richard made another of his impossible promises? Something not in the contract, some unexpected disaster that it would be up to her to carry out when the time came?

He couldn't have, she told herself, not knowing how the bid was already pared to the bone. But he'd done so many other things she'd found hard to believe . . .

She reached for the phone. When she identified herself, she was put through to Howell's office quickly. And, to her surprise, Howell himself answered the phone.

"Ah, Ms. Lockwood. You received the letter, I presume."

"Yes." She hesitated over the phrasing, then jumped in with both feet. "I wanted to confirm with you. To be sure there was no mistake."

"Mistake?"

She bit her lip, then went on. "Mr. Howell, I'm aware that the competition for any contract with your company is fierce. And I'm aware that there were probably other, reputable companies who beat our figures."

She heard a dry chuckle. "I'd heard you were refreshingly frank, Ms. Lockwood."

"If that's a way of saying I like things out in the open, then yes."

The chuckle again, with more amusement this time and, oddly, something that sounded like understanding, although she wasn't sure of what.

"So do I. That's the only way we do business."

"I'd like to believe that. But there is one thing I'd like to know."

"Fire away, Ms. Lockwood."

There was no way to pretty it up, so she just asked bluntly, "Were there any verbal agreements reached between you and my brother that will affect this contract?"

The chuckle became a laugh. "I'd heard you were smart, too. Enough to know how your brother operates. I can assure you that nothing your brother said or did had anything to do with your getting the contract. You might even say you got it in spite of his . . . efforts."

Nicki let out a breath she had barely been aware of holding. She liked this man's voice. He sounded like he was the kind of man she'd pictured, the kind Richard kept telling her didn't exist.

"Put your mind at ease, Ms. Lockwood. We don't do business that way. And there's no mistake. Your figures are a bit high, but you produce the best quality product in the area. The company feels it's worth the extra cost."

"Then . . . your boss—I'm afraid I don't know his name—knows all the details?"

There was a split-second pause in which she sensed the man was carefully deciding what to say. Doubt assailed her. Richard, if you didn't know better, could be convincing. Was this man just another of the same breed?

"Of course," he said finally. "He makes all the final decisions, although he generally takes the recommendations of his staff. It helps him stay where he wants to be, behind the scenes."

A subtle warning that she wasn't going to get a name? Nicki wondered. "May I speak to him? It won't take long." She had to be sure, she thought. Even if it meant proving Richard right. "I'd just like to thank him personally."

"I'm afraid that's impossible. He's . . . out of town."

"When do you expect him back?"

"Actually," Howell said dryly, "I don't know. He's never taken any time off before."

"Ever?" Nicki asked, suspicion biting again. Was it just too convenient that the nameless big boss was gone now?

"Not in the five years that I've been here. But this is apparently... personal business. In any case, I assure you, everything is in order."

Despite his assurances, when she hung up Nicki still had doubts. And she was plagued by a disturbing curiosity about where Chuck Howell had heard so much about her. Surely not from Richard, who, if he mentioned her at all, tended to call her his amusing little sister who was playing at running a concrete plant.

It was horrible, she thought, feeling this way about her own brother, wondering if he'd betrayed them yet again with some foolish, under-the-counter deal that would leave her once again picking up the pieces. It made her sick, almost as sick as it made her to suspect Travis of using her, or of being the perpetrator of the string of mishaps they'd been having.

Nearly as sick as it had made her to believe he'd killed her father. If it hadn't been for her mother, she never would have believed it, but Emily Lockwood had left her no choice. The evidence had been undeniable.

With a sigh, she smothered the old, worn thoughts. She'd never been given to uselessly spinning her wheels, but when it came to Travis Halloran, you'd never know it, she thought bitterly.

She leaned back in her chair. She should clear up this mess, she told herself, looking at the chaotic piles of papers and notes on her desk.

And then it was there, that flashing, vivid image of her and Travis in this room, their passionate embrace broken only by the unwelcome shrill of her phone. And with a flush of heat rising to her face, she realized the word she'd silently used: unwelcome.

The office seemed suddenly too small, too crowded with bright, hot memories. Moving quickly, as if driven, she shuffled through the papers on her desk until she found the excuse she was looking for: a report that had been delivered to her by mistake. It had been meant for Esteban Montero, and she'd planned to give it to the courier that made daily runs between the pit and the offices here. But it was too important, she told herself now, and she would take it herself. She managed to conveniently ignore that it had been sitting in her in tray since yesterday.

She caught herself looking at the empty spot where Travis usually parked, then jerked her head to the front and concentrated on driving out of the yard she knew as well as her own reflection, as if she'd never done it before. Although she denied it every mile of the way, she knew the moment she pulled up at the scale house at the pit and saw his car parked there that she'd been wondering if he might be here.

She thought of leaving before anyone saw her, then set her jaw stubbornly and pulled up to park close beside the black Mercedes. She had her expression carefully schooled, her composure intact as she strode into the office. It fell flat; Travis was nowhere to be seen.

Esteban greeted her a little dolefully, but thanked her when she handed him the report.

"What's wrong, Esteban?" Apprehension furrowed her brow. "More problems?" Please, no, she thought. Not when Travis hadn't been at the plant for the last couple of days, but had apparently been coming back here.

"We lost a spring on the jaw crusher," the superintendent said glumly.

"Anyone hurt?" Her question was swift. She knew the huge springs that ran the crusher that ground the big rocks, not so affectionately called knotheads, into usable gravel were a coiled, dangerous thing if they broke loose.

"No, we were fortunate. It hit a 'dozer, but no one was on it."

Nicki let out a sigh of relief.

"Yes," Esteban agreed, appreciating that her first concern had been for the men, not the property or the time that would be lost. "It could have been very bad. But it will be repaired by tomorrow."

She turned her head to glance out the window of the scale house. She could see the bucket conveyor running, looking like a vertical, elongated water wheel for gravel, could see the earth movers still running, no doubt switched to sand now since the crusher was out of commission. And over near the huge bunkers, more than ten times the size of the ones at the plant, she saw Travis.

He was standing next to a material truck, one of the huge sets of double trailers that transported the rock and sand from the pit, talking to Paul Malone. Paul was nodding, listening intently. Then he smiled, then laughed, gesturing animatedly with his hands as he pointed to something on the cab of the big truck, where the door stood open.

"Esteban?"

"Yes?"

"Do you have . . . any idea why it happened?"

"It happens."

She turned to face him. "Like everything else . . . just happened?"

"I have no reason to think this is connected to the other troubles." He lifted a brow. "Do you?"

She sighed. "Only that this string of . . . accidents keeps getting longer and longer. Here and at the plant."

"You are worried that it is intentional."

It wasn't a question, and she didn't debate the point; she knew Esteban was too intelligent not to see through any dissembling.

"Yes, I am."

"But who? Why?"

She couldn't speak of her suspicions, not even to this man who had been loyal friend and employee for so many years.

"I don't know."

"Is this why we have a second night watchman here now?"

"Yes. And two at the plant." She grimaced. "Not that it's done much good."

"Have you spoken to the police?"

"No!" Esteban's brow shot upward again at her vehemence. "I mean," she amended hastily, "I'd prefer to keep this quiet. It might…damage the company if word gets out that someone's trying to sabotage us."

"Perhaps a private investigator, then?"

"I've thought about it," she admitted, but didn't tell him that the reason she'd decided against it was because she wasn't sure she wanted to know what he might find out. "If it keeps up, I may have to."

Esteban coughed, then looked at her consideringly. "Mr. Halloran mentioned he was thinking about that himself."

"Travis?" She stared at Esteban, startled. "He wants to hire a P.I.?"

"He merely mentioned that he knew one who might be able to find out what was going on."

Nicki turned her head to stare anew out the window, as if by looking at that long, leanly muscled body she could fathom his innocence. He was smiling at something Paul had said, and then leaning over to look at something the older man held out toward him. She saw that it was his wallet, and knew that the proud new grandfather was showing off baby pictures. Frank Reed, the driver of the truck, had joined them, and she could see him shaking his head with the boredom of a man who'd seen those pictures one too many times.

But incredibly, Travis was looking, smiling, and saying something that made Paul beam proudly. Travis, who had always said that he wondered why people brought kids into this crazy world, and who had told her that, except for her, he wouldn't give a nickle for any of them. Including, he'd always added wryly, himself.

"Why?" she whispered, unaware she had let the word slip out audibly.

"Why what?"

She gave a little start and turned quickly back to Esteban. "Nothing," she said, but her mind was racing. If he wanted to hire an investigator, then he couldn't be responsible, could he? Or was it some kind of elaborate cover, with this detective he knew of really being someone he would pay to find what he wanted found?

Pay with Lockwood money? But if it was the money he wanted, why would he try to damage the business? Why wouldn't he just hang on for six months, then take them for all he could when they tried to buy it back from him? That thought brought on the other one she still had no answer for; if that was all he wanted, why was he spending so much time, working so hard at learning all he could? Just so he could know where best to strike?

God, she thought with a shudder, she was sounding more and more like Richard, mistrusting everyone, always suspecting the worst. *I can't live like that,* she cried out silently. *I can't.* And I can't keep riding this merry-go-round of trying to figure out the whys, the possible motives behind what's been happening.

You've got to make a choice, she told herself in despair. *You've got to decide.* Either you agree with Richard—a thought that gave her no more confidence in the theory— that he's guilty, or you trust in him, in what your heart wants to believe. You can't go on like this. Not when it's tearing you apart. Not when—

The explosive sound that split the air ripped her out of her spinning thoughts. Esteban leapt to his feet. He crossed to the window she stood beside in one long stride. The roar continued, lessening but no less ominous.

Nicki whirled to look. A gasping cry escaped her as her hand flew to her mouth to stop it from becoming a scream.

Where the big truck had stood beneath one of the huge bunkers was now only a crazily bent set of trailers buried beneath a mountain of gravel, all of it obscured by a cloud of dust. And nowhere was there any sign of Paul Malone and Frank Reed. Or of Travis. There was only the bent, broken truck beneath thousands of tons of crushed rock below the bunker's swinging, broken gate.

Chapter 10

Nicki was vaguely aware of the men converging on the small mountain of gravel as she ran toward it. Heedless of the uneven ground, she ran as fast as she could, fear lending her speed so that she outdistanced Esteban easily.

She raced to the spot where Travis, Paul and Frank had been standing and began to claw at the gravel with her hands. The men began to arrive, following her actions, some with their hands, some with shovels they'd grabbed.

"Here!"

The shout came from the man to her left, and when she looked over she saw him abandon his shovel and begin to dig with his hands. She saw a glimpse of blue, and remembered the shirt Paul had been wearing. In moments, it seemed they had him by the arms and were pulling him free.

Coughing and sputtering, Paul brushed off their helping hands.

"I'm fine! Get Travis and Frank out of there."

"How close were they?" Esteban asked.

"I don't know. Travis was right beside me; he pushed me out of the way when the gate let go. But Frank was looking at something in the cab... he went down. Travis pulled him clear, but I don't know how far they got before the slide caught them.''

With a smothered little cry Nicki began again, heedless of the scrape of the rock against her tender skin. If the two men had been too close to the truck when the full weight of the bunker's load had hit...

''Hurry!'' she cried, scraping at the slippery mass of rock like a fury. The men jumped to work, digging furiously.

They dug, and dug, and found only more gravel. She knew the enormous bunker held nearly a quarter of a million tons of the crushing rock, and the thought of Travis buried beneath it made panic bubble up inside her. She ignored the scraping of the gravel against her hands, the snapping of her nails, the dust that rose up to choke her. She clawed at the rock, wanting to scream when it cascaded down to fill the spot she'd just excavated.

Esteban tried to pull her away, told her to let the men handle it, but she shook him off furiously. He took one look at her face, and let her go. She clawed some more.

It took forever. Each second seemed days long, and with each of them her desperation grew.

''Please,'' she whispered. ''Please, please...''

She said it again and again, a despairing litany that she couldn't stop. The decision she'd been struggling with seemed so petty now, so superfluous. Nothing mattered, not her father, not Lockwood, not anything, if Travis was dead beneath this pile of rock. She wanted to howl at the unfairness of the fates that had decided that this was the way she was to face how she truly felt. Instead she clawed harder, faster, until her hands were raw, her knuckles bleeding.

When she first saw the movement coming from beneath the surface, she thought she had only imagined it, that she had conjured it up out of her own dread. But then she saw it again, and with a spurt of adrenaline kicking through her system she shifted her position to where she'd seen it.

''Over here!''

Her cry was tiny, strained, but the men leapt to her side as if she'd trumpeted it. And a moment later, when she heard another voice, Travis's voice, hoarse yet steady, the tears she'd been battling began to stream down her cheeks.

"Careful . . . he got hit . . . when the truck went."

Nicki wiped at her eyes, staring as the men worked to free them. She saw Travis hunched over the prone body of Frank Reed, as if he could somehow protect the unconscious man from the crushing weight. When he could move he eased himself off the driver, moving a little shakily until Esteban reached out to help him.

"I'm all right. Get him out."

He slipped a little on the sliding rock, and dropped down to sit on the slope of the small mountain that could have become his grave. He was coated in dust; it sat thick in his hair, dulling the dark sheen. There was a rip in the knee of his jeans, and she saw a trickle of blood tracing down the muscled leg beneath. He coughed, winced, coughed again, then wiped at his eyes with the torn sleeve of his shirt. He looked dazed, only focusing when Paul came over to kneel before him.

"You sure you're all right, son?"

Travis nodded.

"I owe you," Paul said fervently. "If you hadn't moved so fast . . ."

"Forget it."

"Forget that we would have been crushed if you hadn't gotten us out to the edge of that mountain instead of at dead center? Not likely."

"It was instinct. Anybody would have done it."

Esteban approached them in time to hear the offhand dismissal. "Instinct?" he said. "Pushing Paul clear, perhaps. But going back for Frank, knowing there was a good chance you might not get clear? I don't think so."

"We're lucky it wasn't sand," was all Travis said.

"Would've smothered us all for sure," Paul agreed. "But don't make light of what you did, son. I won't forget it, and neither will Frank."

Travis shrugged; it was such an exhausted movement that Nicki shuddered. A small sound escaped her; Travis's head shot up. His eyes, red-rimmed from the dust, narrowed as he took in her appearance, from her sweat-tangled hair to her tear-streaked, grimy face, to her raw, scraped hands.

Esteban watched them stare at each other for a moment, then said quietly to Travis, "She was the first one here. She started digging with her bare hands to get to you, before any of the men could even react."

Travis's gaze, which had flicked to Esteban when he spoke, went back to Nicki. She was trembling, one battered hand pressed to her mouth as if to hold back something trying to break free. Something flared in the gray depths, something akin to the hope she'd seen before. And she saw him fight it in the tightening of his jaw, saw him try to deny it by turning to watch Esteban walk away.

But then his eyes were on her again, and when he whispered her name, it was with all the despair of a battle lost, and all the hope he was trying not to feel.

"I...thought you were dead," she choked out past her clenched fingers. "Oh, God, I thought you were dead."

She knew what she sounded like, knew everything that the tremor in her voice was telling him, but she didn't care. She only cared that he was alive, that he hadn't been crushed beneath that killing weight.

She stumbled forward the three steps between them. She nearly fell as the gravel gave way more under her feet, but she barely noticed. She reached out with one hand. She had to touch him, to feel that hard, living flesh under her hands, to know he was alive.

The moment she lifted that hand Travis was on his feet. With a smothered sound that was half a groan, half a murmur of her name again, he pulled her into his arms, closing them tight around her.

Sobbing, Nicki sagged against him. "God, I'm sorry Travis. I'm so sorry."

"Shh," he soothed, "it's all right. Paul's okay, Frank will be okay, it's all over."

"No, you—"

"I'm fine." He managed a lighter tone. "I need a shower, and I may not be moving real well tomorrow, but I'm fine."

She pulled back to look up at him. He didn't understand, she had to make him understand. "No, that's not what I mean. I have to tell you—"

The sudden silence broke off her words; only when it stopped was she aware that she'd been hearing an approaching siren. They looked up to see the county paramedic van pulling through the gate; someone, probably Esteban, she guessed, had at least had the presence of mind to call them.

She frowned. What she was so desperate to say was going to have to wait; there were other responsibilities she had now. "You're sure Frank will be all right?"

He nodded. "He's just dazed, I think. The door of the cab hit him on the side of the head."

"You're right," Esteban put in; he'd just come back from where the medics were checking on Frank. "They say he has a minor concussion, at most. He's conscious, and talking."

"Thank goodness," Nicki said in relief. "I should call his wife so she can meet them at the hospital— Oh, she doesn't have a car, does she?"

"Not since Frank Jr. drove it into that truck," Esteban said dryly.

"Then I'd better go get her."

"You can't," Esteban said.

She looked at him, puzzled. "What?"

"Don't forget, this was an industrial accident. You know what happens now."

Nicki sighed. Yes, she knew what would happen now. "So it begins," she muttered.

"They'll want to talk to everyone that was here," Esteban said.

Travis lifted a hand to gently wipe at her damp, streaked cheeks. "They?"

"The bureaucracy." She grimaced. "First O.S.H.A., then the Bureau of Mines, then the Bureau of Weights and Measures—"

"Whoa," Travis said. "Occupational Safety and Health I understand, and the Bureau of Mines, but Weights and Measures? What have they got to do with it?"

"They'll be out to make sure that the gravel in that bunker was really the right size and weight, that we didn't overload it, causing the gate to break. It'll take hours," she groaned. "They'll shut us down at least for the rest of the day."

"If we're lucky," Esteban said grimly. Then he looked at Travis. "The medics said they're ready for you."

"Me? Why?"

Esteban chuckled. "I believe it has something to do with you being buried by several tons of three-quarter rock."

"I'm fine."

"Better let them make sure."

His jaw set stubbornly. "They'd better just get Frank to the hospital."

"They will, when you stop holding them up."

"I'm not stopping them. I don't need anything."

"You're starting to sound a bit machismo, my friend," Esteban said sternly. "Let them look at you, as Paul did."

"I—"

"Travis, please." Nicki put a hand on his arm, over the tattered sleeve. "Just let them check? So we'll be sure?"

Travis stared at that slender hand, battered and reddened from her battle to reach him. He reached for it, then the other, lifting them and cradling them gently in his. With a voice made husky by the sudden tightness of his throat, he said, "I think they'd better look at you."

Nicki stared at their hands, all the things she wanted to say welling up inside her. She knew this wasn't the time or the place, but she couldn't help them from glowing in her eyes when she looked up at him.

"I'll go if you will," she said softly.

Travis's breath caught in his throat at the tender undertone in her voice. He opened his mouth, then closed it as if he were afraid to speak. Then he simply nodded, and walked docilely with her toward the paramedic van.

Hours later, when she'd talked to more investigators for more agencies than her tired brain could remember, Nicki felt a wave of weariness ripple through her. She looked around in the twilight-lit yard until she spotted Travis, leaning against the fender of one of the state cars as a hard-hatted Cal-O.S.H.A. representative plied him with questions. The hat was an absurd precaution, she thought, since there wasn't a piece of machinery or equipment moving, but she supposed it made them feel more official.

She watched for a moment as Travis went through it all again; he and Paul had been on the receiving end of the most intensive questioning, having been both the victims and the closest witnesses. His normally straight, powerful body was slumped, and he was looking haggard. Bruises had begun to show up on his face, and she guessed he was feeling them all over. His shirt was stirring in the evening breeze, the torn edges fluttering. Every now and then he would run a hand over his tousled hair, brushing out some of the gravel dust.

Her eyes focused, oddly, on the rip in the knee of his jeans. It brought back forcefully the first time she'd ever seen him. He looked as vulnerable now, yet as determined not to show it, as he had then. He looked battered, beaten, and utterly exhausted.

And quite suddenly, she'd had enough. These men might be official investigators, they might have a job to do, but they'd had six hours to do it, and she was calling a halt. Summoning up every bit of authority she'd ever gained in her years as Miss Lockwood of Lockwood, Incorporated, she strode across the pit yard to the man in the white hard hat whom she remembered was the chief O.S.H.A. man.

"I'm sorry, Mr.—" she paused to glance at the name on the hat "—Clarkson, but I'm afraid that's all for today."

The man looked at her, startled. "We're not quite finished, yet, Miss Lockwood."

"Then I suggest you wind it up in the next fifteen minutes, because that's when this pit closes."

The man stiffened. "Look, Miss Lockwood, this is an official investigation—"

"And this pit is governed by the Bureau of Mines. We don't have a night permit, Mr. Clarkson. These grounds must be vacated by dark. Which is, as I said, in about fifteen minutes."

The man sputtered another protest. Nicki ignored him.

"If you have a problem with that, take it up with Mr. Harknell from Mines. In the meantime, Mr. Halloran has . . . other obligations."

Travis raised an eyebrow as the man protested. "But—"

"You've had him for six hours. That's enough. You know where to find him if you have more questions. Good day, sir."

She took Travis's arm, a little surprised when he came along so easily. When they stopped near their cars, she looked up at him, expecting at the least an argument.

"What obligations?" he asked mildly.

"Some rest. And that shower you mentioned." She looked him up and down, eyeing the reddened spots she knew would be bruises by morning. "Make that a long, hot bath."

Something flickered in his eyes, but he only said, a little wistfully, "Can I wash my hair?"

She bit her lip as she fought back the sudden stinging behind her eyelids. She reached up and patted the thick, dark tousle of hair; a small puff of dust arose.

"Please do," she teased, and was rewarded with a crooked smile.

"You driving me home?" She looked startled, and he shrugged. "I don't think I'm up to it."

She looked at him doubtfully. He *did* look exhausted, but . . . "Are you milking this, Halloran?"

He grinned suddenly. "You bet."

She laughed for the first time on this long, tiring day.

"Only if you let me drive that honey of a car," she bargained.

"Done."

He dug into his pocket and dragged out the keys. He started to hand them to her, then frowned at her hands. The medics had cleaned them, bandaged two knuckles, and given her some salve and told her they'd be fine in a couple of days. But right now, they looked awful.

"Maybe I should drive."

"Oh, no you don't. You're not welshing out now."

He laughed, and got in on the passenger side. She took a moment to enthuse over the luxurious interior of the car, then to familiarize herself with the controls. After she started the engine he gave her directions, then fell silent until, on the freeway heading south to San Clemente, he said suddenly, "Thanks for the rescue act." Then, as an afterthought, "Both of them."

Nicki smiled, but the memory of her terror darkened her eyes for a moment. "I should be thanking you. For saving Paul. And Frank. What you did . . ."

He shrugged off her praise negligently.

"Don't belittle it, Travis. What you did was . . . heroic."

He gave a low, denying chuckle. "Hardly. I told you, it was just instinct."

"And your instinct was to save them instead of yourself."

"Quit trying to make me sound noble."

"I don't have to try. What you did speaks for itself."

"Nicole—"

"Why can't you accept it, Travis? You did something wonderful. Just admit it."

"Okay, okay," he said mockingly. "So I'm noble. The very essence of nobility, that's me."

"Very good, Travis," she said wryly, "that was very convincing."

He grinned suddenly. "Speaking of convincing, was that for real? That stuff about the night permit?"

"Beats me." She smiled again, better this time. "But it sounded good, didn't it?"

His laughter welled up inside the car. "God, you shut him up. Miss Lockwood, at her imperious best."

She remembered the insults they'd traded the first day. "You mean that nose-in-the-air Lockwood glare has its uses?" she asked softly, careful to keep any sting out of her voice. Still, she felt him tense.

"I suppose it does," he said carefully.

"Just like the Halloran tough-guy image does?"

She could feel his gaze on her. "What are you saying?"

"Only that they're both just that—images." Images, she thought that had been battling since the day he'd come back. "They don't have much to do with the real person underneath."

He didn't say anything as she took the off ramp at El Camino Real and began to negotiate the narrow streets of old San Clemente.

"They've been at war, haven't they?" he finally said. "The 'tough guy' and 'the Lockwood'?"

She'd known, somehow, that he would understand what she'd been trying to say. He always had.

"Can we declare a truce, Travis?"

He let out a long breath. "I could use some peace."

She slowed as the headlights lit up the number on the big white house that overlooked one of the most prized views in this coastal stretch. She pulled into the drive, shut off the motor, set the brake, then turned to look at him.

"So could I," she said in a low voice.

"A truce, then." He gave her that crooked smile that sent her heart into free-fall. "A *long* truce."

They got out of the car and went inside. The house was much as she'd expected, spacious, airy, with expansive windows that took full advantage of the view.

"This is lovely," she said as he closed the door behind her and flipped on a light.

"Yes." They walked into the cool, white tile floored living room. Nicki kept going, toward the magnet of the wall of glass.

"It's nice that the owner's letting you use it."

"Martha's a nice person."

"Martha? She's the vice president you mentioned?"

He stretched, tentatively, as if checking for damage. "In charge of marketing. She's a real fireball. She came back to work after her husband died a few years ago, and we wouldn't be where we are without her."

She turned back from the windows, looking at him curiously. "We?"

He flushed, and looked toward the windows that looked out on the sea, sparkling in the gibbous moon's light.

"The company I work for," he mumbled, looking much more flustered than the words warranted. "Can I get you a drink, or something?"

"No. You're supposed to be resting, remember?"

He glanced down at himself. "I need that shower, first." He looked wryly at the pristine white sofa that faced the windows, sitting at an angle on the white tile. "I don't dare touch anything in here."

"You're going to be sore tomorrow. You should make it a hot bath."

He lifted his head to look at her, his eyes glinting. "Only if you volunteer to scrub my back."

Nicki blushed, her lips parting as her breath escaped her on a quick little gasp.

"Pushed the truce too far, huh?" he said ruefully.

She couldn't find the words to tell him it had been the images his words had conjured up that had silenced her, not anger.

"Sorry," he muttered, and started to turn away. Still unable to speak, Nicki made a small, smothered sound. It stopped him cold. He turned back, his eyes searching her face. "Nicole . . . ?"

While her voice still failed her, her feet did not, and she ran to him across the tile floor. He winced when she threw her arms around him to hug him fiercely, but when she saw and tried to pull back, he held her close.

"No. Stay," he murmured, tightening his arms around her.

"God, I was so afraid," she whispered, choking back a sob. "One minute you were there, then ... I thought you were dead. That I'd lost you forever."

He went very still. "I thought ..." He stopped, swallowing heavily. "I didn't think it would ... matter to you."

She leaned back to look up at him, the tears streaming freely now. "I know you didn't. I ... I didn't, either. But when it happened ... when I thought you were probably dead under all that damned rock ... That's when I realized none of it mattered. That nothing mattered, not if you were dead."

"Nicole," he said, his eyes wide as he stared at her, his hands slipping to her shoulders, "what are you saying?"

She drew herself up, sniffing, and wiping at her eyes. She'd had to face her feelings squarely when she'd been clawing at that pile of stones, when she'd feared she was searching for a lifeless body, not the vital, living man before her now. She'd faced them for the first time in her life, and she wasn't going to deny them now.

"I love you."

He stared, then closed his eyes, swaying on his feet as if she'd struck him. His hands tightened until his grip was almost painful on her slender shoulders, but she never wavered. The hellish fear she'd gone through this afternoon had changed her, marked her forever.

"I think I've always loved you. Even when I tried so hard to hate you."

The thick, dark lashes lifted, revealing eyes dark with emotion. "Oh, God, Nicole ... Do you mean it? It's not just ... reaction?"

"I only know that when I thought I'd lost you ... Oh, God, Travis, it all seemed so stupid. So useless." She hugged him again, more carefully this time. "You were right," she whispered against his ragged shirt, "we've lost so damned much already..."

He let out a long, shuddering breath. His arms clamped around her, as if he could pull her inside himself by sheer strength. He murmured her name, over and over, stroking her tangled hair, then lifting her raw, red hands to his lips, kissing them gently. Nicki lifted her gaze, seeing in his dusty face everything he couldn't find the words to say.

"Is that offer still open?" she asked huskily.

"What offer?"

"To scrub your back."

He went rigid, staring at her. He gripped her arms, holding her away from him as he stammered, "Look, I... Just because..."

He released her, his hands curving into fists as if he didn't trust what they might do. "You don't have to do this. That's not why I..."

He trailed off as she smiled at him, a shy yet sensuous curve of her mouth that started his heart hammering double-time in his chest. "I need a bath, too. And I only mentioned scrubbing your back, I believe."

He groaned. "You're a brat, Nicole Lockwood. You always were."

"That's what you liked about me, remember?"

"Always."

"This place does have a bathtub, doesn't it?"

"A huge one," he growled. "With a view of the ocean."

"Big enough... for two?"

"Nicole... don't start something you don't intend to finish. I'm fresh out of nobility here."

"Nobility," she said, holding his gaze levelly, "is not what I want, now."

His breathing quickened, keeping pace with his racing heart. "Exactly," he asked carefully, "what *do* you want?"

"You."

She said it simply, honestly, and it nearly brought him to his knees. He couldn't speak, could barely draw his next breath as his body surged in response to that earnest declaration. Heat rippled through him, searing him to the core. He felt like a man standing at the open gates of paradise, but not certain that they weren't going to slam shut in his face.

His silence shook her confidence, and she drew back a little. "Am I...wrong? I thought you wanted this, too..."

"God, Nicole!"

It ripped from him in the instant he reached for her again, pulling her against him. His mouth came down on hers, hard and demanding. She met his urgency with her own and the fire leapt to life.

Nicki pressed her full length to him, nibbled at his lips, stroked his dusty, tangled hair, savoring every hot, vital, alive part of him. She met his probing tongue with her own, drinking in the taste of him, urging him on until he groaned against her lips.

Her heart was soaring, her blood bounding with triumph, and a joy heightened by the knowledge of how near she had come to never having these precious moments. She tangled her fingers in the thick hair at his nape, pulling him closer, deepening the kiss until all she knew was the heat of his mouth and the stroking velvet of his tongue.

Then she was flying, truly flying, and only after a moment did her hazy mind realize he'd lifted her in his arms and was carrying her up the curved stairway. White carpet, she thought vaguely. Everything in this house seemed white. She didn't care. Travis was all the color she needed in her world; he gave her every shade of the rainbow.

When he set her down beside a huge, sunken tile tub, unexpectedly blue in a spacious white bathroom, he closed his eyes for a long moment, holding her away from him.

"Travis?"

He shuddered at the sound of her voice, low and throaty; it was as if she'd brushed him physically with the feathery sound of it.

"We've got to slow down, Nicole. I've waited too damned long for this to rush it."

She reached up to touch his face, stroking her fingers over the bruise beginning to show on his cheekbone. "Later. We can go slow later," she whispered. "We have all night."

He shuddered again. "Don't," he ground out. "Don't talk like that, or it'll be right here, right now, on the floor, and to hell with the fact that I'm not fit to be touched, let alone touch you."

The flush that crept up into her face had nothing to do with embarrassment and everything to do with the hot, swirling thoughts his words aroused. The heat, the need, glimmered in her eyes unmistakably, and Travis clenched his jaw against the flaming dart of desire that lanced through him.

As if to deny his words about being fit to touch, Nicki slid one hand through the rip that slanted across the front of his shirt, ignoring the dirt and dust. Her fingers sought and found hot, living skin, stretched taut over the ridged muscles of his belly, and she felt an answering quiver in herself as those muscles rippled violently beneath her touch.

"God," he exclaimed, "you're tearing me apart already, and we haven't even begun." He seized her hand and drew it up to his lips, kissing the bandaged knuckle. "We have to talk."

She made a face. "Talk?"

His mouth quirked. "Yes." He released her, then bent to turn the faucet on, sending a rush of water into the big, deep tub. When he straightened, she was watching him with that hunger still in her eyes, and he barely stopped himself from grabbing her.

"Stop looking at me like that."

"Like what?" She was getting impatient with this. "Like I love you? I do. Like I've been waiting for this all my life? I have. Like I'm going to go crazy, wanting you? I am."

She had brought him to his knees then. He sank down to sit on the edge of the tub, marveling at how she could do this to him, he who had clung to his strength when there was nothing else to have pride in. And do it with mere words.

But words he'd never in his life thought to hear, never dared hope to hear.

She came down in front of him, reaching for him. He grabbed her hands before she could touch him, gripping them tightly before the flicker of pain on her face told him he was hurting her and he eased his clasp.

"Nicole," he said seriously, "we *do* have to talk. I never expected this. I don't . . . have any way to protect you."

She colored, but held his gaze. "It's all right."

"It's not. You don't need that complication, not now."

"I mean . . . it's all right. I had some problems, when mother was so sick. My doctor said it was stress, but when it got worse, she put me on the pill . . . to regulate things."

She watched him absorb it, saw the emotions flicker across his face.

"I'm sorry," he whispered at last.

"No. None of that. Not now. Just us, you and me."

After a long, silent moment, he nodded. "Just us," he whispered, standing up and drawing her into his arms.

When he kissed her it was long, and soft, and infinitely tender. He cradled her head in his hands, warmed her with his heat, and stroked that deep, hidden part of her into a glowing pool of molten pleasure. She felt surrounded by that warmth, precious, treasured, in a way she'd never known.

When he at last broke the kiss, she stared up at him, a little shaken. "I'm supposed to be taking care of you."

Passion darkened his eyes, and his voice was somehow dark and hot, as well, when he said, "So go ahead."

With fingers that were trembling she reached for the buttons of his shirt. She fumbled with them until she reached the middle of his chest, then she had to stop to steady herself.

"You know," he said mildly, "this shirt's already shot, anyway."

Her gaze shot to his face questioningly. He shrugged, then tugged the shirt off over his head, heedless of the rest of the buttons popping and the widening of the tears in the fabric. Then he put her other hand back where it had been, braced against his stomach.

She stared at him, at the reddening marks that marred the sleek, satin skin of his chest.

"Oh, Travis."

With a boldness that surprised her, she leaned forward to press her lips to him over the worst of the marks. She felt the hammering of his heart beneath her mouth, felt the searing heat of his skin, felt the undulation of the muscles of his belly once more beneath her hand.

"You do want me back," she whispered in wonder.

He groaned, covering her hand with his and sliding it over the heavy denim of his jeans, down below his waistband.

"God, Nicole," he grated as her fingers instinctively caressed his rigid flesh, "how can you doubt it? I've known it for years. Even when you were fourteen, I knew that someday you'd be the one. That someday, when you were old enough, it would be us, and it would be so damned right..."

He trailed off, his fingers plucking at the buttons of her silk shirt with an urgency he couldn't disguise. And every stroking caress of her fingers, even through the thick cloth, drove him closer to the brink. He didn't know which he wanted to be rid of more, the thin silk that hid her from him, or the heavy denim that kept him from feeling the naked touch of her hands.

Then she solved the dilemma for him, reaching for the snap of his jeans and popping it open; he was surprised it hadn't given way of its own accord, he felt so swollen and hard. The zipper gave way and she freed him at the same moment he finished with the last of the buttons and the pale blue silk drifted away. The combined impact of the feel of her hands on him, tracing the naked, pulsing length of him, and the sight of the sweet swell of her breasts above the delicate blue lace of her bra made him gasp.

He bent to kiss that full, ripe curve, savoring the quivering softness with his tongue. He could taste the grit of the dust that had settled on her delicate skin, but he didn't care. It only made him think of how she had worked so fiercely to get to him, and a flood of tenderness filled him, enabling him to rein in his surging senses.

He straightened, gently gasping her wrist and pulling her hand away from its too sweet caresses.

Nicki looked up at him. "Did I... hurt you? I know my hands are rough right now, I—"

"Your hands," he said thickly, "are beautiful. And having them on me is the most incredible feeling I've ever known. But I can't take much more of it." He kissed her softly. "Time for your bath."

He undressed her as if she were a child, gently, carefully. But the heat that filled his eyes when he looked at her, the sharp intake of breath she heard as he unfastened her bra and her breasts spilled free into his hands, and the low sound that rose from him when he slipped her jeans and panties down over her hips told her he was not thinking childish thoughts.

He slipped off her shoes, taking too long at it to be businesslike, stroking the high arch of her foot, circling her slender ankle with one strong hand, then caressing the taut curve of her leg. She heard him make that sound again, low and harsh in his chest, then he moved quickly, lifting her in his arms and lowering her into the steaming tub.

The heat was a shock at first, but then it began to seep in, meeting with the warmth he'd begun inside her, making her feel deliciously relaxed. She looked up from beneath half-lowered lashes then, and suddenly the heat from the shoulder-deep water was nothing beside the burst of heat that shot out from that glowing pool inside her.

He was sliding his jeans and briefs off, taking his shoes and socks with them, leaving him naked to her eyes. He stood beside the tub for a moment, as if her gaze had frozen him there.

He was beautiful, she thought, filled with wonder at both the sight of him, and how her body seemed to swell and tighten at the same time in response to the sculpted planes of his. She'd known how broad his shoulders were, but not how strongly muscled. She'd known he was lean, fit, but not how the flat, ridged belly would make her own quiver. She'd known his long legs carried him with easy grace, but hadn't realized how powerful they were. She'd seen the way the taut, muscled curve of his buttocks snugged a pair of jeans, but she hadn't expected her fingers to curl with the need to touch him there.

And she had never in her life expected to want, to need, to ache for anything the way she ached for the full, proud, jutting flesh nestled in the dark curls below his belly. He would fill her with that maleness, with himself, until that empty place she'd always thought inescapable didn't exist anymore. That empty place that, until now, she hadn't realized was empty because it was his, and he was gone.

She held her arms out to him, and he slipped into the tub and into her embrace. He tried, she knew he tried to go slow, to give her time. He soaped her body, washing her as gently as if he felt nothing more than a tender concern. But again, the heat in his eyes as her nipples tautened beneath his fingers, and the surging of his naked body when she arched into his hands, betrayed him.

She waited as long as she could stand, then took the soap from him and began to return the favor. She washed the grit from his body, the dust from his hair, and sponged the warm, soothing water over his bruises. And she took no care at all to see that her breasts didn't rub against his skin, that her thighs didn't slip over his as she knelt before him.

When at last she returned her soapy hands to that rigid flesh between his thighs, a harsh, rumbling growl broke from him. He came up out of the water like some mythic god, and she thought him just as magnificent. It was her last rational thought, for his hands were on her stroking, caressing, sliding over her wet skin until she knew there wasn't a nerve ending he'd missed. Then his mouth began, tracing the same path, and she shuddered under its heat.

He lifted her breasts, cupping their weight in his palms, until the crests were clear of the water. His eyes went to her face and she shuddered again; she'd never seen anyone look like that before, so raw, so hot, so hungry. And she wondered if she looked like that herself, as, wrapping her arms around his neck, she convulsively lifted herself upward, thrusting her breasts to him.

He smiled, an ardent, satisfied smile that sent a shiver down her spine before he bent his head once more. When he caught her taut nipple between his lips she gasped, arching even further as wildfire raced along every nerve. He flicked it with his tongue, then suckled deeply. Nicki cried out his name sharply, then again as he repeated the caress on the other tingling peak.

The sound of his name bursting from her on a wave of pleasure sent a rush of sensation through him so hot and fierce he shook with it. His body clenched under its force, demanding to be let loose, to slip the restraints he'd put on it. It took all of his rapidly fading will to hold back.

He suckled her again, savoring the way she rippled in his arms, moaning. Her hands slid down from his shoulders, stroking over his back, sliding over wet skin until he felt on fire with her touch. He slid one hand down her body, over the slight gentle curve of her stomach, stroking, caressing. When at last he slipped his fingers down to her thighs, she parted for him eagerly.

She gasped when he found the spot he'd been seeking, and he felt the convulsion go through her as he began a slow, circular caress. The water around them rippled as she moved in time with his touch, as her hips lifted to him invitingly.

He felt himself tighten unbearably, surging to a hardness he wouldn't have thought possible. And suddenly it was an invitation he could no longer deny. He'd waited fifteen years, yet fifteen seconds more was too much.

"Ah, Nicole, I can't wait."

"Travis," she whimpered, "please."

He gathered her into his arms and stood up. The feel of her naked in his arms, her slick, wet skin sliding over his, robbed him of the strength to do any more than step up out of the tub. He lowered her to the thickly carpeted floor with exquisite care and went down beside her.

"I'm sorry, love," he murmured against the curve of her neck. "I can't make it any further."

In answer she lifted her head, trailing quick, fiery kisses across his jaw and down the corded tendons of his neck. Her hands slipped down his sides, to grasp at his hips and pull him against her. He gasped as his heated flesh slid over the silken skin of her stomach.

"Travis, please," she said again. "I don't want to wait anymore..."

He groaned, lifting himself over her. "Neither do I. God, neither do I."

He slid between her slender thighs, his body probing, seeking her heat. He paused then, looking down at her, hovering on the brink of what he'd waited so many years for.

"Look at me, Nicole," he said thickly.

She lifted lashes still spiked with water from the tub. She wanted to look away from the intensity in his eyes, but as his hot, rigid flesh began to slide into her, she knew he was right, that there should be no concealment between them, that this was only the culmination of all the sharing that had gone before.

And then he was inside her, driving hard and deep and home. Her cry of shocked pleasure blended with his hoarse exclamation as he sheathed himself in her heat. He filled her, stretching her, driving her upward until her hands clenched convulsively on his back as he thrust again and again. She writhed beneath him, caught in a flaming web of sensations she'd never known before.

She couldn't take any more, couldn't take all of him, she knew it, she was filled to bursting. Then he moaned her name, low and deep, and she knew she could never have enough. She arched up to him, taking him deeper, and her hands slid down his back, at last fulfilling that need to curl around the taut curve of his buttocks. She clutched at him as the muscles there flexed with every driving penetration.

"Oh, Nicki! Nicki-ee-ee..."

He'd never called her that. And now, uttered as he bucked wildly against her, gasping out his passion, the nickname everyone else used became something rare and precious. Then, impossibly, she felt him swell inside her, felt him shudder, and gasp her name once more. The sound itself seemed to propel her upward, until she was quivering helplessly.

"Let go, Nicki," he gasped harshly. "Now."

She had no choice, not when he sounded like that. Not when his every movement sent wildfire racing through her. She felt him shudder again, then he arched against her, his head flung back as he drove into her one last time. He sent her flying, whirling off into an exploding world of heat and light and pleasure, and she went with joy in her heart and his name shimmering on her lips.

Chapter 11

Travis knew he was crushing her, pressing her down into the carpet with his full weight, but he couldn't seem to move. He tried, moving his hands to brace himself, but his arms seemed useless. She had sapped him of all his strength, draining him in that shuddering, violent explosion of pleasure that had been unlike anything he'd ever experienced.

At last he managed to lift his head to look at her. He opened his mouth to speak, then stopped when he realized that the drops on her face were not from the bath.

"Nicole? God, did I hurt you? I didn't—"

He broke off as she shook her head fiercely.

"Then what...?"

She shook her head again, and looked away. He turned her chin with a gentle finger. She bit her lip, and Travis felt a sinking, queasy sensation in the pit of his stomach. Was she regretting this, already, when he was still buried deep inside her? How could she? It had been perfect, as right as he'd always known it would be.

"Nicole? Talk to me, please?"

"I wish..."

Wished what? She'd never come here? Never made love to him? Never met him? The queasiness turned to acid, knotting his stomach painfully. But he had to know.

"You wish what?"

She looked at him, then, her eyes bright. "I wish I'd waited."

He froze. She did regret it. His jaw clenched and he looked away, unable to look at the gleam in her eyes that he knew came from tears.

"I'm sorry," he said, low and quiet. "I should have known it was too soon. I should have stopped."

"No!"

Startled, his head came up.

"That's not what I meant."

He looked at her, bewildered. When she spoke again, her voice was a soft, feathery caress, made all the more precious for its shyness, and by the color tinging her cheeks.

"I meant I wish I had waited for you. To be...the first."

Travis sucked in a sharp breath, then closed his eyes, afraid he was going to lose the fight to control the emotion her simple words had aroused in him. His throat tightened until he could barely breathe, and he had to blink rapidly against the stinging of his eyes.

"God, Nicole... If you only knew how that makes me feel."

It made him feel as if he could take on the world. At the least, he could move, and he gathered her into his arms and got up. She draped her arms around his neck, letting her head loll against his chest. She began to press tiny kisses over his breastbone, then let her tongue creep out to taste his skin.

"Nicole," he said warningly.

"What?" she murmured, leaning forward to trail her tongue across his chest, ending with a teasing flick at his nipple. She felt him nearly miss a step, then his arms tightened convulsively around her.

"I'd like to make it to the bed this time," he growled, "but if you do that again, we'll be lucky to make it out of this room."

She looked up at him with a languorous, contented smile that made him smile back with nothing less than pure, male satisfaction.

"I've never felt so lucky," she murmured, moving to repeat the action, laving a path across the muscled curve of his chest to his other nipple, circling it with her tongue until the flat disc puckered and she heard him groan.

He made it to the bed, yanked back the covers and put her down gently. She let her hand trail down his side as he released her, a sliding, brushing caress that made him shiver.

"Remember what you said?" he asked huskily.

"I said a lot of things."

"You said we could go slow later." He stretched out beside her, throwing one leg over hers, cupping a breast in his palm while his thumb crept up to tease her nipple to erect tautness. "It's later, Nicole. And this is going to be very, very slow." He bent to circle that hard little peak with his tongue. "And it's going to take most of that night you said we had."

And it was. And it did.

Somewhere, far away, an alarm clock went off. Nicki murmured a protest, and was pleasantly surprised when the noise stopped. She huddled back into the covers, snuggling up to the heater she was sleeping with, reaching out for the mists of sleep once more.

Her heater was making odd, rumbling noises. She tried to ignore it, but despite her efforts the noises coalesced into almost familiar sounds to her numbed mind. Almost words. Her heater was talking. Because her heater was Travis.

That startled her out of the deep sleep she'd been in, to a still groggy semi-awareness. She realized she was on her side, tucked into the curve of his body at her back. Her head was pillowed on his arm, and she could feel the solid, strong length of him. Just as she had all night.

Color crept up into her cheeks as she remembered last night. Remembered everything he'd done to her, and how she'd responded so fiercely, so wantonly. And then how she'd taken everything he'd taught her about pleasure in the dark and put it to use on him in the dim light of dawn. And how he'd responded in the same way, with a wildness that gave her a sense of feminine power she'd never known before.

He'd been right, she thought. It had been meant to be. That's why it had never been right before, with anyone else. She'd told him, in the moments before they'd at last drifted into an exhausted, sated sleep, about her single, rather grim experiment while in college.

She'd been tracing circles across his chest, through the sweat still sheening his skin from his last explosive climax, when he had shown her how to ride him so sweetly it made her soar to heights she hadn't known were possible.

"I hated it," she told him. "I never wanted to try again. I thought it was just me. After that, when somebody kissed me and I didn't feel anything, I knew there was something wrong with me." Her hand slid down and came to a stop, lying flat on his belly. "But it was just that it wasn't you."

He'd whispered her name and held her close, until, feeling safer than she could ever remember, she'd slipped into sleep. A sleep that had lasted until that darned alarm had sounded. But if it was an alarm, why was he talking to it?

Because it had been the phone, dummy, she told herself, at last surrendering her grip on both sleep and the sweet, hot memories that had flooded her. That was why he was twisted partly away from her now, leaving her shoulders cold and forlorn. She started to move toward his heat again, then stopped. She must have been, on some subconscious level unclouded by sleep and memory, hearing him for some time, for she realized that what he was saying was what had stopped her.

Or rather, how he was saying it.

"I know, Chuck. But I can't do anything about it right now. Things are going to have to stay long distance for now."

He was keeping his voice low, and his head turned away from her to keep, she supposed, from waking her.

"You'll just have to handle it. I'll call him this afternoon and explain. What about the Chandler deal?"

A pause, then. "All right. Let's go for it. Express the forms here. I'll sign them and have them back to you by the next day."

He shifted slightly, adjusting the receiver. "I know, Chuck. I'll try to get back there next weekend. Just hold the fort for me until then, will you? What else?"

She felt him tense behind her, then heard him say, a bit louder, "She what?" He listened for a moment, then she felt a chuckle rumble up from his chest, but he smothered it before it got past his lips. "I should have known." Another pause. "Yes, she is. And you will, I hope."

She lay still as he hung up the phone. He didn't move for a long moment. Then he leaned over to press a gentle kiss on her tangled hair before he disentangled his legs from hers and slipped carefully out of the bed. She heard him moving quietly around the room, felt a rustling at the foot of the bed, but she didn't move.

She didn't understand this. Any of it. Whoever had been on the phone had obviously been waiting to talk to him. Waiting for decisions. And Travis had answered him like a man used to making decisions. And giving orders.

She lay there, turning it over in her mind, until she couldn't stay still anymore. She sat up, glancing around to see if there was a clock on either bedside table. It was there next to the phone, reading a late—for her these days—seven o'clock.

She swung her feet to the floor and stood up, color tinging her cheeks as she became aware of some sore spots on her body she'd never felt before. She looked around the room, wondering if she could find her way back to the bathroom where her clothes were no doubt lying tangled with his on the floor. Then she saw the robe lying across the foot of the bed, and realized what he had done earlier. Touched by his thoughtfulness, she slipped it on.

And stopped still, breathing in the mixture of woodsy after-shave and masculine scent that meant Travis clinging to the thick gray velour. And the memories of the night came rushing back once more as she stood huddled in the garment that he'd worn.

It swam on her, trailing on the floor and over her hands, making her realize again just how big, how strong, how solid the man was, the man she'd turned her body over to for his pleasure, and her own.

After a moment she was able to move again, and padded downstairs, following her nose. He looked over his shoulder at her the moment she stepped into the kitchen, led by the smell of the coffee he was brewing.

"Hi," he said, a soft smile curving his mouth. His hair was tousled, his feet were bare below his jeans, and he looked utterly, boyishly adorable. Except for the fact that he was shirtless, and the muscled expanse of his bare chest was anything but boyish. And made her remember how it felt under her hands. And her mouth.

Stop it, she told herself firmly, or you're going to be hotter than that coffee.

She walked toward him, eyeing with a frown the bruise on his cheekbone, and the worst of the marks on his chest that were already purpling. "Are you all right?"

He grinned, that flashing, devilish grin, and if she'd thought it had incredible effects on her before, after last night it was indescribable.

"I never felt better in my life," he said, and she blushed.

He reached out to touch her hair, and she wished suddenly that she'd tracked down a hairbrush somewhere. It had been wet from the bath, then tangled by his fingers most of the night, until it had dried in a flyaway mass that was probably untamable.

"You look beautiful," he said softly. "All sleepy-eyed, with your hair mussed like it was last night."

He said it as if he'd known exactly what she was thinking about, and a tiny spurt of heat flashed through her. Okay, she muttered inwardly, forget the hairbrush.

"I was hoping you were still asleep," he said. "I was going to bring you breakfast."

She looked at the plate he had out, her throat tightening when she saw her favorite English muffins smeared with boysenberry jam. Even this he'd remembered.

"Thank you," she said. Or tried to; it came out a little squeakily. She sat in the chair he indicated, leaning out of his way as he shoved aside some papers that were piled on the bar. Among them she saw the distinctively striped cardboard envelopes from one of the express delivery companies she occasionally used.

Odd, she thought. He'd said the owner only used the house rarely, yet this was obviously a pile of business correspondence. Then she noticed the top express envelope was addressed to him. Her brow creased.

"Nicole? Are you all right?"

She nodded, reaching hastily for the muffin he'd slid over to her. She had to jerk her arm back when the too big sleeve of the robe headed straight for the jam. Her elbow hit the pile of papers, sending them sliding sideways. With a sigh she reached for them, straightened them, then turned up the sleeve of the robe before reaching for the muffin he'd fixed.

And stopped dead when something midway down in that stack of papers caught her eye. A letter. On letterhead stationery. With a logo she had spent a long time staring at in her office. The logo that summoned up all those long-ago memories of summer days in the shady cocoon of her tree.

She frowned, puzzled. Her gaze was drawn by the small yellow stick-on note at the bottom of the letter. "T—For your signature." it said.

With the speed of a row of toppling dominoes, the pieces fell into place. And the untouched muffin dropped back to the plate. Slowly, she lifted her gaze to his face.

"Travis?"

Her tight, strained tone had his attention immediately. He set down the coffeepot and looked at her. "What?"

"Who's Chuck?"

She saw his jaw tighten, and his eyes flicked instinctively toward the stairway. "You *were* awake."

"Who is he?"

"He's . . . I work with him."

She grimaced at the vagueness. "What's his last name?"

He took a deep breath. He studied his coffee cup. He brushed away an imaginary crumb. He let the breath out, closing his eyes. And then, with an expression that told her he knew exactly what he was about to do, that he dreaded it but was going to do it anyway, he told her.

"Howell."

A tiny gasp escaped her, not of surprise but of stunned confirmation. Her eyes searched out that betraying piece of paper, with the graceful, flowing logo in the corner, printed in the exact green of its inspiration.

"Oh, God. Willow Tree. Willow Tree Corporation. I should have guessed."

"Nicole—"

"I heard how you talked to him. Like a boss. His boss. And he's a vice president." She shivered. "And I guess I know what that makes you."

He let out a long, taut breath. "Nicole, I—"

"Why didn't you tell me? Why did you lie about—"

"I told you I've never lied to you. I couldn't lie to you."

She laughed harshly. "Oh, no? The car—"

"It's a company car. Just like I said."

"And everything else?"

"It's all true. It's just not all of the truth."

"A fine line, isn't it? Why did you let me think . . . what I thought?"

His head came up sharply then. "Why did I let you think what you wanted to? What I knew you were going to think, that I was a—how does Richard put it, a peon? Just a guy breaking his back with honest, physical labor because that's all he knows how to do? That's what you thought, isn't it? What you assumed, with all that Lockwood assurance?''

"What was I supposed to think?"

"Exactly that," he said, bitterness tinging his voice.

"Travis—"

"Well, I've been just that. I started at the bottom, literally. I've dug ditches, carried garbage, all of it. And I'm not ashamed of it, either."

"Did you think I would be? Why didn't you tell me?"

"Why? Because I'm about sick to death of never being good enough for the Lockwoods. And damned if I was going to buy my way in with who I am now."

"The president of Willow Tree Corporation."

He met her eyes evenly. "Yes."

She looked at him, her heart and mind so full of whirling thoughts and emotions that it was long, silent moment before she could speak.

"You were always good enough for the real Lockwoods, Travis," she said softly. "It was only you who didn't think so."

She'd taken the wind right out of his angry sails. She'd made him remember all the time he'd spent wrestling with his feelings of inadequacy back then, feelings he'd thought long behind him. He stared into the dark circle of his cooling coffee.

"I didn't want you to know," he said at last, "because I was afraid you might ... That it might make a difference to you."

"You thought I'd play some kind of phony game, lie about how I felt? So tell me, Mr. Halloran, did I pass your little test? Does last night earn me the right to know who you are really are?"

The coffee in the cup sloshed as he jerked around to face her. "Stop it! Damn it, last night had nothing to do with any of this!"

"God, I want to believe that."

"Believe it. You said it, Nicole. Just us. You and me. Nothing else." His hand clenched around the cup as he stared down into it once more. "Don't defile what we had last night. It was good and pure and right, and nothing can change that."

"That's what I thought. Before I realized that you... thought you had to keep this a secret from me. You have a pretty high opinion of me, don't you?" she finished sardonically.

"Yes," he said, confirming her words, not the tone. "But I learned the hard way to expect the worst, too."

The hard way. He'd done everything the hard way, she thought. He'd had to. It was a moment before she could speak.

"I've read so much about Willow Tree, before we made this bid... How could I not have come across your name?"

She heard him take a breath. "I... Not many people know who I am. Those who do, know I try and stay out of the limelight. And my people do as I say. The last thing I want is a bunch of stories about the boy from the wrong side of the tracks made good. Or about my... record. That's behind me. I want to keep it that way."

She stared at his bent head, for some reason her eyes fastening on the nape of his neck below the thick tangle of dark hair. It made him seem oddly vulnerable, and brought back with a rush the moments when she feared she'd lost him forever. The hurt of his lack of trust still stung, but when she thought of all the reasons he had not to trust, her anger drained away.

"Will you... tell me now?"

The sudden softness in her voice made him lift his gaze to her face, his eyes searching. As if he'd found something in her expression that decided him, he nodded.

"Let's go outside."

She followed him out to the deck that rimmed the ocean side of the house; the salt air carried on the morning breeze and it felt wonderful. The sound of the surf was steady, rhythmic in the distance.

He dropped down on one of the lounges, lifting the leg that had been bruised the most yesterday and stretching it out straight. He rubbed at it as if it were bothering him, and she remembered how she had gently washed the cut on that knee last night. And what had happened next.

She turned her face toward the ocean before he could see the heat pinken her cheeks.

"I haven't kept any of the money from Lockwood," he said suddenly, as if she'd accused him.

She stared at him blankly. "What?"

"It's in an escrow account. It will revert to the company when the six months is up."

With a pang she remembered her nasty words that first day, about him being so successful that he didn't need the Lockwood money. Never would she have guessed how close her angry jab had struck to the truth. Willow Tree. It still stunned her.

"How, Travis?" she repeated.

He gave a self-conscious chuckle. "I don't know where to start."

"Try the beginning."

He ran a finger around the rim of his cup, then lifted his head to stare out at the blue Pacific. The breeze lifted the tousled strands of his hair, then abated to leave them tossed over his forehead.

"I'm not exactly sure where that is," he said at last.

"Did you . . . You were still in school when . . ."

She trailed off awkwardly, and he chuckled again, a little sourly this time.

"Yes, I finished high school. The youth authority doesn't give you much choice. You went, you cooperated, or you wound up in lock-down. A couple of weeks of that, never even seeing the outside, and cooperation was a small price to pay."

She shivered; she never felt so naive as when he talked about this.

"I was . . . lucky, though, I suppose. There was a teacher there, one they brought in from outside. He helped me. He kind of adopted me as his charity case of the year—"

He broke off, shaking his head. "No, I don't mean that. Larry was sincere. And he really did help. When I finished the high school requirements, he made sure I got into the advanced classes. And he got me on the furlough program, so I could work outside . . . I think I would have gone crazy, except for that."

She could think of nothing to say. She'd never been able to deal with the thought of him caged, and she couldn't now.

"Anyway, he got me a job with a construction crew that was building a junior college about thirty miles away. His brother-in-law was the contractor. And when I got out, they hired me."

When he didn't go on, she prodded. "And?"

He shrugged. "You wanted the beginning. I guess that was it."

"Travis," she said warningly.

His mouth curved into a rueful smile. "Not enough, huh?"

"No."

He sighed. "Yes, ma'am," he said dutifully, "but there's really not much more to it. When Bill hired me, it was part of a deal with his brother-in-law. I could work for him as long as I kept going to school." He shrugged again. "So I worked on one part of the college all day, and went to classes in the other part at night."

"That must have been tough."

"I didn't mind. It kept me from thinking too much. I was too tired most of the time."

She didn't have to ask what he hadn't wanted to think about; she knew. She'd spent enough time herself not thinking about it. That old, familiar ache rose in her, but he went on easily enough.

"Anyway, Bill told me that if I stuck it out and got my A.A. degree, he'd make me a foreman. I didn't believe him, but I didn't know what else to do. So I stuck."

Because you didn't have anywhere else to go, she thought with a pang. "Why didn't you believe him?"

"I didn't believe anybody, then."

It stabbed at her again, the pain of realizing what he'd gone through. What had once seemed too little punishment for what he'd done now seemed grim and harsh.

"Did he . . . keep his promise?"

"Yes. And four years later, after he had a heart attack and had to slow down, he offered me a partnership. I told him I couldn't afford it, but he let me pay it off in installments." His mouth twisted wryly. "As long as I went back to school again, for my bachelor's degree. The Schultz boys had a thing about school."

"I'm glad," she said softly.

"That they made me go to school?"

"That there were some good people in your life."

His expression softened as he nodded. "They are good people."

"Do you still have any contact with them?"

He grinned. "Can't avoid it. Bill's my field consultant. He got tired of being retired. And Larry's a counselor at the summer camp we built in the mountains up near Hemet."

Friendship, she thought. His kind of friendship. His kind of honor, and debts paid. No wonder he laughed at Richard's idea of it.

"Anyway, when Bill was ready to retire, I bought him out." He grinned suddenly. "Cash, this time. We were doing okay. That was six years ago." He looked out over the ocean once more. "And the rest, as they say, is history."

"Except you changed the name."

He went very still, then shifted his gaze from the rolling surf to her face. "Yes."

"Why? Why that name?"

"I think you know."

She gave a shivery little sigh. "When I first saw the name, I wondered . . . if maybe it meant something special to somebody, like it did to me. Then I figured it was just something silly, like there'd been a willow in front of their office building, or something." He was watching her too intently, and she looked out to sea. "I keep thinking I should have known."

"Even your radar's not that good, little one. I told you I kept a low profile. And when I knew you were making a bid, I made a point of keeping my name out of everything. Chuck handled it all."

A long moment of silence stretched out before she said, "Travis?"

"Hmm?"

"Would you have...told me? If I hadn't figured it out?"

He sighed. "Yes. I almost did, that day in your office, when you told me why you wanted to deal with Willow Tree."

She looked back at him then. "Why then?"

"Because it... When you said those things, it was like you were telling me you were...proud of what I was doing."

The words were so broken, so hesitant, that her voice was barely a whisper for fear he'd stop talking altogether.

"Why didn't you tell me then?"

"I still didn't want you to know."

"Is that all?"

He let out a long, compressed breath. "I guess I didn't want to admit how much I needed you to be proud of me." He rubbed at his leg again, as if it were aching. "Hell, I almost told you that first day when you were—"

He broke off suddenly, looking away from her.

"When I was being a superior bitch?" she supplied gently.

"You were hurting." His voice was soft, husky. "I had no right to jump you like that. Not then."

"But you were right." She gave a mirthless little laugh. "Lord, were you right."

She fell silent, and he didn't speak as he tried to work the soreness out of his leg. At last, she asked quietly, "It was you who awarded us the marina contract, wasn't it?"

He stopped, his hands frozen just above his knee. "I made the final decision, yes."

"Because you knew we were hurting, financially."

"Nicole—"

"I don't want it, Travis. Not like that."

"That contract," he said dryly, "is not going to help. You won't be making much on it."

"But you know what landing a Willow Tree contract can do for a company. You can't deny its prestige, and that it can give us an edge in the future, even with other companies."

"It's nice to know we can dress up your resume."

"I don't want it," she repeated stubbornly. "Not if you only did it to—"

"Hey," he said, cutting her off, "what happened to the Miss Lockwood who used to climb on her soapbox and lecture me on the quality of Lockwood concrete?"

"She doesn't have a whole lot of faith in her own judgment, at the moment," Nicki said ruefully.

He reached for her then, only now reasonably certain she wouldn't push him away. He hauled her up onto his lap and held her close.

"I'm sorry, Nicole. Maybe I should have told you from the start. But you... I thought you hated me, and I felt like... like a dog who's been kicked but keeps trying to please. I just couldn't do it. It was too much like begging you to be proud of me. And I'll never beg for anything again in my life."

"You don't have to," she whispered, putting her arms around his neck. "I *am* proud of you, if it matters to you."

"It matters," he whispered, burying his face in the gentle curve of her neck and shoulder. "God, it matters so much."

"And I was proud of you before I knew any of this, even though I didn't want to be." She pressed a soft kiss on his hair. "I was proud of the man you've become, before I even realized that's what I was feeling. I'm just sorry it took what you did yesterday to make me recognize it."

"I didn't—" He stopped the denial that he'd done anything special when she put a finger to his lips, and then lowered his head in acceptance. "Okay, okay."

She looked at him for a long moment, then sighed. "It's going to take me a while to get used to this." She added humbly. "I'm sorry, Travis. I *was* being a superior bitch."

He hugged her. "No. You didn't know. And you were in pain. Striking back, like anyone would do."

"That's no ex—"

"Shh," he said. "You're sorry for that, and I'm sorry I didn't tell you sooner. We're even, okay?" Then, looking up at her he added, "I'm proud of you, too, Nicole. You've turned out as smart and strong and beautiful as I knew you would."

"I'm not sure about the smart part right now," she said, her mouth twisting wryly, "but I thank you for the rest."

"You're welcome. Nicole?"

"What?"

"Could you quit moving like that?"

"Like what?"

His hands went to her hips and shifted her slightly, moving the trim curve of her buttocks across his lap, and she realized she had been doing just that, unconsciously.

"Like that," he said. "You're driving me crazy."

"Okay," she said blithely. Then, with a sinuous twist of her body and a quick, graceful movement of her leg, she had straddled him.

"Oh, that helps," he grated out as she rubbed against his quickly responding flesh. "Especially knowing you probably haven't got a damned thing on under that robe."

She lifted one slender hand from where it had come to rest on his shoulder, and held the front of the robe away from her. She looked down the gap, making a mock inspection of her body.

"Nope," she confirmed cheerfully, "not a thing."

He groaned, closing his eyes but unable to stop the instinctive arching of his body up to hers.

"So tell me," she said, her conversational tone belied by the sensuous caress of her hands over his naked chest, and her hips against his, "is there anything between you and your Levi's?"

His eyes snapped open. Slowly, one corner of his mouth lifted into that grin. "Nope. Not a thing."

Heat flared in her clear blue eyes, darkening them to sapphire. She leaned forward and planted a long, hot, wet kiss in the center of his chest. His back arched, his hands gripping her hips tightly, grinding her against him.

"Does this mean you're not mad anymore?"

She didn't answer, just trailed her mouth down over his belly to circle his navel with her tongue. The taut abdominal muscles rippled beneath her, and he groaned deep in his throat. When she reached down and unsnapped his jeans and began to tug at the zipper, the groan became a warning.

"Nicole..."

"Shh. I'm deciding whether I'm still mad or not."

"You're driving me up the wall is what you're—God!"

She'd slipped her hand beneath the denim and found him, her fingers circling and caressing in the way she'd learned so quickly and so well last night. He couldn't stop his body from bowing upward against her hand, seeking that touch that fired his blood.

Sweat beaded on his forehead as he fought for control. He pulled her up his body, away from the surging flesh that threatened to erupt under her sweet ministrations, but all she did was drape herself atop him, and it wasn't much better.

He put his hands to her shoulders and lifted her up. It was a bad idea; the front of the robe gaped open, exposing the firm, full curves of her breasts to his avid eyes. Her pink nipples, already taut at the tips, drew up into hard, hungry peaks under his gaze.

With a movement so swift he hardly realized he'd done it, he parted the front of the robe and pulled her down to him, crushing her bare breasts against his chest. She gave a little gasp of shocked pleasure, then began to move against him, twisting sinuously until her nipples were two points of fire searing them both.

"Oh, Travis..."

"What?" His voice was thick, heavy.

"I want..."

"Anything. Everything. What do you want, love?"

She lifted her head, her eyes dark, her lashes half-lowered with growing passion. "I want to hear you call me Nicki again."

One dark brow lowered. "Did I?"

"You did. Right when you..." She trailed off, reddening.

The brow lifted. "I did, didn't I?"

"It's never sounded like that before. So sweet. So special."

"Ah, Nicole, you're what's sweet. All of you. And I want to taste every bit of that sweetness. From here—" he pulled her head down and pressed a kiss to her forehead "—and to here—" his toes brushed hers "—and every sweet inch in between."

Her cheeks were flaming but her eyes were hot when he gripped her shoulders and lifted her up once more. Although the open robe hid her from the sides, she was bare to his gaze, her breasts swaying, her nipples barely brushing his chest.

With a throttled groan he lifted his head, seizing one of the tempting peaks with his mouth. He sucked fiercely, and the sudden shock of heat and pleasure made her cry out, arching her back to give him more, begging him to take it.

The racing motor of a car out on the street brought him out of the haze of pleasure and back to the reality of where they were. Reluctantly, he released that sweet nub of flesh and lifted his head.

"Have you made up your mind you're not mad anymore?"

"I think you almost have me convinced," she said breathlessly.

"I think," he growled, "I'd better do the rest of my convincing inside."

He carried her in and back to the bedroom. And if he missed a spot in making good on his promise to taste every inch of her, Nicki didn't notice.

Chapter 12

"You're sure you don't want to pick up your car first?"

Nicki shook her head. "I'll get it later. I need to get to the plant. There were a million things I was supposed to do today."

"The day's not over yet," Travis teased. "It's not even noon."

"By three minutes," she returned dryly.

"Are you saying you would rather have been at work?"

She looked over at him as he lounged behind the wheel of the sleek Mercedes. She saw the glint in his eyes, and knew he was remembering the way they had spent this morning. So was she, and her body tingled with the memories.

"No," she said honestly, "I can't think of anything I'd rather have been doing."

That satisfied, male smile curved his mouth, but Nicki didn't mind. He'd earned it, showing her that what she'd experienced last night was only the beginning. Besides, she thought with a slightly smug, feminine smile of her own, she'd done some satisfying herself; she had the memory of his thrashing body and his hoarse cries of pleasure to prove it.

"Damn."

"What?" she asked, startled by the sudden exclamation.

"You look like a cat who's found out where the catnip is stored."

"I have," she agreed, and gave a throaty little purr that had him laughing and groaning at the same time. "And I find I like it very much. It's very... tasty."

The groan won out over the laugh this time, and she could see him remembering the long, leisurely moments when she had set about tasting him as he had her. His hands were tight on the wheel as he made the last turn and headed toward the plant.

"Can we change the subject?"

"Something wrong with catnip?" she asked innocently.

"It's making my jeans too tight," he growled.

"Strange effect," she said in mock surprise, laughing when he made a sour face at her. "Speaking of jeans— Oh, stop," she said at his warning look, "I just wanted to thank you again for the shirt."

"You're welcome."

When they'd found her blouse damp, stained, and impossibly wrinkled on the floor of the bathroom, he'd loaned her a T-shirt. It was pale blue and fashionably huge on her, and she'd pulled up one side at an angle and tied it in a knot so that it wouldn't flap around her knees. It was obviously a man's, and it was probably written all over her face that it was his, but Nicki didn't mind. In fact, it gave her a sense of pleasure new to her, just as wearing his robe had done.

He turned the car into the yard, pulled up next to the office in his usual place and stopped. Then he glanced over at her, and grinned. "It looks a lot better on you."

"Good. Because it looks awfully good *off* you. I might have to borrow *all* your shirts."

"Feel free," he said, his voice low and alive with that husky note that she'd come to associate with that frisson of heat that rippled the muscles of her stomach.

"I *do* feel free," she whispered. "For the first time in so long..."

He leaned across the console toward her; she met him halfway and kissed him hungrily, forgetting, for the moment, where they were. And then she decided she didn't care where they were, or who saw them. Except that when she got out of the car, she felt a crawling sensation at the back of her neck, and turned to see Carl Weller watching them from the window of Richard's office.

Richard would have found out anyway, she told herself for the hundredth time when, long after dark, she finished the minimum of work she'd set for herself. In fact, she was a little surprised he hadn't come bursting into her office with a vintage Richard tantrum.

The thought of explaining to her brother bothered her, and she had no idea how she was going to do it. Not that it mattered. Richard would never understand. But he would have to learn to live with it, she thought. Because she loved Travis Halloran. And he—

She came to a sudden halt, her fingers tightening on the pen she'd just used to sign a formal letter of apology to Sam Shelby. He did love her, didn't he?

Slowly, like a person sifting through the ashes of a burnt-out home for some surviving precious possession, she picked over the memories of the last twenty-four hours. And nowhere could she find a moment when he'd said the words.

But he'd shown her, hadn't he? With every touch, every kiss, every time he'd joined them in the most intimate way possible? Of course he had, she told herself. Stop doubting him. You made your decision yesterday, you're not going to start having second thoughts now. It was too late for that. Much, much too late.

This time when the phone rang, Nicki was already awake. Awake and laying a path of hot, wet kisses over Travis's belly and heading for points south. When the bell clamored, he groaned in protest.

"Ignore it."

Nicki lifted her head and looked at the offending instrument. "If you think it won't stop, it will. If you think it will, it won't. Ma Bell's Law of Opposing Rings."

"Damn."

He groped for the receiver. And Nicki went back to what she'd been doing.

"Chuck, it's 5:00 a.m."

He lifted one shoulder to her mouth as Nicki nibbled across it.

"Who else would call me at this hour?"

He shifted as Nicki traced his collarbone with her tongue.

"Oh. You heard about that, huh? I didn't realize it hit the news. No, I'm fine. My head's harder than a few tons of rock, anyway. You know that."

He let his head loll back as she pressed her lips to the hollow of his throat, where his pulse was beginning to race.

"They said that? Well, yes, there were some weird things going on. I'll tell you when I see you."

Her mouth trailed along his breastbone between the muscled swells of his chest.

"Not much longer. Things kind of...broke loose last night."

Her head moved again, and her tongue found and flicked over one flat, male nipple. He sucked in a quick, audible breath.

"No, nothing's...wrong. Things worked out—" he took in another breath "—better than I ever hoped."

The other nipple received the same tender treatment. Travis tried to control a shudder as he reached for her, meaning to hold her still for a moment until he could get Chuck off the phone, but instead found himself pressing her head to his chest, encouraging that hot, circling caress of his puckering flesh.

"I know I...didn't get those contracts...back to you. I was...kind of busy."

She had started down over his belly again, leaving a blazing trail beneath her soft lips. His muscles rippled in response.

"Chuck, I . . . can't help how I sound at five in the morning. Look...I promise I'll be in—uh—" he couldn't stop the grunt as she reached his navel "—to sign those contracts by this afternoon, all right?"

Her tongue, hot and wet and teasing, circled his navel before she began to inch her way downward once more, gently nibbling, tasting. The thought of where she was going to wind up made him gasp in anticipation; Nicki, he'd found to his incredible pleasure, was a very quick learner. And she'd taught him a thing or two in the process.

"Believe me, Chuck—" he groaned "—there's not a damned thing wrong."

Even from where she was beginning to trace that path of dark hair that pointed the way downward from his navel, Nicki heard the laugh booming out from the receiver.

"About time," she heard, followed by the click of the phone being hung up.

With a quick, determined yank of his hand Travis disconnected the phone from its cord, and let it fall to the floor. Nicki laughed, a low, joyous purr of sound that vibrated against the skin of his lower belly.

"Now where was I?" she murmured, and began again.

She pressed soft, quick kisses across to his hip bone, then back to that arrow of dark hair. She liked that his chest was free of hair, she thought. It made it so hot and silky under her tongue, and made the contrast of the thicket of curls she was exploring now so much more intriguing . . .

He groaned, low and harsh and quick, when her seeking mouth found him, stroked him, then took him inside. Yes, she'd learned quickly, he thought as the incredible heat enveloped him. She'd learned every spot, every way to touch, to caress, until he was twisting helplessly beneath her, lost to anything except what she was doing to him.

She kept on with that hot, wet caress until his hips were bucking convulsively, and her name was a litany on his lips. He knew he had to halt her before the boiling tide became unstoppable. His body screamed in protest, crying out for the beautiful release that was so near, but he fought it down and reached to pull her beneath him.

As if following a map she'd designed, he blazed the same tingling trails over her body, nibbling at her shoulder, lingering in the hollow of her throat for a sweet, drinking kiss. He cupped and lifted her breasts, his mouth moving so quickly from one eager nipple to the other that she felt as if he were suckling them both, sending a wide, leaping ribbon of fire down her body. It cascaded through her, down to that molten pool deep inside her, every flick of his tongue adding another burst until it was overflowing, flooding her.

She watched his dark head move down her body, felt the flexing caress of his lips over her stomach and hips. She became aware she had already parted her thighs for him, and blushed furiously at the realization of how eager her body was for that sweet, intimate kiss only he had ever shown her.

"No, Nicki," he said thickly, his breath stirring the reddish curls his fingers were parting, "no shyness, not between us, not anymore."

Of course he'd known of her embarrassment, Nicki thought. Travis always knew. Just as he knew what to say to ease it. Then his mouth was on her, his tongue probing, stroking, and there was no room for any thought, only hot, rippling pleasure.

He was merciless, drinking her honeyed heat until she was crying out, his name bursting from her throat as her hips arched to him, begging, pleading for the sweet flight that was so close. Then he moved suddenly, coming up over her, and she opened for him urgently.

There were no gentle preliminaries this time, he'd pushed them too far, brought them to within a hairbreadth of the edge. He plunged into her in one fierce stroke.

"Travis!" she cried out, her voice echoing with the pleasure of the sudden, welcome invasion.

"Yes, Nicki! Ah..."

It burst from him the instant her body closed around him, holding him in a hot, sweet grip. He felt the ripple of those deep, inner muscles around him, felt the convulsion of her body as it hit that glorious peak, heard her cry his name once more, the most precious sound he'd ever heard. Then, not caring that it was over so fast as long as she was with him, he thrust hard and deep once more and let himself go, exploding in a burst of heat and sensation and swirling light.

Later, when she could move, Nicki lifted her head to look at him a little uncertainly.

"Is it . . . supposed to happen like that? So . . . fast?"

A laugh rumbled up from deep in his chest. "How would I know?"

"Well, you know more than I do," she said, blushing.

"Not about this, sweetheart. I don't know anything about the kind of bonfire we start together. "Except—" he pressed his lips to her hair "—that it could only be like this with you."

She sighed, a happy, contented sound that made him smile. She reached out a finger to touch his lips.

"What about all those girls in school?" she teased. Her tone was light, but the tiny furrow between her arched brows told him the question wasn't quite as casual as she wanted it to seem.

"To put it crudely, I would have been better off alone in the shower...there would have been more real feeling." He sighed. "I'm not proud of that, Nicole. More than once I took what was offered, even knowing I meant less than nothing to them. I don't know what I was trying to prove."

She'd almost forgotten, it seemed so impossible now, how he'd been treated then. "I'm sorry. I shouldn't have asked."

"You can ask anything." He gently lifted her chin with a finger, and said solemnly, "But there's something else you should know. After I met you, it never happened again. Every time one of those thrill-seeking little society snobs hung out her invitation, all I could think about was you. As young as you were, you were the best, the most honest person I'd ever known. You made me see them for what they were."

"I love you, Travis Halloran."

A soft smile curved his mouth. "It was worth every minute of the last fifteen years to hear that."

"You're going to hear it a lot more. I've got a lot of time to make up for."

"Oh, I hope so," he said fervently, and bent to kiss her.

An hour later, as he lay sprawled sideways on the big bed, Nicki's damp, naked, and sated body draped over him, he surrendered to the inevitable.

"I have to get going. I have some work to do."

Her head came up. "To San Diego?"

He grinned crookedly. "I didn't think you were listening. You were . . . busy."

"Oh, I was paying *very* close attention."

"I noticed." He reached up to cup her face, and lifted his head to plant a kiss on the tip of her nose. "It's only six. Stay here and go back to sleep for a while."

"I need to go to the office."

"You give more than enough time to the office. I don't want you setting foot in the place this morning. Rest for a while." The grin flashed again. "You didn't get much sleep."

She blushed, then her chin came up. "Neither did you."

"Yeah. Can't figure out why I feel so damned good."

She took a swipe at him as he scrambled out of bed, the cocky grin widening. She would, she realized as her eyes lingered on his lean, naked body striding toward bathroom and a shower, give a great deal to see that grin often.

She turned onto her side, snuggling up to the pillow that smelled of him, and without making the conscious decision to, took his suggestion and went back to sleep.

"I hope you're happy."

Nicki finished sorting the stack of mail, made a note, then carefully set the pencil she held down. Only then did she look up at her brother, who had come in and was leaning over her desk.

"Yes," she said simply. "As a matter of fact, I am." At least, as happy as I can be, she added silently, when Travis isn't here to make me think everything's all right.

"He's that good in the sack, huh?"

Her first instinct was to slap him. Only the thought of what glee Carl Weller would get out of it stopped her. Then, driven by some inner demon she didn't quite understand, she gave Richard a decidedly satisfied smile.

"Yes."

It worked. A dull, red flush crept up her brother's neck, and Nicki couldn't help laughing. He'd intended to embarrass her, and wound up discomfited himself.

"You're even blinder than I thought," Richard spat out at last. "Do you know what your . . . lover has been up to now?"

Lover, Nicki thought. What a beautiful word. "He's in San Diego," she said mildly. And wouldn't you love to know that the man you're calling names is the C.E.O. of Willow Tree of San Diego, she added to herself.

"Well, he left us a little present," Richard said with a snarl. "If you'd been here sometime before two in the afternoon, you would have known."

Nicki couldn't help blushing as she remembered why she hadn't been here this morning. She'd awakened hours later, feeling more rested and refreshed than she could remember since her mother's illness. And rather pleasantly sore in intimate places. Quickly she spoke, averting her thoughts before they became even more obvious.

"What are you talking about?"

"This."

Her brother slapped something down on her desk, nearly making her jump. She stared at it, then looked up at him in puzzlement.

"A fuse? I don't understand."

"A two hundred amp fuse. It was on the circuit for the dispatch center."

Nicki's forehead creased. "But those circuits take at least a four hundred amp fuse, don't they? A two hundred would—"

"Blow out in a couple of hours. Just like your boyfriend—" he spat out the word "—knew they would. It took all the computers down, including the load sensors. We were, for six hours, virtually out of business."

Nicki paled. "And you think Travis—"

"I *know* it."

"But he wouldn't! Besides, he's in San Diego," she repeated doggedly.

"And you're fool enough to believe that, aren't you?"

"He wouldn't lie to me." Not now, she thought desperately, not after—

"He was here. He was seen, just before seven o'clock." He gestured sharply at the blown fuse. "Just about the time that would have been put in."

"He was...here?" A chill swept her. Seven o'clock? He'd told her it was six just before she'd gone back to sleep...and he'd told her he was going directly to his office. And he'd been so adamant about her staying at the house. God, this couldn't be starting again, she'd resolved all this, hadn't she?

Quickly she tried to gather her whirling thoughts, to grasp at any straw. "I suppose it was Carl who saw him," she said. "I wouldn't believe him if he said concrete was hard."

"No." Richard smiled, a complacent twist of his lips that told her she wasn't going to like what she was about to hear. "It was Max."

"Max?" The chill turned to ice.

"Go ahead, ask him yourself." Richard reached for her phone. "I'll page him."

She heard the words echoing through the building, surprised that she could hear at all over the hammering of her heart. Max had been at Lockwood for as long as she could remember. He'd been her guardian angel at the plant as a child, when she had been pestering everyone with her questions, and her strong right hand since she'd been working here herself. He would never lie to her. Especially for Richard.

If her brother was confident enough to call Max here, he was sure of what the man would say. So it came as no surprise when the bearded man confirmed Richard's words.

"About ten to seven."

"Did you...talk to him?" Her voice wavered a little, and Max looked at her sharply, as if he guessed there was more going on here than just the suspicions about who was behind the fuse switch.

"Not really. He just waved on his way back to his car."

Nicki bit her lip. "Go ahead," Richard urged, "tell her where he came out from."

Max's brows lowered as he watched Nicki, but when she didn't speak, he answered. "The back door. Downstairs."

He didn't add that that door was right next to the circuit breaker box. He didn't have to; he knew that Nicki knew it as well as he did. And Nicki knew that what his words had meant to her was clear in her face, but she couldn't help it. The chilling, throbbing ache somewhere deep inside her was so fierce it was taking all of her will not to scream with the pain.

"Nicki . . ." Max's voice was gentle. "Maybe he was here for something else. Most of the guys, you know, they don't really believe he's got anything to do with—"

"That's enough, Max," Richard cut in. "You can go now." Max hesitated, but when Richard glowered at him he turned to go. At the door he looked back over his shoulder.

"Maybe he just—"

"That's enough," Richard repeated sharply. "Get back to work."

Max had barely closed the door when Richard turned on Nicki.

"So, are you satisfied now? You can't pass *this* off like you did the rest!"

"Go away, Richard."

"So you can think up more excuses? More reasons not to believe what's right in front of your nose? He's using you!

He's making damned sure you're too charmed to see what he's really up to. Once he gets control of your percentage, he'll destroy us, and then he'll throw you away. It's all part of his revenge on all of the Lockwoods. He can't get to Mother, so he'll use you."

"No." Nicki shook her head helplessly.

Richard snorted in scorn. "God, if I'd known what it would take to keep you in line, I would have found somebody to put in your bed years ago. I've heard of men being led around by their—"

"Get out!"

Something in her face must have convinced him he'd gone as far as he could, because he turned on his heel and left without another word. Nicki sank down into her chair, unable to stop the shudders that gripped her. Her mind was careening wildly, bouncing from the grim facts that seemed to make such an insurmountable pile to the innocent explanations that seemed so feeble in comparison.

And at last her mind came to rest on the one thing that hurt most of all: the gnawing fear that Richard might be right. Ironically, the discovery she'd made about Travis and Willow Tree leant credence to his theory; Travis didn't need a cent of the money her mother had left him. So why shouldn't he destroy Lockwood, if revenge is what he was after? He didn't need the money, so it wouldn't matter to him if he had to ruin the company just to keep Richard from having it?

But could he, knowing that destroying Lockwood would be the same as destroying her? Or was Richard right about that, too, that he was only using her, fooling her into thinking he cared so that she wouldn't look too closely?

But it couldn't be true. It couldn't all be a lie, not the way he touched her, the way he held her, the sweet, hot way he made love to her. Or the way he let her make love to him, the way he let himself go under her touch. That was part of trust, too, wasn't it? He must trust her, if he bared himself both body and soul to her in those vulnerable moments.

But he hadn't told her about Willow Tree. He'd accomplished this miracle in his life, and he hadn't trusted her with it. Even though she understood now why he hadn't, that realization did nothing to ease her doubts. If he'd lied then—even if only by omission—how could she be sure he wasn't lying about what was going on at Lockwood? Or how he felt about her?

But if he was really so twisted, out only for revenge, he wouldn't give a damn about what she thought of him. Yet she couldn't doubt the sheer, genuine emotion that had been in his voice when he had murmured against her skin how much it did matter to him. But he had never actually said that he loved her. Not once. Not even in answer to her own passionate declaration.

"Oh, God."

It was a low, quavering cry, and it echoed in the office. Nicki wrapped her arms around herself, as if she could hold herself together against the chaos mushrooming inside her. She sat there, rocking slowly back and forth, her eyes clenched tightly shut, tears streaking down her cheeks from beneath the wet spikes of her lashes.

She didn't know how long she'd been sitting there, only that when she became aware of her surroundings again, it was dark. Instinctively she reached for the light on her desk, then stopped. She found herself clinging to the dark, as if facing the light meant facing the questions she still had no answers for.

She heard footsteps in the hall, and only then realized that the sound of the outer door closing was what had roused her out of her numbed stupor. She didn't wonder who it was; she knew.

"Nicole?"

She winced as the overhead light flared on as he flipped the switch near the door. He immediately turned it off again, crossed to the desk, and turned on her desk lamp, carefully tilting the shade away from her.

"I figured you'd be here late, but what are you doing sitting here in the dark?"

She was proud of the steadiness of her voice when she answered. "Thinking. How was San Diego?"

"Fine." He chuckled. "They're doing so well without me, they've got me worried."

"Oh."

"By the way, Chuck wants to meet you."

A sudden heat flooded her as she remembered what she'd been doing during Chuck Howell's last phone call. It was followed by an uncertainty that echoed in her voice.

"He . . . does?"

Travis grinned, reading her embarrassment accurately. "I don't think it came as any surprise to him. He's a good friend. And he's known about you for a long time."

She stared at him, startled. "He has?"

He nodded. "Oh, not by name, maybe, but everything else. It wouldn't have taken much for him to put two and two together. He's a pretty sharp guy." He grinned again. "He told me you called him."

"Oh." It seemed to be all she could say.

"He was pretty impressed."

"He said that?"

"Nope. All he said was, 'Now I understand.' For Chuck, that's impressed."

"Oh."

That third short, flat answer got through to him.

"What's wrong?"

"Nothing."

For a moment he didn't move. Then, slowly, he reached out and returned the shade of the desk lamp to its original position, throwing a halo of light that reflected up to her face. He took one look at her red, swollen eyes and sucked in a sharp breath.

"What is it, Nicole? What happened?"

Nicki took a quick breath of her own, steadied herself. "Did you come here this morning?"

He looked at her quizzically. "Yes, I did. I hadn't planned to, but I left some papers here I needed to take back to the office. Why?"

"Did you . . . use the back door?"

She saw his brows lower in puzzlement. "I had to. They had a bunch of trucks pulling out. It was as close as I could get. What—"

"Do you know what this is?" With a shaking finger, she nudged the piece of metal that lay on her desk.

He drew back a little, barely glancing at the burnt-out fuse before returning his intent gaze to her face. When he answered, his voice was tight, strained, as if he had absorbed some of her own tension. Or as if he already knew why she was asking.

"A fuse. So?"

"A two hundred amp fuse, to be exact."

He waited, staring at her.

"They took it out of the dispatch center circuit this morning."

One brow lifted then. "A two hundred amp fuse? That circuit must take at least twice that."

"Exactly."

He picked it up then, turning it around in his fingers. "It blew?"

"And took the whole operation down for hours."

He let out a low whistle. "Whew. What a mess. Who the hell would put that small a fuse in..." His voice trailed off, and his gaze shot to her face. It was one of the hardest things she'd ever done, but she made herself hold his look steadily.

She watched his expression change from puzzlement to disbelief, saw his eyes widen with sick, stunned shock. "My God," he whispered, his voice harsh, catching on the words. "You think I... God, you still suspect me...even after..."

A look of nothing less than agony twisted his face. Then it was gone, replaced by a flat, dead expression that was somehow worse. And somehow, she didn't know why, painfully familiar.

"I never had a chance, did I?" His voice was as dead as the look in his eyes.

Travis tossed the burnt fuse on her desk. He sat up in the chair and squared his shoulders; that he, with his great strength, had to concentrate so hard to do it tore at Nicki, but she couldn't seem to speak. Something was stirring, deep in the recesses of her mind, and she couldn't shake the feeling that grabbing it and dragging it out to the light was the most important thing in her life.

"You win, Ms. Lockwood. I can't fight this anymore." The exhaustion in his voice echoed the tremor that momentarily shook his rigid stance. "In the morning I'll sign the papers turning my share back over to you as soon as the six months is up." Slowly, unsteadily, he got to his feet. "Then the Lockwoods—and San Remo—will be rid of me for good."

A tiny, smothered cry escaped her, but it only echoed off the door he'd closed behind him. Nicki shook with the force of her tangled emotions. Not only could she not seem to stifle that crazy feeling that it was all familiar, there was no way she could doubt his shock, no way she could deny that his agony had been real. It all boiled up inside her, seething, churning, until finally, as if rising on the mist of the maelstrom, the inescapable truth loomed before her.

Grabbing the edge of her desk for the balance she seemed to have lost, she stood up. She had to move, she had to catch him before he walked out of her life again, this time forever. Knowing that it was her own fault for not trusting him lent her the strength she so desperately needed, and she started toward the door.

A sudden clatter and a shout from outside broke the nighttime silence. She ran out and down the hall, toward the sounds. She yanked open the outside door in time to hear Carl Weller's triumphant shout.

"I got him! Red-handed this time," he was exclaiming to a somewhat bewildered-looking security guard. Nicki raced down the steps, vaguely aware of Richard coming down behind her. Why was he still here? she wondered. Late nights at work were not his style.

"Caught him tryin' to break the master switch on the re-claimer!" Weller was exulting. "Somebody coulda got hurt real bad, if I hadn't caught him!"

Nicki skidded to a halt, staring at Carl, who stood with what looked like a bat clenched in his hand, and at the still, dark shape sprawled on the ground in the shadows cast by the headlights of the security guard's truck.

"Maybe you shouldn't have hit him so hard," the guard was saying. "Might have killed him."

"No more'n he deserves," Carl said, and Nicki saw the glint of his eyes as he looked at her. It was more than his usual, avid stare, it was vicious somehow, and made her shiver. Weller laughed; it sounded like that look. Then he reached out with one foot and gave the downed man's shoulder a shove, rolling him over onto his back.

It was Travis.

III. Angstsyndrom oder gesellschaftlicher Spuk

1. Dirk Mende: [»Und immer nur die Zigarre«]

(1980)

[. . .] Zwischengeschlechtliche Beziehungen, eheliche wie
voreheliche, scheitern in diesem Roman Fontanes in allen
Schichten, auf allen Ebenen: bei den Ehelosen, den Jung-
gesellen und Jungfern (z. B. Roswitha, Johanna, Sidonie
von Grasenabb), den Verwitweten (die Zwicker u. a.), den
Verheirateten (die Briests, die Innstettens, die Crampas',
die Kruses u. a.) sowie den halbdutzend Verhältnissen, die
beiläufig erwähnt werden.

Solche Beziehungen scheitern immer dann, wenn Sexualität
zum Problem wird. Beziehungen sind nur dort intakt, wo
der Sexualität Schranken gesetzt sind: in der Liebe zu den
Eltern, in Effis Freundschaften zu den vielen alten Herren
– Gieshübler, Rummschüttel, Niemeyer, dem alten Malpro-
fessor – wie in ihrer Beziehung zu Roswitha.

Effis illusorische wie irreale Vorstellungen von der Ehe
werden durch die Erfahrung zurechtgestutzt. Ihr Anspruch
»Liebe kommt zuerst« [S. 29] bleibt unerfüllt. »Ein Liebha-
ber war er nicht« [S. 102], so klagt Effi über den eisigen
Innstetten, nicht mal ein Kuß, »frostig wie ein Schnee-
mann. Und immer nur die Zigarre« [S. 66], müde Zärtlich-
keiten allenfalls [S. 102 f.], Tristesse des Ehealltags wie
auch der Nächte. »Und fremd war er auch in seiner Zärtlich-
keit. Ja, dann am meisten« [S. 219] – sofern es zu Zärtlich-
keiten überhaupt reicht. »Ich will nichts[!] als dich ansehen
und mich freuen, daß ich dich habe« [S. 147]. Nicht zuletzt
begünstigt Innstettens inszenierter Chinesenspuk, sein
»Angstapparat aus Kalkül« [S. 135], was er eigentlich verhindern sollte: den Ehebruch. [. . .]

*Dirk Mende: Frauenleben. Bemerkungen zu Fontanes ›L'Adultera‹
nebst Exkursen zu ›Cécile‹ und ›Effi Briest‹. In: Fontane aus
heutiger Sicht, hrsg. von Hugo Aust. Nymphenburger Verlagshand-
lung, München 1980, S. 183–213. Hier S. 200. Ausschnitt.*

2. Walter Müller-Seidel: [Die Spukgestalt oder die Gesellschaftlichkeit der Angst]

(1975)

[. . .] In einer unverkennbar humoristischen Tonart werden wir mit ihr [der Spukgestalt] bekannt gemacht. Man
unterhält sich über die slawische Bevölkerung rund um
Kessin, über die Kaschuben, die den heutigen Leser unwei-
gerlich an die Umwelt der ›Blechtrommel‹ erinnern.
Schließlich ist das Gespräch unversehens bei Negern, Tür-
ken und Chinesen angelangt. In diesem Zusammenhang ist
es ein toter Chinese – »sehr schön und sehr schauerlich« –,
über den Innstetten beiläufig, aber in einem humoristischen
Ton plaudert; worauf Effi erwidert: »Ja, schauerlich, und
ich möchte wohl mehr davon wissen. Aber doch lieber
nicht, ich habe dann immer gleich Visionen und Träume
und möchte doch nicht, wenn ich diese Nacht hoffentlich
gut schlafe, gleich einen Chinesen an mein Bett treten
sehen« [S. 43]. Das in gewisser Hinsicht Unernste und
Triviale solcher Erwähnungen ist offenkundig. So jedenfalls
stellt es sich dem in seinen Prinzipien gefestigten Innstetten
dar. Die Art, wie sich der tote Chinese im Haus der jungen
Eheleute einzuleben beginnt, bestätigt das merkwürdig
Spielerische und Beiläufige dieser Hausgenossenschaft. An
einem durchgesessenen Binsenstuhl (damit nur ja auch den
Gegenständen alles Feierliche genommen werde) entdeckt
man eines Tages ein aufgeklebtes Bildchen. Es stellt einen
Chinesen dar: blauer Rock mit gelben Pluderhosen und
einem flachen Hut auf dem Kopf. Effi ist betroffen und
fragt: »Was soll der Chinese?« Worauf Innstetten versi-
chert, daß er das auch nicht wisse: »Das hat Christel
angeklebt oder Johanna. Spielerei. Du kannst sehen, es ist
aus einer Fibel herausgeschnitten.« Effi sieht das ein – und
bleibt doch verwundert, »daß Innstetten alles so ernsthaft
nahm, als ob es doch etwas sei« [S. 59]. Jetzt sind wir
unsererseits ein wenig verwundert, weil wir nicht mehr
recht wissen, woran wir sind. Ist doch nicht alles Scherz,
und ist womöglich dabei doch ein Ernst im Spiel? fragt man

sich, um sogleich zu erkennen, daß der Motivkomplex in der Tat eine sehr ernste Seite hat. Er betrifft Effis rege Phantasie, wie sie ihrer jugendlichen Erscheinung entspricht. Diese sie beherrschende Phantasie produziert Angst, und in ihrer Angst beruht der Ernst der Sache, die 5 Innstetten in dem, was sie für seine Frau bedeuten könnte, hoffnungslos verschlossen bleibt. Von Innstettens »Angstapparat« ist nun die Rede, und was das zu bedeuten hat, beginnt Effi nach dem für sie so erhellenden Gespräch mit Crampas zu begreifen: »was Crampas gemeint hatte, war 10 viel, viel mehr, war eine Art Angstapparat aus Kalkül. Es fehlte jede Herzensgüte darin und grenzte schon fast an Grausamkeit. [. . .] ›Also Spuk aus Berechnung, Spuk, um dich in Ordnung zu halten.‹« [S. 135f.] [. . .]

Auf das Phänomen der Angst war Fontane wiederholt 15 aufmerksam geworden. In seiner Besprechung von Ibsens Drama ›Die Frau vom Meer‹ kommt er auf sie zu sprechen und tadelt das dort angewandte Heilverfahren. Er erwähnt in diesem Zusammenhang eine Tochter des Herzogs von Hamilton, die in den zwanziger Jahren von Angstvisionen 20 verfolgt worden sei: »Es waren Schreckgestalten aus den Propheten oder aus der Apokalypse [. . .] Drachen, geflügelte Ringeltiere, vielleicht auch Satan in Person.« Geheilt worden sei sie durch Dr. Koreff, einen Freund von E. T. A. Hoffmann, Devrient und Hitzig.[3] Es war also ein durch- 25 aus zeitgemäßes Thema, das Fontane aufgriff, um es zur Motivierung seiner Romanhandlung zu verwenden; und dabei handelt es sich um keine zeitlose Angst, sondern um eine solche, die mit der Zeitlage zusammenhängt. Ehe sie um 1910 unter der dann sich ausbreitenden Wirkung Kier- 30 kegaards das alles beherrschende Thema wird, entdeckt sie Fontane für seine Zwecke; und fast ist man geneigt zu sagen, er denkt dabei vor Freud über Freud hinaus: denn er macht aus dem psychologischen ein sozialpsychologisches Thema – dadurch, daß er die Gesellschaftlichkeit der Angst 35

(3) Theodor Fontane, in: Aufsätze, Kritiken, Erinnerungen, Band 2. Carl Hanser, München 1969, S. 795.

sichtbar macht. Denn um eine gesellschaftlich motivierte Angst recht eigentlich ist es Fontane zu tun. [. . .]

Walter Müller-Seidel: Theodor Fontane. Soziale Romankunst in
5 *Deutschland. J. B. Metzler, Stuttgart 1975, S. 362–364. Aus-*
schnitte.

3. Edvard Munch: Angst

Edvard Munch (1863–1944): Angst (1896). Lithographie, 41,5×39 cm. In: Der Expressionismus in Wort und Bild. Text von Wolf-Dieter Dube. Editions d'Art Albert Skira, SA, Genf. Verlagsgemeinschaft Ernst Klett – J. G. Cotta'sche Buchhandlung Nachfolger, Stuttgart 1983, S. 18.

4. Gisela Warnke:
[Der Spuk als Strukturelement des Romans]

(1978)

[. . .] Die Erwähnung des Chinesen, um den der Spuk im
Kessiner Landratshaus kreist, kann demnach einen Ein-
blick gewähren in den Bau des Romans. Unter den Roman-
motiven ist das vom gespenstischen Chinesen das auffällig-
ste, weil dem Verstand anstößigste. Man kann es als »an
und für sich interessant« auf den Grad der Anschaulichkeit
oder Verborgenheit prüfen, man kann sein szenisches
Ambiente untersuchen und seine Kraft, beim Leser Span-
nung zu erzeugen. Um den Spuk als »Drehpunkt« zu
begreifen, müssen die Leistungen erkannt werden, die ihm
für den Handlungsverlauf des Romans und bei der Perso-
nenzeichnung zukommen.

Bezogen auf das zentrale Dreieck der Konfiguration Effi –
Innstetten – Crampas ergeben sich folgende Funktionen:

1. Der Spuk dient der Erfüllung romantischer Sehnsüchte
Effis, die auf Apartes und Abwechslung aus ist. Er bedroht
Effi aber auch in der beginnenden Vereinsamung, beson-
ders bei Abwesenheit des Gatten, durch vielfach erneuer-
ten Schreck und permanente Angst nach dem ersten
Erscheinen des Chinesen.

2. Der Spuk liefert das Gleichnis einer Liebesgeschichte
(mit im unklaren gelassener Art der leidenschaftlichen
Bindung) zu der Affäre zwischen Effi und dem ›Damen-
mann‹ Crampas, wobei die Beziehung den Zug des Unaus-
weichlichen annimmt. Schließlich fällt die Rettungsmöglich-
keit aus der Verstrickung zusammen mit der erhofften
Rettung vor dem Spuk durch das gleiche Ereignis: der
räumlichen Entfernung aus dem kleinen Spukort Kessin an
der pommerschen Ostseeküste nach Berlin, Hauptstadt des
Königreichs Preußen und Sitz des Kaisers und seines Kanz-
lers, des Fürsten Bismarck. Das Mißlingen der Rettung
wird angekündigt durch triviale Handlung: Der Chinese
übersiedelt in Gestalt eines Bildchens im Portemonnaie des
Hausmädchens Johanna mit nach Berlin.

3. Der Spuk dient der speziellen Charakteristik Innstettens. Auf direkte Weise geschieht dies durch die Gesprächsführung Innstettens, halb Aufklärung, halb Bestärkung des Gespensterglaubens, als teils unbewußte, teils bewußte
5 Selbstcharakteristik. Auf indirekte Weise erfolgt die Charakterisierung des Landrats durch gezielte Indiskretionen des Rivalen Crampas gegenüber der begehrten Effi: die Erzählung vom Spuk sei Innstettens Mittel, die junge Frau zu beherrschen zum Zwecke der »Erziehung«, vor allem
10 vor jeder dienstlichen Abwesenheit; das Spukthema sei ferner Innstettens Mittel, sich interessant zu machen zum Zwecke der Karriere. Der Ortswechsel Kessin–Berlin steht im Zeichen der Karriere und diese im Magnetfeld Bismarcks.
15 4. In Parallele zur schwebenden Verwendung der Spukgeschichte durch Innstetten steht Fontanes Handhabung des Motivs ›Spuk‹ im ganzen Roman. Die Stellungnahme Innstettens wird keiner eindeutigen Entscheidung zugeführt, sondern hält sich in der Schwebe. Ebenso bleibt die Gel-
20 tung des Phänomens in der Schwebe: Realität oder Traumphantasie. In dieser Unentschiedenheit, die nicht Schwäche ist, sondern Bündelung von Perspektiven zum Ziele hat, kann eine Analogie zum Ausgang des Romans gesehen werden: auch die Schuld am Mißlingen der Ehe wird als ein
25 Komplex verschiedenster Einflüsse und Handlungen in dem Schlußgespräch der Eltern widersprüchlich vor den Leser gebracht und bleibt ein »*zu* weites Feld« [S. 301].

Fontane »dreht« auch Instettens Haltung gegenüber dem Spuk: Aus der souveränen Verfügung über die Erscheinung
30 wird eigenes Erschrecken, gegenläufig zur Haltung Effis, die vom krank machenden Schreck zu einer Gewöhnung gelangt, statt dessen aber unter dem Schock realer Erlebnisse erkrankt. Was ängstigendes Erblicken des Chinesen für Effi bedeutet, entspricht, vergleichbar, bei Innstetten in
35 der Erinnerung an das Duell mit Crampas dem »Blick« des Sterbenden, »den er immer vor Augen hatte« [S. 290], ein Anblick, der dem zielstrebig Aufsteigenden die beruflichen Erfolge für immer fragwürdig macht.

5. Der Spuk wird zu einer Art ›Orakel‹ mit zwingender

Wirkung, die den Spielraum zwischen Magie, Kraft des Glaubens/Aberglaubens und psychischer Verfassung wechselweise innehat.

6. Der Spuk ist romantechnisch oder ›dramaturgisch‹ ein dem Hauptvorgang zugeordnetes Motiv. 5

Bei der Betrachtung dieser Funktionen fällt auf, daß Fontane bei der Verwendung des Spuks auf die Ambivalenz oder Polyvalenz ihres Einsatzes achtet und der Spukgeschichte eine differenzierte Dynamik verleiht, die Konsequenzen hervorruft. Sie durchwirkt die Folge der Kapitel. 10 Deshalb kann »diese ganze Geistertummelage« [S. 79] ikonographische Hinweise geben, die eine Strukturanalyse des Romans ermöglichen. [. . .]

Gisela Warnke: Der Spuk als ›Drehpunkt‹ in Fontanes ›Effi Briest‹. *Ein Beitrag zur Strukturanalyse des Romans. In: Literatur für* 15 *Leser, 1978, Heft 3, S. 214–242. Hier S. 216–218. Ausschnitt.*

IV. Zeitalter der Prinzipien

1. J. B. Engl: Das hohe Roß

Zeichnung, 1896. In: Facsimile Querschnitt durch den Simplicissimus. Hrsg. Christian Schätze. Scherz Verlag, München 1963, S. 37.

2. Duell-Debatte im Reichstag 1886

Rechtsverstoß

ABGEORDNETER DR. PETER REICHENSPERGER (Zentrum):
»Meine Herrn, ich werde wohl keinem Widerspruch begeg-
nen, wenn ich sage, daß die große Mehrheit der Nation 5
dem immer mehr überhandnehmenden Duellunwesen mit
Unwillen gegenübersteht und Abhilfe erwartet. Ich kann
hinzufügen, daß auch aus der Mitte derjenigen, welche das
Duell nicht grundsätzlich verwerfen, wiederholte und laute
Klagen ausgesprochen worden sind über die vielfachen 10
Auswüchse auf diesem Gebiete und über das Überhandneh-
men der Duelle in der Gegenwart. Es vergeht ja kaum eine
Woche, in welcher nicht die Tagespresse in stehender
Rubrik über Duelle zu berichten hat zwischen Studenten,
Offizieren, Referendaren, Journalisten und anderen Gebil- 15
deten, sowie über die vielfach tragischen Opfer, die hier
fallen. Ich will hierbei auch kein Wort verlieren über die in
letzter Zeit sich wiederholenden Duellforderungen von
Landräthen gegen Selbstverwaltungsbeamte wegen ihrer
amtlichen Wirksamkeit. Ich glaube, daß diese Sache sich 20
von selbst erledigt.
Nun, meine Herrn, bei diesen überhandnehmenden Duel-
len handelt es sich zunächst um einen widerchristlichen
moralischen Schaden, der meiner Anschauung nach nicht
überall ausreichend gewürdigt wird, trotz der vielfachen 25
Warnungszeichen, die uns entgegentreten. Aber es handelt
sich zugleich um eine soziale Frage im eminenten Sinne des
Worts, weil hier einem irregeleiteten Ehrgefühl, ja vielfach
kleinlichsten konventionellen Empfindlichkeiten die Zu-
kunftshoffnungen von Individuen und von Familien geop- 30
fert werden zum Schaden der Gesamtheit. Und endlich,
meine Herrn, handelt es sich für eine politische Körper-
schaft wie die unsrige noch um ein ganz anderes, nämlich
um die systematische Verletzung von Gesetzen, die dieser
Reichstag in Anerkennung ihrer Gerechtigkeit und Noth- 35
wendigkeit mit gegeben hat, und deren Handhabung und
Beobachtung er darum auch mit zu überwachen hat. [...]

Nein, meine Herrn, ich glaube, auf dem Wege kann und darf es nicht fortgehen. Wir sind meiner Meinung nach vor einem kategorischen Entweder-Oder angekommen: entweder muß man die bestehenden Duellstrafen kassiren in den
5 bürgerlichen wie in den militärischen Strafgesetzen, oder man muß diese Strafe ernstlich nehmen, ernstlich anwenden, nicht mit Glacéehandschuhen.

Gebot der Ehre

ABGEORDNETER PAUL VON REINHABEN (Deutsche Reichspar-
10 tei): [. . .] Der Gipfel der Verkehrtheit wäre es aber, wenn man das Duell auf ein und dieselbe Linie stellen wollte. Mit dem gemeinen Mord oder Todschlag, wie das ja, ich weiß nicht ob heute, aber jedenfalls in der Petitionskommission, als über die Frage dort berathen wurde, empfohlen worden
15 ist. [. . .]
Nun, ich meine doch, daß diejenigen, welche in dem Duell weiter nichts erblicken, als Mord, Todschlag oder gemeine Verwundung
(Zuruf: Körperverletzung!)
20 – oder wenn Sie wollen, Körperverletzung, den Charakter des Duells vollständig verkennen, daß diese geflissentlich seine Motive ignoriren, die doch bei Beurtheilung der Strafbarkeit einer Handlung nicht außer Betracht bleiben dürfen.
25 Meine Herren, ich habe die Überzeugung, daß das Duell niemals gänzlich in Deutschland verschwinden wird, und ich glaube, es wäre auch gar kein wünschenswerther Zustand, wenn dies dennoch geschähe. Die ideale Auffassung, die sich im deutschen Volke von dem Wesen der Ehre
30 entwickelt hat, bedingt unter Umständen die Nothwendigkeit des Duells, und wir können nicht wünschen, daß diese ideale Auffassung uns künftig einmal abhanden komme. Durch das Duell soll der Überzeugung Ausdruck gegeben werden, daß die Ehre höher steht als das Leben
35 (Lachen im Zentrum),
und daß ein Leben ohne Ehre keinen Werth hat. – Meine Herren, Sie lachen darüber;

(Rufe: Ja!)

aber ich glaube, wir folgen einem tief eingewurzelten Gefühle, wenn wir uns für verpflichtet halten, sobald mit Bewußtsein unsere persönliche Ehre verletzt ist, durch Einsetzung unseres Lebens das ungeschmälerte Vorhandensein dieser Ehre zu erweisen. Meine Herrn, wenn jemand öffentlich durch Thätlichkeiten oder durch ungerechtfertigte Beschuldigungen einer ehrenrührigen Handlung in den Augen seiner Mitmenschen erniedrigt und dadurch in seiner ganzen moralischen Existenz gefährdet wird, wenn ein Gatte, ein Vater durch Verführung der Frau, der Tochter den denkbar größten Schimpf erleidet, dann, meine Herrn, sagt uns ein kategorischer Imperativ in unserem Innern, daß die uns angethane Schmach mit dem Leben des Beleidigers gesühnt werden muß und nur auf diese Weise gesühnt werden kann. Das Duell ist nach deutscher Anschauung die ultima ratio der ehrenhaften Leute zum Schutze gegen diejenigen, welche ihr höchstes Gut, die Ehre, freventlich antasten.

Allerdings läßt sich nicht leugnen, daß das Duell ein schwerer eigenmächtiger Eingriff in die allgemeine Rechtsordnung ist; aber wenn meine moralische Existenz auf dem Spiele steht, kann ich niemanden anders, wie mich selbst, als Richter über meine Ehre anerkennen. Ich kann platterdings nicht Ehre und Existenz abhängig machen von dem Ausspruch eines Richters; denn es handelt sich um Güter, die ein jeder selbst verteidigen muß.

Diese ideale Auffassung von dem Wesen der persönlichen Ehre ist an keine Klasse und an keinen Stand gebunden; sie ist ein Gemeingut der deutschen Nation. Von dieser Auffassung ausgehend, haben wir in dem Duell nicht anderes als die in bestimmte regelrechte Formen gebannte Prozedur zu erblicken, durch welche der unwiderstehliche Drang zum Ausdruck kommt, die angegriffene Ehre durch den Einsatz des Lebens zurückzuerkämpfen. Wenn wir die Bestätigung dieses Dranges verhindern wollten, zu welchen Zuständen würden wir gelangen? Könnten wir etwa das für einen erfreulichen Zustand ansehen, wenn gegenüber dem Verführer der Frau oder der Tochter der betreffende Gatte

331

oder Vater seine verletzte Ehre dadurch für vollständig
repariert erachtet, daß er vom Richter einige hundert oder
tausend Pfund Sterling zugesprochen erhält? Oder aber wir
gelangen zu Zuständen, wie sie in einigen Gegenden Ita-
5 liens bestehen, wo die Vendetta herrscht, und die alte
Blutrache Landessitte ist. Wir verhüten solche Zustände
durch das Duell mit seinen festen konventionellen Regeln
und Formeln, deren genaue Beobachtung selbst wieder ein
Gebot der Ehre ist. [. . .]

10 *Stenographische Berichte. Verhandlungen des Reichstags. VI.*
Legislaturperiode. IV. Session, 1. Band. Berlin 1887, S. 173–174
und S. 187–188 (10. Sitzung, 13. Dezember 1886). Ausschnitte.

3. Verhandlungen des im Jahre 1848 zusam-
menberufenen Vereinigten ständischen
15 ## Ausschusses zum Ehe- und Familienrecht

JUSTIZ-MINISTER VON SAVIGNY: Wenn jetzt in Frage steht, ob
beide Geschlechter [bei Ehebruch] gleich zu strafen sind,
oder eine Verschiedenheit der Strafe angenommen werden
soll, wie ich glaube, so erlaube ich mir, darauf Folgendes zu
20 sagen: Der Entwurf ist von der Ansicht ausgegangen, daß
der Ehebruch der Frau eine schwerere Strafe verdiene, als
der Ehebruch des Mannes. Die Gründe, welche diesem
Theile des Entwurfs zum Grunde liegen, sind folgende: 1)
die Ueberzeugung, daß durch den Ehebruch die Frau tiefer
25 sinkt als der Mann, weil sie vorzugsweise vor dem Manne
ihren Lebensberuf in der Familie hat, während der Mann in
vielen anderen Beziehungen der Welt angehört. Dazu
kommt 2) ein diese Ueberzeugung bestätigendes allgemei-
nes Gefühl, das Gefühl nämlich, welches dahin geht, daß der
30 Mann in seiner Stellung, in seiner Ehre ungleich tiefer
verletzt sei durch den Ehebruch der Frau, als umgekehrt.
Das ist ein Gefühl, welches allgemein anerkannt ist. Es ist
die allgemeine Ansicht, daß der Mann, welcher wissentlich
einen fortgesetzten Ehebruch der Frau duldet, geringge-
35 schätzt wird, während die den Ehebruch des Mannes still

duldende Frau häufig Anspruch auf besondere Achtung und auf Mitgefühl haben wird. So entscheidet das allgemeine Gefühl zwischen beiden Handlungen. Es erkennt an, daß die Verletzung des Mannes und der Ehe durch den Ehebruch der Frau viel höher 5 steht. [. . .]

ABGEORDNETER FREIHERR VON GAFFRON: Es ist nicht in Abrede zu stellen, daß durch den Ehebruch der Frau ein größeres Unglück in die Familie gebracht wird, als durch den Ehebruch des Mannes, indem dadurch die Reinheit 10 der Familie vernichtet, und unächte Glieder in dieselbe eingeschwärzt werden können. Deshalb haben alle älteren Gesetzgebungen die Frau härter bestraft als den Mann. Ich gebe zu, daß der Mann durch den Ehebruch nicht so tief fällt als die Frau, weil ihm andere Gebiete des Wirkens und 15 Strebens offen stehen. Die Frau fällt aber tiefer als der Mann, weil ihr Beruf als Mutter und Gattin ihr höchster ist. Auf der anderen Seite darf aber nicht verkannt werden, daß die Frau in der Regel stärker an Leidenschaften und schwächer an Vernunft ist, 20
(Viele Stimmen: Oho!)
das heißt, daß die Frau in der Regel die Verführte, daß sie der schwächere Theil, daß das männliche Geschlecht das stärkere und der verführende Theil ist. Aus diesem Grunde stimme ich dafür, daß beide Geschlechter gleich bestraft 25 werden. [. . .]

JUSTIZ-MINISTER VON SAVIGNY: Ich bitte um die Erlaubniß, noch einen Grund anführen zu dürfen, das ist nämlich der: die große Unsicherheit der Paternität[4], welche durch den Treubruch der Frau entsteht, während diese durch den 30 Treubruch des Ehemannes nicht hervorgerufen wird, und diese Unsicherheit ist es, welche das Wesen der Ehe und das natürliche Verhältniß zu den Kindern in hohem Grade gefährdet.

ABGEORDNETER STEINBECK: Daß das Unheil, welches durch 35 den Ehebruch der Frau in der Familie angerichtet wird, viel größer sei, als dasjenige, was durch den Ehebruch des

---

(4)* Vaterschaft.

Mannes angerichtet wird, ist hinreichend beleuchtet worden. Es läßt sich nicht leugnen, daß, wenn man das Unheil allein ins Auge faßt, man dafür sprechen müßte, die Frau härter zu bestrafen; aber es ist schon angeführt worden, daß
5 die Frau in der Regel der verführte Theil, der Mann der Angreifer ist. Dies macht es, daß das, was von dem größeren Unheile des Ehebruches der Frau gesagt worden ist, hierdurch wieder aufgewogen wird, und ich bemerke, daß unsere Vorfahren ebenfalls derselben Meinung waren, und
10 den Ehebruch gleich hart bestraften, mochte er von der Ehefrau oder dem Ehemanne geschehen. [. . .]

Verhandlungen des im Jahre 1848 zusammenberufenen Vereinigten ständischen Ausschusses. Zusammengestellt von Eduard Bleich. Band 3. Verlag der Deckerschen Geheimen Ober-Hofbuchdrucke-
15 *rei, Berlin 1848, S. 411–414. Zitiert nach: Text und Dialog. Hrsg. von Norbert Heinze und Bernd Schurf. August Bagel Verlag, Düsseldorf 1979, S. 197f. Ausschnitte.*

4. Rudolf Morsey: [Bismarcks Bürokratie]

(1957)
20 [. . .] Der Kanzler [Bismarck] ließ im Großen wie im Kleinen des Dienstbetriebs eine strenge Sorgfalt walten, die er umgekehrt von allen Beamten verlangte. Die Aktenerledigung und -vorlage, die Formen der Korrespondenz, von Einladungen, Mitteilungen und Erlassen – kurz, der
25 gesamte Schriftwechsel mit der damit verbundenen Aktenerledigung mußte sich innerhalb genau vorgeschriebener Kurialien und Normen vollziehen. Das Außerachtlassen solcher Formen, die ungenaue Verwendung von Titeln und Anreden oder die falsche Anordnung von Adelsprädikaten,
30 Ungenauigkeiten in Stil, Ausdruck und Schrift: solche »Vergehen« zogen geharnischte Randbemerkungen und nicht selten einen dienstlichen Verweis nach sich. Dabei war der Fürst, wie auch sonst, schnell zum Tadeln bereit, selten zu lobender Anerkennung. [. . .]
35 Ein Erlaß vom 2. Dezember 1881, der die unleserlichen

Unterschriften monierte, wurde den Beamten am 22. September 1885 sowie am 15. Januar 1890 auf dem nicht alltäglichen Wege des Abdrucks in der Presse erneut eingeschärft. Am 28. Februar 1880 verbot Bismarck bei »steigender Ordnungsstrafe« allen Reichsbehörden, sich der neuen 5 vom preußischen Kultusminister v. Puttkamer eingeführten Rechtschreibung zu bedienen. In Reinkonzepten mußten Sätze aus anderen Schriftstücken durch rote und blaue Klammern deutlich gemacht werden (19. Dezember 1867). Jedes Schriftstück, das dem Kanzler zugeleitet wurde – 10 sofern es länger als vier Seiten war, mußte es paginiert sein (20. November 1880, 20. März 1889) –, sollte den Namen des betreffenden Referenten tragen, um unnötige Rückfragen überflüssig zu machen. Kein Aktenstück durfte schwerer sein als 2 kg (14. Februar 1874); eine bestimmte Sorte von 15 roten Aktendeckeln mußte aus dem Verkehr gezogen werden, als Bismarck sah, daß diese abfärbten (11. Juni 1881, 15. März, 7. April 1888). Den Akten beigefügte Anlagen mußten sorgfältig geordnet sein, da für Bismarck durch einen »Mangel an Ordnung in der Form« die Arbeit 20 erschwert wurde [. . .]

Rudolf Morsey: Die oberste Reichsverwaltung unter Bismarck 1867–1890. Aschendorff, Münster 1957, S. 277–279. Ausschnitte.

V. Literarische Techniken

1. Carin Liesenhoff: [Epische Rollendistanz als literarische Angriffswaffe]

(1976)

5 ›Effi Briest‹ ist zu einer Zeit entstanden, wo Fontanes
radikal-kritische Haltung gegenüber der preußischen aristokratischen Gesellschaft ihre extremste Zuspitzung erfahren
hat, wo er, wie er sich ausdrückte, »mit dem Adel, hohen
und niedrigen, fertig« war. Sätze über den Adel als »traurige
10 Figuren«, die nur noch ein Recht haben, als »privateste
Privatleute« zu existieren, waren bereits gefallen. Dennoch
liegt auch mit dem Roman ›Effi Briest‹ keine literarische
›Abrechnung‹ mit dem Adel etwa in Form einer Satire oder
eines dezidiert sozialkritischen Werkes vor. Vielmehr
15 macht Fontane eine bis dahin noch nicht erreichte epische
Rollendistanz zu seiner literarischen Angriffswaffe, indem
er in der Flaubertschen Erzählhaltung der »impassibilité«
den Automatismus der gesellschaftlich verbindlichen Wert-
und Normensysteme der aristokratischen Gesellschaft in
20 logischer Gesetzmäßigkeit bis zur unvermeidlichen Kata-
strophe ablaufen läßt.

Aber der Roman ›Effi Briest‹ ist nicht nur der »Roman der
feinen Gesellschaft«, sondern zugleich auch ein klassischer
Eheroman der zweiten Hälfte des 19. Jahrhunderts, dessen
25 Besonderheit darin liegt, daß ihm die das Bürgertum vor-
rangig interessierenden Eheprobleme und Konflikte zu-
grunde liegen, deren detaillierte epische Ausgestaltung sich
aber angesichts der bürgerlichen Lesererwartungen über
den ›sittlichen‹ Gehalt von Literatur und über eine ›mora-
30 lisch einwandfreie‹ und ›intakte‹ Ehe verbot. Mit der Wahl
des Genres des Gesellschaftsromans und dessen spezifi-
schem Formprinzip der verhaltenen und aussparenden
Darstellung von Liebes- und Ehekonflikten gelingt es Fontane, sowohl den bürgerlichen Lesererwartungen zu ent-
35 sprechen als auch die Möglichkeiten des Gesellschaftsro-

mans bis zum virtuosen Spiel mit ihm zu nutzen, indem er
aus den gesellschaftlichen Handlungsselbstverständlichkei-
ten der aristokratischen Gesellschaft folgerichtig das tödli-
che Ende erwachsen läßt. [. . .]

Carin Liesenhoff: Fontane und das literarische Leben seiner Zeit. 5
Bouvier Verlag, Bonn 1976, S. 103 f. Ausschnitt.

2. Peter Demetz:
Das symbolische Motiv der Schaukel

(1964)
In der Charakterisierung Effi Briests erscheint das Motiv 10
des Fluges, gesteigert durch eine Konstellation gegenständ-
licher Korrelate, zum wesentlichen Elemente erhoben;
offenbar deutet es, wenn man ein vom frühen Fontane oft
zitiertes Wort des achtzehnten Jahrhunderts nachsprechen
darf, auf den hervorstechenden Charakterzug (faculté maî- 15
tresse) ihrer Natur. Verräterisch wieder das Heftige, Flie-
gende, Jugendhafte ihrer Gestik, das mit der konventionellen Jungmädchensitte ihrer adeligen Kreise kontrastiert:
»rasch, rasch, ich fliege aus« [S. 12], ruft sie ihren Gespie-
linnen entgegen; wenige Augenblicke vor der Verlobung 20
noch beobachtet sie der Leser in der Heftigkeit des Spieles.
Der ihr geneigte Erzähler muß gestehen: »sie flog [da]hin«
[S. 13] [. . .]
Die ironische Variation des Bildes von der »Tochter der
Luft« bestätigt auf ihre Weise, wie intim Effis Vorliebe für 25
das Klettern und ihre Leidenschaft für das Schaukeln
zusammengehören. Beide entspringen dem gleichen drän-
genden Impuls; beide entfalten sich, indem sie die Jahre
der Kindheit überdauern, jenseits des eigentlich Schickli-
chen, des Dekorums, der vorgeschriebenen Mädchensitte. 30
Merkwürdig, wie Effi ihre geliebte Schaukel aus den Jahren
der Kindheit in die spätere Epoche ihres Mädchen- und
Frauentums hinüberrettet: Es ist, als wollte Fontane in
ihrer Starrköpfigkeit das eigentlich Unwandelbare ihres
Charakters betonen. Bedeutungsvoll, wie der Autor die 35
altersschwache Schaukel, die so lange Dienst getan, schon

auf der ersten Seite des Romans auf das genaueste lokalisiert. *Dicht* an jenem Rondell, in dem wir Effis zum ersten Male ansichtig werden, steht die »Schaukel . . ., deren horizontal gelegtes Brett zu Häupten und Füßen an je zwei
5 Stricken hing – die Pfosten der Balkenlage schon etwas schief stehend« [S. 3]. Dieses Rondell aber ist der gleiche Ort, an dem der Leser Effi zuletzt verläßt: ihre Grabstätte. Unaufdringlich, so scheint es, hat Fontane von allem Anfang an das Zeichen ihres Verlangens nach dem schwe-
10 relosen Glück emblematisch an den Rand ihres künftigen Grabes gestellt. Ja noch mehr: Fontane hat es sich [. . .] angelegen sein lassen, das Bild der Schaukel dreimal – gleichsam als Effis eigentliches Schicksals- und Todesmotiv – aufscheinen zu lassen: einmal kurz vor ihrer Eheschlie-
15 ßung; ein zweites Mal während ihrer Ehe; zuletzt, kurz vor ihrem Tode. [. . .]
Die vielfältigen Implikationen der symbolischen Elemente im Bilde des Klettermastes und der Schaukel finden ihre Bestätigung in dem an entscheidenden Orten wiederkeh-
20 renden Motiv der Schlittenfahrt. Effis Freude an raschen Schlittenfahrten ist selbst jenen wohlbekannt, die nicht tief in ihre Natur zu blicken vermögen; selbst Instetten, ein eher pädagogisches als psychologisches Talent, verspricht Effi willkommene Aufmunterung von einer Schlittenpartie und
25 erinnert sie an »das Geläut« und »die weißen Schneedek-
ken« [S. 81]. Damit verrät er, wie wenig er sie wirklich kennt; gesellschaftliche Äußerlichkeiten sind für Effi von geringer Bedeutung. Sie selbst belehrt ihn eines anderen: Während der Schlitten dahingleitet, bekennt sie sich uner-
30 wartet zu einem gefährlicheren Genuß – »es ist ja himm-
lisch, so hinzufliegen, und ich fühle ordentlich, wie mir so frei wird und wie alle Angst von mir abfällt« [S. 83f.]; merkwürdige Worte einer Jungverheirateten! Noch deutli-
cher wird Effi, als sie mit der frömmelnden und auf gesell-
35 schaftliche Sicherheiten bedachten Sidonie von einer Weih-
nachtsfeier heimfährt. Halb provoziert von Sidonies Vor-
wurf, daß sie sich recht sorglos aus dem mit keinerlei Schutzleder versehenen Schlitten lehne, bekennt Effi, daß die Gefahr sie bezaubere: ». . . wenn ich hinausflöge, mir

wär' es recht, am liebsten gleich in die Brandung« [S. 159].
Damit ist die dritte und entscheidende Wiederkehr des
Motivs vorbereitet und begründet. Als man die Schlitten
wechseln muß, findet sich Effi in einem Gefährt mit dem in
Leidenschaft entbrannten Crampas: Während es »im   5
Fluge« [S. 163] den anderen Schlitten nachgeht, entschei-
det sich ihr Schicksal.

Hier ist ein für die Organisation des Romans entscheiden-
der Augenblick erreicht – die gesamte Entfaltung des Flug-
motivs und seiner Elemente scheint immer wieder auf   10
diesen einen Augenblick hinzudeuten. Es ist nicht schwer
einzusehen, warum: Wer, meint Fontane, seiner tiefsten
Natur nach den Betörungen einer solchen Schwerelosigkeit
notwendig zustrebt, der kann nicht zu Recht schuldig
gesprochen werden. Effi unterliegt in einem Augenblick   15
süßen Schauerns jenseits bewußter Verantwortung; deshalb
darf sie Anspruch auf Milderungsgründe erheben. Effis
Natur, an deren Zeichnung das Flugmotiv so entscheidenden Anteil hat, ist zugleich ihre Apologie. Da Fontane
innerhalb der literarischen Konventionen eines ›realisti- 20
schen‹ d.h. ›objektiv‹ dargestellten Geschehens nicht
unmittelbar an den Leser appellieren darf, plädiert er meta-
phorisch.

Peter Demetz: Formen des Realismus: Theodor Fontane. Kritische
Untersuchungen. Carl Hanser Verlag, München 1964, S. 210–215. 25
Ausschnitte.

3. Cordula Kahrmann: [Wasser und Rondell]

(1973)
[. . .] Nur in den phantastischen, für ihre Umgebung unverbindlichen und daher wirkungslosen Vorstellungen von der 30
Gefahr des Kletterns und Schaukelns kann Effi eine Sehnsucht nach jener Zerstreuung ausdrücken, die gesellschaftlich nun nicht mehr integrierbar und eine nicht reflektierte
Komponente ihres Wesens ist. Diese Form ihrer Sehnsucht
stellt Effi den Statussymbolen ihrer gesellschaftlichen   35

Sphäre gegenüber: »Er [Instetten] hat keine Ahnung davon, daß ich mir nichts aus Schmuck mache. Ich klettere lieber, und ich schaukele mich lieber, und am liebsten immer in der Furcht, daß es irgendwo reißen oder brechen und ich
5 niederstürzen könnte« [S. 31]. Hier erscheint die Sehnsucht nach Zerstreuung als eine Leidenschaft, die das Leben bedingungslos bejaht und den Tod als Komplement des Lebens, ja sogar als Bedingung seines Werts einschließt. Selbst im Gespräch über die »armen, unglücklichen
10 Frauen«, die »natürlich wegen Untreue« [S. 11] ertränkt wurden, ist durch den voraufgehenden Kindervers: »Flut, Flut / Mach alles wieder gut . . .« [S. 10], der Tod nicht so sehr Strafe, sondern gutes Ende. Nicht von ungefähr steht die Schaukel dicht am Teich; denn auch das Wasser symbo-
15 lisiert Effis Leidenschaft. Auf der Rückfahrt von Uvagla am Strand entlang, kurz vor ihrem Ehebruch, wird Effi von Sidonie ermahnt, sich nicht so weit aus dem Schlitten zu lehnen; aber sie antwortet: »Ich kann die Schutzleder nicht leiden; sie haben so was Prosaisches. Und dann, wenn ich
20 hinausflöge, mir wär' es recht, am liebsten gleich in die Brandung« [S. 159]. Die durch die beiden Symbolbereiche des Wassers und der Luft (Schaukel) versinnbildlichte Wesenskomponente wird für Effi zum Medium ihrer Ver- schuldung. Aber indem diese Symbole als Teil des idylli-
25 schen Bezirks von Hohen-Cremmen erscheinen und indem dieser Bezirk Verweisungsfunktion für Effis Tod erhält, wird jener Wesenszug gleichzeitig als Remedium der Schuld dargestellt.
So erhält schon vor Effis Hochzeit das Rondell im Garten
30 von Hohen-Cremmen seine verweisende Funktion. Effi sagt über den dort blühenden Heliotrop: ». . . ich kann mir den Himmel nicht schöner denken. Und am Ende, wer weiß, ob sie im Himmel so wundervollen Heliotrop haben« [S. 26]. Effi spricht hier im Blick auf ihr bisheriges Glück
35 und den bevorstehenden Abschied. Ihre Trauer läßt sie den Ort, an den ihr Glück gebunden ist, mit dem Himmel vergleichen. Dieser Vergleich macht Hohen-Cremmen kraft der idyllischen Qualitäten zu einer quasi jenseitigen Landschaft. Umgekehrt wird die vage Vorstellung vom

»Himmel« mit idyllischen Anschauungen und Maßstäben,
die Hohen-Cremmen bereitstellt, konkretisiert und bewer-
tet, so daß Idyll und Jenseits hier grundsätzlich füreinander
stehen können. Zudem dient das Rondell der symbolischen
Verschränkung von Tod und Leben: Die Sonnenuhr in   5
seiner Mitte wird am Ende durch Effis Grabstein ersetzt.
Kurz vor Effis Tod geben zwei Sätze von ihr den Blick auf
den komplexen Zusammenhang von Tod und Leben, Dies-
seits und Jenseits frei, indem die einzeln darauf verweisen-
den Elemente miteinander verknüpft werden: »Ich mag   10
nicht mehr weg von Hohen-Cremmen, hier ist meine
Stelle. Der Heliotrop unten auf dem Rondell, um die
Sonnenuhr herum, ist mir lieber als Mentone« [S. 288].
[. . .]

Cordula Kahrmann: Idyll im Roman: Theodor Fontane. Wilhelm 15
Fink, München 1973, S. 126f. Ausschnitt.

4. Ingrid Mittenzwei: [Effis Sprache]

(1970)

[. . .] Der Roman läßt das Bild seiner Hauptgestalt allmäh-
lich aus ihrer Sprache entstehen; dabei demonstriert er das 20
Prinzip des Baron Pentz aus ›Unwiederbringlich‹: »Freiheit
und Unbefangenheit und viel sprechen«. Aus den Gesprächen des Anfangs formt sich dem Leser das »Naturkind«
Effi [S. 34], das viel und virtuos zu sprechen weiß, dabei in
schöner Unbefangenheit seine Phantasie spielen läßt und in 25
ebensolcher Freiheit sagt, was ihm »eben einfällt« [S. 11].
Zur Genauigkeit des Bildes trägt aber neben dieser Form
auch der Inhalt des Gesprochenen bei: Er stellt neben die
Unbefangenheit des Sprechens eine Befangenheit der
Sprache im durchaus Gängigen und Herkömmlichen, neben 30
den originellen Ton das Wort, das so abgenutzt ist in
langem Gebrauch, daß es als Klischee frei verfügbar ist:
Nur deshalb kann Effi es unbefangen im Munde führen,
ohne sich viel dabei zu denken. Nicht nur für »Papas
Lieblingssätze« [S. 6], für alles von ihr Behauptete gilt, was 35

341

ihre Mutter in einem Falle erkennt: Effi spricht es aus –
aber sie »spricht es [. . .] nach« [S. 37]. So kann sie aus den
Mädchentagen ihrer Mutter eine »Liebesgeschichte mit
Held und Heldin und zuletzt mit Entsagung« erzählen,
5 dabei unbekümmert hinwerfen: »Eine Geschichte mit Entsagung ist nie schlimm« [S. 6], und den Ausgang dieser
Geschichte kühl referieren als etwas, das sich von selbst
versteht: »Nun, es kam, wie's kommen mußte, wie's immer
kommt. Er war ja noch viel zu jung [. . .]« [S. 9].

10 Das »Kind«, das vom Spiel zur Verlobung gerufen wird,
braucht zwar einen Augenblick Zeit, um sich im Wechsel
der Sphären zurechtzufinden; in der Reaktion auf die Eröff-
nung der Mutter, Innstetten habe um Effis Hand angehalten, stoßen sie unvermittelt aufeinander: »Um meine Hand
15 angehalten? Und im Ernst?« [S. 14]. Sofort ist ihr indes
geläufig, was eine junge Verlobte von Stand zu antworten
hat auf die Frage der Freundinnen, ob er »denn auch der
Richtige« und sie denn »schon ganz glücklich« sei: »Gewiß
ist es der Richtige. [. . .] Jeder ist der Richtige. Natürlich
20 muß er von Adel sein und eine Stellung haben und gut
aussehen.« Und: »Wenn man zwei Stunden verlobt ist, ist
man immer ganz glücklich. Wenigstens denk' ich es mir so«
[S. 16]. [. . .]
»Mitteilsam« in den Normen und Formen, die die Konven-
25 tion bereitstellt, aber »verschlossen« für das Gefühl, das mit
dieser nicht zu vereinbaren ist, dennoch bestimmt vom
»Bedürfnis zu sprechen« und, als »das Menschlichste, was
wir haben«, Zufluchtsort in menschlicher Bedrängnis, aber
zugleich auch schützendes Versteck, in dem sich solche
30 Bedrängnis verbergen läßt[5] – so zieht sich die Sprache Effi
Briests durch die Dialogkunst des Romans. Je weiter Effi
sich von der Unbefangenheit des Anfangs entfernt, je
kritischer die inneren Vorgänge werden, um so strenger
wird die Kontrolle, der das Bedürfnis zu sprechen sich zu
35 unterziehen hat, um die Konvention nicht zu verletzen,

---

(5)* Vgl. Fritz Martini: Deutsche Literatur im bürgerlichen Realismus
1848–1898. J. B. Metzler, Stuttgart ⁴1981, S. 769f.

und um so verschlüsselter und versteckter wird das, was die Sprache eigentlich meint.

Der Brief der jungen Frau von der Hochzeitsreise an die Eltern enthüllt den Kampf ihrer »menschlichen Schwachheit« mit dem Vor-gegebenen, in festen Sätzen Etablierten gerade im Wort, das ihn verbergen soll. Konfrontiert mit dem, was ›man‹ auf einer Italienreise besichtigt, aber ohne innere Anteilnahme – vielmehr die Tauben auf dem Markusplatz sehnsüchtig mit den Tauben in Hohen-Cremmen vergleichend – schreibt sie brav, pflichtgemäß und verräterisch: »Ach, es ist so schön hier. Es soll ja auch das Schönste sein« [S. 39].

Die Sprache, deren sich die Baronin von Innstetten künftig zu bedienen hat, wenn Effi Briest glaubt, ihre Gefühle verbergen zu müssen, und dennoch dem menschlichen »Bedürfnis zu sprechen« genügen will, ist damit umrissen. »Warum kriege ich keine Staatskleider? Warum machst du keine Dame aus mir?« [S. 5] hatte das »Naturkind« im Matrosenkittel ganz zu Anfang des Romans die Mutter gefragt. Das standesgemäße, das Staatskleid, das aus Effi die Dame macht, die der neuen Stellung entspricht, ist die kontrollierte und den Normen angepaßte Sprache, die man trägt, die das Individuum verhüllt und zu einer Erscheinung macht, die sich sowenig wie möglich von anderen unterscheidet. [. . .]

Ingrid Mittenzwei: Die Sprache als Thema. Untersuchungen zu Fontanes Gesellschaftsromanen. Gehlen, Bad Homburg/Berlin/ Zürich 1970, S. 135–138. Ausschnitte.

5. Richard Brinkmann: Das Gespräch als menschliche Realität

(1967)

[. . .] Das Gespräch erfüllt in Fontanes Gesellschaftsromanen ähnliche Aufgaben wie in anderen, nur bei Fontane mit differenzierterer Kunst als bei den meisten vergleichbaren Schriftstellern: direkte und indirekte Charakterisierung,

Genre- und Milieuvermittlung, unmittelbare Auseinander-
setzung, einzelne Gespräche als Kompositionsglieder im
Aufbau der Erzählungen und so fort. [. . .] Aber es gibt
noch eine weiter reichende Funktion.

5 Eine sehr große Zahl von Gesprächen hat nicht die Form
des auf die inneren oder äußeren Vorgänge direkt bezoge-
nen Dialogs oder Monologs. Breiten Anteil haben die viel
umforschten und gepriesenen Plaudereien, die Causerien,
die sich an allen möglichen Sujets entfalten: Tagesereignis-
10 sen, Politik, Reisen, Kunst, Leuten, Religion, Geschichte,
nicht minder an Quisquilien, Weinsorten, Kleidung, Karriere, Déjeuners und Jeus und tausend Dingen – »Klein-
zeug der Unterhaltung«.[6] Es gibt Unterschiede: Man
spricht verschieden nach Temperament und Charakter,
15 nach Stand, Beruf und Gegend, und wo nur der Zufall bei
der Wahl des Themas zu herrschen scheint, ist er doch oft
schon von solchen Voraussetzungen dirigiert. Auf das Was
der Unterhaltung kommt es aber sehr oft gar nicht an.
Nichts Wesentliches würde sich zuweilen ändern, wenn man
20 zum Beispiel statt über Mantegna, alte Familien und die
Sozialdemokratie über Havannas und Poularden, statt über
Chablis und Lafitte über Bismarck, Theater und Konzert
plauderte. Gleichwohl gibt es kaum ein Gespräch, das
nichts anderes als Genrevermittlung, nichts anderes als
25 Charakterisierung wäre oder Ausbruch des baren Vergnü-
gens am Parlieren – *auch* das kommt vor, aber nie als
Selbstzweck.
Die neuere Forschung zur Erzählkunst und zu Fontane hat
gezeigt, was Gespräche solcher Art im Roman zu leisten
30 vermögen, als was sie fungieren: Gesellschaftskritik,
»Medium einer lebendigen Wechselwirkung zwischen Individuum und Gesellschaft«[7], Vergegenwärtigung von umfas-
senden Aspekten des Wirklichen und der »aktuellen Ge-
schichtszeit« in »partikularen oder bagatellmäßigen De-

---

(6)* Theodor Fontane: Brief an Friedlaender.
(7) Horst Turk: Realismus in Fontanes Gesellschaftsromanen. Zur Roman-
theorie und zur epischen Integration. Jahrbuch der Wittheit zu Bremen. IX,
S. 441.

tails«[8] und so fort. Nun ist da aber noch etwas Grundsätzliches, das hier in unserem Zusammenhang interessiert.

Im vordergründig ganz gleichgültigen Geplauder realisiert sich oft Entscheidendes von dem, was man überhaupt in einem Roman Fontanes »Geschehen« nennen kann. Wenn die Leute sich unterhalten, ereignet sich etwas, häufig mehr, als sie ahnen und wollen. Belangloses Geplauder verlassen sie oft als entschieden Veränderte. Das festzustellen ist weder selbstverständlich, noch heißt es nur an der Sprache psychologische Studien treiben, den Seelen durch Interpretation ihrer sprachlichen Äußerungen auf die Schliche kommen. Vielmehr ist das Gespräch in der Tat Medium des Vollzugs von Menschlichem im eigentlichen Sinn, es ist – wenn man so will – die »geistige«, die menschliche Realität im Roman Fontanes. [. . .]

Alles im eigentlichen Sinne *menschliche* Geschehen entscheidet sich bei Fontane gültig nur im Gespräch. Im Gespräch kommt das menschlich Bedeutsame in die Welt und fängt an zu wirken. Außerhalb des Gesprächs geschieht nichts anderes als die innere oder äußere Vorbereitung dieser sanktionierenden Entscheidungen, die sich im Gespräch verwirklichen, und die Exekution des Entschiedenen. [. . .]

Richard Brinkmann: Theodor Fontane. Über die Verbindlichkeit des Unverbindlichen. R. Piper & Co., München 1967, S. 127f. und S. 129. Ausschnitte.

(8) Wolfgang Preisendanz: Humor als dichterische Einbildungskraft. Studien zur Erzählkunst des poetischen Realismus. 1963, S. 234, 237.

VI. Fontanes Selbstinterpretationen

1.Theodor Fontane: [An Clara Kühnast]

Berlin, 27. Okt. 95
Potsdamerstraße 134 c

5 Mein gnädiges Fräulein.
Ihr liebenswürdiger Brief, für den ich Ihnen herzlich danke,
war verkramt worden, – das ist der Grund, weshalb ich so
spät erst antworte.
Ja, Effi! Alle Leute sympathisiren mit ihr und Einige gehen
10 so weit, im Gegensatze dazu, den Mann als einen »alten
Ekel« zu bezeichnen. Das amüsiert mich natürlich, giebt mir
aber auch zu denken, weil es wieder beweist, wie wenig den
Menschen an der sogenannten »Moral« liegt und wie die
liebenswürdigen Naturen dem Menschenherzen sympathi-
15 scher sind. Ich habe dies lange gewußt, aber es ist mir nie
so stark entgegengetreten wie in diesem Effi Briest und
Innstetten-Fall. Denn eigentlich ist er (Innstetten) doch in
jedem Anbetracht ein ganz ausgezeichnetes Menschenex-
emplar, dem es an dem, was man lieben muß, durchaus
20 nicht fehlt. Aber sonderbar, alle korrekten Leute werden
schon blos um ihrer Korrektheiten willen, mit Mißtrauen,
oft mit Abneigung betrachtet. Vielleicht interessiert es Sie,
daß die *wirkliche* Effi übrigens noch lebt, als ausgezeichnete
Pflegerin in einer großen Heilanstalt. Innstetten, in natura,
25 wird mit Nächstem General werden. Ich habe ihn seine
Militärcarrière nur aufgeben lassen, um die wirklichen Personen nicht zu deutlich hervortreten zu lassen.
In vorzüglicher Ergebenheit Ihr

Th. Fontane.

30 *Theodor Fontane: Briefe. Vierter Band, s. o., S. 493/494.*

2. Theodor Fontane:
[An Josef Viktor Widmann]

Berlin, 19. Novb. 95
Potsdamerstraße 134 c

Hochgeehrter Herr.

Herzlichen Dank für Ihre Besprechung. Sie werden aus
eigener Erfahrung wissen, daß einem *die* Kritiker die liebsten sind, die das betonen, worauf es einem beim Schreiben
angekommen ist. Es geht das, für einen leidlich vernünfti-
gen Menschen, weit über das bloße Lob hinaus, das, wenn
nicht *Leben* drin ist, überhaupt sehr leicht langweilig wird.
Ich habe das diesmal reichlich erfahren. Obenan an
Schreckniß stehen die, die einem die ganze Geschichte
noch mal erzählen und nur gerade das weglassen, worauf es
einem angekommen ist. Sie sind der Erste, der auf das
Spukhaus und den Chinesen hinweist; ich begreife nicht
wie man daran vorbeisehen kann, denn erstlich ist dieser
Spuk, so bilde ich mir wenigstens ein, an und für sich
interessant und zweitens, wie Sie hervorgehoben haben,
steht die Sache nicht zum Spaß da, sondern ist ein Drehpunkt für die ganze Geschichte. Was mich ganz besonders
gefreut hat, ist, daß Sie dem armen Innstetten so schön
gerecht werden. Eine reizende Dame hier, die ich ganz
besonders liebe und verehre, sagte mir: »ja, Effi; aber
Innstetten ist ein ›Ekel[!]‹.« Und ähnlich urtheilen alle. Für
den Schriftsteller in mir kann es gleichgültig sein, ob Innstetten, der nicht nothwendig zu gefallen braucht, als famo-
ser Kerl oder als »Ekel« empfunden wird, als Mensch aber
macht mich die Sache stutzig. Hängt das mit etwas Schönem
im Menschen- und namentlich im Frauenherzen zusammen, oder zeigt es, wie schwach es mit den Moralitäten
steht, so daß jeder froh ist, wenn er einem »Etwas« begeg-
net, das er nur nicht den Muth hatte, auf die eigenen
Schultern zu nehmen.

Zu »Lacrimae Christi«. Ich glaube, es giebt Strudel in
stehenden Gewässern. Ich kenne zwei kleine Seen in unsrer
Mark, in denen sich Springfluthen und Trichter bilden,

347

wenn in Italien und Island die Vulkane los gehn. Auch aus
andrer Veranlassung kommt es vor.
Nochmals besten Dank. In vorzügl. Ergebenheit

Th. Fontane.

5 *Theodor Fontane: Briefe. Vierter Band, s.o., S. 506.*

3. Theodor Fontane:
[An Hermann Wichmann]

Berlin, 24. April 1896.
Potsd. Str. 134 c.

10 [. . .] Ja, die nicht-verbrannten Briefe in Effi! Unwahrscheinlich ist es gar nicht, dergleichen kommt immerzu vor,
die Menschen können sich nicht trennen von dem, woran
ihre Schuld haftet. Unwahrscheinlich ist es nicht, aber es ist
leider trivial. Das habe ich von allem Anfang an sehr stark
15 empfunden und ich hatte eine Menge anderer Entdeckun-
gen in Vorrath. Aber ich habe nichts davon benutzt, weil
alles wenig natürlich war, und das gesucht Wirkende ist
noch schlimmer, als das Triviale. So wählte ich von zwei
Uebeln das kleinere. [. . .]

20 *Theodor Fontane: Briefe. Vierter Band, s.o., S. 556 f. Ausschnitt.*

4. Theodor Fontane: [An Unbekannt]

Berlin, 12. Juni 95
Potsdamerstr. 134 c.

Gnädigste Frau.
25 Ergebensten Dank für Ihre liebenswürdigen Zeilen, die ich
schon früher beantwortet hätte, wenn ich nicht gerade mit
dem Abschluß einer Arbeit beschäftigt gewesen wäre.
Natürlich ist alles Recht auf Ihrer Seite, natürlich alles sehr
unplatonisch. Ich bin schon ohnehin gegen todtschießen,
30 Mord, aus dem Affekt heraus, geht viel eher, aber nun gar
todtschießen wegen einer 7 Jahre zurückliegenden Cour-

macherei – an die sich in der Regel ein anständiger Ehe-
mann mit Vergnügen miterinnert – das wäre denn doch über
den Spaß. Auch so geht Innstetten, der übrigens von allen
Damen härter beurtheilt wird als er verdient – sehr ungern
'ran und wäre nicht der Ehrengötze, so lebte Crampas noch. 5
Es ist nämlich eine wahre Geschichte, die sich hier zugetra-
gen hat, nur in Ort und Namen alles transponirt.
Das Duell fand in Bonn statt, nicht in dem räthselvollen
Kessin, dem ich die Scenerie von Swinemünde gegeben
habe; Crampas war ein Gerichtsrath, Innstetten ist jetzt 10
Oberst, Effi lebt noch, ganz in Nähe von Berlin. Vielleicht
läge sie lieber auf dem Rondel in Hohen-Kremmen. – Daß
ich die Sache im Unklaren gelassen hätte, kann ich nicht
zugeben, die berühmten »Schilderungen« (der Gipfel der
Geschmacklosigkeit) vermeide ich freilich, aber Effis Brief 15
an Crampas und die mitgetheilten 3 Zettel von Crampas an
Effi, die sagen doch alles.
Gnädigste Frau, in vorzüglicher Ergebenheit
                                              Th. Fontane.

Theodor Fontane: Briefe. Vierter Band, s.o., S. 454f.   20

5. Theodor Fontane:
[An Georg Friedlaender]

Berlin, 12. April 94.
Potsd. Str. 134 c.
[. . .] Ich habe nichts gegen das Alte, wenn man es inner- 25
halb seiner Zeit läßt und aus dieser heraus beurtheilt; der
sogenannte altpreußische Beamte, der Perrückengelehrte
des vorigen Jahrhunderts, Friedrich Wilhelm I., der Küras-
sieroffizier der mehrere Stunden Zeit brauchte eh er sich
durch sein eignes Körpergewicht in seine nassen ledernen 30
Hosen hineinzwängte, die Ober-Rechenkammer in Pots-
dam, der an seine Gottesgnadenschaft glaubende Junker,
der Orthodoxe, der mit dem Lutherschen Glaubensbe-
kenntniß steht und fällt, – all diese Personen und Institutio-
nen finde ich novellistisch und in einem »Zeitbilde« wun- 35

dervoll, räume auch ein, daß sie sämmtlich ihr Gutes und
zum Theil ihr Großes gewirkt haben, aber diese todten
Seifensieder immer noch als tonangebende Kräfte bewun-
dern zu sollen, während ihre Hinfälligkeit seit nun gerade
5 hundert Jahren, und mit jedem Jahre wachsend, bewiesen
worden ist, das ist eine furchtbare Zumuthung. Von mei-
nem vielgeliebten Adel falle ich mehr und mehr ganz ab,
traurige Figuren, beleidigend unangenehme Selbstsüchtler
von einer mir ganz unverständlichen Bornirtheit, an
10 Schlechtigkeit nur noch von den schweifwedelnden Pfaffen
(die immer an der Spitze sind) übertroffen, von diesen
Teufelskandidaten, die uns diese Mischung von Unver-
stand und brutalem Egoismus als »Ordnungen Gottes«
aufreden wollen. Sie müssen alle geschmort werden. Alles
15 antiquirt! Die Bülows und Arnims sind 2 ausgezeichnete
Familien, aber wenn sie morgen von der Bildfläche verschwinden, ist es nicht blos für die Welt (da nun schon ganz
gewiß) sondern auch für Preußen und die preußische
Armee ganz gleichgültig und die Müllers und Schultzes
20 rücken in die leergewordenen Stellen ein. Mensch ist
Mensch. Goethe würde sich gehütet haben, es zu bestreiten;
aber jeder agrarische Schafzüchter prätendirt eine Sonder-
stellung. Indessen der Krug geht so lange zu Wasser bis er
bricht; in den eignen Reihen dieser Leute wird es zur
25 Revolte kommen und alle die, die das Herz auf dem
rechten Flecke haben, werden sich von den selbstsüchtigen
Radaubrüdern scheiden. [. . .]

Theodor Fontane: Briefe. Vierter Band, s. o., S. 341 ff. Ausschnitt.

Zeittafel zu Leben und Werk

1819 30. Dezember: Henri Théodore (Theodor) Fontane in Neuruppin geboren.

1827 Juni: Die Familie zieht nach Swinemünde.

1832 Ostern: Eintritt in die Quarta des Gymnasiums in Neuruppin.

1833 1. Oktober: Eintritt in die Gewerbeschule K. F. Klödens in Berlin.

1836 Beginn der Apothekerlehrzeit. Konfirmation in der französisch reformierten Kirche.

1839 ›Geschwisterliebe‹.

1840 Apothekergehilfe. Gedichte im ›Berliner Figaro‹. Roman ›Du hast recht getan‹ und Epos ›Heinrichs IV. erste Liebe‹ (beide nicht überliefert).

1842/43 Gedichte und Korrespondenzen in dem Unterhaltungsblatt ›Die Eisenbahn‹. Ab 1843 Gedichte im ›Morgenblatt‹ (Cotta). Anfang August Rückkehr nach Letschin, Defektar in der väterlichen Apotheke. 30. Juli 1843: Gast (›Rune‹) im Literarischen Sonntagsverein ›Tunnel über der Spree‹.

1844 1. April: Beginn des Militärjahres. Mai–Juni: Erste Reise nach England. 29. September: Aufnahme in den ›Tunnel‹.

1845 8. Dezember: Verlobung mit Emilie Rouanet-Kummer.

1847 Approbation als Apotheker erster Klasse. Trennung der Eltern ohne Scheidung.

1848 Teilnahme an den Barrikadenkämpfen am 18. März. Die ›Berliner Zeitungs-Halle‹ bringt vier Aufsätze Fontanes. ›Karl Stuart‹ (Fragment). 15. September: Anstellung im Krankenhaus Bethanien.

1849 30. September: Fontane verläßt Bethanien. ›Freier Schriftsteller‹. Korrespondent der ›Dresdner Zeitung‹ (bis April 1850).

1850 ›Männer und Helden‹: ›Von der schönen Rosamunde‹. Eintritt ins ›Literarische Kabinett‹. 16. Oktober: Heirat.

1851 ›Gedichte‹. 14. August: Sohn George Emile geboren.

1852 ›Deutsches Dichter-Album, hrsg. von Theodor Fontane‹. 23. April–25. September: Aufenthalt in London.

1853 ›Unsere lyrische und epische Poesie seit 1848‹.

1854 ›Ein Sommer in London‹; ›Argo‹. ›Belletristisches Jahrbuch, hrsg. von Th. Fontane und Fr. Kugler‹.

1855 10. September: Beginn eines mehrjährigen Aufenthalts in London.

1856 Halbamtlicher ›Presse-Agent‹. 3. November: Sohn Theodor geboren.

1857 Emilie übersiedelt mit den Kindern nach London.

1858 August: Reise mit Lepel nach Schottland.

1859 15. Januar: Rückkehr nach Berlin. Beginn der ›Wanderungen‹.

1860 ›Aus England‹; ›Jenseit des Tweed‹. Eintritt in die Redaktion der ›Kreuzzeitung‹. 21. März: Tochter Martha (Mete) geboren.

1861 ›Balladen‹.

1862 ›Wanderungen durch die Mark Brandenburg‹ (bis 1882 vier Bände).

1864 5. Februar: Sohn Friedrich geboren. Reisen nach Schleswig-Holstein und Dänemark.

1865 13. August: Tod Wilhelm Wolfsohns[9] in Dresden. 26. August–21. September: Reise an den Rhein und in die Schweiz. Scott-Lektüre.

1866 ›Der Schleswig-Holsteinische Krieg im Jahre 1864‹. Reisen auf die böhmischen und süddeutschen Kriegsschauplätze. ›Reisebriefe vom Kriegsschauplatz‹ im Deckerschen ›Fremdenblatt‹.

1867 5. Oktober: Tod des Vaters.

1869 13. Dezember: Tod der Mutter.

1870 Bruch mit der ›Kreuzzeitung‹. Theaterrezensent der ›Vossischen Zeitung‹. 5. Oktober: Festnahme in Domrémy. Internierung auf der Île d'Oleron. Anfang Dezember: Rückkehr nach Berlin. ›Der deutsche Krieg von 1866‹ (Bd. 2: 1871).

1871 ›Osterreise‹ nach Frankreich. ›Kriegsgefangen‹; ›Aus den Tagen der Occupation‹.

1872 ›Willibald Alexis‹ in ›Der Salon für Literatur, Kunst und Gesellschaft‹, hrsg. von Julius Rodenberg. Umzug in die Potsdamer Straße 134 c, Fontanes letzte Wohnung.

1873 ›Der Krieg gegen Frankreich 1870—1871‹ (Bd. 2 in zwei Halbbänden 1875/76).

1874 Italienreise mit Emilie über Verona, Venedig, Florenz, Rom, Neapel, Capri, Sorrent, Salerno, Rom, Florenz, Piacenca, Verona.

---

(9) * Wilhelm Wolfsohn: Fortschrittlich demokratischer und jüdischer Schriftsteller und Publizist (1820–1865), mit dem Fontane seit gemeinsamer Mitgliedschaft im ›Herwegh-Verein‹ in Leipzig (1841) befreundet ist.

Chapter 13

"Oh, God." Nicki went down on her knees beside him. "Told you it was him!"

Nicki heard Carl's words, but she was too worried about the blood streaming down Travis's temple to care. She looked up at the guard, squinting against the headlights' glare.

"Go and call the paramedics!"

"Just call the cops, man," Carl chortled. "They'll cart him away and throw him back in the slammer where he belongs."

"Shut up," Nicki snapped.

"I think it's time you shut up, Miss High and Mighty. The Miss High and Mighty who's sleeping with the guy who killed her old man and tried to close down his company."

If she'd been less worried about Travis, Nicki knew she'd be enraged at Weller's filthy mouth. But there was no room for anything but fear now. She reached out to touch him; he groaned, and the dark lashes fluttered.

"Aw, I didn't hit him that hard," Carl drawled. "Just enough to stop him from tamperin' with that switch. Why, somebody could get chewed up real bad if that thing came on at the wrong time." He glanced at the big auger that turned with crushing power to reclaim the unused cement from the returning mixers. "Cops might even look on that as attempted murder or somethin'." He laughed, that malevolent laugh again. "'Course, he's been there before, hasn't he?"

Nicki ignored him. Travis had opened dazed eyes to peer at her through the darkness.

"Ni—Nicole? What...?"

"Shh, don't move. It's all right."

"I'll say it is, Halloran," Carl crouched beside them. "I got you good, this time. You won't slide out of this one."

A puzzled look lowered dark brows, then he winced as the movement tugged at the wound on his temple. "I... don't..."

"Go ahead and play dumb, it won't do you any good. Not with the evidence still in your hand."

Carl's words made Nicki glance at Travis's outflung right hand, the fingers curled around the handle of the heavy, twelve-inch, flat-bladed tool. Something about it made her brow crease, but before she could think about it Travis made a small sound, and her gaze flew back to him. Then it was there again, that uncanny sense of familiarity about the heart-wrenching combination of fear, anger, and desperation in his face.

"I didn't," he whispered.

"Shh. I know you didn't." He stared at her, doubt clouding his eyes. "I know you didn't do any of it," she said emphatically. "I'm sorry I ever doubted it."

He let out a breath, lowering his eyes, but she saw the relief, the joy leap in the gray depths before they were masked by the thick, dark lashes.

She meant it. In those taut, strained moments in her office, she'd worked her way through the morass of confusion and returned to the one thing she knew for certain: Travis was incapable of pulling those sneaky, petty tricks. Not just because he was the man who'd risked his life for two men he barely knew, not just because he was the man who'd built Willow Tree into one of the most prestigious companies in the state, but because he was, simply, Travis. Her Travis. He always had been.

"You're siding with him. Again."

Richard's words, the first he'd spoken, drew Nicki's eyes to his face. As there had been with Travis, there was something familiar about his expression. And about the whine in his voice.

"He didn't do it, Richard. Any of it," she repeated.

"How can you say that? Carl caught him in the act!"

Travis moved then, lifting himself gingerly up on the left elbow that had been bent awkwardly beneath him when he'd fallen. He stared at the screwdriver in his other hand, still looking a little dazed. Nicki saw the bewilderment in his eyes, and glanced at the long, silver blade of the tool.

Then she went very still. Slowly she lifted her gaze to Carl. "You caught him like this? Just like this?"

"Yeah." Carl grinned again. "I saw he was monkeying with that switch, so I popped him."

"What else did you do?"

Carl looked at her, suddenly wary. "Nothin'. I just yelled for the guard. And then you showed up."

"You didn't move anything? You left him just as he fell?"

"Yeah," Carl said angrily, "just like that. I caught him, he's guilty as hell, and you spreadin' your legs for him won't change that."

"You bastard." Travis moved sharply. His eyes had cleared now, were hot with anger, and she knew he was going to try to get up. She stilled him with a hand flat on his chest, gently pushing him back.

"So tell me, Carl," she said, almost conversationally, "just what were you doing here so late?"

"Watchin' out. For more trouble."

"And you just happened to be carrying that?" She nodded at the heavy, wooden club he held, which looked like a small baseball bat.

"Hey, I got to protect myself."

Her eyes flicked to the guard. "Did you see Carl?"

"Sure," the man said.

"Didn't you . . . wonder what he was doing?"

"Why should I? Mr. Lockwood said he was okay, and he's always around at night."

Nicki felt Travis tense beneath her palm. Her gaze went to his, and she saw the same glow of realization in his eyes that she knew must be in hers. Richard said nothing, as usual, letting someone else deal with things. She looked a query at Travis, but he gave a slight shake of his head.

"Go for it, Nicki." Pride and—unmistakably—love, lit his eyes. It warmed her, as did the name he used, and gave her a strength she'd never known. She looked back at Carl.

"When was the last time you were at the pit, Carl?"

The man stiffened.

"When, Carl?"

"I haven't been there—"

"I wonder what the guard would say about that? The one who told Esteban that only our people have been in and out."

"I told you—"

"He keeps a list, Carl."

"That doesn't prove nothing! I got a right to be there!"

"It proves you just lied. And makes me wonder why you've been skulking around here nights, like perhaps the night the conveyor motor belt broke. And why you conveniently disappeared and forgot to sound the alarm when the acid leaked."

"I told you," Weller squeaked, fear beginning to take the place of his blustering anger, "I got a phone call—"

Nicki went on as if he'd never spoken. "And where you were when that call was made to mess up the Shelby run, that call from a 'familiar' voice. And the slurry tank valve—will that have your fingerprints on it? Like—" she was bluffing, hoping Carl wouldn't guess "—the broken bunker gate at the pit? They already know it was tampered with. O.S.H.A. is very thorough, you know."

Carl's eyes widened; fear was uppermost now. "You're not going to hang me to save your lover, bitch! I caught him red-handed—"

"Right-handed, you mean. And that's what's going to hang you, Carl, not me."

"What the hell does that mean?"

She gestured at the screwdriver. Travis grinned at her, hefting it against his right palm.

"He's left-handed, Carl."

Weller paled, and backed up a step. "I'll get the gate logs from the pit, Carl. And I'm sure this gentleman—" she gestured at the guard "—will be able to remember just what nights he saw you here. And maybe I'll just have you call Ed Hartman on the phone, to see if he recognizes your voice—"

"Hey," Weller sputtered, "I'm not taking the heat for that! It was Richard who wanted him out, he's the one who said to do what I had to do!"

Four pairs of eyes turned on Richard Lockwood, but he saw only one set, cool, gray, and full of knowledge.

"No! No, I didn't!" He pointed a shaking hand at Travis. "He did it! I didn't, he did! He did!"

There, in the shaft of light projected by the truck's lights, Nicki watched her brother tremble, heard his mewling accusation. She recognized the pattern, recognized Richard's old, familiar tactic of shifting the blame. He'd always done it, from when they were children, blaming her for breaking the crystal lamp, for leaving the door open, or for any number of childhood misdeeds he'd committed.

She saw the expression on Richard's face, and remembered that awful look in Travis's eyes, and how they both seemed oddly familiar. Time seemed to shift for her. Memory swept over her like the shock wave from an explosion, and she shook under its force.

"It was him!" Richard had been screaming. "It's all his fault, he was going too fast!"

Her mother, eyes wide and dark in her chalk-white face, staring at her son. And herself, cowering in her favorite chair in the library, staring at the ominous men in uniforms and guns, who had just, in gentle but impersonal words, blown her world to bits.

"You're...certain?" Her mother's voice was shaken, something Nicki had never heard before.

"I'm afraid so, Mrs. Lockwood. We found the other boy, Travis Halloran, at the car, trying to get Mr. Lockwood out, but it was already too late."

"I had to go for help," Richard yelped. "Travis wanted to run, but I made him stay."

Nicki huddled deeper into the chair, her dazed young mind seizing only on the absurdity of the idea of Richard making Travis do anything.

"It appears your son's car was traveling at high speed, on the wrong side of the road. Your husband's car was forced over the side."

"It was Travis," Richard whimpered. "He always drives too fast, you know that—"

"He doesn't!" Nicki burst out. "He's always careful when I'm with him!"

Richard whirled on her. "Shut up, you little brat! It's just like you to side against me, you always do! Ever since he started hanging around here, you've been on his side!"

"I don't care what you say, Travis wouldn't do that! He would never hurt anybody! And he would never run!"

"What do you know about it? He's always fighting, hurting people—"

"Be quiet."

Emily Lockwood silenced them both; they'd never heard her sound like that. She shivered, and it frightened Nicki even more; never had she seen her mother so shaken. She turned to the uniformed man with the stripes on his sleeve.

"You will see that . . . he's moved?"

"Of course, Mrs. Lockwood. We'll handle it."

Nicki shuddered, barely able to comprehend that the "he" they were talking about as if he were a thing, not a person any longer, was her father.

"I'll make . . . arrangements as soon as possible."

"Yes, ma'am."

Nicki saw her mother's head turn toward the library door, then heard the sound of steps, one set firm and even, the other unsteady, as if someone was hurt, or being dragged. The door burst open, and she cried out as another uniformed man shoved Travis into the room. He stumbled, and Nicki scrambled out of her chair to go to him, to help him.

"Sit down, Nicole."

Her mother's voice was quiet, still shaken, but some undertone in it held Nicki fast, and she dared do nothing but obey. Trembling, she sank back down in the chair, her shock-filled eyes fastened on Travis.

He looked horrible. His clothes were torn, even more than usual, and stained with grease. And blood, she realized. He *was* hurt. He was breathing hard, his chest rising and falling visibly as he pulled in air. His hair was tangled, falling over his forehead, and sweat shone on his face. He was standing awkwardly, his arms...

She realized with a sick little jolt that he was handcuffed, his hands held tightly behind him in the merciless steel grip. Her gaze flew to his face, to his eyes. They were wild, full of fear and anger and desperation as he looked around the room. His eyes found her mother, and he seemed to straighten somehow, despite the caging of his hands.

"I'm sorry, Mrs. Lockwood," the sergeant said quietly, "but we are looking at a possible manslaughter case here. I'm afraid I have to ask you a couple of questions."

Emily Lockwood looked at Travis for a long, drawn out moment. Then she turned to the sergeant and nodded.

"You saw your son and the Halloran boy leave the house? In your son's car?"

"Yes," she answered flatly.

"Do you remember what time?"

"Shortly after nine."

"Could you be a little more exact?"

"Nine-fifteen, perhaps. My daughter had just gone to bed."

A glance passed between the sergeant and the deputy who had brought in Travis. The sergeant's eyes flicked to Travis, who glared back at him defiantly.

"Mrs. Lockwood," he said slowly, "this is very important. The accident occurred at nine-eighteen. When you saw them leave... who was driving?"

''He was, I told you!'' Richard cried, pointing a shaking finger at Travis.

Nicki saw Travis's eyes widen as if he'd been struck. He drew back slightly, as if bracing himself. ''What the hell are you trying to pull, Rich? You know damned well you were driving! I told you not to take that turn so fast—''

''We've taken your statement, young man,'' the Sergeant said sternly. ''I'm speaking to Mrs. Lockwood now. Ma'am? Who was driving your son's car?''

Emily looked past her son to Travis for one long, silent, strained moment. With an expression tinged with something oddly like remorse, she looked at Nicki. Then the slender, regal woman drew herself up straight, and without another glance at any of them, said frozenly to the sergeant, ''Travis was.''

The noise Travis made, not a word but a strangled, anguished chunk of sound that tore like red-hot talons into Nicki's heart, drew her eyes back to his instantly, irresistibly. Disbelief twisted his face, and an agony so great she could feel it radiating off of him in waves. She must have made a sound of her own, because he looked at her, his eyes filled with a pleading she'd never thought to see in them.

''Nicole, no,'' he choked out, ''I didn't—''

''Will you please take him out of my home?''

Her mother's cold words did nothing to ease the effect of his look. In all the times he'd come to her, beaten and battered, knowing she alone knew why, he'd never looked like that. The day she'd found out the truth about his father, when he'd looked at her with such anguish, he hadn't looked like that. She'd never seen anyone look like that.

And then, even as she watched, she saw the chill begin. She saw his eyes go cold, the life withdraw, even the pain fade, as he retreated into himself until there was nothing left but the flat, hard gray of granite. He drew himself up, just as her mother had, and without waiting for the deputy who had handcuffed him, he turned and walked out of the library. And out of her life.

''Nicole? Nicole, what's wrong?''

It was Travis, his voice soft and worried in her ear, bringing her back to the present. She tried to shake off the horror that had engulfed her, then realized she was already shaking so hard it was a lost cause. She met his troubled gaze, her eyes wide with wonder.

"You didn't do it," she whispered.

"I know. So did you, remember? You knew, in spite of everything." A note of pride, of joy, crept into his voice beneath the worry. "Come on, snap out of it, honey."

"Don't believe it!" She heard Richard vaguely, through the mist that still clouded her mind. "You fell right into his bed, didn't you? You bought it all. I suppose he told you he loved you, and you believed him."

Nicki shook her head, clearing away the last of the vivid memories.

"No," she said softly, "he never told me that."

She felt Travis stiffen beside her. "I never—?" He stopped, realization of the truth of her words striking home. "Oh, God, I thought you knew—"

"Of course I knew," she said. She turned wide, pained blue eyes on him. "But I can see why you'd think I didn't. I haven't been very smart at all, have I?"

"Shh, it's all right. It doesn't matter anymore."

She reached up to touch his face. "God, Travis, you're so strong. How can you love me? After the fool I've been?"

Travis stared at her, sensing that the shock in her face, the pain in her eyes, went far beyond the events of this night. "Nicole—"

"You make me sick," Richard burst out. "Look, he's guilty, we caught him at it, and I'm calling the sheriff."

"Please do, Richard."

Nicki's voice was ice over the heat of anger, and it made Richard take a step back from her as she rose to her feet. Slowly, using the hand she subtly offered in support to steady himself, Travis rose beside her. Carl took one look at his face, dropped his bat, and took off running.

"Stop him," Nicki said to the guard. The man didn't question her, but turned and went after the sprinting Weller.

Richard looked uneasily at them both. "Look, maybe we don't have to call the cops. We can work something out." He put on his best wheedling tones as he turned to Travis. "You just sign back your percentage, and we'll forget everything."

"No," Nicki said before Travis could speak, "I think we'd better call the sheriff."

Richard gaped at her. "You *want* to call them?"

"Yes."

"I don't understand," Richard said, that whiny undertone creeping back into his voice.

"I do. At last."

"What are you talking about?" Richard sounded bewildered now.

"I'm talking about," Nicki said coldly, "who really killed our father."

Nicki crossed the room to stand in front of the wide expanse of glass, staring out into the morning light where the white curls of foam marched in long lines onto the beach. She sensed his presence, felt his heat close behind her before Travis spoke, handing her a small glass filled with a rich brown liquid whose sweet aroma tickled her nose.

"Martha's private stock of Amaretto. You need it."

She took the glass and sipped, the honeyed warmth burning its way down her throat to her stomach, where it expanded and made her muscles shiver with the outer chill.

"Sit down, Nicole. Before you fall down. It was a long night."

She did, had to, and when he dropped down beside her, she looked at him through eyes bright with moisture. "I should be taking care of you," she said, looking at the cut on his head he'd done little more with than clean and cover with an adhesive bandage.

"I'm fine. You're the one who's been through the wringer."

"How—" Her voice broke, and she had to swallow and blink rapidly before she could go on. "How can you say

that? My God, Travis, we took two years of your life from
you!''

"It's over and done with. It doesn't matter.''

"But it does! God, I can see now, it's just what I should
have expected from Richard. Why didn't I see it then, I
should have known—''

"Honey, you were just a child. Too smart for your own
good, but a child nevertheless. Believing me would have
meant hanging your own brother.''

"And hating my own mother,'' she said bitterly.

"Nicole—''

"She lied!'' It burst from her on a despairing cry. "She
supposedly cared about you, I thought she loved you, and
she betrayed you! God, I wish she was alive so I could—''

"Nicole, no.'' He reached for her, pulling her over next
to him across the soft cushion of the couch.

"Yes! I hate her for what she did!'' She pulled her knees
up and huddled against him like some wounded wild creature burrowing for shelter. He just held her, gently, croon-
ing soothing words she barely understood. It was a very long
time before she spoke again.

"Travis?''

"What?''

"After...the accident...they told me you never said
another word about it, after that night. That you never tried
to defend yourself. I think that's why I...thought you must
have really done it.'' She looked up at him, eyes wide and
dark. "Why didn't you fight it?''

He gave a mirthless chuckle. "A Halloran against the al-
mighty Lockwoods? Who was going to believe me?''

"But the police—''

"By the time they got there, I was the only one there.'' He
looked away suddenly, his voice dropping. "I tried to get
him out, Nicole. I really tried. But—''

"I know you did. They said they found you trying to...''

When she trailed off, he took a deep breath and went on.
"Next time I looked up, Rich was gone and the sheriff was
there. I told them I hadn't been driving, but once the deputy recognized me, it was all over but the paperwork.''

And the betrayal.

He didn't have to say it, Nicki knew it, and it stung viciously. The fury welled up in her again.

"Especially when my sainted mother swore before God you'd been driving. God, I will *never* forgive her for that."

"Shh," Travis soothed, gathering her close. He stroked her hair, then, with the backs of his fingers, her cheeks. He felt her tremble, and held her silently until the quivering stopped. When at last he spoke, his voice was as soft and soothing as his touch.

"Don't hate her. She did what she thought she had to do, to protect her son."

"Richard," Nicki grated out in repugnance, remembering how her brother had crumbled when the truth had come out. How he'd blubbered out his confession, both about the long-ago accident, and the assault on Travis. Carl had told him about their late arrival that first morning, looking, he'd said, like they'd been making love all night. Carl, of course, had a much cruder word for it. Richard panicked, thinking that the sister he'd always envied for her quick mind and the man he'd wronged so long ago were going to unite against him. He'd told Carl to get rid of Travis once and for all, and to hell with how he did it.

"Forget Richard," Travis told her gently. "He doesn't matter. He never did."

"No," Nicki agreed unexpectedly, "he doesn't. All he did was run true to form. But my mother... All that preaching about what it meant to be a Lockwood, how we had to be better... And then she...she... I hate her! I hate her, and I wish she was alive so I could tell her!"

"Nicole, don't. You don't mean that."

"I do!"

"You might think so now, but later you'll understand—"

"I'll *never* understand!"

"That's what I thought. Before I knew... how far someone will go for someone they love."

Nicki sat up sharply, cutting him off. "How can you sit there and defend her, after what she did to you?"

"Because," he said simply, "her hell was worse than mine."

"How can you say that?" Nicki's voice was incredulous.

He shrugged. "I got out of my jail. She never did."

Nicki frowned, puzzled.

"She had to live with what she'd done. The kind of woman she was . . . it ate at her, every day of her life."

"How can you know that?"

Travis gave her the look of a teacher whose cleverest student hasn't yet made the final leap of logic. "She left me half of Lockwood," he said gently.

Nicki gasped, realization and chagrin filling her eyes. "God, I didn't— How stupid can I be? Of course . . ." Then, with a sudden return of anger, "Did she really think that could make up for what she did?"

He shrugged again. "It was the best she had."

"It isn't enough," Nicki exclaimed bitterly. "She only did it out of guilt. She lied, she pretended to care about you, then threw you into hell . . . and for Richard!"

"Nicole—"

"I wonder if anything she ever felt was real. If she ever really loved anyone. If she ever really loved me—"

"Stop it! You know she loved you!"

"Do I? I thought she loved you, too, but it was a lie. She never felt a thing, or she couldn't have done it. I don't think she ever felt anything, for anyone. She didn't love you, and she didn't . . . love me. It was all lies, all of it . . ."

She looked at him, agony darkening eyes that were more devastated than he had ever seen them. It ripped at him with glowing hot claws, deep into that last solitary place he'd kept sheltered and hidden for so long. He couldn't stand it. He'd tried to keep from destroying her image of her mother, and had wound up doing something even worse, making her doubt that mother's love.

He knew what he had to do, as surely as he knew he didn't dare do it. But he had to. He couldn't bear to see her like this, not his brave, beautiful Nicole. He had to do it, and—God help him—trust that she would understand. Trust. Such a small word. Such a damn small word to strike such terror inside him. But he still had to do it. Even if he lost her forever, he had to make that look in her eyes go away.

He made himself move, made himself cross the room. His hands trembled as he reached for the book, the rich green leather feeling oddly cool beneath his unsteady fingers. He took out the letter and turned back. Nicki was staring at him, as if something about the way he was moving had penetrated even her raging grief and anger.

"Travis...? What is it? You look..."

"Scared? You bet I am." It was barely audible, but it was taking all his strength to come back to her, to hand her that folded paper. Nothing in the two years of hell he'd spent in prison had prepared him for this kind of fear.

He handed her the letter. "What your mother felt was real," he said, not quite able to hide the tremor in his voice. "Don't ever doubt that. Or that she loved you."

Nicki unfolded the letter slowly, her eyes never leaving Travis until it was open before her. She began to read, and Travis knew his time of joy was down to moments. When he heard her gasp, he knew it was over.

She raised haunted, tortured eyes to him. "She wrote this... all this time you had this... you could have shown me... but you let me go on thinking you were..."

With a strangled cry she stood up, the letter fluttering to the floor. He took a step toward her. She whirled, and ran out of the room. He raced after her, but by the time he reached the bottom of the stairs, all he could hear was that echo of the slamming front door.

She couldn't have gotten far, he told himself. She hadn't taken her purse, so she had no cash, or even identification. And she'd been on foot. Not, he thought grimly, that that had stopped her from disappearing thoroughly.

Panic welled up inside him as he tried to quash the image of never finding her, never seeing her again. Tried to quash the little voice inside him saying that he'd been a fool to think that anyone could really trust him, that someone might really love him. His mother, his father had both loved their alcohol more than him. Emily Lockwood had loved Richard so much more she'd sent him to hell. Why did he think Nicki might be different?

The world seemed forbiddingly silent, except for the sound of some kids shouting over an odd, rolling sound coming from just out of sight around the corner. Maybe, he thought. He started that way at a run.

The sound was composite rubber wheels on plywood; a large, ingeniously built skateboard ramp was taking up most of the dead end of the narrow cul-de-sac. The group of five boys, all about fifteen, he guessed, stopped their racing, flying stunts and eyed him suspiciously.

"You guys been here long?"

"What's it to you?" the tallest one asked, glaring at him from beneath a fall of blond hair that reached almost to his nose.

Travis recognized that defiant tone. Halloran, meet yourself, he thought as he took in the boy's defiant stance.

"I'm not going to rat you off for cutting school, if that's what you mean."

The boy looked taken aback, then a grin flashed across his face. "It's a holiday."

"Sure. It's, er, National Ground Squirrel Day, right?"

The grin again, genuine this time. "You got it."

The others laughed, and Travis felt them relax. "I just need to know if anyone went by here in the last few minutes."

"Why? You lose somebody?"

"God, I hope not," Travis muttered.

"Uh-oh." The boy chuckled. "Must be a girl, huh?"

"Not just *a* girl. *The* girl."

For a moment the boy looked oddly mature, as if he'd taken on years with Travis's frank, man-to-man admission.

"She about my height, great bod, hair about Timmy's color there?"

Travis glanced at the boy who groaned at the attention; fiery strands of dark copper lit his hair in the sun. His eyes shot back to the blond.

"Yes. Exactly."

The boy jerked a thumb over his shoulder. "Toward the beach. A while ago."

Travis let out a sigh of relief. If she was on the beach he'd find her, somehow.

"You tick her off or something? She looked pretty stressed, man."

"I," Travis said fervently, "am the biggest idiot this side of the Pacific." He started to move, then stopped, glancing once more at the cleverly designed, curving ramp. "You build that thing?"

The boy nodded. "I drew it, cut the pieces, and Timmy helped me put it together."

"Remember Willow Tree."

"Huh?" The boy looked at him blankly.

"That's my company. When you need a job, come see me."

Then, leaving the boy gaping after him, he took off at a run toward the beach.

It didn't take long for him to realize that a couple of miles of running every other day did not condition one for long treks in soft sand. He turned to walk closer to the water, where the sand was damp, and harder. And empty, except for a few morning walkers.

He kept on, the number of people dwindling the further he went. His feet were wet, and the bottom of his jeans halfway to his knees, a souvenir of his misjudgment of an incoming wave. He was thinking of all his misjudgments in general when he spotted the lone figure.

Something about that figure tugged at him, something about the way it was huddled in the sand made him think of a slim, trembling body drawn up next to his, seeking shelter. He stopped, staring at the windblown hair, and how the sun lit it with bright fire.

Then he was racing up the beach, forgetting his tired muscles. He was half afraid she would run, but she never even looked up as he dropped to his knees beside her. He searched for the words to say, to make her understand, but all he could manage was an inane, "I'm sorry."

She looked at him then, and he saw the traces of tears on her cheeks. "About what? That I know now that you could have proved your innocence since the day of mother's funeral?"

"I didn't—"

"I went through hell, Travis. I felt like I was being torn in half. I knew... thought I knew you'd killed my father, but I still couldn't stop myself from caring about you. I felt like I was betraying my father's memory, and my brother, the only family I had left, every time I even talked to you."

"I know."

"But most of all I was confused. I didn't understand why my mother had done this thing. She had to know how hard it would make things for me. I even wondered if she'd been angry at me, at the end, for something I didn't know about—"

"Please, don't."

"You could have saved me all that, Travis. You could have just shown me that letter, and I would have understood."

"I... Oh God, Nicole, I'm sorry. I wanted to, at first. Hell, I wanted to shove it in your face that first day, under the tree. I wanted to force you to read it, just so you'd stop looking at me like I'd crawled out from under a rock."

"Why didn't you? It would have saved so much pain..."

He sighed, and shifted in the sand to stare out at the ocean. Finally, in a voice barely audible above the steady sound of the incoming surf, he spoke.

"Pride, Nicole. Damned, stupid pride. I told myself you should have known that I hadn't killed your father. That if you didn't believe in me then, you sure as hell wouldn't now. Especially if you hadn't changed your mind in fifteen years."

Travis let out a compressed breath. "I was wrong, then. I wanted you to trust in me. God, you knew me better than anyone in the world, but you still believed I was guilty. Knowing you believed it hurt more than anything else. I didn't realize... maybe I was too young to realize that I was expecting too much."

"Too much?"

"You were only fourteen. To expect you to jettison your brother and believe your mother a liar, when you'd just lost your father..." He shook his head.

"You wanted me to trust you...but you didn't trust me enough to show me my mother's letter. Or to tell me about Willow Tree."

He dug a hole in the sand with a taut fist. "I just didn't realize...how unfair it was."

"You want to talk about faith and trust? Well, remember, I loved you even when I thought you *had* been responsible for my father. And when I still suspected you might be behind the accidents at Lockwood."

"I know that. God, I know."

"I loved you so much that none of that mattered. But that still wasn't enough, was it?"

Pain twisted his face at the deadly finality of her words. "Nicole—"

"I had to believe you on faith alone to satisfy you."

His jaw tightened, but he held her gaze steadily and nodded. "I admitted that. I know it was pure pride. But when you've been down to none at all, pride is a precious thing."

His words made her eyes sting with more tears. He saw it, and it seemed to give him the drive to go on.

"And later...when it started to seem like you didn't hate me so much after all, I was afraid to show it to you."

"Afraid?"

"Because I...didn't want you to be with me for the wrong reason. Because you thought that you...owed me something."

Nicki flushed, staring at him. "Something that could be paid back...in bed?"

Travis paled, his eyes widening with shock. "I didn't mean—" He stopped, as if hearing his own words, and how they'd sounded. "God, I've really been a fool, haven't I?' He let out a harsh, bitter chuckle. "I've hurt you, kept secrets from you, and insulted you. God, no wonder you ran. I don't blame you for changing your mind."

"I— What?"

Travis shivered. He picked up a handful of sand, and watched it slip through his fingers with a set, intense expression. Then he looked at her, his eyes dark with the same intensity.

"I said before that I knew how far people will go for someone they love. Well, I was wrong. I didn't know. I do now. Because I swore fifteen years ago I'd never beg anyone for anything again. But if that's what it takes to get you to give me another chance, then I'll do it."

"Another chance? Travis—"

"I don't blame you, but please, just listen. I love you. I love you, Nicole." He lowered his eyes. "I'm sorry I didn't say it before. I guess I thought...it was obvious." She heard his breath catch. "And I am so damned sorry. About everything." He looked at the tiny pile of sand he'd dropped. "I guess I don't have any pride when it comes to you. Not if it means losing you."

"Losing— Travis, what—"

"I can't lose you now, not when I've just found you again, please Nicole, I—"

"Travis!" she cried. "Don't sound like that! You're not ever going to beg anyone again, not me, not anyone."

"It doesn't matter anymore. Nothing does without you."

"But you're not without me."

"But...you said..."

"I said what?"

"That you...loved me."

"I know." She stared at him, perplexed.

"Not love. Loved. Past tense."

Her eyes widened in understanding. "And you thought I meant I didn't anymore? God, Travis, how could you think that? Do you think it's just a word I throw around? It's not something that's only there when things are sunny, it doesn't disappear when I'm angry, or—"

She stopped suddenly, an ugly, stark vision in her head of Travis, dodging a blow from his drunken father. What did he know of a love that was constant, that solid, untouchable core that survived bad times and anger? The closest he'd ever come to it was in the Lockwood house, only to have it coldly and cruelly betrayed.

Nicki stared at him in understanding. He looked away, but not before she saw the shimmer of moisture in his eyes. It slashed at her already battered emotions. "Travis," she whispered, "why did you show me that letter now?"

For a moment she didn't think he was going to answer. Then it came, low, thick, and barely audible. "Because of what you were thinking. That your mother didn't . . . love you."

"But . . . you must have known how I'd react."

He shuddered. "I knew."

"Oh, Travis," she whispered. Emotion flooded her; they'd joked about nobility, but at this moment she saw more of it in this man than she'd ever known in anyone.

She reached out to cup his bruised face with her hand. He didn't move, but there was an odd look in his eyes, the look of a creature in pain who wasn't sure if the hand extended to it was to heal or do more harm.

"Nicki . . . ?"

That he used that name now, the name so common from others, so special from him, until now heard only in their most intimate moments, told her all she needed to know. And what she needed to say.

"I love you, Travis. And I'm sorry I didn't realize until now that you gave me the greatest trust of all when you showed me that letter. You trusted me to understand."

He stared at her, a shudder rippling through his lean body. Then he swallowed heavily, his eyes closing for a long moment. Then the thick, dark lashes lifted. "I thought . . . when you ran out . . ."

"I was angry, yes," she said, "and I needed to work through it. I didn't understand so many things . . . but I never stopped loving you." She saw a shiver ripple through him, and her voice went soft and warm. "That's not my kind of love, Travis. Or yours. I know that. It doesn't change when the wind changes, or burn up in the heat of anger."

A parade of emotions flitted across his face; pain, doubt, wonder. She knew when he'd at last reached acceptance, for he reached out and pulled her into his arms.

"I love you. You. Travis Halloran. The boy you were, the man you are. No matter what the trappings are. No matter that, for a while, we both forgot that to truly love you have to trust ... But please, no more secrets."

"No." His agreement was heartfelt. "No more." She felt him shiver, then his arms tightened around her. "I'm sorry. I underestimated you." He smiled wryly. "And I had a pretty high opinion of you in the first place."

She let out a little sigh. "Thank you."

"Will you forgive me if I'm still a little bit glad that you came to me even when you thought the worst?"

She wiggled closer, burrowing into the warmth of his embrace. "You're lucky. I'm in a forgiving mood."

"Nicki, love, I know just how lucky I am."

"And I know how lucky I am, to have a man who can say that and mean it, after what you've been through."

He went still, then took a deep breath. "Will you have me, Nicole? Forever?"

She lifted her head to look at him, her eyes shining. "I couldn't face forever without you," she whispered. Then, her face alight with love and a teasing joy, she said, "After the last fifteen years, forever should be a snap."

And as easily as that, the long, hard years were dismissed, vanishing in the glow of the future before them. And today shimmered in their hands, bright and shining and precious; they held it as tightly as they held each other, two solitary figures making a single silhouette against the soft, white sand.

Epilogue

"Who?"

"He says his name is Kevin Hayes."

Travis's brow furrowed as he searched his memory. Nothing materialized, no peg to hang the name on. He shifted the receiver on his shoulder as he finished signing the letter on his desk.

"He asked for me?"

"Not by name," the receptionist said, sounding amused. "But he did describe you . . . rather accurately."

"He did?"

"'Tall, dark hair, good looking dude, but real intense,' I think were the words."

Travis laughed. "You trying to flatter me into a raise, Jenny?"

"No, but now that you mention it . . ." she said with a laugh. "Anyway, he insists you told him to come."

Travis sighed. "Okay. Send him in."

When the door opened, a tall, lanky, blond young man of about eighteen stepped in. He looked around the office, and Travis could see him fighting not to be impressed. And I still don't have a clue who he is, Travis thought. He stared at him, again searching his memory. The boy took in his blank expression.

"I should'a known you didn't mean it." The boy scowled and turned to go.

Something clicked into place at the surly attitude, and Travis stood up. "Wait a minute."

The boy looked back over his shoulder. "What for?" he asked sourly.

"Because if you want a job here, you're going to have to learn some patience."

The boy's angry brown eyes widened. "You mean...you did mean it?"

"I said it."

"Sometimes that doesn't mean much."

"It does around here."

The boy turned back. He was taller than he'd been that day, but just as thin. And just as scared, Travis thought, and hiding it behind a screen of surliness. Again, he recognized himself in the boy before him.

"You still in school?"

"Graduated. Barely. They wanted to get rid of me."

Travis gave a short bark of laughter. "I know the feeling."

The boy glanced around the office once more. "You?"

"Me. The boy most likely to fail. The only thing I was good at was 'not living up to my potential.'"

The boy gaped at him. "You, too?"

"Me, too." Travis walked around his desk. "You ready to work?"

"Yeah."

"I mean really work, not goof off, not get into trouble, not walk around with an attitude—"

"I don't have an attitude—"

"Not talking back to the boss is part of that patience I mentioned."

"Well, just forget it, then."

"Knock it off, Kevin. I've been there. I know every smart-mouth remark. I've used them all. And I know what's behind them. I know you're scared that there's no place for you in this damned world. And there won't be, unless you make it yourself.''

Kevin was staring at him, wide-eyed.

''If you really want a job, you've got it. But it isn't free. Nothing is. You want to work here, you keep your mouth shut. I did it, and so can you. You think what you want, but you don't say it around my people. Got that?''

The boy nodded silently.

''And you keep going to school.''

''What?'' It was an astonished squeak. ''I'm out of school.''

''It's called college.''

''Me? I barely made it through high school!'' He gave Travis a look that was half frightened, half defiant. ''My folks kicked me out the day after graduation. I can't afford to go to college. They wouldn't let me in, anyway.''

''So you start with a junior college.''

''But . . . that costs money, too.''

''That's your boss's problem.''

His eyes widened. ''You?''

Travis nodded.

''Me . . . ? College?''

The boy's wondering expression told Travis he'd made a good call. He held out a hand. ''Do we have a deal?''

Moving with stunned slowness, the boy nodded as they shook hands.

''Good,'' Travis said. ''You can—''

He broke off as his office door was flung open and a small, denim-clad whirlwind burst in. A fiery ponytail bounced as the bundle of energy flew across the room and flung herself at Travis.

''Daddy!''

''Hi, baby.''

He lifted the exuberant toddler up in his arms and kissed her bright hair. She giggled and planted a wet, sloppy return kiss on his cheek. His own gray eyes looked back at him from beneath the coppery hair, a striking combination that he realized with some ruefulness would have him shopping for a shotgun in a few years.

The child suddenly noticed the stranger in the room, and a tiny finger went to her mouth as she stared at him. The boy looked back, his eyes lingering on the gleaming red highlights in the pert ponytail. Then his eyes went to Travis.

"I guess you found her, huh?" he said softly.

Travis nodded, hugging the little girl. "Not bad, for the guy most likely to fall on his face."

Kevin nodded slowly, and for the first time Travis saw hope shining in the brown eyes.

"Sarah? Sarah Emily Halloran, where are you?"

"In here, Mommy," the toddler chirped. "You look funny, Daddy," she added when she looked back at Travis.

"I'll bet I do," he admitted, acknowledging silently the odd little tumble his heart still took when he heard his daughter's name in Nicki's voice.

And when Nicole Lockwood Halloran appeared in the doorway, her blue eyes bright with the joy that was constant now, her lips curving with the smile he knew was for him alone, her slender body beginning to show his son growing inside her, he knew their forever would be brighter than he'd ever dared hope.

* * * * *

From the popular author of the bestselling title
DUNCAN'S BRIDE (Intimate Moments #349)
comes the

LINDA HOWARD

COLLECTION

Two exquisite collector's editions that contain four of
Linda Howard's early passionate love stories. To add
these special volumes to your own library, be sure
to look for:

VOLUME ONE: *Midnight Rainbow*
Diamond Bay
(Available in March)

VOLUME TWO: *Heartbreaker*
White Lies
(Available in April)

 *Silhouette Books*®

SLH92

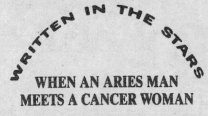

WRITTEN IN THE STARS

WHEN AN ARIES MAN
MEETS A CANCER WOMAN

Aggressive Aries businessman Alexander
Donaldson III did *not* appreciate being
wakened at dawn by a huge sheep outside his
bedroom window! But upon confronting its
owner—child psychologist Hannah
Martinof—Alex knew his love phobia was
instantly cured! Now, if only Hannah would
admit she wanted *him!* Carla Cassidy's
WHATEVER ALEX WANTS... is coming
this April—only from Silhouette Romance.
It's WRITTEN IN THE STARS!

NORA ROBERTS

Love has a language all its own, and for centuries, flowers have symbolized love's finest expression. Discover the language of flowers—and love—in this romantic collection of 48 favorite books by bestselling author Nora Roberts.

Starting in February, two titles will be available each month at your favorite retail outlet.

In March, look for:

Irish Rose, Volume #3
Storm Warning, Volume #4

In April, look for:

First Impressions, Volume #5
Reflections, Volume #6

Collect all 48 titles and become fluent in

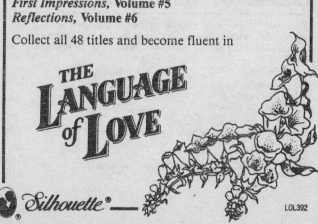

THE LANGUAGE of LOVE